CANYON WIND

Canyon Wind

For information contact: Shalako Press
P.O. Box 371, Oakdale, CA 95361-0371
http://www.shalakopress.com

ISBN: 978-0-9798898-5-1

Cover Artist: Nancy Ruybal
Cover design: Karen Borrelli
Editor: Judith Mitchell

Dedication

To Wes and Nancy Ruybal, who are just plain good folks.

Acknowledgments

This book is a combined effort of many people. I would like to thank Nancy Ruybal, Josie Costa, Kelly Phillips and Deborah Cone for their input and helping to correct my mistakes.

And as always, hugs and kisses to my editor-in-chief and wife, Judy, who always turns my hieroglyphics into something readable. Thanks kid.

CANYON WIND

By Major Mitchell

Shalako Press
Oakdale, CA

CANYON WIND

South Dakota, 1888

"Ya! Get in there!" Katherine Eleanor Parker yelled as she swung the end of her rope in tight circles, driving the stubborn steer back toward the mouth of the canyon. She really couldn't blame him for wanting to escape. The feed in the winter pasture had been mostly eaten off, and the cattle inside the canyon were looking half-starved. But it was early January and the open pastures in South Dakota were no place to be grazing cattle that time of year. They would be lucky if the entire herd survived the winter. The narrow canyon shielded from the harsh winds had been fine when their herd was small. Now they had a thousand head to care for, and the grass had been grazed off before mid-winter. Some of the ranchers, like Clayton Jones, were growing and storing feed for the long winter months. But pulling heavy wagons loaded with hay through snowdrifts was difficult and hazardous work. They would have to decide what to do before next winter. If they couldn't find some better way of feeding the cattle, they might have to sell half the herd.

The sound of gunfire drew her attention to the north rim of the canyon where her eldest son, Matthew, waved his rifle in the air, motioning for her to join him. She spurred Culpepper into a ground-eating lope toward the trail leading up to where her son waited. She had bought the large gray stallion on a hunch from a cattleman passing through a year earlier, and had to endure her husband's jibes and teasing for eight miles, from Denby to their ranch.

"I still can't believe you paid seventy dollars for that crow-bait," he said with a snicker.

"Culpepper's worth more'n that, James, and you know it."

"You think so?"

She nodded.

"He's old, honey. And about wore out. He's been down more trails than a whisky peddler. That old horse thief you bought him from probably traded a Comanche a jug of moonshine for that critter."

"I don't care. He's mine, and I like him."

"Why, in God's name? We've got better looking horses at the Flying K."

"Because he's got sand. I can see it in his eyes. This horse isn't going to let me down in a pinch."

And Culpepper had not only proven her right, he was more than Katherine had ever hoped for. It hadn't taken but one ride for James to change his mind about the animal, and Katherine had to fight to keep him or one of their sons from running off with her horse while she washed the breakfast dishes or did some other menial task around their rambling ranch house.

Culpepper short-loped up the steep trail to the rim where Matthew sat waiting. Katherine caught her breath as a frigid breeze slapped her in the face.

"Look, Ma," her son said, pointing the Henry rifle toward the northern horizon. The boiling black clouds that spanned the sky were enough to cause her alarm, but the solid sheet of white beneath the clouds was what really concerned her. Nothing could be seen through the sheet, and it was moving rapidly toward them. The temperature had already fallen several degrees since she had crested the canyon's rim. Culpepper stomped his large hooves and snorted nervously.

"Oh my word! Better get down from here and warn the others. It's a big one and it'll be here any minute. We'll be lucky to make it to the house. Hurry now," she said as

Matthew spurred his brown and white paint over the rim and down the trail.

Katherine surveyed the canyon floor once more, hoping to see her family. She spied James, casually trotting his horse beside Steven and Joshua near the creek. Timothy was loping his horse toward them. The only one she couldn't see was Abby, but since the girl never seemed to wander far from her father, Katherine figured she must be somewhere close. She drew her rifle from its sheath and fired several shots into the air, then waved it as James and the boys looked up, motioning them toward the house. She immediately urged Culpepper down the steep trail, and the anxious animal almost overran Matthew's pony as they reached the floor. She had trouble holding him in check as James and the three others joined them.

"What's wrong, Kate?" James asked.

"Blizzard's coming…a big one. Matt saw it first and showed me. It'll be here quick. We'd better be heading to the house."

James glanced toward Matthew who nodded. He looked up as a few random snowflakes began dropping around them. The sky overhead was filled with a mass of swirling white. "Move," he yelled and spurred his horse forward.

Katherine glanced around her quickly before urging Culpepper into a full run. It didn't take long for the large horse to overtake her husband.

"James," she yelled over the pounding hooves. "Where's Abby? I don't see her."

"I sent her up to the east rim early this morning. You can see forever up there, Kate. I'm sure she saw this coming, and is probably at the house by now."

Katherine nodded and let Culpepper have his lead. The horse quickly pulled away from the others, and Katherine had the barn door opened by the time James and the boys rode into the yard. The temperature was falling quickly now, and clouds of steam appeared with each breath as they turned the horses loose inside the stalls.

"Matt, you and the boys drive the animals in the corral inside the barn," James ordered.

Katherine ran to the house and dashed through every room. "Abby! Abby! Where are you? Don't do this to me, Abby!"

The wind gave an eerie howl as it hit the house like a battering ram. She ran to the front door as James and the boys struggled inside, covered with snow. Katherine gazed through the open door before Matthew forced it shut. It seemed as though the corrals, barn and tack house had disappeared, leaving only a solid, swirling mass of white. She felt the blood drain from her face as she turned toward her husband.

"Abby isn't here, James. She's still out there somewhere."

He stared at the closed door without saying anything.

"James? James? Did you hear me? Abby's still out there."

He continued staring as the wind grew louder. The inside temperature had fallen to freezing as Joshua struggled to build a fire. An empty hole grew inside Katherine's stomach as James stared at the door. Her daughter was somewhere on the east rim of the canyon, caught in a blizzard.

CHAPTER 2

One year later

Katherine used her weight to sink the shovel, then wiggled the handle to loosen the dirt. She was past the layer of rocks and gravel that had given her trouble a few minutes earlier. The soil was soft and damp and the digging would go much faster now. She hoisted the load and tossed it onto the growing mound at the edge of the grave. She estimated she was now close to five feet deep. She remembered reading somewhere that graves were supposed to be six feet deep, but doubted this one would be much deeper than it was at that minute. Being only five-foot-seven, she would have difficulty climbing out of a six-foot hole with straight sides. Besides, she reasoned, James wouldn't know or care how deep his grave was. He was dead.

Katherine removed her soil-stained hat and wiped the sweat away with her sleeve as she adjusted the leather gloves on her calloused hands. She shoved the hat down tight and continued her digging, methodically, like a machine. She had four healthy boys, ranging from thirteen to seven who had offered to help, but she had chosen to do it by herself. Losing their father had been hard enough on them, let alone having to watch him quit living and pine away like he had done. Besides, they had built his coffin themselves, using leftover planking from the barn. She had been James' wife for nineteen years, so she reasoned the task of digging his grave should fall to her. She couldn't help but feel there must have been something else she could have done to save James. She shook her head as she hoisted another load of dirt over her head. If she had missed something, she couldn't think what it might be.

Losing Abby had simply killed James on his feet. He'd been a good husband and father, especially to Abby. She was their first-born. She had arrived shortly after they had finished building the house, and quickly became the center of her father's attention. Their place was small back then, but they had plenty of land and room to grow. The house had been added onto with the addition of each child, and they had planned on another addition perhaps next year. Those were happy times that quickly changed when they lost Abigail.

James acted as though their daughter had belonged to him personally, and that her disappearance in the storm shouldn't have caused her or the boys any grief. They all had cried, and searched for Abigail for months, but she was simply gone without a trace. James quit working the ranch and seldom talked to anyone. He would ride out in the morning looking for his daughter and not return home until after dark, leaving her to raise their four sons and run the 75,000-acre ranch by herself. He seldom ate, growing thin and gaunt, with sunken dark eyes that gave him a skeletal look. The boys, especially seven-year-old Steven, grew frightened of their father, and would leave the room when he came home. He hadn't come home at all the previous night and Katherine had ridden out that very morning before sunrise to find him in the winter canyon, where he had fallen off his horse and hit his head on a rock.

She paused and looked at the grave. It was deep enough. She wiped her eyes against her soiled sleeve and choked back a sob. She had been a good, loving and faithful wife. James had no call to die on her like that. It would have been one thing if he had gotten killed by a Sioux raiding party, or caught cholera, or died in some terrible accident. But he hadn't done any of those things. It was as if he never considered the rest of his family important enough to live for.

The very thought angered her. She laid the shovel across the width of the narrow grave and used it to hoist herself up.

"Matthew…Timothy?" she called to the boys who had been watching from the front porch. "You boys find your brothers and bring your father."

Timothy poked his head into the house and Joshua and Steven suddenly appeared in the doorway. She couldn't hear what was being said as the boys engaged in a quick hushed conversation. Matthew seemed to take charge and directed his brothers into position as they hoisted the crude box and slowly crossed the yard toward her. Katherine glanced at the sandstone marker to the left of the newly dug grave. The inscription caused her eyes to water and spill down her dusty cheeks.

Abigail Susana Parker, Beloved Daughter, June 24, 1874 – January 12, 1888.

That had been the cause of the worst argument in their long marriage. "You shouldn't have done that, Kate," James yelled when he saw the marker. "Abby ain't dead! I know she ain't."

"James," Katherine had argued, "she isn't coming back. It's been too long, and we've looked everywhere. All of us...even people from town and other ranchers. Something bad happened to her, and she's gone."

"No she's not. I can still hear her, Kate. Our Abby's still alive, and I'll find her sooner or later."

Abigail wasn't the only person caught in that storm. The newspapers and periodicals had called it the *School Children's Blizzard of 1888.* While Katherine never paid much attention to things written in the papers, she figured they had gotten this one right. The storm swept in so suddenly it had caught children on their way home from school. While most of them had been rescued quickly, quite a few children had frostbite and dozens had to spend the night trapped inside school buildings.

She watched her sons carrying their father and considered that folks carried their grief in different ways. While she found her solace in working from sunup until complete exhaustion overtook her, her eldest son, Matthew, had grown withdrawn and sullen, and certainly never smiled. Not that he shirked any of his duties…none of the boys did that. Matthew simply withdrew into himself and seldom talked, unless it was to answer a question or something needed saying.

Joshua and Timothy, who were now eleven and nine respectively, became pranksters and were continually horsing around. They worked hard around the ranch, but worked equally hard teasing and pestering not only each other, but especially their seven-year-old brother, Steven. Their pranks never seemed to stop, regardless of how they were threatened. She finally gave up. There were worse things than hearing them laugh while Matthew or Steven yelled and threatened them with murder.

Steven seemed to take Abby's disappearance and James' mental state worse than any of the boys. He grew timid and followed her around like a lost puppy, until she gave him a project to occupy his time. Then the lad would do his level best to please her. She thought the boy would be willing to walk into a burning building carrying a can of kerosene if she asked him to.

The boys set the coffin beside the grave and stepped away, waiting for her direction. Katherine took her time, surveying every little detail of the tiny cemetery. She had chosen the shade of the large willow tree behind the barn to place Abigail's headstone several months earlier. Abby wasn't really there, but she and the boys needed some sort of closing, and it was only fitting they have a monument to remember her by. James, on the other hand, had never found closure and kept looking for an entire year. She figured he should have a spot next to Abby's, and then maybe he could find peace. She'd have a matching marker made for him next time she went to town. Perhaps the blacksmith could make a wrought-iron fence to surround their graves. That'd be nice.

She nodded and the boys slowly lowered their father into the grave with ropes, then stepped away to remove their hats. Matthew's eyes were moist and his jaw was clamped tightly shut. Otherwise, he gave no outward sign of grief.

Joshua and Timothy had somehow lost their sense of humor, but seemed to be holding up well. Steven was the only one crying openly.

Katherine removed her gloves and swiped at both of her eyes with her palms and cleared her throat.

"Lord, James was a good man…weak in some ways, but still good. He was a good husband and father, up to this past year when he abandoned us to look for Abby. He never drank more than his proper share, and was honest in his business. He had a good eye for land, as this ranch will testify. He also had a good eye for cattle and horses, and he loved his children, especially Abby. Maybe he loved her too much.

"But he had no reason to treat us like he did this past year and pine away and die like this. I guess he didn't really care how me and the boys felt. And I'm having a hard time forgetting how you sent that storm that took Abigail from us. First I lost my daughter, and now my husband. And these boys are good boys. You know that. Now, they are without a father or sister, and it was uncalled for. What you allowed to happen was meaner'n a sack full of snakes in my book, so I'm not likely to forget anytime soon.

"All that aside, I'm asking you to remember the good that James did, and forget his weakness and failures when you tally the books. Amen."

Katherine waited until each of her sons had tossed a handful of dirt on James' coffin and said their goodbyes. She pulled her gloves back on and sobbed openly as she cast the first shovelful of dirt onto the box.

"Bye James." She shoveled as she cried.

CHAPTER 3

1893

Katherine rode the ginger-colored mare past the rambling ranch house and dismounted in front of the corral. She arched her back with a soft groan, and swatted at spots of mud dotting her tan riding skirt and brown leather jacket with her gloves. It seemed unreasonable that she should have gotten this dirty, while patches of snow still huddled under the brush and shady areas surrounding the elm and cottonwood trees. She could see her breath as she worked at the task. Early spring was always cold in South Dakota.

It had been a particularly hard day for her and she was already feeling fatigued. Herding four growing boys, who ranged in age from twelve to eighteen, was hard enough, but the ranch had begun to feel like a prison. The thought of spending another winter like the last one, cooped inside while the freezing canyon winds blew snow horizontally and battered the ranch house, seemed overwhelming to her. And, to add to her sour mood, she had discovered they had been losing cattle. She expected to lose the occasional cow to a hungry wolf or coyote, but they always left the bones as a thank you, and they had found precious few bones lying around. She didn't consider herself a harsh or selfish woman, and had never minded a hungry drifter or Indian killing one of her beeves to feed his family. She could stand to lose a few head and survive. The ranch had been long paid for, and she had been debt-free for years. After a quick survey of the winter canyon, she figured they might have lost ten percent of the herd, and it didn't take much imagination to know where the cattle had gone. A cattle ranch without cattle was something Katherine would simply not tolerate, especially when she had worked so hard to make it what it was.

She allowed her tan hat to hang against her back by the leather drawstring, and ran her fingers through her shoulder-length sandy-blond hair, then flung the gate open with a sigh. If she took time to be honest with herself, there was no reason for the blue feeling that had plagued her throughout the day. She had her beautiful ranch and her sons. The boys had become her constant companions and joy. She also had Charlene Thompson, her housekeeper, who was her closest friend and confidant. She had more than most people she knew, and laughed at herself as she removed her saddle and turned the mare loose inside the corral. Such thoughts were silly, and must have something to do with being middle-aged. It could also be attributed to the harsh winter that had just ended. But that had been nothing compared to the blizzard that had swallowed Abby, leaving no trace of her or her horse. Katherine paused to stare at the tiny cemetery under the willow. Losing Abby had nearly killed her.

She gave Ginger a friendly swat on the rump and closed the gate. Abby had been missing for five years, and James died nearly four years ago. The time for mourning had long passed. She had spent twenty-two winters on her South Dakota ranch, and simply didn't have time for such foolishness. The boys were rounding up the remuda in preparation for the spring roundup, and were close enough to eat their midday meal at the house. They would be hungry, as always, and the good Lord knew teenage boys worked better with a hot meal in their stomachs.

She leaned against the gate and watched as her two youngest sons, Timothy and Steven, raced their horses toward her and dismounted in a leap, arguing over which had won the race. The boys stopped when they realized their mother wasn't listening, but staring past them.

"Know who he is, Ma?" Steven asked.

"No, I don't. Do either of you know?"

"Never seen him before in my life," Timothy said with a grunt as he removed the saddle from his brown and white paint and draped it over the top rail of the corral.

"Neither have I," Steven said, and turned his attention toward his horse.

"Well, guess we'll find out soon enough, won't we?" Katherine said as the man drew closer. He was taking his time, walking a dark brown Mustang with a coal black mane and tail. The horse looked almost as tired as the man slumped in the saddle. "I can tell from this distance he could stand a bath. You boys finish up here while I see if Charlie's got your dinner ready."

"Yes, ma'am," the boys said in unison as she hurried toward the house.

Katherine called for the housekeeper as she stomped and scraped the mud from her boots on the metal boot scraper and opened the door to the mudroom.

"Charlie?"

"Yes, Mrs. Parker?" Charlene appeared from the kitchen wiping her hands on a white apron. The house smelled of roast beef and hot biscuits.

"Steve and Timmy are here, and if I know Matt and Josh, they'll be along any second."

"Yes, ma'am. Those boys never miss a meal," Charlene said with a laugh.

"No, they don't, but it looks as though we might have a guest joining us today." Katherine pushed the door open even wider as the stranger walked the horse toward the house.

"Don't say? We don't get many folks visiting way out here. Fellow looks half starved to me."

"Or sick. Do we have enough to feed him?"

"Oh, don't you worry about that, Mrs. Parker. I always cook more than enough with those boys of yours." Charlene laughed and returned to the kitchen. The decision to hire the housekeeper had been one of Katherine's better ideas. She had met the aging widow three years ago during one of her infrequent trips into Denby, and discovered she was destitute. She invited her to the ranch more out of pity, but the fifty-year-old heavyset woman, who walked with a limp from an arthritic hip, had proven indispensable.

"Afternoon, ma'am." The rider stopped at the steps and tipped his hat before dismounting with a grunt. He was a large man. Katherine guessed him to be six-foot-four or five inches tall, and two hundred pounds. He was dressed shabbily with a dirt-stained jacket that had seen better days. His rugged features were well hidden behind dirt and a week's worth of whiskers. "Is the owner or boss-man around?"

"You're looking at her. Name's Katherine Eleanor Parker and I own this spread. State your business." Katherine's words came sharp and crisp as she stepped onto the porch.

"Well, ma'am," he removed his hat to reveal a shock of unruly brown hair, "I was hoping to find a job, or maybe a hot meal if that isn't possible."

"I don't know about the job, seeing as I already have four strong boys. But I've never turned anyone away hungry. You may put your horse in the corral with the others and wash up at the washbasin by the tack house. Looks like that horse could stand some feed also."

"Thank you, ma'am." He turned toward the corral, then stopped and looked over his shoulder. "Phillip Anthony Denning, ma'am."

"I beg your pardon?"

"You never asked my name. It's Phillip, only most folks call me Arizona, because that's where I was born."

"You're a long way from home," Steve said as he passed quickly toward the house.

"Yes sir, I am certainly that," he said with a chuckle. Then giving a gentle tug on the reins, he said "Come on, Lucky," and led the tired animal toward the corral.

Katherine watched from the porch as the stranger unsaddled his mount and wiped it down with straw before turning it loose in the corral. He then pitched several armfuls of hay into the feeding trough for the animals before pouring water from a bucket into the metal washbasin perched on a bench next to the tack house. He was just finishing when Matthew and Joshua galloped into the yard and dismounted. The boys shook hands with the stranger and talked as they washed. Phillip motioned with his head toward the house a time or two, and she knew they were discussing her, but she couldn't hear their words clearly. With a shrug, Katherine turned back through the doorway and walked briskly toward her bedroom to wash for dinner. Feeding a filthy saddle tramp was not something she had placed on her agenda that morning.

~ ~ ~

Phillip Denning excused himself when Timothy invited him inside, saying he was pretty rank and not properly dressed to sit at a table. He could hear the boss-woman's laughing retort from inside when her son explained. "Being dirty never stopped any of you from sitting at the table, or plopping your filthy bodies on the furniture." He jumped to his feet as the cook came out with a tray holding a plate of roast beef with mashed potatoes and gravy, several biscuits and a large mug of steaming coffee.

"Thank you, ma'am. That's real kind of you."

"You're quite welcome, and my name's Charlene Thompson. But everyone around here just calls me Charlie."

"Yes, ma'am. Thank you."

The cook lingered as he sat on the edge of the porch and dug into the tasty food. She grabbed a broom leaning against the side of the house and chased the dog away as he came looking for a handout, then paused at the doorway.

"Let me know if you want seconds."

"Yes, ma'am," Phil said over a mouthful of biscuit, and she disappeared inside. He paused with the mug of coffee halfway to his mouth and listened as her voice drifted through the open door.

"That poor man's eating like he's half-starved."

"Probably is, from the looks of him," the boss-lady said.

"So am I, so pass the potatoes," one of the boys chimed in.

~   ~   ~

He was sitting on the edge of the porch rolling a cigarette when Katherine came through the door pulling her gloves over her long, slender fingers. She was a handsome woman, but not in a delicate way. He knew, by the very look of her, the lady could handle herself in any scrap. He guessed her to be about five-seven, and a hundred and twenty pounds, give or take a few, and he was usually right about such things. She had fine features with steel-blue eyes and a smattering of freckles across her sculptured nose.

"Ma'am?" He jumped to his feet as she came toward him. Mealtime was over. He could hear the sound of clinking dishes from inside, mixed with the housekeeper's voice as she belted out an Irish ballad. Her sons were saddling fresh mounts for what the youngest said was "emptying the canyon of broncs."

"Well, Mr. Denning…was it?" she asked with her head cocked to one side.

"Yes, ma'am, Phillip Denning."

"I hope you enjoyed your meal, and I do wish you the best of luck. I'm afraid I don't really have any work available. I won't be hiring for another two or three weeks, and I'll only need a couple of seasonal hands when I do. My boys and I run this place mostly by ourselves."

"Oh," he said with a nod, "I thank you for the meal anyway. It was real nice of you."

"You're welcome. Sorry about the job. You can check back in a few weeks if you haven't found something by then." She stepped off the porch but stopped at the sound of his voice.

"I just figured since you're selling cattle, you might need an extra hand or two."

"Selling?" She turned to stare. "I'm not selling any cattle this time of year. No one does. Whatever gave you that idea, Mr. Denning?"

"Well, I cut across four drovers herding twenty-five or thirty head off your place back up the trail a ways, and took it for granted they were working for you. That's what made me decide to come here." He struck a match on the soul of his boot and lit his cigarette, then tossed the match away as he headed toward the corral.

"Wait a minute!"

"Ma'am?" He turned to face her.

"Just where did you see these cattle? I didn't hire anyone to herd cattle off my range. The only people working my ranch are right here in this yard."

"Well now," he turned the corners of his mouth downward and arched his eyebrows, "guess that puts another twist on things, doesn't it? They must be *independent* cowhands hoping to make a profit off your stock."

"Are you sure? Did you get a look at the brand? How do you know they were our stock?"

"Well, I really don't know, ma'am. I just took it they were, seeing as they were following the trail out of here, and there's a busted-down sign saying this is the *Flying K Ranch*, with a set of wings on the *K*. Most of the steers I passed all had brands that looked sort of like the one on that sign."

"Busted-down sign? The sign leading into our ranch is perfectly fine. I was just up there myself yesterday."

"It's broken now."

"Sounds like rustlers, Ma," Joshua said.

"What do you think, Mr. Denning? Could they be rustlers?" Steven said.

"Well now, what do you think, son? They don't work for your ma, and they've got her steers. You'd best go get them back, unless you like giving your cows away."

"No! They are not going to get away with this. I will not lose one more if I can help it." Katherine felt her blood rush through her veins as she ran toward her horse. She leaped into the saddle and turned the animal around to face Denning.

"Well, are you going to show me where they went?"

"Do you want me to come?"

"How do we know he isn't one of them?" Matthew asked.

"You don't," Denning said with a shrug. "I'll show you where I cut their trail, and you can handle it from there. I owe you that much. Fair enough?"

"Fair enough," Katherine said with a nod.

She waited impatiently as the man tossed the saddle across his tired horse. He grabbed the rifle he had leaned against the tack house and calmly shoved it into the scabbard, then strapped on a gunbelt and checked the cylinder for loads in his pistol. *Guns.* There was always the chance shooting would be involved. Katherine had tangled with more than one rustler, and even a couple of Sioux raiding parties. And while she never had feared for herself, one of her sons might get hurt or killed, and she wasn't sure any amount of cattle would be worth that. Sweat beaded on her brow as Joshua and Timothy came from the house carrying several boxes of shells and handed one of them to her.

CHAPTER 4

"Well, here's where we part company, ma'am," Phillip said, wiping his hatband with a soiled neckerchief. "Those men took the cattle down that fork." He pointed with the neckerchief then tied it around his neck. "Towards the badlands."

"Why would they want to do that?" Katherine asked.

"Well, I don't rightly know. You can ask them when you catch up with them."

"You're not coming?" Steven asked wide-eyed.

"No, son, not unless your ma wants me to. Otherwise, I'm heading toward Denby to see if I can't scare up a job someplace." He turned his horse as if to leave, then gave Matthew a hard stare.

"You look like you're the oldest and strongest of the lot."

"Yes, sir. I'm eighteen."

"Well, I had me a good look at the men you're after, and they're not your normal cut of rustler. You'd best keep an open eye and help your ma look out for the others. It isn't likely they're gonna hand over your cattle without some sort of tussle. Make sure your rifle is cocked and loaded when you confront them. Don't face them all bunched up. Come at them from all different angles," he said with a sweep of his arm, "and be willing to shoot the first one who reaches for his gun. Understand what I'm saying, boy?"

"Yes, sir. I think I do."

"Mr. Denning, please wait. I would like you to come with us." Katherine urged Ginger closer and gave him a steady stare.

"What made you change your mind?"

"Just a hunch. Will you go with us to get our cattle?"

"I reckon."

"Good, we'd better get moving."

She took the lead and set Ginger into a fast canter, slowing only over rough, rocky areas or to maneuver through thick brush. She could hear her sons' chatter as she walked her horse across a particularly rough area.

"I'm sure glad you're coming with us, Mr. Denning," Steven said.

"Yeah, maybe we can talk ma into giving you a job," Joshua said. "We've always got more than enough work to do."

"It appears you've handled it pretty well by yourselves," Phillip said in a low voice. "But, you'd best hold the talking down, unless you want to tell the rustlers we're coming. A man's voice carries out here, and I've got a hunch we're getting close."

Katherine nodded her agreement and urged her horse into a gallop as the ground smoothed out.

~ ~ ~

It was mid-afternoon when they smelled the smoke of a campfire and dismounted. She led her horse slowly through the brush until she could see their camp. They had stopped to rest the cattle by a brisk stream where patches of spring grass were sprouting toward the warm sun. There were four of them crowded around a coffee pot and waiting for it to boil. Katherine thought it would have been a lovely spot for a picnic under different circumstances. Their horses made no sound on the damp earth. The men were laughing and talking, and evidently had not heard Katherine and her sons approach. She drew her rifle from the scabbard as Phillip slipped quietly to her side and whispered.

"How do you want to play this, ma'am? It's your call."

She motioned her sons into a tight circle and talked in a loud whisper.

"Mr. Denning? You take Matthew and move off to the left. Joshua and Timothy will cover us from the right. I'll keep Steven with me. I'll give you time to get set, then confront them. Okay?"

They gave her a firm nod and slipped silently through the damp grass. She could hear Steven's heavy breathing as he stood close to her side. She watched Matthew and Phillip Denning from her vantage point, as they ran hunched over from bush to bush. The cowboy patted Matthew on the shoulder and pointed to a clump of brush, then ran a few yards farther to crouch behind another clump. She stole a glance to her right and received a wave from Joshua. Katherine took a deep breath and laid a hand against Steven's shoulder, then stepped into the clearing.

"Excuse me," she said in a loud voice. "I believe those cattle belong to me, and I'd like them moved back onto my range."

All four men leaped to their feet and grabbed for their guns, but stopped when Matthew stood and injected a shell into his Henry rifle.

"Whoa, hold on there, son," the largest man said, holding out his hand. He was a heavyset man with a long unkempt black beard and a sweat-stained red flannel shirt. "There's no need for shooting. There's got to be some mistake here. Those cattle don't belong to you, ma'am. All you've got to do is check the brand on 'em, and you'll see."

"I doubt what you're saying is true. Why would your cattle have been grazing on my property?"

"Well, you know how cows are, ma'am," he said turning sideways as he swept his left arm in an arch toward the stolen cattle. "They'll wander off…"

He was lifted from his feet and pitched backward as Phillip fired from behind the clump of brush. Her heart skipped a beat as the man's pistol discharged into the air as he hit the ground. She had not seen him draw the gun.

"Okay, the rest of you highbinders, drop your gunbelts and step away from the campfire."

"Now, wait a minute…" one of the men started, but jumped backward as another shot hit the coffee pot, showering the men with half-perked coffee.

"Ow, geez," one of the men shouted. "That's hot!"

"Not half as hot as hell's gonna be. I can kill all three of you from where I'm standing, so what's it gonna be, boys? Drop your belts and step back from the fire."

They instantly obeyed and Phillip appeared from behind the brush. He walked briskly toward the rustlers. "Now, get face-down in the dirt."

"I'm not laying face-down for…" the pock-faced man's protest was cut short as Phillip drove the butt of his rifle into his mouth. He landed on his back and rolled over coughing and spitting bloody teeth into the dirt.

"Who's next? You two want to join him, or get in the dirt by yourselves?"

The men turned and leaped belly-first to the ground.

Phillip glanced at Katherine and gave a firm nod. "Matt, you'd best get some rope and tie their hands behind their backs. And do a good job of it, understand?"

"Yes, sir." He ran to grab a rope from his horse.

"You," he pointed toward Joshua, "keep your rifle pointed at their backs, and shoot 'em if they so much as scratch an itch."

"Shoot them?"

"That's what I said."

"And you, Timothy, isn't it?"

"Yes, sir."

"Collect all their guns, including the rifles they've got on their saddles."

Katherine walked slowly to stand over the dead rustler. A thin line of smoke still drifted upward from the gun lying next to him.

"I'm really thankful you decided to come along, Mr. Denning. This would have turned out badly if you had not seen him draw his gun. I completely missed it. I almost got us killed."

"You weren't supposed to see it." Phillip calmly reloaded his rifle. "That's why he turned his gun hand away from you. It's an old gunfighter's trick, and he pulled it off pretty slick. Bet you won't let that happen again," he added with a grin.

"Aye, that's a good bet, Mr. Denning," she said with a nod and a smile.

"All done, Mr. Denning," Matthew said. "What do you want us to do now?"

"Well, if we were in Arizona, I'd hang 'em from the grove of cottonwoods over yonder. Seeing as they were stealing your ma's cattle, I reckon they're her rustlers. Better ask her how she wants to play this hand."

"Oh God, lady! Please don't let him hang me," one of the rustlers cried. He didn't look any older than her Joshua.

"Mr. Denning, could I hire you to accompany one of my sons and hand these men over to Sheriff Crutchfield in Denby? There'll be a job waiting when you get back," she said."

"Yes, ma'am. Reckon I can do that." He turned to Matthew and Joshua. "Get 'em up on their horses, boys. Reckon your ma's gonna let the sheriff do the hanging."

"I ain't going to no jail," the pock-marked man growled as Matthew helped hoist him into the saddle.

"It's either that, or I'll let Mr. Denning hang you from that grove of cottonwoods." Katherine said. She turned to Phillip as her sons helped the other rustlers onto their horses.

"I want to thank you, Mr. Denning, for lending us a hand."

"You're welcome, ma'am."

"On this outfit, I pay forty dollars a month plus room and board, which is ten dollars more than you'll get any place else. I'll also supply all the fresh horses, ammunition and supplies. I allow no drinking during working hours or fighting amongst my riders, including my sons. I never ask anyone to do something I wouldn't do myself. And anytime you feel you can't stand up to the work, I'll give you the wages you've earned and two day's grub, and show you the way down the road. What do you say to that, Mr. Denning?"

"I reckon that's fair enough, Mrs. Parker."

Their handshake was cut short as the pock-marked rustler yelled "Ya!" Phillip flung her out of the way as the man charged his horse through the middle of the camp with the other rustlers following. Katherine grabbed for her gun, but rushed to help Steven instead as the boy yelled. He had been knocked into the campfire and his pant-legs had caught fire. Katherine jerked off her jacket and helped Phillip beat the flames out as Joshua and Timothy fired several shots at the fleeing rustlers with no luck.

"Are you okay, son?" Katherine asked, and received a nod. She hiked the burnt pant-legs, then cut the seams for a better look.

"It don't look too bad, ma'am," Phillip said. "He's gonna be sore for a few days, but he's tough as rawhide. Ain'tcha cowboy?" He also got a silent nod.

"I'd better get him home and put something on those legs. You stay here with Matthew and round up our cattle. I'll take Joshua and Timothy with me. You and Matthew can drive the cattle back in the morning. You don't think those men will be back anytime soon, do you?"

"Na, it'll take them most of the afternoon to find new guns once they get themselves untied. And the one who tried to eat my rifle needs some tending. They'll more than likely lick their wounds awhile before deciding to try their luck again in a week or two. That's when you all need to keep your eyes and ears peeled. They'll be looking to get even. I've seen fellers like them before. They're not just thieves. They'd just as soon kill you as look at you."

"Come on, son, let's get you home," she said, helping Steven to his feet. Joshua…Timothy…" she called in a loud voice.

"Yes, ma'am?" Timothy raised up from studying the dead rustler.

"You two come with me. Matthew?"

"Ma'am?"

"You and Mr. Denning will stay and round up strays. I think several steers bolted when Mr. Denning fired his rifle. After you camp here for the night, bring the cattle back to the ranch first thing in the morning."

"Yes, ma'am."

"What about him?" Steven asked and pointed toward the dead rustler.

"Matt and I will take care of him. You go get your legs fixed up. A ranch the size of your ma's needs a good drover like you," Phillip said with a grin and crammed Steven's hat down onto his head.

Katherine watched as her boys collected the rustlers' guns and tied them onto their horses. Phillip walked calmly to the grove of trees and returned with his horse. He unsaddled the tired animal and patted him on the rump.

"Well, Lucky, today's your lucky day. You get to rest some."

He whistled a tune and rebuilt the campfire, then scrounged around in the rustlers' pack to produce a sack of coffee and some jerked beef. He checked the damaged pot before deciding it might still be useful. He was in the process of making a fresh pot when the boys were finally ready to go. He had gone about his tasks as one might if they were preparing for a picnic on a pleasant afternoon. It was as if he had not killed a man a few minutes earlier. Katherine shook her head.

She had had several encounters with rustlers and Indians in the past, and had personally killed several defending her property. She had felt nauseated for days afterward, knowing she had taken a life. But this man had simply brushed the incident aside as though it were nothing.

Oh well, she shrugged. *To each his own.* She had her cattle back and more importantly, outside of Steven's minor burns, her sons were alive and well. That's all that mattered.

CHAPTER 5

Phillip's idea of burying the dead rustler was to drag and toss his body into a shallow wash and cover it with a few stones. He then took the first watch. He sat by the campfire listening to the crackling logs as he watched the sparks ascend toward heaven. Matthew was fast asleep, rolled in his saddle blanket and snoring softly. Phillip allowed his mind to retrace the long, weary trail that had brought him to this place, and didn't particularly like what he saw. He had foolishly cast aside a career as a lawman, and wasted the past three years on a trail of vengeance that had left him a hard, broken shell of the man he had once been. He ran a hand across his face and heaved a sigh. He was financially broke, ragged and half-starved, and worse yet, he had resorted to begging for food…something the old Phillip Denning would have never done.

He couldn't really blame the woman for not wanting to hire him at first. Staring at his reflection in a small pool by the stream had given him a frightful sight. As far as the rustlers were concerned, what he had done by lending her a hand was only right. What he hadn't counted on was spending half the night thinking about Mrs. Parker. Her son had explained over a supper of beef jerky and coffee that his older sister and pa had both died, so the woman was unattached, which was something he couldn't figure out. Why a rich, handsome widow like her didn't have half the men in the Dakotas hanging on her caused him to wonder.

He had met a lot of women the past few years, both young and old, but none of them were like Katherine Parker. She reminded him for all the world of his sister, Ruth. He began rolling a cigarette. He'd stop and visit Ruth when he finally wormed his way back to Arizona. All he needed was steady work for a few months to make it happen.

Katherine Parker and Ruth were the same height and build. They even had similar coloring, and Ruth had several sons also. The trouble was, Phillip was responsible for killing Ruth's oldest boy, Robert. He had constantly reminded himself the past three years that he hadn't actually killed Robert, although he might as well have. Pinning a badge on a seventeen-year-old boy was the same as pulling the trigger, even if he had done it in ignorance.

He held a smoldering twig to his smoke and lit it. No, the boss-lady was different from Ruth, or any woman he'd met. Her handshake was as strong and firm as any man's, and calloused, which was something most city women tried to hide. She was used to hard work. Phillip admired that in a woman. Her handshake had given him more than a job. It was the kind of handshake that let him know she was his equal, and not someone he could easily forget.

Ah, you old saddle bum. You ain't got time to be thinking about no woman. Besides, Mrs. Parker wouldn't take note of you anymore than she would be interested in catching typhus. You've been living too long on the trail with coyotes and lizards.

~ ~ ~

It was mid-afternoon when Phillip stopped to stare at the sign. Mrs. Parker had only given it a brief notice the previous day before following after the rustlers. But the sign now stood tall and erect on a brand new post displaying the entrance to the Flying K Ranch.

"You'll discover ma won't tolerate having anything busted or out of place too long around here," Matthew said with a snicker.

"That's the way it should be, I reckon."

Katherine joined them with two fresh cups of coffee as they unsaddled and turned their tired mounts into the corral. She waited as they washed away the grime in the metal washbasin. She handed one of the cups to her son and received a quick, "Thanks Ma," then waited as Phillip dried his face on the soiled towel.

"Well, how'd it go? Did you meet up with any more rustlers?"

"No, it was just like Mr. Denning said, Ma. We took turns sleeping, then drove the cattle to the spring range and turned them out with the others."

"Well, that's good news indeed. Now, rustle along, both of you. Your brothers have already eaten and gone to wrangle the remuda, and Charlie's been holding dinner for you quite awhile now." She gave the second cup to Phillip as Matthew hurried across the yard toward the kitchen.

"Thank you, ma'am." He took a sip and grinned as Matthew clumped his way across the wide porch and disappeared inside.

"Guess he must be hungry. Beef jerky and coffee isn't much of a meal for a growing boy."

"Growing?" Katherine glanced toward the house. "Lord, I'd hoped he was finished with that. He eats more than a prize hog. Do you have any idea what it costs to clothe four teenage boys?"

"No, I only know what store-bought clothes cost me," he said with a snicker. "I considered joining the Injuns the last time I had to buy new boots and some britches, but thought better of it when I realized I'd be running around in a breechcloth." He paused at the porch and took another sip from the cup. "I didn't think folks would care to see me that way."

"No, I daresay not," Katherine said with a giggle. "Plus, it might get cold during the winter. Come inside before Charlie gives your dinner to the dog."

"Thank you, ma'am." He held the door for her, then stood in the middle of the living room, surveying every detail, from its huge rock fireplace to the rugged but comfortable leather furniture. Several racks of deer antlers were mounted on the walls, and several photographs were proudly displayed on the mantle over the fireplace. Phillip picked up one of the pictures to study and glanced toward Katherine.

"Your wedding?"

"Yes, I was sixteen," she said with a sigh. "Boy, that seems like an age ago." She laughed and joined him. "And that's James," she said, giving the glass a quick swipe with her handkerchief. "I thought he was the most handsome man on earth. The truth was, he was only a child, one year older than me."

"You made a handsome couple." He placed the photo back on the mantle and picked up another. "And who's this?"

"That's my daughter, Abigail." The soft expression on Katherine's face disappeared and she suddenly looked old and grief-stricken.

Phillip replaced the photograph and asked, "Mind my asking what happened to them?"

"Abby died in a blizzard, and James died about a year later. Their graves are beneath the willow behind the barn." The grief disappeared, leaving something cold and unapproachable in its place. She turned on her heel and walked briskly toward the dining room. "You'd better get to the table before Matthew eats your portion. Everyone else is finished."

~   ~   ~

"Ah, it's nice to have a good man around this house to cook for," Charlene said as she refilled Phillip's coffee cup. Katherine had vacated the house shortly after he had asked about the picture of Abigail, leaving a chill behind. Matthew was busy gulping the last of his food by the time Phillip had seated himself.

"Well, if I was Matt, I might get offended by that."

"And why's that, Mr. Denning?"

"Ain't he a man?"

They both looked toward Matthew, who washed the last of the biscuit down with a swig of coffee and said, "Huh?"

"Nothing, boy. Just finish eating so I can clean this place up," Charlene said.

Phillip watched as the boy shoved his hat down tight and shuffled out the door.

"Well, you've got it half right," Phillip said, lifting the cup to his lips. "Thank you, ma'am."

"What was that you said?" The housekeeper paused with the pot in her hand.

"I said, thank you."

"No, no…I don't care about that part. One of your "thank you's" have more than made up for these roughneck boys around here. I'm asking about what you said before, about my being only half right."

"Oh," Phillip lowered the cup and grinned. "I was only saying that I *am* a man, but it remains to be seen exactly how good I am."

"Oh don't you worry yourself none about that," Charlene said with a giggle. "You're good alright, I can tell."

"Well, let's hope so." He spooned a healthy portion of red beans and ham into his mouth and paused, then gave the woman an excited nod.

"Lord Almighty, these are good," he said over a mouthful. He scooped another spoonful into is mouth. "If I knew you'd feed me like this every day, I'd marry you and steal you away from here."

Charlene laughed loudly and scooped more beans and fried potatoes onto his plate. "The offer sounds tempting, but I'm afraid I've had my eye on someone in town for quite awhile. But if he keeps dragging his feet I just might take you up on that offer. I'm also a wee bit older than you, but I'm guessing you and Mrs. Parker are about the same age. If you're looking for a woman, that's the one you should be looking at."

Phillip paused with a mouthful of potatoes. "Not hardly. I'm not the marrying kind, and I don't think she's interested in having a man under foot for very long. No sir, I don't think she's looking for any kind of man, especially an old saddle tramp like me."

"She might not be looking, and I'll grant that she thinks she doesn't need a good man, but she does." Charlene poured herself a cup of coffee and sat across from Phillip. Her intent gaze made him uneasy. "Go on, eat. I'll get you more when you're finished."

"Just wondering what you're driving at, ma'am." He lowered his eyes and shoveled more beans into his mouth.

"I'm just teasing you some, Mr. Denning, I'm not driving at anything. And I certainly wouldn't be saying anything to give you the wrong impression about Mrs. Parker either. She is a fine woman who took me in and made me part of this family when nobody else cared whether I lived or died. She's a good, loving woman who's had some real hurt and sorrow in her life. And you're a fine gentleman. I know that because the boys told me last night how you helped them get their cattle and saved their lives in the process."

"Well, you can't believe everything a boy will tell you, ma'am. They'll embellish the story until you'll never know what is true and what's an outright lie."

"No, except Mrs. Parker told me, and I don't think she was lying."

"Maybe not, but I still don't get what you're driving at."

"Not a thing. I'm just happy she's hired someone to help her and the boys. She's done a right smart job of running this spread. It's starting to wear on her, though. She's starting to look tired and haggard. I'm glad you're here. Please don't do anything to hurt her."

Phillip choked on his coffee and wiped his mouth on his shirtsleeve before speaking.

"You throw a mighty big loop, woman. What makes you think I'd do anything to hurt her?"

"Not a thing, Mr. Denning. Now me personally, I don't have anything but the highest respect for an honest hand. Mrs. Parker usually hires her hands a little later when she figures it's close to spring roundup. You're the first she's hired this early, and I suspect it was because you lent her a hand with the rustlers." She studied him intently before she continued.

"The thing is, I don't know you, cowboy, and I don't know what you're capable of. From what I gathered by listening to them talk last night, you might have a dark side to you. I want you to understand that Mrs. Parker is a special person, and I'd do anything to protect her and them boys."

"Charlie, hurting Mrs. Parker and her boys is the last thing on my mind. She was generous enough to hire me, and when I take someone's money, I ride for the brand. I don't know any other way. And I don't intend to ruin it by doing something stupid." He scooted away from the table and grabbed his hat.

"Thank you for a fine meal, ma'am. It was real good, and some interesting conversation if I do say so myself."

"You're quite welcome, Mr. Denning, and I'll count it a privilege to cook your meals."

Charlene sat at the table sipping her coffee long after he was gone. She could see the corral through the window from her vantage point, and watched as Mrs. Parker and Mr. Denning rode out together, leaving her alone, with the dog begging for table scraps at the kitchen door.

"Okay, okay. Hold your fur on, I'm coming." She rose slowly and raked the leftovers into a chipped bowl for the yapping animal. "Feeding those boys is bad enough. I don't need you raising a fuss."

CHAPTER 6

Nathan Thomas sat at a rickety card table inside The Snake Den dealing a hand of Five-Card Stud to himself and four empty chairs. The green felt covering the tabletop was torn in several places and decorated with stains. Nathan was positive at least one of the stains had to be blood. Earl Tucker, the bartender, was busy rinsing glasses in a pan of amber-colored water and drying them on a soiled towel. The old man seated at a corner table with an empty bottle was snoring loudly. One of two "ladies" who worked at The Snake Den sat at the bar, which consisted of several planks stacked atop empty barrels. She was smoking thin cigars and coughing. Nathan didn't know where the other one was, and could care less.

The Snake Den existed solely for the inhabitants of what was called End Of The Line, a smattering of cabins, shacks and a few tents, nestled in the rugged badlands. End Of The Line wasn't a recognized community of any sort, with a population that usually consisted of less than a hundred bandits, rustlers and murders on any given day. Nathan figured it might be a fitting place to be, given the circumstances in which he found himself. There was a time when he could have walked into most any respectable establishment and been well received, but he had taken the wrong fork in a trail and found himself here, dealing cards to no one and drinking whisky not fit to remove boot polish.

The Lakota had aptly called this erosion-chiseled portion of South Dakota *Mako Sica*, or "bad land," and Nathan figured it fit. It was a maze of deep canyons, rocky spires and jagged buttes that could swallow an entire army and never spit them out again. Riffraff running from the law loved the country, knowing few lawmen would ever follow them in. End Of The Line was one of several such villages created by, and catering solely to, these men and women. It had actually become the end of the line for many who were either killed by Indians or other outlaws over a card game or some other senseless dispute. Nathan kept to himself, talking to few and refusing to play cards with others. It was safer that way.

He poured himself another drink, more to pass the time than anything else. It had been a long and twisted journey that had brought him here, and he needed to find a way to return to a normal way of living. Nathan figured he would have long done so except for one man, Phillip Denning. He had considered killing the man, except he knew and liked Phil, and more or less agreed that Denning had a reason to dog him. Nathan might have thought it a comedy of errors that brought him to this point, except it hadn't actually been funny, just odd.

He had become acquainted with Denning during the Lincoln County War, and the two men had fought on the same side. They were friendly with each other, and Nathan had begun calling Denning one of his pards. They had somehow drifted apart after the dust and the gunsmoke had settled. Denning had become sheriff of Crown Point, while Nathan drifted aimlessly from town to town, gambling and raising hell. Then, he woke up one day with empty pockets and an equally empty stomach. He needed money to survive on, but ranching jobs were hard to find, and he'd burnt a lot of bridges since his Lincoln County days. He remembered drifting through Crown Point and running into his old pard Denning about six months earlier. It wasn't much of a town, with a mostly Navajo population, but it did have a large bank that serviced the coal mines in the area. He remembered standing next to Denning as the Wells Fargo stage rolled into town and offloaded a strongbox full of cash.

Nathan had never wanted to cause his old pard any trouble, so he devised a foolproof plan, where no one would get hurt, and Denning would never know who had robbed his bank. He found three men who were equally as hungry. A shady Mexican by the name of Francisco Torres, a half-breed Navajo named Jesus Tapia, and Carl Lilly, who was a half-wit looking for quick money. Carl was his biggest mistake, and the main reason he was in The Snake Den.

It was a simple plan, and should have worked. They were to wait until the day the stage was to roll into Crown Point. Part of the gang would ride out to one of the coal mines and cause a little diversion, then wait until Denning left town to investigate. They would rob the bank while he was away, and be long gone before he even knew what hit him. And best of all, no one would get hurt. That was the plan, and it worked well up to a point.

Nate arrived a couple of days early and made sure of the stage schedule by pretending to want passage to Albuquerque.

"The stage arrives day after tomorrow, and leaves for Albuquerque early afternoon. A ticket will cost you five dollars, young man." The man behind the counter was a shriveled prune with a balding head, who hardly looked at Nate as he shuffled stacks of paper from one side of the counter to the other.

"Thanks. I'll be in day after tomorrow and get one."

"I wouldn't wait too long, sonny," he said as Nathan turned away. "The stage usually leaves full, and you'll be waiting until Friday if you miss this one."

"Thanks. I'll keep it in mind," Nate said, closing the door.

Things went like clockwork. Francisco and Tapia rode out to the mine two hours before the stage was due, and cause a ruckus by lobbing several sticks of dynamite and taking several shots near, but not hurting any workers. They rushed back to town under the cloak of confusion, and were sitting quietly drinking a beer with Nate and Carl when several people from the mine arrived. They could hear their loud, angry voices across the street as they told Denning they were attacked by neighboring mine owners. Nate chuckled to himself as Denning rode out of town with the miners. Half an hour later, the stage rolled into town. It was twenty minutes late, but still close enough for his purposes. They finished their beers as the driver and guard carried the strongbox into the bank.

Nate waited another ten minutes, to make sure the box and safe had been opened, then strolled calmly toward the door, only to be informed by the guard that the bank was closed until they had finished counting the payroll for the coal mines.

"Really?" Nate said. "I think you might want to let us in anyway," he added as Carl Lilly shoved a gun in the man's back. Nate took the driver's shotgun and ushered him inside.

"Okay, gentlemen, as you can tell, we're robbing this bank. Now, I don't want anyone hurt, so just bag up the paper as quick as possible." He pointed the driver's shotgun at the bank teller and grinned. "Come on now, move it along." They had the money in a matter of minutes and were out the door. That was when things went wrong.

The teller rushed to the door yelling, "They're robbing the bank! They're robbing the bank!" Carl Lilly was already on his horse, but swung around and shot the man in the chest.

"Dammit, Carl. I said no killing," Nate yelled, to no effect.

A young deputy, no more than a kid, rushed into the street yelling, "Halt! Drop your guns!" Carl swung back around and shot him in the head.

Nate leaned low across his horse's neck and dug his spurs into its flanks. They rushed full speed out of Crown Point amid a hail of gunfire. It was a miracle they escaped unscathed. They divided the money several hours later, as they sat hidden among some rocks and trees.

"Here's where we part, boys, and I'd recommend you clear out of New Mexico. Our sharp-shooting friend here just stirred up a hornet's nest. There wasn't supposed to be any killing, but he saw fit to kill the teller and deputy both."

"Well, I ain't used to leaving witnesses around to point me out. Besides, you didn't say anything about a deputy, now did you?"

"He didn't have one six months ago, but it doesn't matter. I'd recommend we don't sit around here arguing about it, either. Phillip Denning will be hot on our trails by now."

"So? I just might wait around and kill him too. That'll solve all our problems, now won't it?"

"Huh," Nate said with a smirk as he stuffed his share into his saddlebags. "You don't know Denning. I do, and he doesn't die too easily. Adios, amigos." He touched the brim of his hat and rode north.

That was three years ago, and the bank money was long gone. Word drifts fast when you ride on the wrong side, and he'd heard rumors that Carl Lilly had waited for Denning and suffered the consequences. Denning had also caught up with Francisco Torres in Gallup and sent him to his maker with three forty-four slugs before the Mexican could clear leather. The same thing happened to Jesus Tapia last year in Wyoming. Nathan was the last one left, and he knew Denning was close...he could feel him. Nate rolled his last twenty-dollar gold piece in his fingers, wondering if Francisco and Jesus might not be the lucky ones after all.

The door crashed open with a bang as Moses Martin helped Pox to the nearest table. The front of the man's shirt and vest was covered with dried blood.

"Jesus, Pox, what the hell happed to you?" Earl asked. He tossed the dirty towel on the counter and made his way from behind the bar to take a closer look. Nate thought the man might have been shot, until he tilted his head back to reveal his smashed lips and missing front teeth.

"That woman we've been stealing cattle from has herself a new hired hand," Randy Houk said nervously. "We'd stopped around midday to rest the cattle and make some coffee. First, it was just the woman and her boys. They came on us out of nowhere. Jerry started talking some line of horse manure about the steers belonging to us, then he decided to pull his gun. That's when he shot him."

"Talk some sense, boy," the bar keep barked. "Who shot who?"

"That new man working for the woman shot Jerry," Moses said. "Used a Winchester and killed him deader'n a doornail. Then, he bashes Pox in the mouth and starts to hang us."

"Hang you?" The whore set her glass on the counter and swished her ample hips as she sauntered toward Randy. She was in her mid-twenties and past her prime as a prostitute. Her dark eyes were deep-set in her heavily painted puffy face, which was accented by a set of tobacco-stained teeth. "How'd you boys escape hanging?" she asked as she ran her fingers through Randy's damp hair.

"He started crying and begging. The woman felt sorry for him and ordered them to haul us off to the sheriff in Denby," Moses said with a snort.

"Them?" Earl asked. "She had more men working for her?"

"Naw, you idgit! She was barking orders to that new guy and them boys of hers. They had us all tied up with our hands behind our backs and loaded on our horses. Then Pox digs his spurs in and yells. He takes off right through the middle of them and we followed. They took a couple of shots at us, but we got away just the same."

"Get me some whiskey," Pox mumbled. His real name was Walter Tivo, but he had been given his nickname after surviving a case of smallpox in his teen years.

"Sure, Pox. Sorry, I should have poured you one when I first seen you." Earl rushed to fill a glass and set it before the big man who sipped, but cried in pain the instant the liquid touched his lips. Nate laughed out loud and received angry looks from the group.

"This new man got a name?" he asked casually.

"The woman kept calling him *Mr. Denning*," Randy said, brushing the whore's hand away from his long blond hair.

"Nate snorted as he laughed again. "Thought it might be him."

"Why? You know him?"

"You might say that." Nate took time pouring another drink and toasted the group. "I met him awhile back in Lincoln County. You'd best stay clear of him, boys. He's meaner than a rattlesnake."

"The hell you say!" Moses Martin puffed his chest and tossed back a drink. "I'm gonna kill the son-of-a-bitch first chance I get."

Nate smiled and nodded.

"What's your name, son? Randy, isn't it?"

"Yes sir, Randy Houk."

"Well, Randy Houk, you'd be better off shedding yourself of their company. They're only going to get you killed."

CHAPTER 7

Katherine sat on a rugged bench under the shade of her porch sipping a cup of hot tea. The afternoon ride with Phillip Denning had been profitable. She had simply planned on showing him the lay of the land and the canyon where the boys were working, but he had insisted on searching the brush himself, and had produced several strays. He knew ranching and was not afraid of hard work.

"So, Mr. Denning, tell me about yourself," she said on their ride back to the house.

"I've told you just about everything there is to tell, ma'am. I'm just a no-account saddle bum."

"Okay, let me ask you this one question. You're not wanted by the law for murder or something I should know about, are you?"

"No, ma'am, I'm not. Guess that's the whole point of cowboying. No one's really looking for you, and you're as free as a bird."

He followed that statement with a crooked grin that made her wonder how true it really was. She decided that he was either hiding or running from something, and she would eventually discover what it was, one way or the other. She just hoped it would not be something that would bring danger to her sons or this ranch. In the meantime, she resigned herself to keeping an eye on the man to decide for herself how much trust to give him. At the present, she could hear him clunking around inside the tack room and singing a song about an old slave named Uncle Ned. The fact that he had been in there for nearly ten minutes had her curious.

Timothy came from the barn and walked lazily toward the house, stopping several times to glance toward the tack room. He sat on the bench beside his mother and stared toward the small building with weathered siding.

"What's Mr. Denning up to, Ma?"

"Cleaning the tack house, I guess."

"Why? I mean, I just swept it yesterday, and we hung everything just the way you like it."

"I know. I checked when you were done."

The statement brought a scowl from her son.

"I'm your mother. I have that right. Evidently, Mr. Denning thought he needed to move things around to make room for his own grip."

"Well, you don't need to be checking on me like that. Check on Matt and the others, if you want. My room's always cleaner than theirs." The boy gave her an indignant glare.

"Timothy Eugene! Telling lies is a sin that God frowns on, and you know it."

"My room's clean. Just go look, if you don't believe me," he said pointing toward the house.

"I don't have to. I know it's clean, because I caught Charlie cleaning it for you. She did the same for your brothers. I don't know what you boys are going to do if that woman ever leaves here, or falls over dead. Guess you'll have to clean up behind yourselves, or find wives that'll work like slaves picking up after you." She gave him a grin.

They grew silent as the man came outside to shake several blankets then disappear back indoors singing a different tune.

"Still would like to know what Mr. Denning is doing."

"Well, I can't help you there, because he didn't tell me. Why don't you go ask, if you're so curious?"

"I probably won't have to," Timothy said as Steven stopped on his way from the barn and poked his head inside the tack room. "He's always sticking his nose into someone's business."

"Oh, and I guess it's better to go around puzzled about something and asking questions of people who don't know, than to simply ask the right person."

Timothy waited until Steven had reached the porch before asking.

"I don't know. Rearranging the tack room, I guess," the boy said with a shrug and bounded past and into the house.

"Well, you're a lot of help," Timothy yelled after him.

"Oh, you boys, I'll go ask him myself." Katherine said, and crossed the yard at a brisk pace.

"Mr. Denning?" she said, poking her head through the open door.

"Yes, ma'am?" He wiped his face with a bandana.

"The boys and I are curious as to what you are doing."

"Just moving things around some, ma'am."

"Yes, I can see that, and you're doing a fine job of it. But Timothy just cleaned the tack house and everything was in its place." She stepped inside and gazed at the neatly hung gear and saddles stacked on sawhorses along one wall. A fine dusty haze hung in the air from the vigorous sweeping, and the floors and window sills were dirt-free. "You've done a fine job, Mr. Denning, but what possessed you to take on such a project? Everything already had a place, and I'm certain there was plenty of room for your grip."

"Yes ma'am. I just reckoned it would be a fine place for me to bunk at night. I'll toss my bedroll along that wall," he pointed as he talked. "I think it'll be just fine."

Katherine stared at the blankets neatly folded in the corner and felt her cheeks flush. The subject of sleeping arrangements was something that hadn't crossed her mind.

"Oh, I'm terribly sorry, Mr. Denning. I guess with the stolen cattle and everything going on…well, I simply forgot to tell you, but we do have a spare room in the rear of the house that our hands used. I'll have Charlie lay out some fresh blankets for you."

"No need to bother with that ma'am, this will work out just fine. I'm an early riser, and I'd probably wake everyone up clumping around inside your house in the dark. Besides, for the past couple of years, I mostly tossed my war bag on the ground. This is bound to be more comfortable than sleeping on the ground. As long as I can keep the dog off my bed." He stomped his boot against the wooden floor and yelled as the dog wandered through the opened door.

"Ya! Get outta here you mangy flea-bitten bag of bones!"

"Well," she cleared her throat, "the choice is yours, Mr. Denning. The offer of the spare room still stands. Charlie will have supper ready in about an hour, so make sure you're on time, or my boys won't leave anything for you."

"Yes, ma'am, and thank you."

She paused at the door and looked over her shoulder. "Thank me for what?"

"For hiring me and giving me a place to stay."

"Oh, you're quite welcome, Mr. Denning. I'll see you at supper."

She walked briskly to the house and shouted from the middle of the living room.

"Matthew…Joshua…Timothy…Steven! You boys get in here…now!"

"Yes, Ma. What's wrong?" asked Matthew, as they scrambled into the room to face her like soldiers. Charlene, holding a large spoon, came from the kitchen to see what was happening.

"Everything. I forgot about sleeping arrangements for Mr. Denning, and he's taken it upon himself to turn our tack house into a bunk house for himself."

"The tack house? Why?" Steven scrunched up his nose.

"Yes, the tack house, and he has done a fine job of it too. Now, you boys are going to have to remember it's his bedroom, and don't enter without knocking."

"That might get kinda hard, if you've got a handful of saddle and bridle," Joshua said with a laugh.

"Do it anyway. Use your foot, if you have to. There may be times I ask him to work nights, and if I find you've been busting in and disturbing his sleep, you'll be sleeping in the tack house, and Mr. Denning will be sleeping in your bed. I'm serious. Does everyone understand me?"

"Yes, ma'am," all four answered in unison as Charlene returned to the kitchen laughing.

"Now, I want you boys to climb up into the attic, and get Abby's bed down and take it to Mr. Denning."

"Abby's bed?" Matthew cocked his head to one side. "I thought you said no one was to touch it. Why can't we give him one of the cots from the spare room?"

"The last time I checked, those cots were in sad shape and need replacing. Besides, I simply will not have someone who just saved our lives sleeping on a cold plank floor. Hurry up now, you've got time before Charlie says it's time to eat."

"Now? Why not after we eat?" Timothy whined.

"Because I said so, and I'm your mother."

"Yes, ma'am."

Katherine waited until the boys were scurrying to carry out her orders before entering the kitchen.

"Why in the world didn't you say something, Charlie? You let me make a fool out of myself. I could have had the boys get Abby's bed this afternoon."

Charlene cocked her head and raised her eyebrows as she stirred the pot of stew.

"Sorry, ma'am. I thought you had the sleeping arrangement taken care of, or I would have taken it upon myself."

"Really? You didn't see me doing anything, so where was he supposed to sleep?"

"That, I cannot answer, ma'am. I guess it *has* been a long time since we've had any hired hands to care for." She grinned and turned to check on the bread baking in the oven.

~   ~   ~

Katherine lay awake studying the pine ceiling planks, and musing how they looked different in the moonlight than in the day. Several of the boards above the wood-burning stove were dry and were cracking. Someday, she would have to buy a jug of tongue-oil from Jordan's store in Denby to help preserve them.

She had no idea why Mr. Denning's sleeping in the tack house instead of the spare bedroom had bothered her. Perhaps it was that she didn't want him to think her thoughtless and uncaring. It didn't really matter, seeing as he was, in his own words, *a no-account saddle bum*, and had only been hired for the season. When fall came, they would have another roundup to drive the cattle back into the winter canyon for protection from the cold winds and snow. Then Mr. Denning would be free to wander where his heart might dictate.

Charlie's words had been an irritation to her. The woman had been insinuating for quite awhile now that Katherine had been too long without male companionship. She had to admit there were times she had thought briefly on such things, but she never allowed herself the luxury of dwelling on the subject very long. It didn't help solve the problems that rose daily on this ranch. Besides, James hadn't really been much company the year between Abby's disappearance and his own death. He simply moped around, longing and looking for his lost daughter, then finally pined away and died. No one else had existed or mattered as far as he was concerned. He acted as though losing Abby hadn't hurt her and their sons just as much. He was so wrapped up in his grief that Katherine was left to handle her own mourning in hard work and solitude. He had no loving arms to console her with, so in reality, she had lost both her daughter and husband at the same time.

No, she didn't need another man in her life, especially one as shiftless as Phillip Denning. She had raised four hairy-legged men of her own, and they were plenty to have under foot. Mr. Denning's converting the tack house into a bunk house had been a waste of time and effort. They had perfectly good sleeping quarters, built specially for hired hands at the rear of the house. The large room was something James had insisted on. He believed they would never have more than two or three seasonal hands, and a separate bunkhouse would become wasted space. Instead of converting the tack house, what Mr. Denning should have been doing was giving his clothes and body a good scrubbing in a hot tub of water.

Katherine's eyes drooped and finally closed as she yawned. That was a subject she would approach him with tomorrow.

CHAPTER 8

Katherine was awakened by Charlie's loud angry voice in the yard. She was giving someone a good scolding and not mincing her words. *What'd my boys do to her now?* She crawled out of bed, opened her window and leaned out to see what was bothering the housekeeper. The sun had barely begun to creep over the canyon wall, and Katherine had to adjust her eyes to the dim light, then cover her mouth to smother her laughter. Charlie was giving Mr. Denning a good scolding as the man attempted to bathe in the freezing-cold watering trough with his long-johns on.

"Get yourself out of there before you catch your death of cold! Besides, those poor animals have to drink this water."

"Maybe so. But I always wash up in a water trough, and it hasn't killed any animals yet. Besides, I've only got one extra shirt, and it's not fit to wear in front of a coyote."

"Oh, my word," Katherine said as the man lifted his shirt out of the trough and began wringing it. She opened the bottom drawer of her dresser and retrieved one of James' shirts and a pair of corduroy britches. They were still arguing as she opened the front door.

"Hey, you two," she yelled and made her way to the trough in her bare feet. "I realize I over-slept, but that's no way to wake a person in the morning. What is going on, here?"

"This woman won't let a man take a bath and do his laundry in peace, ma'am."

"And this man," Charlene motioned toward the trough in disgust, "is trying to catch pneumonia and poison your horses at the same time."

"Well," Katherine said with a nod, "oddly enough, I can agree with both of you. Mr. Denning did need to bathe and wash his clothes. However, I also agree with you, Charlie, the horse trough is no place to wash your clothes, especially since I don't see a bar of soap in sight. Here," she handed the maid the change of clothes, "Mr. Denning can wear these, *after* he bathes with soap in the wash tub. Then, if you'll be so kind, perhaps you can see if his shirts and britches are worth washing. I think they could stand a good boiling."

"With pleasure, ma'am." Charlene took the clothes and stood like an army guard at her post. "You heard the boss…get out of that trough and come to the house. I've already got water heating."

"Well, I can't, not with you women watching."

"Why not, I've seen grown men buck-naked before."

"Yes, ma'am, but not this one."

Katherine couldn't help herself and burst out laughing. "You're dressed in your long-handled underwear, Mr. Denning, and far from being naked. So please get out of my horses' water."

She could see all four boys snickering from the living room window as she made her way back to the house.

~   ~   ~

"That shirt seems to fit you pretty well," she said as Phillip joined them for breakfast. He had bathed, shaved and combed back his hair, making a striking difference between the Phillip Denning they knew, and the one seating himself at the table.

"Yes, ma'am, and I thank you. I know I must have made quite a sight when I first rode up here."

"Yes, you did, and I'm sure we all welcome the change."

"Well, I don't," Matthew snarled as he pushed away from the table.

"Matthew, that was rude! Apologize to Mr. Denning," Katherine said.

"No, I won't. Those are Papa's clothes. You're letting him wear them, just like you gave him Abby's bed. He's not even part of the family."

"Your ma's just lending me the clothes, son, until mine get washed."

"I'm not your son, so don't ever call me that again!"

"I'm sorry."

"And," Matthew turned to yell at his mother, "I don't need you bringing some saddle tramp into the house to take the place of Dad."

"Matthew, I'm not doing that at…"

He stormed out of the dining room and slammed the front door.

"Ooo, that boy…I'll give him a piece of…" Katherine started after him, but stopped when Phillip grabbed her arm.

"Let him be, ma'am. Going after him now will only make things worse. I'll take care of it myself, later."

She sat back down and began picking at her pancakes and moving bite-sized pieces around with her fork. Joshua and Timothy did the same, while Steven just sat, staring at Phillip for a great while before breaking the silence.

"I don't feel like you're taking my pa's place, Mr. Denning. You're a whole different person."

"Glad to hear that, son, because I never intended to try. I never knew your pa, but from the looks of this ranch he built, and this house, and knowing your ma and seeing you boys, I'd wager he was a pretty good man. One I could never measure up to."

CHAPTER 9

"Ride 'im high, Ma," Timothy yelled as Katherine adjusted herself in the saddle. They had spent the past week rounding up the remuda, and were now selecting the individual string each rider would be working with. Katherine had chosen a particular grey called Smoke. He was a large, unruly horse who had been sired by Culpepper.

"Don't let him get you to the back of the saddle," Timothy continued as she gripped the reins in her gloved hands. She waved off his comments as Smoke snorted and pawed the ground nervously. Phillip tugged downward on the bridle to hold him steady. Timothy had chosen Smoke previously, but had never been able to stay in the saddle longer than a few seconds. After being tossed several times, he happily chose another animal more suited to being ridden.

This was her specialty. Katherine loved each and every horse on her ranch, and considered them to be part of the family. Larger ranches might have remudas with ninety to a hundred horses, but no one had better horses. She personally chose each horse bought and sold on her ranch. She had an eye for good horseflesh, and knew within seconds whether or not a horse was fit for ranching. James used to call it her "sixth-sense," and happily left the horses to her. Ginger was a living testimony to her ability to breed good stock. Ginger was a large, muscular mare, with both speed and heart. The horse was intelligent, and cattle ranching came natural to her.

Neighboring ranchers had been trying to buy the mare the past several years, but she was Katherine's personal favorite, and not for sale at any price.

"Ready ma'am?" Phillip asked. Katherine nodded. "You've got him," he yelled, and released his grip on the bridle.

Smoke shot across the corral heaving like a tormented sea. Katherine was only vaguely aware of cheers and whistles coming from Phillip and her sons, who were perched atop the fence. She rocked in motion with the beast trying to throw her. Some horses were inclined to pitch regardless of their years in service, especially during the spring when the grass was green. Sometimes it was best to saddle a particular animal and allow him to "soak" for awhile, but this was not the case with Smoke. The gelding had his father's temperament, and did not want to be ridden, period. Katherine had been Culpepper's favorite human, and she thought it might be the case with his son.

Her neck and shoulders ached from a previous ride on a bay, but that was normal for a bronc-buster. This was not a rodeo, it was cattle-ranching. Clayton Jones had said during a combined roundup years earlier, "When you fork one of them babies, you'll learn to live with busted bones and constant back pain, 'cause that's what you'll get as a reward." Clayton walked hunched-over with a limp as testimony that he knew what he was talking about. The old man was her closest neighbor and personal friend. She often wondered if she'd walk hunched-over when she reached his age.

The horse leaped high into the air and came down stiff-legged, causing her teeth to clack inside her mouth. He then jerked hard to the left, dislodging her from the saddle. Katherine felt her breath leave her body as she slammed face first into the dust.

"You okay, ma'am?" Phillip asked. She pushed his hand away as he tried to help her to her feet.

"She alright?" Steven yelled.

"Yes, yes, I'm okay. I just got the wind knocked out of me. Give me a minute and I'll get back on." She leaned heavily against the fence as Matthew tossed a loop around Smoke's neck and herded him into a separate corral. Phillip instantly mounted a coal-black mustang that snorted and pitched around the corral, trying to shake its rider loose.

A good horse went into the remuda when he was four years old, and by the time he was six, he would be fairly trained for cow work. He wouldn't reach his full usefulness until he was about ten years old. A good and faithful horse would be pensioned for a life of ease and only be ridden for pleasure. Others wound up pulling wagons and plows. Any horse not meeting her standards was culled from the herd and sold. Each rider would need seven or eight head in their personal string, consisting of two "morning horses," two "afternoon horses," two "cutting horses," and a "night horse." Everyone could have as many broncs as they wanted to ride. Any bronc that could not be broken was useless for working cattle, and she would eventually sell them, along with those past their prime for farm work.

"He's pretty good," Matthew said sullenly as he leaned next to her, watching the spectacle.

"Yes, he is."

They watched until the mustang grew tired and trotted around the corral, snorting his displeasure at being ridden.

Katherine figured an outfit would never be any better than its horses, and she had the best. She ordered her boys to check on them and give her a daily count, to make sure none were hurt or missing. She also expected everyone to be responsible for the condition of his string, and would not tolerate anyone abusing her horses. She had hired a cowhand two years ago, and fired him the following day for beating a gelding that had pitched him while cutting cattle. She never allowed any horse to be overworked or overlooked. These animals were the power that moved cattle ranching forward, and they would be handicapped without them.

"By the way," Katherine turned to Timothy as she adjusted her gloves. "Wasn't I the one who taught you how to ride?"

"Yes, ma'am."

"I thought so. Now, bring Smoke back inside."

"You sure? I can ride the dun and give you a break, if you want."

Katherine glared at him.

"Okay."

She waited while Timothy led the large animal to the center of the corral. Her remuda would consist mostly of geldings, with a few exceptions. Two of the exceptions were Ginger and Culpepper, which she occasionally rode during roundup simply because she loved the animals. Mares however, were generally considered bunch-quitters and failures as saddle horses. Clayton claimed that "Lady horses are like most women. They get the notion of goin' home, and no gentleman cayuse is gonna think of lettin' a lady go alone." She had found the saying to be true for the most part, but she also discovered that stallions were like a bunch of rowdy boys, and fought one another. She would have her boys single out any new males from the herd once they had finished choosing their string, and decide which ones were fit to become geldings or breeding stock, and cull the rest.

She climbed onto Smoke's back while Matthew tugged down on the bridle, holding the horse's head low. She could hear Phillip's voice as she adjusted herself in the saddle.

"Well, she's sure got sand, I'll give her that."

CHAPTER 10

"He's a fine little man, ma'am," Phillip said, rubbing the glossy chestnut-colored colt. Katherine felt a lump in her throat as the tiny animal stood on wobbly legs trying to receive its first meal from its mother.

Joshua had rushed into her bedroom at four o'clock the following morning and proceeded to shake her awake.

"I'm awake!" she yelled. "For goodness sake, quit shaking me and let me get my robe. You woke me when you banged my door open." She groaned and held a hand against her aching back as she stumbled out of bed, almost tripping over his feet. "What's wrong? Is someone sick?"

"The mare is having her colt…right now!"

Katherine stared at her son through squinty eyes before inhaling deeply and releasing the air slowly.

"You burst into my room this time of night shaking the dickens out of me to tell me the mare is having her baby? What is the matter with you?"

"You said you wanted to know the minute it happened."

"Yes I did, I'm sorry to admit." She pulled the robe tight and tied the sash into a knot. "Who's with her?"

"Mr. Denning," he said as they hurried down the hall. Matthew, Steven and Timothy all had their heads poked into the hallway.

"What' wrong, Ma?" Matthew asked as they passed.

"Your brother says the mare is foaling."

"Is that all? I'm going back to bed," Timothy said as he disappeared back into his room and shut the door.

"Might as well get up," Katherine said, shoving the door back open. "It'll be time to jingle your spurs before you know it."

Katherine passed through the kitchen, hoping that by some miracle Charlene would be awake and have coffee made. She heaved another sigh when she discovered the kitchen dark and the stove cold.

"How did you find out about the mare, and what are you doing up this early anyway?" she asked as she opened the door.

"I was coming back from the outhouse and saw the lamp inside the barn. I took a peek and saw Mr. Denning. She was almost done giving birth when I looked."

She stopped in the open doorway at the sound of Phillip's voice and watched as he helped the newborn to his feet.

"You're a fine lady, ma'am. Take a look at what you've done. You've given birth to a fine son. He looks something like you. Take a look at those eyes."

She crept silently toward the stall and watched as he worked with the mother and baby. It seemed strange that someone who had recently shot a man and offered to hang three others could be so kind to a horse and her newborn colt. It was Joshua opening the gate that made Phillip jerk around with a start.

"Oh, good morning, ma'am. I see your son woke you. I didn't know you were standing there. You should have said something."

"No, Mr. Denning. I was enjoying myself just watching. How long have you been out here?"

"Most of the night. I heard her whimpering and came to take a peek. She just needed a little help, and did most of the work herself. I think she just wanted the company, to tell the truth. She delivered a fine little boy for you."

"Yes, he is beautiful, Mr. Denning. Thank you."

Phillip made sure the newborn was standing on its own before washing his hands in a bucket of water. "What are you going to name him, ma'am?"

"I don't know. Since you're the one who spent most of the night delivering him, perhaps you should give him a name."

"Me?"

"Yes you, Mr. Denning. What is the first thing that comes to your mind?"

"Not much." He shrugged.

"Well, what are you thinking right this minute?"

Phillip squinted toward the beam of sunlight seeping through the open door and snickered.

"I was thinking that it's already morning. That's the sun rising, if I'm not mistaken."

"Sunrise it is," Katherine said with a nod of her head. She squatted on her heels beside the sucking colt and grinned.

"Hello, Sunrise. Welcome to the world. You're going to become part of our family."

Phillip dried his hands on a soiled towel and shook his head.

"Sorry 'bout that boy. If I'd had a couple of cups of coffee in me and been thinking straight, I would have given you a more proper name, something like Comanche or Bandit. Hope being named Sunrise doesn't turn you into a sissy."

He shoved his hat down on his head and headed toward the smell of fresh coffee coming from the kitchen.

CHAPTER 11

Katherine found Phillip mid-afternoon in the winter canyon sitting on his heels and rolling a cigarette, while Lucky searched for something to graze on nearby. They were supposed to be flushing the remaining strays out in order to give the ground a chance to replenish itself before the next winter hit.

"Well, looks like you're hard at it, Mr. Denning," she said, sliding out of the saddle. "Did delivering the colt wear you out, or do you think those strays are going to join the others on their own?"

"No, ma'am, I think we've got nearly all of them right now. The boys are beating the brush right now to make sure."

"So, my boys are busy working, while you sit here resting. Is that the way it works?"

"No, ma'am, I was just thinking about something."

"It doesn't have anything to do with the way Matthew's been acting lately, does it? Because I've had enough of his snippy attitude toward everyone, and I'm especially angry at the way he's been treating you."

"No, ma'am, it doesn't have a thing to do with your son. I'll take care of that when the time is right and now isn't the time. I was just thinking about this canyon, and how you drive all your cattle down here each winter."

"Yes, the wind gets mighty cold here. It can freeze you to the bone, if you're caught out in it. A lot of cattlemen have found any number of their stock frozen to the ground. We discovered the high walls give them quite a bit of protection."

"Yes, I grant it's a right nice little canyon, and probably does most of the things you say it does. You've got a year-round stream, plenty of grass in the summer, and nice high walls. The only thing you don't have is enough of those things to keep all the cattle you've got. Quite a few of the steers we've been driving out of here are skin and bone."

"Yes, I realize they are thin. I really don't know what else I can do. This is the best place I have to winter them in. I guess I could sell half my stock this fall. I didn't really want to do that, though."

"I don't think there's any need to do that." He rose to his feet and crushed the cigarette under the toe of his boot. "You might sell some, but not half. Come on, I want to show you something."

He jumped on his horse in one fluid motion and spurred it into a gallop across the valley toward a high rocky wall, bordering the north end of the canyon. Katherine followed as he rode halfway up the slope and dismounted where the wall became steeper. "Come on," he said with a grin, and began climbing. Philip stopped every once in awhile to offer his hand, but Katherine shook her head.

"Keep going, Mr. Denning, I'm doing just fine," she panted as she struggled up the slope. He stopped to grin several times and climbed faster. She finally forgot her pride and grabbed his hand, and was easily pulled upward onto a ledge, sweating and panting, to find him sitting and looking almost as fresh as he was at the breakfast table.

"Okay, Mr. Denning, what was it that made you decide to climb all the way up here? I hope you didn't think I needed the exercise or excitement."

"No, ma'am. Look behind you."

She turned to spy a black hole in the side of the hill.

"A cave? You made me climb up here to see a cave? There are small caves all over this ranch. We could have seen one not too far from the house."

"Granted, but this one can become useful.'

"Useful? How so, Mr. Denning? I would like to hear."

"Come on, and I'll show you." He grabbed her by the hand and led her into the mouth of the cave, then stopped to light a small candle. They pressed deeper into the mouth and it suddenly opened into a wide cavern with solid rock floor that seemed to go on forever.

"My word, I never realized this was here, and I've lived on this ranch more than twenty years."

"I'll bet your boys have never been up here either," Phillip said turning in a small circle. "Come here, I want to show you something." He pulled her toward a wall to reveal ancient cave drawings.

"Some Indians used this cave hundreds, maybe thousands of years ago. I'll bet we're the first humans that have come here since. You can't see the opening from the canyon floor at all. The only way I knew about it, was I rode down here late last night, after you folks had gone to bed. I happened to see some bats flying out of here."

"Bats?" Katherine jerked around in a circle. "We're in a hole with bats?"

"Don't worry, they won't bother you. They're asleep right now, and only wake when it gets dark. Come on." He took her by the hand and led her back out into the sunlight.

"Well, sit down and rest a minute and tell me what you think." He leaned against a rock and patted another with his gloved hand.

"Tell you what I think about what? It's a large hole in the side of my canyon wall," Katherine said with a shrug. "Is that what you want to hear?"

He laughed and took his time rolling a cigarette while he talked.

"Well, the way I see it, there's no reason to graze this valley to the dirt and starve your cows half to death in the winter. You've got plenty of grassland to the west and this cave."

"That's quite true, but as you well know, if you've spent a winter in South Dakota, the grassland is exposed to some of the harshest wind and freezing snow around. It's not fit for man or cattle when the weather turns. We need to bring them to a sheltered canyon, such as this, or stand a chance of losing them."

"Uh-huh, I agree," he said with a nod and struck a match against the rock to light his cigarette.

"Well, I'm glad you agree. So what was your point of dragging me up to this cave?"

"The way I see it, ma'am, is you stock this cave with as much feed as you can lay your hands on. Then, when the canyon's been grazed off during the winter months, have the boys fork a ton every now and then down to the steers."

"What?" She gave a short laugh, and scooted away as though she thought him insane. "And just how are we going to get the feed up here in the first place?"

"Let me explain."

"Please do, Mr. Denning."

"You hire a bunch of workers who know something about carving out a roadway. You might even be able to get some Chinese who worked for the railroad. They already know such things, and you won't have to keep an eye on them. They can cut a trail from the mouth of the canyon up to this cave."

"Are you sure you know what you're talking about? We had to climb up here on hand and foot. I don't see how any team of horses or mules could make such a climb."

"They can't, if they try coming the way we came. I reckon if you cut a trail along the edge of the cliff, starting at the mouth," Phil laid a hand on her shoulder as he pointed, "and followed the cliff, it wouldn't be much of a climb for a team of mules at all."

"I see what you mean, but do you have any idea how much that would cost?"

"A bundle, I'm sure."

"Yes it would…more than I have. I guess I could charge admission to our cave of bats to help pay for it. And where do you suppose we're going to get the amount of feed you're talking about?"

"I haven't figured that one out yet. That's your department. I'd say cut hay from the grassland, but you've got mostly short grass, and I don't think you'd get enough to matter. If you could lay hold of it somewhere, and store it in here…it might work. Josh says the snow gets too deep to drive a wagonload of hay down in here come midwinter."

"That's true, once we've had a couple of good storms. The trail's too steep and gets covered with ice. It's a good way to break a horse's leg or worse."

"Well, it's just an idea, ma'am," Phillip said, crushing the cigarette under his heel. "If it could be done, those boys of yours could come up here and fork a ton or so over the side every so often to feed your critters. Come spring, they should be in better shape and you'd have a head start on the summer feed. They'd put on more weight and bring a bigger profit when you got them to market."

Katherine raised her eyebrows and nodded slowly as she allowed his words to roll around inside her head. What he said made sense. It would be a monstrous undertaking, and one that could fall flat. There were a million things that could go wrong. She might not be able to find workers to cut the road in the side of the cliff, or be able to come up with the financing if she did. Just buying the feed to carry them through the winter months would take a huge bite out of her budget. She had quite a sum in savings at the bank, but she was sure that wouldn't be enough, and she'd rather not deplete her account and be crippled in some emergency.

Then, there would be the task of buying or renting other wagons and drivers to stock the cave. There were a million reasons not to even try such a crazy scheme. Katherine reasoned that it was bold and made sense. If it worked, it could become a wise business undertaking. It could possibly make a ton of money for her sons after she was gone and forgotten. But, if it failed…it could also bankrupt her.

"Let me think about it," she finally said, jumping to her feet and dusting her skirt. "I can see what you're talking about might work, Mr. Denning. I need time to consider it from every angle before I commit myself to such a plan."

"Yes, ma'am. I thought you might like to think on it for awhile. Come on, we'd better start back before your boys think I kidnapped you and come looking for us."

The climb down to where the horses waited was much easier, and Phillip had to keep cautioning her to slow down. She was waiting when he finally reached bottom.

"I can see you're half mountain goat," he said with a grin.

"I've been climbing these hills the past twenty years, Mr. Denning. You, evidently, haven't done much climbing at all."

"Not so fast that I stood a chance of breaking my neck. Besides, what's the use of me climbing when I can get Lucky to do it for me?" He slid into the saddle and turned his horse as she caught his bridle.

"I do have one question for you before you ride off. Just who are you, Mr. Denning?"

"Me? I'm just a no-account cowpuncher, ma'am," he said with a grin, then turned his horse and galloped through the brush.

"Not hardly, Mr. Denning, not hardly." She watched his horse weave its way to the canyon bottom before climbing onto her own mount. "A *no-account cowpuncher* would have little knowledge of road-building, or the ability to think up such a plan."

CHAPTER 12

Matthew had been sullen and morose most of the day, and preferred riding by himself. He would have normally carried more than his load, doing the work of two men, but today was not such a day. Instead of being his normal, energetic self, he rode into the brush and, finding a large flat rock, dismounted and sat. And that was how he chose to spend the majority of his day, letting the others do his work.

He had no idea why seeing Phillip Denning in his father's clothing bothered him so. The man seemed nice enough, and had confronted the rustlers, killing one of them, and possibly saved their lives. He had doubted several times since the incident whether he would have had the nerve or ability to pull the trigger of his Henry rifle, even though he had already injected a shell into the chamber as Mr. Denning had said. Matthew had to admit that, just like his mother, he had not seen the man pull his pistol when he turned sideways. There was little doubt the rustler would have killed Joshua, and perhaps every one of them. The very thought made his stomach knot up while he sat on the rock brooding. If Phillip had not gone with them, they might have all been lying by the creek dead, or carted off by some wild creature. Matthew had the impression his father had been a weak man. The thought that he might be just like him, and useless when it came to a fight or facing danger, made the raging storm inside grow darker. That was when he saw them.

They passed not fifty yards from where he sat, evidently without seeing him or his horse in the thick brush. Phillip Denning was pushing his horse at a good clip, weaving his way toward the north side of the valley, with Matthew's mother close behind. Matthew thought there might be trouble brewing, perhaps more rustlers, but that made no sense. The canyon had already been cleared of most cattle. The few strays they might find here and there would not be enough for a rustler to bother with. If it were rustlers, they would be busy cutting cattle from the summer range.

Matthew scampered to the highest point of his rock to see if he might get a handle on what the emergency might be. He could only see a growing trail of dust kicked up by the horses, and an occasional glimpse of a hat bobbing up and down. The riders left the brush and began climbing their horses higher toward the bluff. Matthew shaded his eyes against the sun and scanned the hillside in search of what they were after, but could see nothing.

Thinking perhaps one of his brothers had ridden up the hill and gotten hurt, Matthew thought of following after them. He watched as his mother and Phillip dismounted. He paused to get a good bearing as to the spot they had stopped. He saw them climbing even higher on foot. Seeing a taller rock farther to his right, Matthew jumped from his rock and climbed to a higher vantage point to get a better view. Shading his eyes he watched them climb upward. He wondered if they weren't simply trying to reach the top. Matthew watched as Phillip crawled onto some sort of ledge or flat spot on the cliff, and reached down to haul his mother up. Then they sat to rest. Matthew thought how stupid it was for grown people to climb hillsides when they should be working; then he witnessed the most incredible thing. Phillip Denning took her hand and the two disappeared into the side of the mountain. They were gone for what seemed an eternity. When they came back into the sunlight, they were still holding hands.

They sat talking for awhile, and Phillip placed a hand on her shoulder and kept it there while he pointed at something. Matthew thought it was a pretty friendly gesture, especially for someone his mother hardly knew. He didn't need to think hard to imagine what they had been doing hidden back in the rocks. His father had been dead for five years now, and he had often wondered why his mother had never shown any interest in other men. She was still fairly young and attractive, for a mother, and several of the men they knew had been single, and at least one or two were rich. She had never shown an ounce of interest in anyone, until now, and it infuriated him.

First, she had given him Abby's bed, which she had refused to share with anyone, not even Matthew or his brothers. Next, she was letting him wear his father's clothing, which had not been moved from the drawer he had been using the day he died. Matthew felt his blood boil. No one had to explain what they were doing hidden in the rocks. It didn't take much imagination for him to see it all. He knew very well what had been going on. He'd kill them both if he ever got the chance.

CHAPTER 13

Katherine was coming out of the house carrying a cup of coffee when Matthew brushed past, causing her to slosh the hot liquid over the brim and across her hand.

"Hey! Matthew?"

He ignored her and made his way to his room. Katherine set the cup on the bench and wiped her hand with her bandana, mumbling about her son's rudeness. The boy returned a few minutes later swatting a well-used pair of gloves in his left hand, and bounded off the porch without speaking.

"Matthew?" Katherine said, but he kept walking. "Matthew Henry, you stop right now and talk to your mother," she said forcefully. The boy turned slowly to glare as she came from the porch to face him. Steven and Phillip were busy latching the corral gate and came to watch, standing a few feet away.

"Yes, Mother," he said sullenly.

"What is bothering you? You've been acting like this since yesterday afternoon. You're rude, and making everyone miserable."

"You know."

"No, I don't know. How can I know, if you won't tell me?"

"I happened to see you two yesterday. The both of you."

"You saw me with who yesterday? What are you talking about?"

"Him," he pointed his gloves toward Phillip. "I saw you riding through the brush, and I saw when you climbed the hill, and I saw when you held his hand and went into that cave hidden in the rocks. You were in there an awful long time, Mother. What were you doing in there? Hum? No, don't answer…I know."

"What?" Katherine said with a laugh. The laughter and smile faded quickly as the full impact of what he had accused her of took effect, and she gave him a resounding slap.

"Don't you ever accuse me of something like that again!"

"And don't you ever hit me again, because I'm not your son anymore." Matthew spun on his heel and started for his horse, when Phillip grabbed his arm.

Whoa, son, you've got it all wrong. Your ma and I…" Matthew spun, swinging a wild left haymaker that took Phillip by surprise and knocked him to the ground.

"I warned you to never call me that again. I'm not your son!"

"Okay, boy," Phillip rose from the ground, rubbing his jaw. The look in his eyes frightened Katherine. "I'll let you get away with it this time, because I forgot and deserved it. But don't ever do it again. And as far as your ma is concerned, you've got it all wrong. Nothing happened that she should be ashamed of."

"I don't believe you. Neither of you," he added with a disdainful glance toward Katherine.

"I don't care what you believe, boy. I'm just telling you the truth."

Phillip brushed past Katherine without speaking, to disappear through the kitchen door. Matthew cast a second disdainful glare at her before leaping on his horse and spurring it into a full gallop out of the yard. She started toward the house before noticing Steven staring open-mouthed toward his quickly disappearing brother.

"Come on," she placed a hand on his shoulder, "don't let it bother you. Your brother just misunderstood something and got angry. Let's see if Charlie hasn't baked something sweet for us."

"What the heck is he talking about, Ma?"

"Oh," Katherine heaved a deep sigh, "Mr. Denning was simply showing me a cave he found in the north side of the winter canyon. I guess your brother happened to see us climb the hill and go inside. I spent quite a bit of time studying some old drawings left by Indians who used to live in that cave hundreds of years ago. Your brother, evidently, thought Mr. Denning and I were…well, to put it bluntly…sparking, making love, inside that cave. But I promise…" She was cut short by Steven's laughter.

"What? He's dumber'n a dog turd!"

"Steven!"

"Well he is, Ma. There's a million places better to go sparking, if a couple's got a mind to, instead of an old musty cave that you've got to climb to. If it was me, and I got curious, I would have just climbed up there myself and surprised you."

Katherine arched her eyebrows and nodded. "You're a wise man, Steven Michael. But you still shouldn't call your brother a dog turd. It isn't nice."

"Well, he's acting like one."

"Perhaps, but you shouldn't say it. It isn't nice."

~   ~   ~

"Yeah, and I said he was dumber'n a dog turd, but Ma got mad." Steven finished recounting the tale with a laugh.

"Yes, and if I hear you say it one more time, I'll wash your mouth out with lye soap."

"Well, he *is* sometimes," Timothy said over a mouthful of fried potatoes. They were gathered around the supper table sharing the evening meal, minus a sullen Matthew, who had chosen to have his meal in the privacy of his room.

"He actually thinks Mr. Denning and you were making love inside that musty old cave? Ewww." Joshua crinkled his brow and allowed his glance to dart between Katherine and Phillip.

"What's so awful about that?" Phillip asked as he cut the steak on his plate. "I know I'm not much of a catch, and it'd be quite a stretch for your ma to think in those terms, but she is a handsome woman. I'm sure a lot of men have had that thought."

Katherine allowed her fork to fall to her plate with a loud clink. She retrieved it with trembling fingers as her eyes bounced from Phillip to her plate and back several times before settling on her biscuit. Katherine decided it needed buttering.

"Yeah, but that cave ain't no place to take a girl," Joshua said with a snort.

"That's what I told Ma," Steven said.

"Well, I didn't go there with any of those intentions, although I'm sure a lot of women have looked on Mr. Denning that way." Katherine gave Phillip a nod.

"Thank you, ma'am." Phillip grinned before taking the bite of steak he'd been holding on his fork.

"Besides," Katherine continued, "how would you boys know what that cave is like anyway?"

"Because we've all been there, everyone except Matthew. I don't think he has," Joshua said.

"I stand corrected, ma'am," Phillip said with a nod.

"Really?" Katherine laid her fork aside and held her cup for Charlene to refill with coffee.

"Yeah, Josh found it a long time ago, and showed us," Steven said. "Matthew said he wasn't gonna climb that hill to see a dumb hole in the ground, when he could find dozens of better ones anywhere on this ranch."

"Sounds like someone else I know," Phillip said with a snicker.

"Well, Mr. Denning suggested that we stock that cave with feed for the winter. Then, when our cattle have grazed off the land, we could toss it down for them to eat. What do you boys think about his idea?"

"Might work," Joshua said thoughtfully, chewing a piece of steak. "It's big enough."

"That's what Mr. Denning said. He also suggested that we hire someone to build us a road along the hillside, beginning near the canyon entrance, for wagons to haul the hay in. That's the only part that worries me. I think it might be too costly."

"Why go to all that trouble?" Timothy asked, stuffing half a biscuit inside his mouth.

"You're going to need some way of getting the hay to the cave," Katherine said.

"Yeah, but," Timothy swallowed his biscuit, "the canyon rim has a pretty gentle slope down to the grassland. I've been up there. Why don't you just drive the wagons up there and toss the hay down to that ledge? It's big enough."

"Yeah," Joshua said. "He's right. It's pretty flat from the rim all the way from there to the grassland. You might even be able to cut some prairie grass, if you had a mowing machine."

"Na, it's way too short," Steven said as he buttered his third biscuit.

"It might work. Then it could be tied into bundles and tossed over the cliff. Someone could already be down there to stack it inside," Timothy said, and reached for more potatoes.

"Huh, the boys have it all worked out. Guess my work's done." Phillip gave Katherine a grin.

"Except one thing," Steven said.

"What's that, squirt?" Joshua said.

"How are you gonna get up there during winter to toss the feed down, when everything's frozen and the hill's got snow and ice everywhere? Huh? You're gonna slip and break your stupid neck. I almost broke mine going to the barn last winter."

The table grew silent as everyone pondered the question. Timothy started, but quickly stopped, saying "No, that won't work." Then Phillip, grinning, stabbed another hunk of steak onto his fork and held it up to study.

"It appears the lad has given us an obstacle to overcome." He popped the hunk of meat into his mouth and grinned as he chewed.

CHAPTER 14

Katherine sat on the front porch sipping a cup of coffee in the evening breeze as she watched Phillip exercise the mare and her colt. He had a halter on the mare and a loose-fitting rope on her colt, and talked softly to them as he led them slowly around the corral.

"Yes, ma'am, I know you just had a baby, but you want to keep your girlish figure, don't you? You're still young, and you don't want that old stallion of yours to completely forget about you and go looking at all the other females, do you? Besides, your boy needs his exercise. We don't want him growing up lazy, do we?"

Charlene came from the kitchen with the coffee pot and extra cup. She warmed Katherine's cup, then poured herself one, before leaning against a post to watch.

"He sure has a way with animals, doesn't he? He even has that old mongrel dog following him around like a puppy."

"Yes, I sometimes think he likes animals better than people." Katherine nodded thoughtfully.

"Well, I suppose that could be true. I've known quite a few men like that. Most of the old trappers and prospectors...even a few scouts like my husband were like that."

"Your husband liked animals better than people? How did he treat you?" Katherine shifted to stare at the housekeeper.

"Oh, George treated me fine. Especially after he came home drunk one night and proceeded to slap me around. I grabbed a cast iron pan and beat him senseless and set a few things straight. He treated me pretty well after that. But he did cotton to horses and dogs quicker than humans."

They watched the hired hand awhile longer as he fed the mare a carrot and rubbed her glossy coat.

"Yes, he certainly has a way with animals," Charlene finally said. "I reckon he'd better quit raiding my pantry to give them treats, or I might take a cast iron pan to him and set a few things straight."

Charlene returned to the kitchen, leaving Katherine to her thoughts. She allowed her gaze to drift from the corral to the kitchen door and laughed out loud as she tried to envision her housekeeper and friend chasing Phillip Denning with a frying pan. She had to agree with her though. The man certainly had a way with animals, especially the new colt. He had removed the rope, and the young horse was following after him like a dog.

CHAPTER 15

Matthew urged his horse well ahead of the rest and galloped through a stand of cottonwoods. His mother had insisted that everyone stay within eyesight of each other as they checked on the herd. He was having no part of it, though. Being in close proximity to his mother and her lover was something he refused to do. The fact was, he hadn't spoken a dozen words to Phillip Denning or his mother in the past two days, and was intent on keeping it that way.

He crested a small rise and brought his horse to a halt. Three men were busy cutting a couple of dozen cattle from their herd. Matthew recognized one of them as having been with the group of rustlers that were stealing cattle the day that Phillip Denning arrived. Matthew had never forgotten what happened that day either. He glanced over his shoulder, but Phillip and the rest were nowhere in sight. He drew his Henry rifle and galloped toward the rustlers.

"Hey, what do you guys think you're doing?"

He had no more than gotten the words out of his mouth, when one of the men jerked a pistol from his belt and fired. Matthew felt his heart jump as the bullet passed his ear with a buzz. His horse jerked to the left at the sound of the gunshot, causing Matthew to lean awkwardly in the saddle. The action more than likely saved his life, and the next bullet whine as it clipped a chunk of leather from the pommel on his saddle. He rolled from the pitching horse, losing the rifle in the process.

He crawled quickly toward the rifle as a volley of gunfire rang out from atop the small rise he had just ridden down.

Finally getting control of his mount, he raised his rifle only to see the rustlers fleeing at a full gallop, leaving the cattle behind. The beat of horses' hooves charging across the soft earth caused him to look over his shoulder. Phillip Denning was at a full gallop, coming toward him, with his mother and his brothers trailing behind. He retrieved his hat with a mumbled curse and used it to dust his pants.

The angry cowboy dismounted and began yelling. "I thought your ma told you to stick with the rest of us."

Matthew look past him as his mother and brothers rode up. She sat calmly watching as Phillip continued.

"I'm talking to you, boy."

"I don't want to hear anything you've got to say." Matthew turned his back on Denning, only to be jerked back around and slammed backward against his horse. The startled animal bolted, causing Matthew to fall. He started to rise, but thought better of it as an angry Phillip Denning stood over him, pointing his finger like a gun at his face.

"Boy, I don't give a damn if you want to ride off and get yourself all shot to hell. The way you've been acting, I'd say good riddance. But I do care what happens to your ma, and your brothers. And, I happen to give a big damn about what happens to me. So while we're out here, you'd best be doing exactly like your ma tells you. Do you understand me?"

Matthew glanced toward his mother who simply raised her eyebrows and grinned. Deciding she would be no help, he shot a sullen glare toward his antagonist.

"We're going to settle this right here and now, so you'd better answer me, boy. Do you understand me?"

"He's right," Katherine said. "You almost got yourself killed, and for what? To prove you know how to ride right up on a bunch of rustlers by yourself like an idiot? I've taught you better than that, Matthew Henry."

Her expression changed as he turned his back on her. Katherine dismounted and grabbed him by the arm, spinning him around.

"Don't you dare turn your back on me while I'm talking. Unless you want to be stuck at home helping Charlie with the housekeeping, you're going to do exactly what I say, when I say it. Do you understand me?"

"Yes," Matthew mumbled.

"What?"

"I said, yes," he yelled.

"Good. Now get your horse and stay within earshot from now on." She grabbed the trailing reins of her horse and yelled at Steven, who had decided to retrieve Matthew's horse which was now grazing thirty or forty yards away.

"Let that animal be, son. Your brother can fetch it himself. He created this mess, now let him clean it up."

"Yes, ma'am," Steven said, and trotted his own horse back to where they were.

Matthew slouched toward his horse. He had hoped she would have been frightened at his getting shot at, and maybe even thrown her arms around his neck, thanking God he was alive. Instead, she had taken her boyfriend's side and disciplined him for confronting the rustlers. He shoved his hat down on his head, knowing nothing had changed. He still hated them both.

"Okay, which one of you killed my steer?"

Matthew's horse shied away when he first approached, and stopped a few feet away to resume its grazing. He stood watching as his brothers gathered around the dead calf his mother was standing over.

"Well, which one? I don't think it shot itself."

"Are you sure you didn't kill it?" Steven asked. "There was an awful lot of shooting."

Katherine glared at him. "You know better than that."

"What about Mr. Denning? He fired several shots," Joshua said.

"Mr. Denning?" Katherine asked. The cowboy looked up from rolling a cigarette.

"No ma'am, I didn't kill it. I was shooting at the varmint who tried to kill your son. I would have had him too, if someone hadn't of bumped into Lucky."

"The squirt killed him," Timothy said with a snigger.

"Na-uh," Steven said indignantly. "I was shooting at one of the rustlers."

"You still killed the calf," Timothy said. "I saw it fall the instant you pulled the trigger."

"How do you know? Everyone was shooting. Even you," Steven yelled.

"Boys, boys…it doesn't matter. The calf is dead and arguing isn't going to bring it back to life," Katherine said.

Matthew caught the horse by the bridle on the third try and made sure the cinches were tight. The bullet nick in the pommel made his stomach queasy. He mounted the horse quietly and watched the spectacle.

"Your ma's right." Phillip said. "Toss the calf on Steve's pony and tie it down. He can ride double with me. We'll take it back to the house and clean it, so Charlie can cook it into something. No reason to let good beef go to waste."

"Why do I gotta ride double? Why not one of them?" Steven said with a whine.

"Because, you more'n likely killed it. Besides, you and me are pards, aren't we?"

"Yeah," the boy said with a grin, and ran to help with the dead calf.

Phillip removed his hat and wiped the sweatband with his neckerchief as he approached Katherine.

"Ma'am? When we've finished cleaning that animal, I'd like to have a confab with everyone, if it's alright with you."

"A confab? I guess it would be okay. What about, Mr. Denning?"

"About those rustlers. The way I see it, these highbinders aren't gonna leave you alone. They're acting like this is more personal than simply stealing. And," he paused and cocked his head to one side with a grin, "well, let's say I've got a hunch about some things."

"Okay…certainly, Mr. Denning. We'll have your confab."

Matthew waited for his brothers to follow and nudged his horse into line. *Huh*, he thought, *this might be kind of fun to watch.* He'd never seen his mother take orders from any man, unless it was his father. If Phillip Denning started telling their mother what to do, he just might be getting more than he bargained for.

~ ~ ~

Everyone had gathered in the yard and watched as Phillip placed six empty cans along the back. He turned toward Charlene when he had finished and asked, "Do you know how to shoot, ma'am? I know you said you could. I've seen the others, and know they are more than tolerable with a rifle. Can you honestly shoot?"

The housekeeper took Phillip's rifle and knocked an empty peach tin from the fence post with one shot. "Does that answer your question, Mr. Denning?" She handed him the gun.

"Yes, ma'am, it does. Spoken like a true westerner."

"What's the point of all this, Mr. Denning?" Katherine asked with a hint of irritation in her voice. "We know how to shoot."

"Yes, ma'am. I'm sure you do." He cleared his throat. "First, I need to start by offering my apology for acting out of line back there and yelling at the boy. He's your son, and I had no place doing that. I overstepped my bounds."

"Yes you were out of line, Mr. Denning. I accept your apology, and fully understand why you did what you did. Is there anything else?"

"Yes ma'am, there is."

"Let's hear it then."

Matthew started to speak, but Phillip quieted him with an upraised hand.

"Just let me have my say, then you can say anything you want. The thing is, these men you're dealing with are just a little different."

"You've already said that, several times." Katherine put her hands on her hips.

"Yes ma'am, I reckon I have. To put it bluntly, I've ridden on both sides of the law, some. And a man learns a few things along the way. I remembered seeing that pock-faced rustler a few years back when I was wearing a badge. I couldn't remember where until this morning. It was on a wanted poster. Now, there's a chance it might not be the same skunk, but I reckon it is.

"To make it short, this man's a mean one. He was going about killing folks and taking what he wanted, when he wanted, all over parts of Texas and New Mexico. They never caught up with him, so I reckon it's him. All of you, including Charlie, had best be ready and shoot to kill when you lay eyes on him. I figure we've been lucky so far, but our luck won't last long with him on the loose."

"You were a lawman?" Katherine asked.

"Yes, ma'am. Sheriff of Crown Point, New Mexico. It was after the Lincoln County fiasco."

"You were at Lincoln County? You didn't get caught up in that mess down there, did you?" Charlene asked.

"Yes, ma'am, I was."

Charlene whistled.

"That's when I reckon I might've ridden on the opposite side of the law. Some folks didn't think the side I took was the right one. We just figured we were trying to set things right.

"Anyway, back to what I was saying. We all figured the man I killed that day was the leader of this bunch, but I don't think he was. I think the pock-faced man is. And if I'm right, he aims to settle a score. I killed one of their own, and busted his teeth out. They're gonna keep coming back. They won't stop until they've cleaned you out and killed you all…every one of you."

"So, if what you say it true, how do we stop them?" Katherine asked with a sigh.

"Kill 'em. That's the only way."

"Are you saying we're into something like the Lincoln County range war?" Charlene said.

"No, that was a matter of right and wrong. This is simply wrong. My guess is, by the amount of cattle they're taking, they're trying to stock a ranch somewhere. You can bet you're not the only one they are rustling from. That ain't all. They're killers and cutthroats. I'd suggest you make these boys heed your advice, Mrs. Parker. No one goes out by themselves. Ride in twos and threes, and keep your eyes peeled and your rifles handy. And, for God's sake, be ready to shoot first. You've seen what happened to Matt out there today. That feller tried to kill him right on the spot, and would have if we hadn't come along."

"I believe that's fair, Mr. Denning," Katherine said with a nod. "You heard him boys. No one goes out alone. Is that all, Mr. Denning?"

"No, ma'am. I'd recommend stocking up on .44 cartridges next time you're in town."

"Mom says we're going day after tomorrow for supplies, anyway," Timothy said.

"I'm going to get a pistol while we're there," Matthew said matter-of-factly.

"What for?" Phillip turned to stare at the youth with his hands on his hips.

"To protect myself," Matthew said, and braced himself for the remark he knew was coming. When it didn't arrive, he added, "I've saved enough money."

"I didn't ask if you had the money. I only asked what you'd want one for."

"Ask yourself. You've got one."

"Sure, but I know how to use it. Besides, they're no good, unless you're right up close to someone, and rustlers aren't gonna let you get that close. And, if you ever get that close, you'd better be both real quick and accurate, because you'll wind up decorating a plot of ground inside a cemetery if you're not.

"Look," he continued as the boys stared, "I'm only telling you this because it's true. You strap one of these on," he pulled the Colt peacemaker, twirled it once and dropped it back in the holster, "and you're free game for anyone looking to build a name, or itching for a fight. Out here, they're not much use anyway. They're only accurate for thirty, forty, or maybe fifty yards, if you're really good. I heard Bill Hickock killed Davis Tutt at seventy-five yards with one shot from his Navy .36. If that's true, it was an exceptional shot, from an exceptional marksman, and it doesn't happen very often.

"Most gunfights happen by someone shooting someone in the back, or ambushing them in a dark room or alleyway. Or, they happen up real close and fast." He whipped the Colt from the holster and shot the five remaining cans in rapid secession.

"Geeze!" Joshua said as Timothy whistled. Matthew felt his knees weaken as he remembered striking the man who had just shown a display of lightening speed and deadly accuracy.

"Now," he said, calmly reloading the gun, "you might buy one, but I'd advise you not to show off by wearing it around town, unless you think you can beat what I just did. Because there are men out there who are quicker'n me, and just looking for a fight." He slid the gun back in its holster. "Now, I reckon I've said about all I've got to say, unless someone's got something to add."

Matthew spied his mother standing to one side, looking stunned. "No, Mr. Denning, I don't believe I have anything to add. I would honestly like to know who in the world you are."

"Me? I'm just nobody." He touched the brim of his hat and wandered toward the tack room.

CHAPTER 16

Katherine spent another night studying the cracked boards in her bedroom ceiling. She had replayed the events of the day a hundred times inside her head, trying to make sense of each and every tiny detail, and came to the same conclusion. Phillip Denning handled Matthew's rebellious and snippy attitude perfectly. It was certainly a foolish act to face the rustlers alone. He could have gotten himself killed or seriously hurt, and all for a few cows. No amount of cattle was worth the lives of her children. She had already lost her only daughter, and would fight to her last breath for the lives of her sons.

Some amount of danger or trouble was always present working a ranch this size. Anyone, including her sons, could be hurt or killed at anytime. On any given day, a steer might hook you, or you could get thrown from a horse or snake bit. Katherine had exchanged shots with more than one Sioux raiding party, and a rustler or two. James always carried a rifle, and insisted on teaching the children how to shoot by the time they were strong enough to hold a gun. Abby was almost as good a shot with a Henry rifle as her father. Katherine herself never gave danger a second thought. She figured the boys would have to learn to face it if they were going to run the ranch when she was gone. The fact that Phillip Denning kept insisting this particular band of rustlers were cutthroats and killers, and somehow different, caused her to wonder if the man had ever faced an angry Sioux warrior. How different could they be?

No rancher with any sense ignored missing cattle, or they didn't stay in business very long. Ranchers could expect the loss of a few steers to wolves or other predators, but they never ignored such things, and shot every four-legged predator they saw. These rustlers were another matter. They had gotten bolder, striking in broad daylight and had tried twice to kill her boys. She couldn't help but feel her decision to turn them over to the sheriff in Denby had been the wrong one. She heaved a sigh just thinking about it. Her decision had given them a chance to escape. She should have allowed Mr. Denning to hang them on the spot.

The sound of hooves against packed ground caused her to leap out of bed and pull the curtain back. Phillip Denning was returning after riding night watch, protecting her cattle. She held her alarm clock in the moonlight seeping through the window. It was twelve-thirty. The man would be exhausted in the morning with only a few hours of sleep. He was the one though, who had made the decision to use the tack house as his sleeping quarters. The boys would be waking him shortly after sunrise.

Katherine crawled back under the covers and pulled them against her chin. The crack in the ceiling looked the same. She couldn't decipher who Phillip Denning really was, any more than she could will the cracked board to heal itself. The man was completely closed on the subject of his past.

Me? Why, I'm just a no-account saddle bum, ma'am. I'm just a cowpuncher, happy to have a job. The man did know his way around cattle and the workings of a ranch. She had to give him credit for that. But he was far more than a saddle bum or cowboy. He was better educated than most ranch hands she had known, and she had met quite a few since coming to South Dakota twenty-one years ago. He was also polite, as most cowboys were, but poised, with proper table manners, which few had. The most disturbing part was the glimpses into a dangerous side that Denning kept well hidden. Katherine hated to admit that these small glimpses both frightened and thrilled her. It was something that James never had, and it was unfamiliar territory to her. She told herself she should be repulsed by it, but the mystery of it drew her to him somehow.

She was still wondering who she had invited into her home when she fell into deep slumber. Steven's shrill voice woke her long after the sun had risen. She staggered to draw the curtains open and stared. A team had been hitched to the wagon, and the boy's horses were saddled. Today was the day she had promised they were going shopping in Denby. She drew the curtains shut with a grumble, not understanding how Phillip Denning could survive without sleep. She desperately needed four our five more hours herself. Besides being dangerous, the man must not be human. The smell of strong coffee gave Katherine encouragement and she buttoned her white blouse. Her image in the mirror over the dresser was frightening.

She would be riding in the wagon with Charlie today, so she slipped on a full skirt instead of one of her riding skirts, and chose a pair of high-buttoned shoes instead of boots. She was in the process of brushing her hair when she stopped. She remembered Matthew telling Phillip he was going to buy a pistol when he got to town. That was just before Phillip demonstrated a frightening display of accuracy and speed with a hand gun. She laid the brush to one side and stared at her image, no longer seeing the purple bags under her eyes from a lack of sleep. She wondered if there was any way possible of preventing her son from buying a hand gun and becoming what Phillip had warned against, decoration inside a cemetery.

CHAPTER 17

Phillip rose long before sunrise, fed and watered the horses, pampered the new colt a few minutes, then hitched the team to the buckboard before saddling his Mustang. A lamp inside the kitchen cast a yellow light through the window. Charlie was stirring around, getting breakfast ready. He rinsed his hands in the washbasin and paused with the towel in his hands to stare at the stately willow on the hillside behind the barn. He had only given halfhearted notice to the fenced-in area beneath the tree. He knew it contained the graves of Mrs. Parker's husband and daughter, and decided to pay a visit this morning, simply out of curiosity.

He hung the towel on its peg and walked briskly up the small incline toward the tree. The fence was made of wrought iron, and must have cost a sizable amount of money. The paint had long worn away in places, and the gate gave a groan of protest as he opened it. The sandstone markers were overgrown with weeds, and Phil had to pull several to read the writing.

The larger stone was dedicated to her husband and simply read: James Eugene Parker, April 3, 1855 – December 26, 1889. He had been dead nearly five years and that explained a lot about Katherine. It took a lot of courage for a woman to raise four boys and run a spread, especially one as large as the *Flying K.* Phillip nodded his approval. She was not only attractive, but tough and willing to roll up her sleeves to see the job got done. It was the smaller marker that left him feeling cold.

Abigail Susana Parker, beloved daughter, June 24, 1874 – January 12, 1888.

She was only thirteen and had had her whole life ahead of her. *Much too young for a woman to die*, he thought. She should have lived, married and raised children of her own…had grandsons for Mrs. Parker to enjoy spoiling.

"It's sad to see them go like this, isn't it?"

Phillip jumped and turned to see Charlene standing behind him.

"I saw you hitching the team. Thought you were coming in for coffee before those boys started making a lot of noise. Then, I saw you up here, so I brought it to you." She held two steaming mugs in her hands and offered one for him to take.

"Thanks, you're an angel. You also sneak up on a person as quiet as an Indian. Anyone ever tell you that?"

"I was married to an army scout, Mr. Denning." She took a sip and nodded toward the graves.

"Mrs. Parker hasn't been up here weeding and planting flowers this year, and it's kind of surprised me. This place looked real nice last year, but she hasn't shown much interest this year. The fence could stand some paint, too."

"Well, it's still early. She may whip it back into shape. She was pretty young, wasn't she?"

"Thirteen." Charlene took another sip and nodded thoughtfully. "She froze to death in a blizzard. What an awful way to die."

"Any way is awful when you're that young." Phillip squatted on his heels to pull several weeds from Abigail's grave. "I might sneak up here some evening and get rid of the weeds, but it'll be up to you to plant flowers." He gave Charlene a crooked grin.

"I can do that. That would be real nice, Mr. Denning." Charlene squatted on her heels next to Abby's grave and sipped her coffee thoughtfully.

"Kate buried more than her husband and daughter here. She buried a whole way of life. I knew them, back when James and Abby were alive. She was a fun-loving and happy girl. He left her with four boys and a lot of responsibility. She handled it all by herself. But she buried a good part of herself here without realizing it. There are some things she's completely forgotten."

"Like that old surrey parked inside the barn?"

"Exactly," she said and struggled, trying to get to her feet. "Here, help me up." She extended her hand. Phil pulled her to her feet, where she heaved a sigh.

"Thanks. I should have known better than to squat with this hip of mine. Where were we? Oh, the surrey. James bought it for Kate right after they arrived from back east and set down roots. Avery Jordan said it had to be special-made because of the third seat he wanted. James somehow knew they were going to have a litter of young-uns, and was proud as punch whenever Kate got pregnant. I remember he would bring the whole family to town two or three times a month for shopping, and show up at church every Sunday, just for the fun of it. Kate hasn't touched the surrey since Abby died. She quit going to church, except on special occasions."

A door banged as someone yelled, drawing their attention toward the house.

"Well, guess they're awake. Come on down to the house and have breakfast, if you're brave enough."

CHAPTER 18

Matthew spent most of an hour studying the shiny weapons inside the gun case in the hardware store, before pointing toward a .36 caliber Smith and Wesson.

"I can see you have an eye for fine weapons," the clerk said with a grin. "It's light, with a breakaway barrel and cylinder to make loading fast and easy." He handed the pistol across the counter for Matthew to look at. Matthew fondled the weapon gingerly a few moments, opening it to examine the loading system, then snapped it shut.

"I'll take it."

"Good choice. Now, what about a holster? What do you prefer? A shoulder holster?" He pulled one from a rack and held it up for Matthew to see. "They're popular with gamblers and some lawmen nowadays. Or, maybe you'd prefer something more traditional, like a cartridge belt to hang on your hips."

Matthew considered his choices a long minute before pointing toward the clerk's left hand.

"I'll take the cartridge belt. A shoulder holster might get in my way doing my chores around the ranch."

"You're probably right. I'd think it would rub your arm raw roping and branding cattle. Now, you'll need a couple of boxes of shells," he stacked the cartridges on the counter and turned to grab another box, "and a cleaning kit. Now, make sure you give the gun a good cleaning before loading and using it the first time. I try keeping them clean, but it does get dusty in here. And make sure you clean it every time you use it. In fact, living on a ranch like you do, I would recommend a good cleaning and oiling every night before going to bed. That way, it will always work and last a lifetime."

He laid forty-two dollars on the counter and thanked the clerk. The clerk wrapped the gun and holster in brown paper and tied it with string. Matthew walked proudly toward the wagon, making plans to start practicing tomorrow morning. He shoved the package under the seat as Avery Jordan came from the store and hoisted a barrel of flour into the buckboard with a grunt.

"Good morning, Matt," the storekeeper said, wiping his brow with a hanky.

"Mr. Jordan." Matthew gave the man a nod. "It's actually afternoon, isn't it?"

"Ah, so it is." He laughed and stuffed the hanky into his pocket. "I knew that. I guess I forgot."

"Kind of busy today?"

"Yes, yes," he nodded, "we got a shipment in, and everyone seems to want first pick." He motioned toward the crowded store. "Your mother and Mrs. Thompson gave me quite a list. Since you folks only come to town once a month, I guess you start running out of things, don't you?"

"I don't go into the pantry very often, so I never know. But, yeah, I reckon we have big appetites. Plus Ma decided to hire herself a man to help run things."

"Really? I guess that was the big fellow I saw helping her out of the wagon when you folks got here. Who is he?"

"He says his name is Phillip Denning. We don't know much about him. I don't know," Matthew said with a shrug.

"Well, it's been nice chatting with you, Matt. I'd better get back to work. Come around and see us sometime."

"I'll do that," he shouted as Avery scurried back inside.

Matthew leaned against the buckboard watching people pass on the plank walkway in front of the store, wondering if he wanted to chance entering the crowded store. He had just about made up his mind to enter when Avery's sixteen-year-old daughter, Rebecca, came through the door with an armload of packages.

"Hi, Matt. Would you please give me a hand? These are for your mother."

"Sure." He hurried to take the load from her arms. "I was hoping to see you."

"I heard you were in town, and I've been waiting for you to come around. What kept you so long?" The petite girl flashed him a smile and batted her large, dark brown eyes, before tossing her long chestnut hair over her shoulder. She was positively the most beautiful creature he had ever seen.

"Well, I had some things to get at the hardware, but I'm here now. I was hoping to see you alone. I guess that's out of the question today." He stared forlornly at the store.

"Yeah. Maybe you could ride in here some day and have supper with us. I'd really like it if you did."

"I'd like that too, Becky."

"You still hanging around my girl?"

Matthew snapped upward as Silas Norton pushed several people aside to reach the buckboard. Silas was an entire head taller and twenty pounds heavier than Matthew. And for some reason Silas had considered Rebecca Jordan his private property, although she claimed to hate the blowhard.

"I warned you, Parker, the next time I caught you trying to make time around her, I'd pound your sorry ass into the ground." He grinned to reveal a set of crooked teeth set inside an oversized mouth, decorating a large puffy-looking head.

"I am not your girl!" Becky screamed, and several people exited the store, including her father.

"Hush, and stand back while I teach this knot-head a thing or two." Silas pushed Rebecca aside as he removed the hat covering his unruly red hair. Several of Silas' friends laughed and urged him on. The bully had pushed his weight around Denby long enough, Matthew decided. He had seen him strong-arm and give several weaker men vicious beatings more than once. Seeing him push Becky was the last straw.

He charged, throwing wild blows that caught Silas on the arms and shoulders. The punches that bounced off his head were glancing blows that had no effect. The crowd of bullies cheered and laughed, urging him onward. The attack was short-lived, when Matthew walked right into a hard right that landed flush on his nose. He staggered backward, landing against the side of the buckboard. The next blow caught him in the stomach, and was immediately followed by a series of punches that left him senseless. The attack was stopped as quickly as it started, and Matthew vaguely remembered loud, angry voices as he sank to his knees and fell face-first into the street.

CHAPTER 19

Katherine and Charlene had finished eating fried chicken and mashed potatoes at Beth's Café, and were on their way back to the mercantile when they saw the milling, noisy crowd surrounding their buckboard.

"What in the world….?" Charlene exclaimed.

"Matthew?" Katherine said as she caught a glimpse of her son through a break in the crowd. Silas Norton was giving him a vicious beating. "Matthew!" she screamed and ran toward the milling mob. She had almost reached the wagon when Phillip charged past her, driving his shoulder into one of the cheering spectators, knocking him into Silas. The blow delivered by Phillip sent both men sprawling on the plank walkway. Silas glared at Phillip and uttered a string of curses as he scrambled to his feet, but Phillip delivered a vicious kick that caught him under the chin. He fell back and lay unconscious. Phillip stood over the second man pointing a finger.

"Enough. It's over. Understand? You just sit there until the sheriff arrives."

"Yes, sir."

"Matt?" Katherine knelt in the dusty street and held her son's battered head in her lap.

"Oh, Matthew, I…I'm sorry." Rebecca fell to her knees beside Katherine and held her tear-streaked face against Matthew's bruised cheek. The girl then turned just as quickly to scream, "I hate you!" toward the unconscious bully, as she stroked Matthew's hair. "I'm sorry, Matthew. I'm sorry."

"How is he, ma'am?" Charlene said, squatting beside her. "That boy needs a doctor."

"I know. Where's Josh and Timmy? See if you can find the boys and send them to fetch Doctor Krucker."

"Yes, ma'am." Charlene pulled herself up by the side of the buckboard and hollered.

"Joshua, Steven? There you are. Where were you when your brother needed you?"

There came a muffled reply from the other side of the wagon, and the housekeeper nodded, saying, "uh-huh…uh-huh. Well, I see three healthy young men standing there without a scratch on them. Don't try to weasel out by telling me the three of you together couldn't have offered your brother a hand when he needed it."

"Charlie, the doctor!" Katherine pleaded.

"Yes, ma'am," she said with a glance toward Katherine. "Now, go fetch the doc like your ma wants. Hurry, or you'll be eating dirt for your next meal."

"He'll be here in a minute, ma'am." Charlene squatted beside her again and dabbed at Matthew's cut lip with her handkerchief. "Yes, he's beat-up some, but I think he's going to be just fine."

"Well hello, Arizona, what brings you to Denby?"

Katherine looked up to see Sheriff William Crutchfield, with his hands on his hips and grinning as he eyed Phillip up and down.

"You look a little worse for wear. Still looking for Nate Thomas?"

"I was, but I got tired of starving, so I took a job punching cows for Mrs. Parker."

The sheriff gave Katherine a quizzical look. "That right, Katherine? You hire Phil out on your place?"

"Yes," she nodded, "is there something wrong?"

"No, no. Just asking."

"I didn't say you could get up." Phillip gave Silas' friend a shove with his boot. "You just lay there quiet-like until Crutch says you can get up."

"I see you're still as cantankerous as a wounded Comanche," the sheriff said with a chuckle. "Maybe you can tell me what's going on here, since you seem to be involved in some way."

"I don't know the particulars, but that buffoon was pounding on young Matt, and decided to turn on me when I protested. And this jughead was egging him on."

"That right, George?" Sheriff Crutchfield asked the young man at Phillip's feet.

"No, I just seen the fight, and stopped to watch when he hit me in the back and knocked me into Silas. Then he kicked Silas for no reason."

"Liar!" Rebecca Jordan screamed. "You were right there cheering as Silas beat Matthew, simply because he was talking to me. You're always following him around and cheering when he hurts people. I hate you. I hate the both of you!" She jumped to her feet as Silas Norton moaned and sat up.

"I'm not your girl…I have never been your girl…and I'll never be your girl. I'd rather catch cholera." She gave Silas a swift kick and returned to kneeling beside Katherine.

She patted the girl's arm and smiled. It felt both sweet and strange to know this girl had strong feelings for her son, especially when he had taken a beating before Katherine found out. Her boys were approaching manhood, and would soon be finding mates. She suddenly thought it strange how she'd never pondered the subject before. They would certainly be moving out and starting families of their own. They could choose to move completely away from the ranch, leaving her and Charlene alone. The thought overwhelmed her, and she heaved a huge sigh, as Rebecca threw her arms around her and cried against her shoulder.

"Huh, I think that's gonna make your pa real happy, George. Especially seeing as he's on the Town Council, and been begging you not to go hanging around with troublemakers like Silas. Speaking of which," Sheriff Crutchfield glanced up, "here he comes now."

"My boy get himself mixed up in something, Will?" a large red-faced man asked as he made his way through the crowd.

"A bit. Seems he's been following Silas Norton around, cheering and egging him on as they cause mischief. Silas just finished giving Katherine's boy a good pounding, and according to Phil, who saw the whole thing, your George was right there cheering him on."

"I'm terribly sorry, Katherine. If there's anything I can do, just let me know," the angry father said.

"No, Harry. I'm just waiting for the doctor."

"Tell him to send the bill to me." He gave a disdainful glare at his son before turning back to Sheriff Crutchfield.

"You need to lock him up, or can I take him home and give a beating of my own?"

"No, I ain't got nothing against him, except knowing he's stupid. Have at it."

"Come on, you numbskull." The angry man grabbed his son's arm and gave him a shove. "Just wait until your mother hears about this."

"Pa...," George whined and slinked through the laughing crowd as his father gave another shove. The crowd parted as Doctor Krucker made his way toward Katherine, carrying his medical bag. He knelt and examined Matthew momentarily, as the boy moaned and rolled his head. Matthew's eyes fluttered open and Rebecca covered her mouth and uttered a happy sob.

"He's got some cuts and bruises, and more than likely a concussion. Who gave him this beating?"

"He did!" Rebecca yelled, and rushed to give Silas another kick.

"Whoa, hold on, honey," Avery said, wrapping his arms around his daughter. "Let's let Sheriff Crutchfield handle this."

"He ought to be locked up," Benjamin Krucker mumbled and turned his attention back to Matthew.

"That's exactly where he's going. Wanna give me a hand here, Phil? Silas sometimes can be a handful."

"Be happy to, Crutch," Phillip said, and grabbed Silas Norton by the shirt.

"Hey, get your hands…" The protest was cut short by Phillip driving the heel of his boot hard against Silas' toes and bringing a cry of pain from the big man.

"We can do this easy, or hard. It's entirely up to you."

"Some of you men help me take this boy to my office," Doctor Krucker said, and several bystanders rushed to offer their services. Katherine paused long enough to watch Phillip Denning drag the protesting bully as he followed the sheriff toward the jail.

"Coming Ma?" Steven asked, tugging against her sleeve.

"What? Oh yes, and let's hope Doctor Krucker finds nothing seriously wrong."

"I still say three healthy young men like you three should have pitched in and given your brother a hand," Charlene scolded as they fell in line behind the doctor. "I've never been so ashamed of you boys as I am right this minute."

CHAPTER 20

Katherine sat in Dr. Krucker's living room fidgeting with her handkerchief while the doctor and his wife tended to Matthew inside a bedroom that had been converted into an examination room. Charlene sat in a chair across the room sipping tea from a dainty china set the doctor's wife had brought, before leaving to aid her husband. Katherine's tea was growing cold, and she hardly noticed the fine blue flower print on the white porcelain cups and saucers. She had expelled Matthew's brothers from the doctor's house after they refused to sit quietly, especially after Timothy had spilled his tea during a scuffle with Joshua. Charlene mopped the spilt tea from the floor and sat quietly as Katherine tied her handkerchief in knots.

Rebecca Jordan arrived shortly after the boys had been sent packing. Her father had ordered her to come because she had suddenly become useless. The girl's eyes were red from crying, and she instantly sat on the sofa beside Katherine, and laid her head against Katherine's shoulder. Katherine stiffened, not knowing how to react to this strange girl, until she remembered Rebecca was hardly a stranger. She had known the Jordans long before Rebecca's birth, and had watched the girl grow during her frequent visits to town. As far as Katherine knew, Rebecca was a nice, polite, hardworking God-fearing young woman, who attended church regularly. She was also beautiful, and someone most mothers would be proud to have their sons marry. It was, Katherine reasoned, that she had no idea until the scuffle in the street, that Matthew and this girl felt this way toward each other. This was all new to her. Then, remembering how her own mother and James' parents were shocked when they announced their engagement, Katherine slid her arms around Rebecca and held her against her breast.

"Shhh," she said as Rebecca sniffed, "he's going to be alright. Doctor Krucker is a fine doctor, and he'll take good care of him. Do you love my son?"

"Yes." She nodded and blew her nose on a soiled hanky.

"I see. How long has this been going on?"

"All my life."

Katherine raised her eyebrows and looked at Charlene who smiled like the cat who ate the mouse.

"You knew about this, Charlie?"

"Yes, ma'am. Where've you been? A blind man could have seen what's been going on between these young folks."

"And is my son in love with you too, Becky?"

The girl's snapped her head upward and flashed her large dark brown eyes inches from Katherine's face.

"Lord I hope so. It will just kill me if he isn't."

"Don't worry, honey, he does," Charlene said, pouring another cup of tea. She passed the cup to Rebecca. "You take anything in your tea, honey?"

"Just cream. You think Matt likes me, Mrs. Thompson?"

"The boy's crazy about you, he told me so." Charlene grinned at Katherine. "His mama might have known all this too, if she'd slow down long enough to pay attention once in awhile."

"I've got work to do Charlie. That ranch doesn't run itself, you know."

"Yes, ma'am, and you've got help...plenty of help. Just tell those boys what to do and relax once in awhile. They know what they're doing. And you *could* toss a little more Phillip's way. He seems to know how to cowboy."

"That's another worry, Charlie. Who is he?"

"Phillip Denning, at least that's the name I got. Why, did he give you another?"

Katherine shot Charlene an angry glare as the woman sat back laughing. The door opened and Phillip entered with Sheriff Crutchfield.

"How's the boy?" Phillip asked, removing his hat.

"We don't know. The doctor is still with him," Katherine said as Rebecca choked back another sob.

Phillip smiled warmly and squatted as he took the girl's hands. "Hey, look at me."

"Yes?" She turned toward him, still leaning against Katherine.

"That boy's big, and tougher than a bag of horseshoes. He'll be the same old stubborn knot-head he's always been before you know it."

The comment brought a giggle from the girl as the door to the examination room opened. Katherine stood as Matthew came into the living room, followed by Doctor Krucker and his wife, Rose. Rebecca flew to give Matthew a hug, which brought a whimper of pain from his swollen lips.

"Easy, Rebecca, he's got some sore ribs," Doctor Krucker said with a chuckle.

"Is he going to be okay, Doctor?" Katherine asked, as she tried desperately to find a way to hug her son. The boy now had both arms around Rebecca, making the process difficult.

"Sure. He'll be sore a few days, but he should heal just fine. He does, however, have a mild concussion. I'd make sure he stays awake several hours, and you folks keep a close eye on him. If he starts passing out, or having trouble walking or slurring his words, perhaps acting strange, you bring him right back here in a hurry."

"Well now, that'll be a difficulty in itself," Charlene said with a chuckle. "He's a teenage boy, Doc. He and those brothers of his are always acting strange."

"Ow!" Matthew said and covered his bruised lips. "That hurts, Charlie. Don't make me laugh."

"That's another thing. You'll have to feed him soft food for a few days, because he'll have trouble chewing until the inside of his mouth heals. Here," Doctor Krucker grabbed a small paper sack from a drawer and handed it to Katherine, "dissolve one teaspoon of this in a cup of water several times a day, and have him rinse his mouth. It'll sting, but it will keep it from getting infected."

"Can we take him home?"

"Sure, as long as he rides in the wagon. I don't want him on horseback for a couple of days. He'll heal up fine, as long as he doesn't get in anymore fights for awhile."

"What do we owe you, Doctor Krucker?" Katherine asked, rummaging inside her handbag.

"Not a thing," Sheriff Crutchfield said. "Harry Norton said to send the bill to him. His son did the beating, so I reckon Harry has plans to collect it from his hide someway."

"Thank you. Thank you both for everything," Katherine said, giving the doctor and his wife a quick hug. "We have a long ride home, so I guess we had better get started." She paused and gave Sheriff Crutchfield's hand a gentle squeeze.

"Thank you too, Bill."

"What for, arresting Silas Norton? I've been hoping to have an excuse to do that for years. You folks take care now."

"Guess I'd better find the others and get the horses and buckboard ready," Phillip said. He turned to leave, then motioned toward the teenagers still locked in an embrace. "You'd best find a way of prying those two apart, unless you plan on taking her with you." He left the door open and yelled loudly as he strode toward the buckboard.

"Hey, Josh. You numbskulls fetch the horses and bring 'em to the doc's place. We're leaving. I'll get the buckboard. And, hey, make sure mine's saddled right, or I'll make you walk."

Katherine stood in the shade of the porch watching, as her sons rushed to carry out his orders. "Bill?" She grabbed Sheriff Crutchfield's arm as he joined her side.

"Hum?"

"You seem to know him. Who is he, really?"

"Who, Phil?"

"Yes, Phillip Denning. I've asked him several times, and all I get is, "Well, gosh ma'am, I'm just a no-account saddle-tramp," she mocked in a low voice. "Then, a few days ago, after we had a run-in with some rustlers, he put on a shooting display with his pistol that was simply amazing and frankly, frightened the dickens out of me."

"Huh, sounds like Arizona," Crutchfield said with a grin. "I met him back when we were both riding for Tunstall down in Lincoln County. We rode together some, but not much. We used to call him Arizona back then, 'cause he was always bragging on how pretty it was. I told him once he ought to go back there if he liked it so much. Anyway, I left shortly after Tunstall got killed. Phil on the other hand, hung around and got caught up in the Lincoln County War. I lost track of most that went on, and I don't know a whole lot about Phil myself. I don't think anyone does."

"I heard the killer Billy Bonnie worked for Mr. Tunstall. Did you and Mr. Denning ever meet him?" Katherine asked.

"Yes, I knew Bonnie quite well. So did Phil. Have you ever heard him mention a man named McCarty?"

She nodded.

"Well, McCarty was Bonnie's real name, or at least that's what I've been told. Phil could tell you more about him. He knew Billy quite well, and they rode together, ate together and fought side by side. But if you're worried that Phillip Denning is anything like Billy Bonnie, get that idea out of your head. Phil and Billy the Kid are as different as night and day. Arizona's a good man. He'll stick by you 'til hell freezes over, then skate with you on the ice.

"As I said, I don't know a whole lot of what happened after Lincoln County, but I do know at one time Phillip Denning was about the best law-dog in New Mexico. After the war, he took over a small town near Gallup that had been plagued with rustlers and thieves, and cleaned it up. Even hired a young deputy, his sister's son from what I hear, not much older than your Josh. They had a right peaceable little town going.

"I ran into a fellow we both knew back in the Lincoln County days, who filled me in on a few things. He said some hombres decided to rob the bank in Phil's town one day, when he was away checking on something at a mine."

Crutchfield paused to wipe the sweat from his hatband with his handkerchief. He shot a glance down the street as Phillip turned the buckboard in a circle and walked the horses their way.

"One of them killed his young deputy on their way out of town. That was when Phillip quit being a sheriff and went on the prod. Last I heard, he'd found and killed all those men but one."

"Nate Thomas, the man you were asking him about?"

"Yes, ma'am. I hear he's the last of the bunch. I hope he doesn't find him, because someone is sure to get killed when it happens."

Phillip stopped the wagon in front of the doctor's house and helped Katherine and Charlene into the seat before pausing to give Matthew a crooked grin.

"Well, you'd better kiss her and climb into the buckboard. We ain't got all day."

"Ah," Rebecca gasped as everyone laughed. Matthew followed Phillip's advice by giving her a quick peck on the cheek that caused her to flush bright red. She slapped a palm over the spot Matthew had kissed and dashed from the porch, sprinting toward the store amid a rustle of her grey skirt and white petty coats.

"The boy's not so dumb after all," Phillip said, and mounted Lucky. He gave Sheriff Crutchfield a thoughtful stare.

"You haven't heard of any rustler trouble going on around here, have you, Crutch?" The sheriff's reply was a loud laugh.

"Hell, Arizona," he glanced toward the women to offer a "pardon" before continuing. "You're in the Dakota Badlands. The place is full of rustlers and murderers and all kinds of riffraff. It goes on all the time. I've got enough trouble just keeping a lid on this town. Why, you folks run into some trouble?"

"Not too much, but we did catch a few red-handed. One of them tried pulling a gun and I sent him home to Jesus. I can show you where he's buried, if you're interested. I would have hung the rest, but they got away. They came back a few days later and tried killing Matt. Just wondering if you had any idea about 'em?"

"No, sorry I don't. But keep in touch and I'll let you know. And if you find out anything, come get me. I'll be happy to give you a hand."

"Much obliged." Phillip touched the brim of his hat and urged his horse down the street. Charlene slapped the reins with a "yah!" and the buckboard jerked forward with the boys following close behind.

"Isn't that gentleman who frequents the post office and eats in Beth's Café named Nathan Thomas? Could he be the same man Mr. Denning is looking for?" Rose Krucker asked in a soft voice.

"Oh yes, he's the same man alright. I wasn't bound to tell Denning about him, not just yet anyhow. He'd never go back to that ranch, and Mrs. Parker needs the help. Besides, he'd just be hanging around waiting for Nate to show up, sticking his nose into my business and trying to tell me how to run this town." He gave a chuckle. "No, they'll run into one another soon enough, and someone's going to die when that happens. I'd rather have Denning out on Mrs. Parker's place as long a possible before they meet. He'll rout out that band of rustlers and save me some trouble."

CHAPTER 21

Matthew sat sullenly at the dining room table cleaning and oiling the gun. His mother had given him a good piece of her mind when he produced the weapon. The heated exchange only lasted until she yelled, "You'll only wind up getting yourself killed," and stormed into the kitchen.

Normally, her anger and threats might have worn him down, but it only added to his already blackened mood. To make things worse, he had to sip warm beef broth for supper, while the rest ate steaks with baked potatoes, biscuits and gravy. The growling in the pit of his stomach was a constant reminder of the happenings in front of Jordan's Mercantile. Being beat up by Silas Norton might not have been pleasant, but it was something he could have swallowed easily enough. He'd suffered beatings from larger boys before. Being beat senseless in front of Becky however, was unbearable. He felt the cloud grow darker as he rehashed the scene in his mind.

"If I'd had this gun with me when Silas showed up…" he started, and was cut short by Phillip's snort from the other side of the room.

"You would've gotten your blamed head shot off."

Matthew jerked up to see him sitting in his father's chair, smoking and grinning back at him. "What'd you say?"

Phillip tossed the cigarette into the fireplace.

"You heard me. You probably can't use that pop-gun any better than you can fight with your fists. That ox would have killed you quicker'n spit."

His brothers laid the book they had been sharing on the floor as his mother and Charlene came from the kitchen to stand in the doorway to listen.

"I can learn. Then I'll show you."

"Show me what? That you know how to die? Dying isn't anything special, boy. We're all going to do it sooner or later. The secret is in learning to stay alive. Besides, I've seen dying plenty of times before; too many times, to tell the truth. I told you the other day that thing won't be any good unless you're right up on someone, and none of those rustlers are going to give you that privilege. Practice with the Henry rifle, if you want my advice. It will do you more good in the long run. Why do you want to carry that thing around, anyway?"

"Well, because everyone's got one."

"No they don't." Phillip paused to take a sip of coffee. "Wyatt and his brothers passed an ordinance in Tombstone against carrying a loaded weapon in town. Most towns I've been in have similar laws. Everyone is required to check their guns at the sheriff's office or leave them home. Even the Earps go unarmed, unless they are arresting someone. But that's still no reason for you to carry one. Why do you want one?"

"He's only trying to…" Katherine started, but Phillip quieted her with a hand motion.

"You can't really answer that, can you, anymore than you could answer me if I asked why you tore into that big tub of guts back in town."

"Yes I can!" Matt yelled. "He said Becky was his girl, and I couldn't see her anymore. Then he pushed me."

"So? The pushing might have had a little reason attached to it, but saying you couldn't see that girl? Na," he said with a shake of his head.

Matthew jumped to his feet and yelled, "Are you saying Becky's not good enough?"

"No, I'm saying she was already your girl, and what that buffoon said didn't matter anymore'n a busted poker chip. She told your mother right there in that doctor's office that she's been in love with you all her life. And I believe it by the way she was acting. You have her anyway you look at it. Now, if he'd grabbed her, or touched her inappropriate-like, that might be another story. Now, I did hear he pushed her, but you didn't say that. So you didn't have any call to get all puffed up and go swinging like a windmill at him." He finished with a laugh.

"I know I can't fight too good with my hands," Matthew said sullenly.

"So you want to carry a gun to make up for it, is that right?"

"You carry one," he said pointing toward Phillip's gunbelt hanging on a coat-peg near the door.

"Yeah, I do. But that's a little different. I came here looking for a man. He and I aren't exactly friends, and I'll need that gun when I find him. Na, carrying one won't make you a man. In fact, if that's the only reason you've got for buying it, you might as well return it to the hardware store next time you're in town."

"What's a good reason for having one, Mr. Denning?" Steven asked.

"The same reason for fighting with your fists. Protection for you or your family, mainly. Lawmen carry them as a deterrent against crime. Sometimes, in rare cases, simple honor might be a big reason. A pistol will never make you a man, and if that's the only reason you've got, you'll wind up dead." He paused to point a finger at Matthew.

"You think about it, boy, before you strap that thing on. I'd learn how to use my fists first, if I were you." He set his cup on the table and turned as if to go. "Because you're fist-fighting is about as effective as a fart in a tornado," he added with a chuckle.

"Mr. Denning!" Katherine said as Joshua and Timothy burst into laughter.

"Turn around, you…you…!" Matthew kicked his chair and yelled. Phillip turned with a grin and pointed at him.

"That's your first lesson. I don't know what's got you so angry son, but you let your temper control you. I was able to get you all huffed-up with a few simple words, just like that lard-belly in town today. When that happens, you're not thinking straight and get yourself into trouble. Anger's a good thing, as long as you control it. Go ahead and get angry. Do it for the right reasons though, and learn to harness it. A man who controls his anger is clear-headed and deliberate about what he's doing. He becomes powerful…even dangerous. You think about it, and let me know when you think you're ready for lesson two."

Phillip paused at the door long enough to drape his gunbelt across his shoulder and shove his hat down on his head. "See you folks in the morning," he said without looking back, and closed the door as he stepped into the dark.

"Well now, that's a mouthful to swallow," Charlene said, and returned to her dirty dishes. Katherine stared silently at her son for a long minute, before following her housekeeper.

Matthew set his chair back at the table and stared at the Smith & Wesson. His brothers had begun conversing in a low, mumbling chatter, speculating who Phillip really was, and how many men he had killed. One of them scooped the book from the floor and closed it with a snap, tossing it on the table. Their mother had instituted a regimented time of evening studies, because the distance to the nearest school was prohibitive to their attending. Studies were long forgotten this evening. He sat in the chair and wiped the excess oil from the gun, then stuffed it, unloaded, into the holster. He decided to ask Phillip if he knew anything about fighting with his fists first thing in the morning. If he did, and was willing to teach him, maybe he could also get him to teach him how to shoot.

He placed the gun and ammunition in the trunk beneath the window in his bedroom. He didn't know where his anger and rage toward Phillip Denning had gone. He had trouble dredging it up again, and discovered he didn't even want to. He was no longer angry with his mother either. He suddenly thought his suspicions of her dalliances with Phillip inside the cave were silly. Not that such a thing was far from possible, but Steve was right. There were much better places for such a romance, and he was certain his mother would insist on one.

He paused to study his battered reflection in the mirror hanging over his dresser, and cringed at the sight. He wasn't too sure if Phillip could ever teach him how to control his temper. He really did hate Silas Norton. Matthew knew he'd have to work on that one.

CHAPTER 22

"Don't you think that colt's a little young to be trained?" Matthew asked as he joined his mother on the porch. She had formed a nightly ritual of sitting on the bench next to the mudroom door and enjoying an evening cup of coffee while she watched Phillip work with the colt and mare.

"I thought so, but he does seem to know what he's doing. I've had my eye on him, and I haven't seen him do anything I thought might harm Sunrise. I'll stop him if I do."

They watched in silence as he trotted the mare in wide, slow circles inside the corral. He had a rope tied loosely around the mare's neck and to her colt, who galloped happily after its mother.

"He's got that colt pretty spoiled, if you ask me. It starts neighing and jumping around inside the stall every time it sees him coming. The way he treats it, you'd think it belonged to him."

"Well, it doesn't. Besides, is spoiling the animal such a bad thing? If he treats it like his own horse, he won't do anything to hurt it, will he?"

"No, I don't suppose he would."

Phillip removed the rope from the colt and ran the mother faster. The colt let out a high-pitched whistle and galloped after her.

"Would you mind much if I did give Sunrise to him?"

"What? You've been waiting for that mare to birth a colt for a long time. Now you want to give it to Mr. Denning?"

"No, I didn't say I was going to give Sunrise to him. I just asked if it would bother you much if I did. Would it?"

"Huh, I don't know," he said, hugging the post. "He belongs to you. I suppose you can do what you want."

"Thank you. I just wanted your support and approval. You're my oldest son and your support happens to be important to me."

"I didn't know that." He arched his eyebrows thoughtfully.

"You should have."

They watched silently awhile longer before Matthew leaned to kiss the top of his mother's head.

"I think I'm going to read awhile before crawling into bed." He paused at the mudroom door to study her profile.

"You gonna give Sunrise to him?"

"Now, that would depend on a lot of things, wouldn't it? I'll let you know first before I do anything. Is that fair enough?" He nodded and disappeared inside.

CHAPTER 23

The rope snaked easily through the air and looped over the calf's neck. Katherine jerked the rope tight and formed a quick dally around the saddle horn. The brown gelding she was riding pulled back and the calf was instantly jerked off its feet. This was spring roundup, Katherine's favorite part of the year. She had no idea why, but the bawling of cattle, shouts of working cowboys, the smell of scorched hair and hide were all music to her. Perhaps it was a combination of things, but the roundup was the most important function in cattle ranching. She considered the spring roundup the cattleman's planting season, when several ranchers joined forces and branded the calf crop. The fall roundup was their harvest, when they gathered the beeves for shipment and the branding of any late calves or those they might have overlooked in the spring.

Each rancher furnished men and bore his share of labor and the general expense according to the number of cattle they owned. The Flying K wasn't the largest ranch, but it certainly wasn't the smallest. Katherine discovered, as the roundup progressed, that she was becoming quite competitive in the business. Each of them furnished a sufficient number of horses, but only the larger outfits were required to send a chuck wagon. Cleanup detail was rotated on a regular basis. This evening it would be Katherine's turn to help Clayton's cook, and to wash dishes. She could do without the washing dishes, but evenings around the campfire, drinking strong coffee and listening to the hands display their talking talents was one of her favorite times. One of the most colorful men was Curly, a newcomer with kinky red hair.

"Yes sir," Curly said, as they sat around the campfire the previous evening. "Old George had heered that some feller up in Wyoming had hisself a pet buffalo, that he'd trained to do tricks like a dog. He said the danged thing would lay down and roll over, and even follered him around while he was doing his chores.

"Well, George, he finds hisself a young buffalo calf wandering around one day bawling for its mama. He sees where a bunch of hiders have made a sweep of the area and left the carcasses, so he takes the calf home to raise. When the thing gets big enough, George figures he's gonna teach this buffalo to do something useful, and hitches it to a plow.

"Well, sure enough. That buffalo takes off, pulling that plow pretty as you please. Only thing is, when they reached the end of the field, he couldn't get it to turn. It just kept right on a going. Last I heered, George was saying that buffalo was plowing fields somewhere down in Mexico."

"Lord-a-mighty," Dusty snorted. "You're so full of wind Clayton could use you just to keep the windmills going."

Katherine drug the bawling calf toward the campfire where Jerry McCoy grabbed its rear legs and yelled, "Another Rocking J calf." Steven grabbed the Rocking J iron from the fire and held it against the calf's hip. Smoke and the smell of burnt flesh carried across the camp on a gentle breeze as the calf bawled loudly. Dusty Moore quickly castrated the bellowing calf and tossed the testicles into a bucket.

"Oh, okay. I guess you earned it," he growled as Phillip's dog began whining. The dog had quickly turned into an excellent cow-dog and an important part of their roundup. Dusty fished one of the testicles out of the bucket and tossed it to the hungry animal. The contents of the bucket happened to be on that evening's menu. Katherine grinned as Dusty slipped her lariat from the calf and turned the animal loose. She remember gagging at the mere thought of eating a calf's testicle her first year as a rancher. She had since gotten past the thought and developed a taste for mountain oysters, especially the way Clayton's cook rolled them in flour and cornmeal and fried them in hot bacon grease.

Jerry McCoy and Dusty Moore both had worked for Katherine at the Flying K, and she had the highest respect for them as honest hands. It was on her recommendation that Clayton had hired them both when her boys were big enough to take their place. She shook out another loop as Phillip drug a bawling calf toward the fire.

"Reckon this one's a Flying K," he said. "At least that large mossy-horn with Kate's brand kicked up a fuss when I tossed a cotton-patch loop around her young'un."

Katherine walked her gelding toward the milling cattle boxed in the canyon. She guided the horse toward an unbranded calf and began cutting the animal from the rest of the herd. Phillip's dog darted in, barking and nipping at the calf's heels. The calf bolted forward and Katherine tossed her loop.

"Ya! Get back in there," Matthew hollered at the angry cow trying to come to the aid of its baby. He glanced at the cow's brand and yelled "Box D."

"Box D calf," Dusty repeated and Steven grabbed the Box D iron from the fire as Katherine drug the animal toward it.

CHAPTER 24

Phillip was awakened in the blackness of pre-dawn by the shaking and rattling of pots and pans hanging on the side of the chuck wagon. The wind gave a haunting moan as it seeped through the brush and trees, bringing with it a tang of dust and manure from the temporary corral at the edge of camp. The canvas on the chuck wagon was making popping noises as pots and pans banged loudly around with the wind.

"Agh, damn it!" Phillip said as he tried yawning and got a mouthful of dirt and dried grass for his effort. He spit several times and shoved his hat down on his head as Jerry McCoy chased his battered Stetson through the brush cursing. Phillip snorted a short laugh and pulled the drawstring tight to keep the hat on his own head and pulled his corduroy britches over his long legs. He then buttoned them around his waist and sat on the edge of his blankets and shook out his boots in an attempt to evict any critter that might have set up homestead during the night, before pulling them on.

He could see Mrs. Parker's silhouette as she crawled out from where she had bedded down under the chuck wagon. The pots and pans hanging on the wagon's side were now beating an uneasy rhythm as the howling increased. The dog raised his head and whimpered, as one of the pans jumped loose from the wagon and rattled across the campsite.

"Don't you go complaining, it'll be just as tough on all of us. Ain't none of us who gets to sleep in all day. Don't reckon I'd want to in this mess." He quickly rolled his grip and stored it out of the wind inside the tack wagon. Jerry McCoy finally caught his hat and returned, giving the wind a few new names that may not have been uttered before. Phillip buttoned his flannel shirt as he crossed the camp toward the chuck wagon. He looked up just in time to duck a metal plate, and quickly scooped it from the dust before it decided to take flight a second time.

"Huh," he said, handing the errant plate to Katherine, who ducked a tumbleweed and uttered a couple of oaths under her breath. "Seems I just heard Jerry call the wind the same set of names. Is that some new lingo up here?"

"I figure it fits," she said with a scowl. "I hate wind." She gave the plate a quick wipe and shoved it inside the wagon.

"Reckon none of us like working in it. Even the dog's got a grouch on this morning."

"Smart dog," Katherine said as she grabbed pots and tossed them inside the wagon out of the wind.

"Need a hand making coffee or something?" Phillip asked.

"That'd be nice. You might grab one of the boys and help George build a windbreak so he can build a fire. We might have a cold camp this morning if this keeps up. Where's Steven? He's supposed to be George's helper this morning."

Phillip left to lend a hand building George a windbreak, and Katherine walked through camp calling her youngest son's name. She grabbed Matthew's arm as he hurried past.

"Where's your brother?"

"Which one?"

"The one was I've been calling. Steven! Where is he?"

"I don't know. He still might be rolled in his blankets for all I know."

"Well, go find him. He's supposed to be helping."

~   ~   ~

Katherine's prediction of a cold camp proved to be accurate as the wind continued to howl. No one was willing to chance building a fire and having the wind ignite a prairie fire. They ate a cold breakfast of dried fruit and jerky, washed down by water from their canteens. Katherine and Bill Donovan from the Box D helped drive the cattle and horses into a large draw shielded by high walls as Clayton oversaw the moving of the camp.

"I don't like it," he complained as they joined him at noon. They had the chuck wagon neatly tucked against the east wall of the draw, with the coffee pot on. "I just don't like the idée of camping in a wash. I've seen too many folks and cattle get swept away in a flash flood."

"It doesn't look like rain, Clay," Donovan said, scanning the sky.

"Don't have to rain anywhere near here. It could rain up in the hills, and the water will still come rolling down here and take everything with it. That's why you don't see no trees growing in the bottom. Only drift wood and what not."

"I don't know what else we could've done. We need a fire for branding, if nothing else." Donovan shrugged and sipped his coffee.

"Well, you're both right, and I vote we move the camp back on top just as soon as the wind quits blowing," Katherine said, then sneezed several times before sipping her coffee.

"Alright, you hungry galoots, come and get it before the wind carries it to Mexico," George yelled as he rang the bell. Steven promptly appeared with a plate of steaming biscuits smothered in thick gravy and chipped beef.

"Huh," Clayton said as Katherine perched herself on a rock and began scooping hot food into her mouth. "I guess there are some advantages to being a woman, ain't there, Kate?"

"Maybe." She swallowed and grinned. "But it also helps if your son is the one helping the cook."

CHAPTER 25

The mood around the campfire was angry and sullen. Every rancher had noticed missing stock, but the Rocking J had suffered the worst. The amount of cattle Clayton had lost astounded Katherine. Unless he could recover some of his cattle, the poor man would be close to bankruptcy.

"It has to be the work of some bloody rustlers," Bill Donovan growled.

"That's about as obvious as a boil on a pug nose," Phillip said with a snort.

"Yeah, it doesn't take much to figure that one out," Jerry McCoy agreed.

"Think they're the same ones that tried to kill Matt?" Steven asked.

"It might be the work of several bands of rustlers, son," Katherine said. "But you're probably right in assuming those men were involved."

"Well, I'd like to know what we're going to do about it," Jerry asked.

"I say we hold a necktie social when we catch that bunch of thieves," Donovan said. He poured a generous amount of Irish whiskey into his coffee and passed the bottle to Clayton.

The bottle made its way around the fire, with Katherine and her boys being the only ones to pass on its contents. Dusty figured Donovan's remarks were mostly a combination of Irish temper and Irish whiskey talking, but had no doubt the big Irishman would back his threat to hang any rustler he could lay his meaty hands on.

~   ~   ~

Dusty Moore had been riding for Rocking J for a little over two years and had ridden for the Flying K several years prior to that, but had never seen anything like this. The rustlers were bold enough to try to steal thirty head in broad daylight. Dusty wiped dust from his eyes as a gust sent a tumbleweed sailing past his head. The weed ricocheted off an elm tree and a boulder before rushing westward toward the Black Hills.

Jerry McCoy said he had seen a good number of their stock inside the wide wash bordering the Rocking J two weeks earlier, and Clayton had taken his two most trusted riders to make a sweep of the area.

Dusty pulled his rifle and injected a shell into the chamber as he walked his horse zigzag down toward the stolen cattle. He had dealt with rustlers and highbinders before. Most rustlers waited until later in the season when the ranchers had done most of the work of feeding and caring for the cows. Then they would swoop in during the night and make off with nice fat cattle that would bring a healthy price to a buyer who wasn't too particular where the cattle came from. The Rocking J's cows had been fed during the harsh winter, but they were still too thin to bring a good price at market. None of it really made sense.

Once he reached the bottom of the draw, Dusty spurred the steel-dust gelding through a grove of cottonwood lining the creek to get ahead of the stolen cattle. There were two men, a large stocky man and a boy not quite in his twenties who looked vaguely familiar. He would have rather faced them with his saddle pard, Jerry McCoy, at his side. But McCoy was at the other end of the wash. The rustlers would be long gone by the time he found him and returned to this spot.

He dismounted and fired a shot into the air as he stepped into the open.

"Alright, drop your guns and keep going. The cattle stay."

"Wait a minute, mister. These cows belong to us. I just bought 'em from a fella back yonder." The man was positively the ugliest human Dusty had seen, and maybe the dirtiest.

"You made a mistake if you did. They're Rocking J cattle, and they're staying. I'd say you just lost your money." He took a better look at the boy and shook his head.

"Randy Houk. How in the hell did you get tied up with this outfit?"

"I was out of work and hungry, Dusty. I see you're still working for the old man. I thought you would've moved on long ago."

"It's steady work Randy and I'm sorry you're mixed up in this. Now I'm asking nice. You and your new partner drop your guns."

"I'll tell you what, sonny," Pox leaned against the pommel with both hands, "since we're all friends here, I'll just keep the cattle and we'll call it even."

"You touch that hogleg and you're a dead man." Dusty leveled the Henry at the man's chest. The shot came from behind a clump of rocks to his left and slammed into his back, knocking Dusty to the ground. He let out a groan and lay still, listening but not moving or speaking. He didn't think he could have done either, even if he tried.

"Boy, you sure called that one, Pox," Randy said as he dismounted to have a better look. "Dusty was a good man. Too bad we had to shoot him, but you sure called it right."

"Sure did, didn't I? I knew this was the place they'd try stopping us. You grab his horse while I see what he's got on him."

Dusty held his breath while the man rifled through his pockets. He smelled of a combination of stale whiskey, tobacco and body sweat. He had removed Dusty's gunbelt and boots by the time the boy returned with the gelding. A third man walked his horse up to the men and dismounted.

"Good shot Moses. Hit 'em right in the brisket. He must've been between paydays, though. The poor son of a bitch only had three dollars on him."

"Had a good horse, though," Randy said. "It'll be worth something."

"Yeah, well let's round up our cattle and get going before anymore honest folks show up and cause us trouble."

Dusty waited until he was sure they were gone before clawing his way to the creek. After taking a long drink, he gathered a clump of dry grass and a few twigs to a rocky area shielded from the wind. Fishing a box of matches from his shirt pocket, he lit the grass on fire and piled on more sticks until the flames shot upward. He then topped the flames with clumps of green grass and twigs.

It was all he could do to stay awake. He leaned back against the rock to watch the smoke ascend upward to get whipped away in the wind. He was losing blood and knew he would soon pass out. It wasn't that Dusty expected that Clayton Jones would see the smoke. He knew Jones was somewhere to the west of the draw, and perhaps had heard the gunshot. If he had, and came looking, he just might see or smell his fire. If he didn't, Dusty figured he would bleed to death and become coyote bait, and that was one thought he had never cherished.

CHAPTER 26

Katherine began the day with a splitting headache that kept her indoors. She nibbled at her breakfast and drank a half a cup of coffee before retreating to her office, where she simply stared at the ledger. The wind still howled outdoors, making her mood worse. She finally retreated to her room midmorning, thinking a short nap might ease the pain in the top of her head, and woke late in the afternoon to a quiet house. She stretched lazily and lay watching the shadows caused by the wind-torn trees dance against the wall opposite her bed. Her head still felt as though it was ten times its normal size. Gratefully though, the sharp pain had eased to a dull ache. Someone, probably Charlie, had covered her with a comforter as she slept. The house was totally quiet. She rolled on her side grabbing the alarm clock from her nightstand and held it in the stream of sunlight from the window. It was ten to three. She had been asleep nearly five hours. Katherine jerked upright and returned the clock to the stand with a bang that caused the alarm to go off.

"Shut up, you stupid thing," she snapped as she fumbled with the alarm mechanism. Feeling as if she had slept her life away, she quickly pulled on her boots and opened the bedroom door. The smell of beef stew and baked bread accosted her nostrils as a loud clank of a metal lid against a pot told her she was not entirely alone.

"I thought you were up." Charlene looked up from the cookie dough she was cutting as Katherine entered the kitchen. "Only you would set your alarm to take an afternoon nap."

"I didn't set it. I accidently bumped it and it went off on its own."

"No matter. I was just pulling your leg. Set yourself down," Charlene said as she spooned some honey into a mug and filled it with hot tea. She slid the steaming concoction in front of Katherine. "Here, drink this. It'll make you feel better."

"Thank you, Charlie," Katherine said, blowing across the rim of the cup.

"You had yourself a good nap. Feeling any better?" Charlene asked as she fumbled inside the cupboard looking for something.

"Some. My eyes don't itch as much, but my nose is still running in a stream." She quickly set the mug on the table and blew her nose.

Charlene returned with the bottle of whiskey she had purchased in town and poured a couple of tablespoons into Katherine's tea.

"Charlie! What…you just ruined my tea."

"Don't argue with me," she said corking the bottle. "It's an old remedy that's been around for centuries and it'll make you feel better. Folks normally use it for colds and such, but my pa used to say it was good for most anything." She shoved the bottle back into the cupboard and paused to grin. "Of course, he used to catch a terrible case of something nearly every night."

Katherine took a sip and felt the warmth wash down inside her. She had never liked the taste of liquor to begin with, and had liked the results it caused in most men who drank even less. But Charlene's tea remedy was sweet and did warm her insides, as well as clear her head.

"I guess the boys went back to the roundup. The house was so quiet when I woke, I began thinking Jesus had come and taken everyone to heaven except me. Then I remembered where everyone was." Katherine took another sip, savoring the effect.

"No, I figure you'd most likely be the first one of us he'd pick." Charlene slid a plate of warm sugar cookies on the table in front of Katherine and sat across from her with a cup of coffee. "Actually, the boys came home shortly after you fell asleep. They're here now."

"Here…?" She set the cup down hard, sloshing some of the toddy over the rim. "Why aren't they out with the cattle?" She started to scoot away from the table, but Charlene laid a hand on her shoulder and stared her in the eyes.

"Everything's okay, Kate. They said Donovan and Jones called the roundup off until this wind dies down. They said it was blowing sparks from their branding fire, and they were afraid of causing a prairie fire. They all went home. They'll finish in a day or two, when the weather cooperates."

"Oh." Katherine sipped her toddy as Charlene filled her own mug with hot tea and chuckled. "What's funny?"

"Oh, I was just remembering something Phillip said when the boys mentioned the fire. He said calling a halt to the branding was a good idea, because "a burned-out range is a sad sight, and looks like hell with the folks moved out."

"I guess it might." She grinned and took another sip. "Where are they now?"

"Phillip's got them involved with something inside the barn."

"Doing what?" Katherine took a dainty bite of a cookie and looked at Charlene with wide eyes. "My word, these are delicious. What did you do that gives them that taste?"

"I added a few nuts and a couple of tablespoons of Kentucky corn, same as you're drinking. As far as to what they're doing in the barn, I don't have the foggiest idea. He's sent Steven back here several times to refill his coffee mug, and the boy seemed downright happy. Whatever it is, it can't be work-related. You'd better eat a couple of cookies before he makes another run for coffee, because they'll disappear like magic."

The door flew open with a bang as Steven bounded in holding an empty mug.

"Speak of the devil and he pops right up," Charlene said. The boy started for the coffee pot sitting on the stove, but paused as he passed the table.

"Mmm, cookies." He stuffed a fistful inside his coat pocket then filled the cup. He reached for another handful of cookies as he passed the table on his way back toward the door and received a rap across the knuckles with Charlene's wooden spoon.

"You've already got a coat-full. Save some of those for your mother." He laughed and opened the door.

"Steven Michael Parker, you just wait a minute."

"Ma'am?" He turned slowly, wondering what transgression he had committed that had caused his mother to use his middle name.

"Close the door."

"Yes, ma'am." He shut the door and stood timidly facing her.

"Are you going to pass right by your mother without saying a word?"

"Yes…I mean, no ma'am. Are you feeling better?"

"Yes I am. Thank you very much. Now, what are you boys and Mr. Denning doing inside the barn that is so important that would cause you to be rude?"

"Phil's teaching us how to fight. Bye," he said, and left by closing the door with a loud bang. Katherine stared at Charlene a pregnant minute before scooting away from the table.

"Would you like to go with me?"

"I'd like to see you stop me. Just give me a second to stir the stew before we leave."

CHAPTER 27

"No, no, no! You're fightin' just like your brother did when he got hisself punched silly."

Katherine stood just inside the barn door next to Charlene, sipping her toddy and watching the spectacle. The boys had only given them a casual notice when they entered before continuing their training. They had hung several grain sacks from a rafter, and were using them as punching bags. Phillip was presently showing his frustration with Timothy, who seemed to be ignoring his instructions.

"But I can get more power if I put everything behind it."

"Who says you can? When you rear back and swing wild like a windmill, you're not getting anything behind it except your arms. Let me show you. Hold your hand up like this." Phillip held a hand with his palm outward as if telling someone to halt. Timothy mimicked him and received a resounding smack on his palm that caused him to yelp with pain. The part that amazed Katherine was the speed with which Phillip had delivered the blow. His hand had been a blur.

"Hurt, didn't it? Now, that was my left hand, thrown from right here." He held his fist several inches from his body just below his chin. "When you keep your hands here, in tight, and throw your punches like this," he hit the grain sack with a flurry of punches, "you get your entire body, shoulders, chest and even legs behind the blow. But most importantly, you stand a better chance of blocking the other fellow's blows. But if you swing wild like you were doing, you're going to be wide open and easy to hit. Let me show you. Come here, all of you."

He squared off with Timothy as the other three watched. "Come on, hit me."

"Huh?" The boy stood dumbfounded.

"I said hit me."

"I don't wanna hit you."

"Come on, you're not going to hurt me."

"But…" He was cut short as Phillip slapped him. Timothy's mouth dropped open in shock, and he received two more slaps. Katherine started forward, but and pulled back by Charlene.

"Let 'em be, ma'am. He's teaching them how to handle themselves."

"But…"

"Let 'the boys learn."

Timothy's face reddened with anger and he charged swinging like a mad man, but his blows only found air as Phillip ducked and dodged, delivering a slapping-blow with nearly every move. The exhibition only lasted momentarily before an exhausted Timothy broke down in frustration and tears. Phillip pulled him close in a bear hug and patted him on the back.

"You okay, boy?"

Timothy nodded with a sniff.

"Good." Phillip gave him another pat before releasing his hold. "Now, I did that to show you what happens when you try throwing your punches all the way from Texas. That's what Matt was doing in town the other day. The sad part was the clown he was fighting was doing the same thing. It might have been funny, except Silas was bigger and stronger than Matt. He happened to land a couple of lucky blows, then beat the stuffing out of Matt while he was out on his feet. If Matt had been punching like I've been trying to teach you boys, it would have been a different story. Matt, come here."

Matthew walked timidly toward him.

"We're going to do this real slow so these brothers of yours can see. I want you to act like you're going to hit me with a haymaker like you did in town."

The boy gave a lazy swing that seemed to wrap around Phillip's shoulder as he moved in close.

"See, even if he did land that blow, it really wouldn't hurt. Look where it's landing."

"Yeah, but he could grab hold of you, if he wanted," Steven said.

"Not if I'm landing blows of my own." Phillip demonstrated by acting as if he were punching Matthew. "He's swinging wild, while I'm in close, causing him to move away and lose power with his punches. In the meantime, I'm hitting him in the body and face anytime and anywhere I want. But, that's enough for today. We'll work on it a little more tomorrow, after you've had time to digest what you've learned today."

He grabbed his hat from a pile of straw and draped his gunbelt over his shoulder.

"When are you going to teach me how to shoot?" Matthew asked.

"After you've learned how to control your temper," Phillip said. "I don't want to hear some day that you've killed someone or gotten yourself killed, simply because you didn't like what some idiot said."

"Well, how will I know when?"

"I'll let you know. I have a knack for getting you all heated up. I'll find out when the time's come and let you know."

He stopped at Sunrise's stall as the colt whistled and snorted happily.

"Yeah, I saved you one." He dug into his vest pocket and gave the colt one of Charlene's cookies.

"Now, I've seen everything. I didn't slave over a hot oven all afternoon so you could feed my cookies to a bunch of farm animals, Mr. Denning," Charlene said.

Phillip turned and gave the women a grin.

"Sorry, ladies, you were so quiet I forgot you were standing here."

"Oh, she started to get noisy when you slapped Timmy a time or two, but I threw a muzzle on her," Charlene said.

"It's not easy watching one of your children getting hit, Mr. Denning," Katherine said.

"No, I don't reckon it would be. I don't have any children, so I really wouldn't know." He held the door open for the women and joined them as they rushed to the shelter of the front porch.

"Is there any chance you might have a few of those cookies left?" he asked as he opened the kitchen door.

"Yes, I do, and if I catch you feeding another one to that horse, I'll break both of your hands," Charlene said. She glanced out the window and cocked her head with grin. "You both had better get what you want now, 'cause the boys are headed this way. Those cookies are going to disappear quicker than a scared jackrabbit."

~   ~   ~

The few minutes Katherine had spent inside the dusty barn and the dash across the yard in the wind had caused the headache to return. She was forced to leave the supper table due to her sneezing and a queasy stomach. She sat near the toasty fireplace holding several handkerchiefs in her lap and sipping broth from a cup. Matthew gave her a crooked grin as he joined her after supper.

"I know exactly how you feel. I hated every minute of drinking soup and watching everyone eat steak. I feel for you, Mama."

Katherine scowled as he patted her on the arm. "Now, why do I doubt that?"

"No, it's true, 'cause you're my mother and I love you."

The boy retrieved the Bible from the shelf and sat beside his brothers on the sofa to begin their nightly ritual of reading. She would have offered him a tender reply, except the pounding in the top of her head and a runny nose took precedence. Charlene came from the kitchen with a warm towel and a mug filled with her tea remedy.

"No, not anymore, Charlie. I've already drunk enough of your medicine." Katherine shook her head, as Charlene gave her a stern glare.

"You may be the boss-woman and run this ranch, but here inside this house I'm the boss. So don't argue with me young lady. Drink some of this."

"I'm not that much younger than you, Charlie," Katherine said with a chuckle.

"I'm still the oldest. Drink it." She held the mug in front of her.

Katherine obeyed grudgingly and took a swallow, then gasped for air as the fiery liquid burnt a path to her stomach. The toddy was mostly bourbon. She coughed and gave the house-keeper an angry glare.

"What are you trying to do, kill me? Besides, you know I never drink."

"You felt better after that weak toddy I gave you earlier today, so I'm increasing the dosage. Go on, take another drink."

"No, I can't Charlie." She set her mouth into a thin line and shook her head.

"You can't or won't? It's not going to make you a drunk, so quit making things difficult and drink it." Katherine grudgingly took another sip as Phillip came from the kitchen rolling a cigarette.

"Does that stuff really stop rag-fever?"

"Rag-fever? What's that?" Charlene asked as she forced Katherine's head back onto a pillow and covered her eyes with the hot towel.

"That's what my ma used to call it when your head got all stuffed up with the dust and junk from hay or ragweed."

"Well, I've never know a little dirt or pollen to bother Kate. I've seen her still working when she was so caked with grime you couldn't tell her from the dirt. I'd say she caught something else, and I don't know if my tea will cure it,"

Charlene said with a shrug, "but It'll certainly make her feel better. Now, excuse me while I clean the dishes."

Phillip waited until she had left before smelling the concoction inside the cup. "Yep, I'd say you'll be feeling pretty good in a few minutes. Probably sleep real good too."

"Sleep actually sounds good," Katherine said with a slight grin. She couldn't see him with her eyes covered beneath the towel, although she could feel his presence as he pulled a chair next to hers. "The inside of my head feels like it's going to explode."

"You get this way often?"

"No, I seldom get under the weather."

"She don't," Steven said from the couch.

"She doesn't." Katherine corrected him without removing the towel.

"Okay, she doesn't get sick. She slipped on the ice a couple of winters ago and cracked her left arm. Doctor Krucker had her arm in a splint, but do you think that'd slow her down? Na, she kept right on working."

"Ma will be herdin' cattle long after she's dead." Joshua chuckled.

"Makes sense," Phillip said as he lit his cigarette. "I'd probably do the same thing, when there's work to be done."

"Exactly, Mr. Denning. That's why I can't get sick, especially now. It's spring roundup. You know as well as I do, it's the heart of cattle-ranching…"

"Yeah, and you're not feeling right. You could let me and the boys handle things for a couple of days."

She removed the towel to look at him. "Maybe, but I've always done my part. That's what I do."

"And you want everyone to know who's boss," he said with a grin.

"I do not!"

"Now, don't get all puffed up over something I said, ma'am. I can see where your son gets it from. All I meant was there's no need in you going outside and making yourself worse. Those boys know what to do. And as far as I'm concerned, you can trust me, Mrs. Parker."

"Can I, Mr. Denning?"

"When I hire on with someone to do a job, I do my job the best I know how, Mrs. Parker. I don't know any other way." He tossed his half-smoked cigarette into the fireplace and scooted his chair away.

"Now who's getting all puffed up over something I said?" Katherine sat upright and tossed the towel onto the floor.

"Okay…you got me. I just figured y'all should know me by now."

"I'm sorry if it offends you but no, we don't. I learned more about you in the few minutes I spent talking to Sheriff Crutchfield than I've learned from you, and you've been with us for over a month."

"You've seen my work. There's not much more to know."

"Oh, I think there is." She paused to take another sip of Charlie's medicine, and gasped. "I hate to admit it, but it does make me feel better."

"I reckon it might at that." Phillip pulled the chair closer and crossed his legs as he sat studying her. "What would you like to know?"

"A lot of things. For instance, what you were teaching my boys this afternoon. Where did you learn to fight with your fists?"

"Oh," Phillip said, nodding slowly. "I learned that when I was a kid, about Matt's age. I was riding for John Tunstall down in New Mexico. Tunstall was an Englishman who'd bought a big ranch and hired a bunch of us boys on to cowboy for him. He also owned a bank and a store…I guess he was into most everything, but he was one of the nicest God-fearing men I've ever met.

"One day, a bunch of people from his native England showed up in fancy wagons. I don't think he really knew them. They'd heard about him and just showed up. They had their women, and all of them were dressed up like they were going to a wedding. They even had a private chef, if you can believe it, and one of the wagons was stocked with fancy food and wine, including champagne. They asked Tunstall if he would send a few of us boys to work as guides and take them on a hunting expedition for sport. So, Tunstall picked me, Jim Greathouse and McCarty to go. We led them up to the hills, where they could hunt such things as cougars and mountain goats. Turns out, their form of hunting was for us boys to go up into the rocks and flush the game down, where they'd be waiting near the wagons, dressed in their fancy clothes. There wasn't much sport to it at all, and they never kept anything they killed, except for a few cougar hides and some antlers. None of us cowboys cared a whit for what they were doing.

"Anyway, they had this big shambles of a man traveling with them, who had huge scarred hands, and scars around both eyes. Turns out he was a bare-knuckle fighter from England. He was as much a spectacle and entertainment for them as anything else. They would stop in every town they passed and take bets as to whether anyone could best him in a fight. No one ever did. To make a long story short, he and I became friends, and he taught me most of what I've been showing your boys. Hope you don't mind, ma'am. It's important that they learn how to protect themselves."

Katherine had finished drinking the toddy as she listened, and the whiskey made her head feel light. She smiled and studied him through half-closed eyelids. He wasn't what she would have considered an overly-handsome man, but still attractive in a rugged sort of way. Besides being quite tall, he had strong, broad shoulders supporting a well sculptured head. His droopy moustache was well trimmed and complimented his shoulder-length brown hair.

"No, I don't mind you teaching my boys, Mr. Denning…not at all." She took a deep breath and sighed. "Look, I can breathe and my head quit hurting. Charlie's concoction worked. Get me another one."

"Ma'am?" He grinned slant-wise. "Are you sure?"

"If one worked, perhaps a second will help me get a good night's sleep."

"I'm sure it would," he said with a laugh.

"I heard," Charlene said from the kitchen and appeared seconds later with another steaming mug. She also had a small snifter of bourbon which she handed to Phillip.

"Here you go, honey," she handed the mug to Katherine. "Drink up, and we'll put you to bed."

Charlene retrieved the towel and empty cup before heading toward the kitchen, and stopped as Joshua asked, "Can I get one of those?"

"Why, are you sick?"

"Yeah, I have a terrible cough." He gave several forced hacks. "See?"

"Huh, Matthew can have one if he wants, but you'll get regular tea and honey. Finish your studies."

"That ain't fair. I'm almost as big as he is."

"You're still younger, and I said no. Besides, it *isn't fair*, not *ain't fair*. So finish your studies."

Katherine giggled as she took a sip of her toddy. It burned all the way to her toes, making her feel warm and fuzzy. She glanced at the man seated next to her in James' favorite chair, sipping from the snifter and watching the crackling logs in the fireplace. For an odd moment, he seemed to fit. She closed her eyes, trying to remember James in the chair, to hear his laughter once again as he teased Abby and the boys. She had no idea when she dozed off, but vaguely remembered being cradled in James' arms as he carried her to her bedroom. She inhaled his scent and slipped her arms around his neck as he laid her on the bed, hoping to taste his mouth, but he untangled her hold and told her goodnight. It was Charlene who removed her boots, skirt and blouse and covered her with the blanket. Charlene kissed her on the forehead saying, "Goodnight, dear," and closed the door. She suddenly felt lonely and her bed grew as large and empty as the South Dakota prairie. She rolled over hugging her pillow and fell into a deep sleep.

CHAPTER 28

Sixteen-year-old Charlie Carpenter had gone into the bushes to seek some privacy and do his evening toilet before supper. His mother was busy cooking the meal while his father chopped more firewood. Charlie's younger sister Sally was occupied inside the wagon making the beds. He had just finished and was buttoning his coveralls when he heard the voices.

"Hello in the camp. Mind if I join you for a spell?"

"No, we don't mind, if you come friendly, pilgrim," Charlie's father answered back.

"Mister, there's folks around here claim Walt Tivo is the friendliest man you'll ever meet."

"That's good. Come and sit yourself awhile. My woman's almost got supper fixed."

The Carpenter family was on their way south from North Dakota after experiencing only one winter in Fargo. Charlie's father, George, had sold the family farm and moved his family to Fargo with the dream of opening a general store and pharmacy. But the harsh winter and his wife's ill health had drained their finances and dashed their dreams. They were now on their way back to Pine Ridge with a promise from friends and relatives for help to start over. George had made camp for the evening beside a deserted and seldom used road, and Charlie was surprised to hear the stranger's voice. He made his way through the brush, and stopped just short of the camp as the stranger walked into the clearing leading a dun-colored mare. In the firelight the man's features were frightening, and almost monster-looking. Charlie squatted behind the bush and peered through the branches.

"You sure are a welcome sight," the pock-faced man said. "You ain't traveling alone way out here, are you? I don't see another wagon around."

"No, we're all there is. Are you hungry?"

"I sure am. Let me tie my horse to that dead tree over yonder and I'll join you." The stranger ambled toward the tree whistling and Charlie had almost decided it was safe for him to return to camp when the man spun and shot his father through the heart with a pistol. That was followed by a volley of gunfire from the trees on the opposite side of the camp. His mother and father had both fallen where they had been standing. Sally jumped from the wagon screaming and the ugly pock-faced man shot her. Two men, a large middle-aged man and a young man not much older than Charlie himself emerged from the trees. The older man was laughing, but the younger one was pale and sick-looking. Charlie bit his tongue until the taste of blood filled his mouth, knowing if he uttered the slightest whimper they would kill him also.

"You sure called that one right, Pox," the middle-aged man said.

"I'm always right, heck there weren't nothing to it, Moses. Why don't you and Randy climb into the wagon and see what you can find while I sneak a peek into this feller's pockets?"

Charlie wiped his eyes against his shirtsleeve and watched as the man rifled through his father's coveralls, stuffing anything he considered valuable into his own pockets.

"We hit the jackpot," the middle-aged man said, jumping from the wagon. He had found his mother's jewelry case, and Charlie knew that was where his mother had kept the remainder of their savings hidden.

He eased back into the brush, not wishing to see anymore. It took the men most of an hour to rifle through their belongings. At one point, the men stopped their thievery and ate the supper his mother had been preparing. He waited until he was certain they had gone before returning to the wagon to discover they had scattered anything they didn't consider of value. They rode away, leaving his little sister and parents lying on the ground. Finding the shovel, Charlie dug three shallow graves and buried his family. Then he sat by the wagon and watched the sunrise above the distant hills.

He remembered his father saying Denby lay along this same trail approximately eight miles to the south. Since the thieves had taken the horses, Charlie decided he had better get an early start. Stuffing several dried crackers and some beef jerky in his pockets, Charlie slung a canteen of water over his shoulder and started walking. Perhaps Denby had a sheriff who would know what to do.

CHAPTER 29

Randy Houk sat sullenly inside the cabin replaying the events of the previous night in his mind, while Pox Tivo and Moses Martin drank and played cards for the woman's jewelry.

"What's the matter with you boy?" Pox asked as he poured himself another drink. "You're not feeling too perky. Take a slug of this *who-hit-John* and it'll fix you right up."

He didn't answer, figuring Pox was either too hard or too stupid to understand what he was feeling. He had told Dusty the truth about his joining up with Pox. The past two winters had been hard ones, and most of the cattlemen had suffered something fierce. Besides losing large amounts of their herds to the cold, the price of beef had fallen to the point they were laying their ranch hands off in droves. Randy, because of his age, had been one of the first to go.

He had looked most everywhere for work, and even done odd jobs, such as sweeping floors and emptying spittoons at the saloon. But he figured that wasn't fitting work for a cowhand, and he began drifting from one place to another, looking for something better. That was when he ran into Pox Tivo on the trail to Buffalo Gap. They had ridden only a short distance when Randy mentioned something about how tough times were, and that he'd been out of work for quite a spell. That was when Pox told him about his ranch, and how he was planning to build a herd of his own and asked Randy if he was interested in working for him.

Naturally, he had jumped at the idea of steady work as a cowhand and there was nothing wrong, in his mind, with pilfering a few strays here and there to help Pox build a herd. And the man had picked a perfect spot for a ranch. It was a beautiful little valley with plenty of water and grass. It even had an abundance of wild game to tide a man over until he had his herd built. The real kicker had come when Pox promised he would have a permanent job.

"Anyone working to help build my ranch can work for me as long as they want," he had said. "In fact, they'll be sort of like partners and own a piece of the spread."

What Tivo had not mentioned was they would be participating in out and out rustling instead of branding a few mavericks here and there. Every rancher he knew of threw a wide loop and put their own brands on mavericks. But they also frowned on outright rustling, and rustlers usually paid with their lives when they got caught. And while Randy had hated the idea of rustling, he hated worse seeing a nice guy like Dusty Moore getting plugged in the back. The worst had come with the outright murder of that poor family the previous night on the trail. There had been no call for it, and the vision of the pretty little girl's lifeless body on the cold ground was permanently branded in his mind.

"Aw, don't pay no attention to him, Pox," Moses Martin said with a laugh. "He just ain't got no stomach for killin'."

"That right, Randy? You didn't like me plugging that pilgrim and his folks?"

"She was just a little girl, Pox. She couldn't have caused us any harm."

"Well, there was some mighty young boys just about her age killing men during the war. You can believe that before anything else. I was there and seen it."

Pox downed his drink and poured himself another, then dealt the cards.

"Well, I'll tell you what, sonny. I'll let the next cute little girl live and you can take care of her. How's that?"

Randy didn't answer and lay back on his cot as they laughed. What he needed was a way out, but you just didn't quit a man like Pox Tivo. The only way you left him was dead, like Jerry Sloan. The man was mean as a snake and Randy had only seen him show fear twice since joining up with him. The first time was when Phillip Denning had ordered them hung. And for some reason that Randy could never figure out, he knew Pox was deathly afraid of Nate Thomas. To his reckoning, the man had never threatened any of them. Randy was certain, however, that Pox feared him.

All he knew was he needed out, but couldn't figure how without getting himself killed.

CHAPTER 30

Katherine woke with the clank of the metal door on her small wood stove in her bedroom. She bolted upright in bed to discover she had a splitting headache, and flopped back with a groan to cover her face with a pillow.

"Sorry to wake you, honey," Charlene said. "There's a little nip in the air, so I thought I'd build you a fire."

Katherine peaked at the woman from beneath the pillow. "What time is it?" she asked in a raspy voice.

"Mmmm, I don't rightly know. It was close to eight o'clock when I last checked in the kitchen. It's hard to tell inside this house, since every room has a clock, but every clock tells a different time."

The fire inside the heater caught and Charlene closed the door with a clank.

"Take a look at that noisy alarm clock on your nightstand."

"I can't. I can't see anything. That stuff you gave me last night caused me to go blind."

"You might have a little hangover, but I hardly think you're blind. That's what you get for asking for one more, instead of stopping with the toddy I gave you. You still sound stuffy. How are you feeling this morning? How's your head?"

"I feel like I got run over by a herd of buffalo. I don't want to talk, Charlie. I'm dying." She pulled the pillow down tight and moaned.

"It only feels like your dying," Charlene said, patting her on the leg. "If a herd of buffalo had actually run over you, you wouldn't be feeling a thing. Stay in bed and I'll get you some coffee and something for your head."

"No more of your toddies."

"Got you, no more toddies, at least not this morning." Charlene opened the bedroom door and paused as Katherine spoke in a muffled voice from under the pillow.

"Get the boys their breakfast and tell them I'm still sick. I'll see them later."

"The boys ate two hours ago and left with Phil. They all know you're not feeling well."

"Two hours ago?" Katherine sat up quickly and tossed back the covers. She grabbed for her house coat and was attempting to put on her slippers when the room started spinning as her stomach churned. She fell to her knees, grabbed for her chamber pot under the bed and heaved. The heaving continued until she lay exhausted on the floor with her cheek pressed against the cool wood. She was still there when Charlene returned with a tray.

"Katie? Oh, my word!" She set the tray on the dressing table and knelt beside her. "Did you fall, honey? Are you hurt?"

"No, just sick," Katherine said, shaking her head. She grabbed for the pot as another bout of heaving struck her. "I'm sorry…Charlie. I…I'm making a mess."

"That's okay, honey, go ahead. It'll make you feel better."

Charlene rubbed Katherine's back and shoulders until the heaving ceased and helped her back into bed and covered her. "I think you might have a little more than a hangover, young lady," she said, wiping Katherine's face and hands with a damp towel. She felt Katherine's forehead with the back of her hand, then leaned over to place her lips against her temple.

"Mmmhumm," she said with a nod. "You've either got the first hangover in history that came with a fever, or you caught something. I'd say you caught something. Do you feel like you can drink some coffee?"

Katherine squeezed her eyes shut and shook her head. The very mention of coffee caused her stomach to churn.

"I didn't think so. I'll come up with something else. In the meantime, I brought you some headache powders. Drink this," she held a glass of water to Katherine's lips, "it'll stop your head from hurting."

She drank half the glass and covered her face with the pillow as the caterpillars inside her stomach began crawling.

"I'll set the glass here next to your clock and you can finish it later. In the meantime, you can use this, if you feel sick again." She laid Katherine's washbasin next to her. "It'll be cleaner and more pleasant than sticking your face in a chamber pot. Stay in bed and holler if you need anything. I'll clean this mess up."

"I'm sorry, Charlie," Katherine said weakly.

"Don't worry about it, honey. You'll eventually do the same for me one of these days. There isn't a person alive that doesn't get under the weather once in a while.

~   ~   ~

Katherine fell in and out of sleep the rest of the day, only waking when Charlene forced her to drink some water or broth. The moments of being disturbed were an irritation that caused both women to lose their tempers.

"Good God, Charlie, please quit bothering me, and let me be!"

"I will as soon as you drink something. You're going to dry up and blow away like a leaf."

"Good, then I can sleep without you bothering me."

"Okay," Charlene glared down at her, "I'll leave, but since you won't mind me, I'm sending Phillip Denning in here with your supper. Maybe you'll mind him."

"You wouldn't dare," she yelled as Charlene closed her door with a bang.

She fell back to sleep to be awakened by the banging of a door and the loud voices of her sons. The light inside her bedroom looked strange, and it took her several minutes before she realized it was late afternoon, and the sun had begun to wane. She crawled out of bed and staggered to her dressing table on shaky legs to stare into the mirror. The unfamiliar figure looking back at her had dark bags under her eyes and an unruly mess of damp yellow straw instead of hair sticking out of her head.

"You're a frightful sight," she said, and staggered to retrieve her washbasin from the bed. Katherine washed herself and brushed her teeth, but the action exhausted her. She sat for a long while, holding a hairbrush and staring into the mirror. Washing hadn't changed a thing. The woman in the mirror was still frightful to look at. She laid the brush aside and crawled back into bed and pulled the covers under her chin. Her head had quit hurting, that was a good thing, and there was a slight hunger in her stomach. She couldn't tell if the caterpillars had entirely left, but at least the heaving had stopped. She stared at the ceiling, listening to the noise down the hall. Steven was excited about something, and his squeaky voice carried like an out-of-tune violin, although Katherine couldn't quite make out what he was saying. She was thinking about how much she loved them when she dozed off.

She woke with the loud banging of a door and Matthew yelling at Joshua and Timothy. The boys had pulled another prank and their brother was furious. She crawled out of bed with a sigh and pulled on her robe and slippers. Brushing her hair did absolutely no good, so she shuffled down the hall and into the living room and purposefully between the arguing boys. The arguing ceased immediately as she sat in one of the chairs.

"Huh," Charlene said, poking her head into the room. I see you went and disturbed your mother. Are you happy now? You boys need a good thumping."

"I don't want to hear who did what," Katherine said quietly, "I only want it to stop this instant. Do you understand?"

"Yes, ma'am," came the unison reply.

The smell of pot roast caused the caterpillars to resume crawling. Katherine closed her eyes sitting in the chair and drifted back to sleep. She heard Phillip Denning's voice in her dream several times before realizing it wasn't coming from her dream.

"Wake up, sleepyhead, it's time to eat."

Katherine pulled the robe tightly around her neck and straightened herself in the chair. Someone had retrieved her pillow from her bedroom and tucked it neatly into the chair for her to lean on. Phillip placed the tray on the small table beside her chair and sat on a stool.

"Charlie said I'm supposed to make sure you eat this soup."

"She did, did she?"

"Yes, ma'am. It ain't quiet as filling as her roast, but it looks mighty tasty."

"I'm going to kill her when I get over this."

"Kill who?"

"Charlie. She's been bossing me around like a child."

"No, don't do that," Phillip said with a grin. "Sheriff Crutchfield will have to put you in jail. Besides, Charlie's the best ranch cook I've ever run across, and believe me, I've seen a few." He sat quietly for a minute studying her.

"What? I know I look a sight. Are you trying to decide if you should run, or laugh?"

"No, you're actually beautiful."

"And you, Mr. Denning, are a big liar."

"I've been called a lot of things, ma'am, but I've never been accused of being a liar. I was just trying to decide if I should feed you, or if you're well enough to feed yourself."

"I am quiet capable of caring for myself, thank you."

"Okay, let me see."

"What?"

"Charlie wasn't joking when she ordered me to make sure you eat. She's in a mood I've never seen before. Those boys wandered off into the kitchen the minute you went to sleep and started up arguing again. She went on the warpath and thumped them real good with a wooden spoon."

"She did, did she?"

"Yes, ma'am, she did."

Katherine dropped her spoon into the mug of chicken soup and covered her mouth laughing. "Lord, I'd have given anything to see that."

"It was pretty funny. Me and Steve split a gut laughing," Phillip said as he dabbed at a dribble on her chin. He talked in low tones while she ate, filling her in on the events of the day. The cattle had scattered during the windstorm, so everyone had spent the day locating the wayward cows. They would drive them back to camp tomorrow and resume branding. He made sure she drank her hot tea, and again dabbed at a dribble on her chin. He was a rather nice looking fellow, she thought, with his hair combed back and a clean shirt. But this tender side of Phillip Denning was something new, and had thrown her for a loop. His actions with the rustlers and the shooting demonstration had given her a different impression of the man. Now she didn't quite know what to believe. It had been quite awhile since she had simply sat and talked to a man, and he had a way of making her feel comfortable. She had enjoyed her talks with James. He had been gone four years now, and she still missed him. She vaguely remembered how she had felt when James carried her to her room the previous night, then caught her breath as she realized it wasn't something she had dreamed.

"Is something wrong, ma'am?"

"No....yes...I mean..."

"You mean what, ma'am?"

"I had the strangest dream last night. I dreamed that my husband, James, carried me to bed after I fell asleep in this chair. But it seemed so real..."

"Yes, ma'am?"

"Tell me the truth, Mr. Denning. Did I fall asleep, and did you have to carry me to bed?"

"Yes, ma'am, but Charlene was there every step of the way, and she's the one who tucked you in. I just laid you on the bed. Honest."

"I'm sorry if I made myself a nuisance, or did anything inappropriate. I seldom drink anything with alcohol, and Charlene's remedy really packs a wallop. I can't remember if I did or said anything embarrassing or..." She trailed off as he grinned. "I did, didn't I?"

"No, ma'am. I was just thinking how cute it was seeing you like this, and knowing what a strong woman you are. I just thought it was funny." He took the empty cup from her hand and placed it on the tray. "Now, if you're done, I'd better take these dishes back to the kitchen. Is there anything else you would like me to get you?"

"No, Mr. Denning. I think I've eaten all my stomach will allow. And thank you for being so kind."

"You're welcome," he said with a grin. He held the tray in one hand and paused at her voice.

"Mr. Denning?"

"Ma'am?"

"Are you sure I didn't do or say anything embarrassing last night? You'd tell me, wouldn't you?"

"I don't know if I'd tell you, but no," he shook his head, "you were a perfect lady. Although," he cocked his head to one side and chuckled, "I was pretty sure you were going to kiss me when I laid you on the bed."

"Aaaah!" she yelled and threw a pillow. He laughed and disappeared into the kitchen. She covered her face with both hands. "Oh God, please let me die."

CHAPTER 31

William Crutchfield leaned his elbows against the battered desk in his office and cradled his forehead in his hands. He had just talked to Charlie Carpenter and was in the process of filling out a report. He would take a few townspeople and a team of horses first thing in the morning to retrieve anything left of the boy's family's belongings. Of course, none of that would either help the boy or bring their murderers to justice.

One thing he could not do was go chasing after Pox Tivo and his gang with a bunch of untrained townspeople, no matter how honest or big hearted they might be. Pox was a killer, and so were those riding with him. If he went after them with a makeshift posse he would only get them killed. What he needed was someone who could be equally as vicious when the chips were down. He figured that he needed at least two men besides himself, and he only knew of two in the area that came close to matching that description--Phillip Denning and Nathan Thomas. The only trouble with trying to recruit them would be in preventing them from killing each other before they had killed Pox Tivo.

He ran his fingers through his graying hair before pouring himself a drink. He'd have to figure a way of doing exactly that, or go after Tivo alone. Tangling with Pox and his gang by himself was an idea Crutchfield did not cherish.

CHAPTER 32

The wind that had driven them indoors had died to a pleasant breeze. Steven draped the blanket and saddle gently across the blue roan's back and snugged the cinches, then climbed up onto the corral fence and sat. There was no doubt the two-year-old was her mother's daughter. The way she tossed her head, the intelligent flash of her eye, and the unabashed fearless curiosity she possessed were proof of that. Everything about her was exceptional, from her beautiful face to her graceful movements. She even presented herself in a way that made her stand out from other two-year-olds. Her long legs and well rounded rear end told him she was going to be a runner.

He watched as the young roan cavorted in the crisp morning air. Cowboy Willie had told him his mother was *La Jinete*. "That's someone who knows horses. Knows them intensely. They're just born with it, kind of like they can talk to 'em and know what they're thinking. It ain't something they learned along the way. They're just born with it. Yep, your ma's *La Jinete*."

Willie had told Steven that several years ago and he had never forgotten it. Everyone claimed Katherine Parker was the best wrangler in the area. She didn't just ride horses, she made them. She bred them for intelligence, workability and color. She could bring out the best the animal had to offer, and trained them to become the best they could be. She was known for her string of bridle and savvy working horses. "Yer ma could've trained her horses the old vaquero way, if she'd been born in the right place," Willie had told him. As it was, she made fine horses. His mother and the old vaquero shared a bond with the horses. She used his knowledge, and lately the old man had been asking her questions. They respected each other.

Willie had been coming around as long as Steven could remember…even before his father died. The old man would show up in the spring, then vanish in the fall. No one seemed to know where he went. He was just there. Steven had heard him mention Texas once, but figured that was too far for an old man to travel. Regardless, Willie had mourned with the family when Abby went missing, and told them he had lost a wife and daughter of his own to Comanches. Willie said he figured Steven's dad had never given up looking for Abby to ease his own soul. Willie hadn't arrive at his normal time last year, and it wasn't until late fall they heard he had been drug to death during a stampede on a ranch somewhere in Wyoming.

Steven had looked forward to Willie's arrival each year. The old man was one of the few people his mother trusted in judgment and friendship. The old man knew a million stories, and gave lessons on braiding horse hair and working leather. He had learned more about cattle and horse breeding listening to Willie and his mother talk, than he could ever have learned from reading books. The fact that they had allowed him to sit in on these conversations, and asked his opinion, made him proud.

Steven watched as the two year-old pranced around the corral. His mother had named the mare Smokin' Ripplin' Rio the day she was born, more for its smoky-blue coat. His heart almost stopped when she turned toward him and said, "This little girl is yours, Steven. I know you'll make a fine horse out of her." He glanced toward Willie, and the old man gave him a confirming nod.

He had worked the horse daily since, picking up her feet at every turn, giving gentle tugs on her tail, taking her along patiently, and trying to bring out the best in her. As soon as the filly and her mother could go out, he took them on every job he could. He loved watching her frolic and play, running to catch up as they went out to mend a fence or go fishing. He eventually took her farther from home, and stayed longer. Steven had to tie her to a lead rope, because she was curious and would stray. She was now two years old and had covered the entire ranch. She had encountered wolves and bears and skunks, holes and caves, shifting shadows, jumping things, flying things, and swimming things. He discovered the horse loved to swim, and knew he'd have to teach her not to lie down in the water while she was under the saddle.

She trusted him implicitly. He had done all the ground work in teaching her to lead well, to stand still and have good manners. She had been free-lunged and driven under saddle, learned voice commands, and how to bend and be supple. He had stepped in and out of the saddle on either side. He couldn't think of anything he'd forgotten. Today, though, he was going to ask her for more.

Steven glanced up as Phillip and his brothers rode into the yard and dismounted at the neighboring corral.

"Ooo, looks like the squirt is gonna try riding her," Timothy said.

"Yeah, I gotta see this," Joshua said.

"Quiet down, you lunk-heads. Don't rile the mare," Phillip said.

"I bet he's gonna get tossed on his butt," Joshua snorted.

"I'll take that bet," Phillip said.

"Me too," Matthew said with a nod. "I'll do your after-dinner chores for a week, if he gets bucked off. If he stays, you do mine."

"Yeah, it's a deal," Joshua said.

"I'll do the same for you, Tim," Phillip said, then gave Steven a wink.

He wasn't afraid of being bucked off a horse. He'd been face down in the dirt his fair share each spring while he and his brothers were snapping out new ones. But Rio had not been ridden, and he felt that was his first step in becoming *La Jinete* like his mother. He didn't have to look over his shoulder to know his mother was watching from the window by her desk where she kept the daily books. He could feel her.

He jumped down from his seat and Rio came to stand facing him, then followed a few steps, then reached around to lip at his cuff when he gave the cinches a final tug, telling him they were tight enough.

Steven glanced toward the house and saw his mother standing quietly next to Charlie near the porch rail. He had not told her, but she had somehow known this was the day, and was offering her support in a way he understood.

Steven slipped the bosal over Rio's nose then behind her ears. This was nothing new to her, and she was used to this activity. He pulled gently to bring her head back around to the near side. When she complied and relaxed with her nose nearly on the fender leather, he reached up and took the saddle horn. Keeping a firm hold on her head, he stepped into the stirrup, paused for the count of ten and stepped down, releasing her head. He petted and stroked her neck and praised her softly, "What a good girl you are. Now, we're going to do it again and see what we both are made of."

He stepped into the stirrup and paused for a minute, allowing Rio to balance under him. Then he swung his leg over and gently settled into the saddle. He sat quietly before urging her to move forward in the direction of her head. When she began to move out in a tight circle, he let go of her head and they walked crisply around the pen, once, twice, and three times. He breathed out slowly and kept focused, knowing anything was possible at this point. It was far from being over. They were off to a good start. Stephen knew that it was always the third ride that told the truth. They kept moving forward, in large circles, then through the middle of the pen. He talked constantly to the mare, assuring her she was being good. He pulled her head back around to her off-side and stopped, then let her go again. After several more starts and stops, they sat quietly in the pen, horse and rider. He dismounted, dropped the rope and walked away. Rio followed closely on his heels, almost bumping him when he reached the rail. He turned and stroked her face and kissed her nose. He waved at his mother and received a wave and cheer back.

"I want my saddle soaped nice and clean," Phillip said, and slapped Timothy on the back.

"Me too." Matthew gave Joshua a nod. "And check the bridle. It needs a little attending."

Steven stroked Rio's neck. She was beautiful. Maybe he was *La Jinete* like his mother.

CHAPTER 33

Phillip could see the smoke from a campfire from a quarter of a mile's distance. He and the boys had eaten their breakfast and left the ranch before daylight, and split up once they had reached the washes in which the cattle had taken their refuge from the wind. The ranchers had decided to save time and split their forces. Instead of driving the cattle into one area for a massive branding, they would have several smaller brandings. The Box D had set up in an area they would use as headquarters that evening. Matthew had chosen the wash where they had discovered cattle the day his mother had taken ill.

Phillip had been scouting around, locating wayward cattle, when he got an uneasy feeling crawling up the back of his neck. There was no explanation for it, but he had learned over the years never to ignore such feelings. They had proven right and saved his skin in more than one situation. He pulled the Winchester from its scabbard and walked his horse closer. The smoke was coming from a draw where a dead tree had fallen. He dismounted and led the horse forward cautiously. The campfire was in the area where Matthew said they would be branding, but the fire could have also been built by rustlers or Indians, although Indians seldom built a fire away from their village during daylight hours. They had long ago realized the smoke could give their location to their enemies as easily as it had been telling them the location of unsuspecting white men who had been encroaching on Indian land for years. Most rustlers on the other hand, would wait until they had driven their stolen stock away from where they were stolen before burning brands, although he had known a few who did not follow this rule. He could hear the lowing of cattle as he approached the brim of the wash and saw where a single rider had entered. Peering over the edge, he spied Matthew seated on a deadfall brewing a pot of coffee as a small herd milled not too far away.

"Hey, down there in the camp," he yelled. The boy waved and Phillip led his horse into the draw.

"Coffee's done," Matthew said as Phillip approached.

"Yeah, sure smells good." He pulled a battered tin cup from his saddlebag. Phillip leaned his rifle against the deadfall and squatted on his heels as he poured a cupful. He glanced around as he took a sip and sat on the log beside Matthew, quietly enjoying the coffee.

"Where's everyone?" he asked after a long minute.

"They went up the wash to see how far the cattle have drifted. They should be pushing them back this way by now."

"Sure is a pretty place you folks have. Plenty of grass and water. Yes sir, a good place to put down roots."

"My pa had it picked out before he and ma got married. He'd been out here with the Army during a Sioux uprising and staked a homestead claim. They moved here right after they were married."

"Huh, he's lucky he still had his scalp when they got hitched." Phillip took another sip and shook his head. "The Sioux are plenty to deal with. I had a run-in with them a time or two myself, and don't cherish the idea of doing it again. Yes sir," he said looking in a half circle, "sure pretty land."

"I always thought it was kind of lonely, being stuck out here by ourselves," Matthew said with a snicker.

"Well, you can cure that easily enough."

"How's that, Mr. Denning?"

"I don't pretend to be telling you what to do, but if it was me, I'd build me a nice cabin not too far from your ma's, then marry that storekeeper's daughter and move her in there. You'd have plenty of company then, and still be able to work your land. A fellow would also be close enough to take care of his ma in her old age. A man should take care of his folks when they're old." He nodded and gave Matt a sideways grin. "You can do what you want, but that's what I'd be doing."

They sat quietly for a minute, sipping coffee.

"I've thought about it. I just don't know if she feels that way about me. Think I should ask her?"

"I'd do it right soon. Maybe next time you're in town. Then me and your brothers could pitch in and build the cabin while you're engaged. Have yourself a fall wedding and spend the winter months cuddled in a warm bed next to your pretty wife. Yes sir, makes good sense. That's exactly what I'd do."

The sound of horses and cattle caused Phillip to grab his rifle. He relaxed as Tim and Steve pushed a small herd of ten or twelve steers toward their camp.

"Where's Josh?" Matthew asked as the boys dismounted.

"He's coming," Tim said as he grabbed a cup from his saddlebag and headed toward the coffee pot. "He rode up to the top to have a look-see if any cows wandered up there."

"How're the cattle downstream doing?" Phillip asked as they boys filled their cups.

"About the same as yesterday," Steven said. "The ones I saw were in the same spot."

"Mmm, that's good. They'll be moving around soon enough," Phillip said, and grabbed the rifle once again as Joshua rode into the draw.

"You sure are jumpy," Matthew said. "Are you expecting trouble?"

"Well son, I don't rightly know. I just got a feeling things aren't like they should be. Besides, you might not know this, but your campfire told me where you were a quarter of a mile away…maybe even farther. Now, if I saw it, I'm sure Indians or rustlers have also seen it." The boys glanced at each other as Joshua dismounted.

"We didn't know. We need a fire for branding. Besides, we always make coffee around noon," Matthew said.

"You see anything, son?" Phillip asked, as Joshua reached for the coffee pot.

"Yeah, I saw some men about a half a mile from here."

"See who they were?"

"Not really. I figured they might be from the Box D.

"Or, they might be the same ones stealing your cattle."

Steve and Timothy both began talking at once, and Phillip asked them to hush. Matthew quietly retrieved his Henry, checking the loads as Phillip continued.

"Did they see you?"

"I don't know. Why?"

"They did," Matthew said as he pointed toward the top of the draw. Three men sat on horseback staring at them. One of them had a rifle pointing their direction. A branch pointing upward from the deadfall exploded as Steve gave a cry of pain, covering the right side of his face as he fell to the ground.

Phillip whipped his Winchester up and fired. The man with the rifle slumped awkwardly in the saddle and dropped his gun as they retreated. Mathew fired several times before they were out of sight. A second man grabbed his right arm.

"How's the boy?" Phillip asked, kneeling beside Timothy and Joshua as they tended to their brother.

"He's alright, I think. He's got some scratches and splinters, but the bullet didn't get him," Timothy said.

Phillip wet his neckerchief with his canteen and held it to the boy's right cheek. "Yeah, you're one lucky son-of-a-gun. He barked you pretty good. One inch closer, and you'd be joining your pa and sister under that willow." The boy had tears in his eyes but hadn't been crying that Phillip could see…at least not out loud. He was a gutsy lad, Phillip had to grant him that.

"How's your eyesight? Close your left eye and tell me how many fingers I'm holding up."

"Four."

"Yeah, you're okay," Phillip said, patting him on the shoulder. "Now, when you see your friends in town you can brag about being involved in a shootout with rustlers."

"I think you got one of them, Mr. Denning," Joshua said excitedly. "He dropped his rifle and hunched over."

"Yeah, I winged him alright, but didn't kill him. That means he'll probably be coming back, unless he bleeds to death first. Matt also got a piece of one as they were riding away."

"I did?"

"Yes sir. The one on the far left grabbed his arm while you were firing off your Henry. You handled yourself real well. But I'd recommend we give up this idea of having separate camps. It might take a little longer, but having all the hands armed and bunched together's safer than being out here by ourselves. They blowed a hole in Dusty, and almost killed Steve. These fellers ain't likely going away until we kill 'em. You might give up brewing anymore noonday coffee. You can drink your coffee at the main camp with everyone else. And keep your rifles loaded and handy. That means having them right at your side even when you're taking a leak. That also means identifying yourselves before you ride into camp. Someone could mistake you for a rustler some night and put a hole in you." He shoved the Winchester back into its scabbard and tightened the cinches on his saddle as the continued.

"Now, we'd best follow those yahoos to make sure they've left off rustling your cows today, then decide which one of us is going to see that your brother gets home safe and face the music."

"Face the music?" Timothy asked. "Why, do you think Ma's gonna get mad 'cause we ran some rustlers off?"

"No, I think she'll get angry when she sees your brother's face. Oh," he added as an afterthought, "one of you fetch that fellow's rifle on the way out."

CHAPTER 34

Nathan Thomas was seated at the bar inside The Snake Den enjoying a bowl of elk stew and cornbread when Pox flung the door open with a loud crash.

"Dammit, Pox, some day you're gonna knock that door completely off its hinges," Earl Tucker growled and slammed a clean beer mug against the plank counter. "What the hell's the matter with you anyway?"

"It's Moses. He's hurt bad," Pox roared.

Nate didn't know whether to consider the missing front teeth as an improvement for the rustler or not. He would be ugly either way you looked at him. He dropped his spoon back into the bowl with a clink as Randy Houk struggled through the door under the weight of a much larger Moses Martin. He helped him into an empty chair and heaved a sigh. The front of Moses' shirt and vest was soaked with blood that oozed between the fingers of Moses' right hand as it clutched a bloody neckerchief against his chest.

Rose slid her ample posterior off a stool at the far end of the bar and rushed toward the wounded man to stare, then glanced at Earl in horror. "He's hurt Earl! Do something!"

Earl removed the neckerchief and opened Moses' shirt to reveal a bullet wound about midway on the right side of the man's chest. A deep rattling came with every labored breath. Earl shoved the neckerchief back over the wound and returned to his mug at the bar.

Nate took another bite of his stew and glanced toward Pearl, the other whore. He had no idea how or why Rose had come to End Of The Line, but he'd heard rumors that Pearl had been married once to a gambler in Sioux Falls. They claimed the man used to come home drunk and beat on her almost nightly, until she stabbed him to death with a butcher knife. At the moment, she was sitting on a stool smoking a cigarillo, and watching the scene as though it were some curious form of entertainment.

"You son-of-a-bitch," Rose yelled. "Aren't you gonna do something? Are you just gonna stand there and let him die?"

"There's nothing I can do, Rose," Earl said in a low voice. "The man's already dead. He just hasn't stopped breathing yet."

Rose jumped backward and gasped as Moses coughed, spraying droplets of blood across the card table.

"Oh, Jesus!" Earl grabbed a towel from a box beneath the bar and rushed to wipe at the soiled felt, making the stain worse. "Lay him on the floor. My tables look bad enough as it is."

Randy labored with Rose, who only offered token help, to get the big man prostrate on the floor.

"Shit, Pox, he's your friend. Couldn't you even offer a little help, you lazy bastard," Pearl said with a snort, and blew a cloud of smoke into the air. Nate thought Pearl might be ten years older than Rose, somewhere in her mid to late thirties, and harder, but better looking and packing more common sense than the younger woman. While he hadn't slept with either of them, he had talked with Pearl from time to time, and enjoyed her company.

Moses coughed again, then issued a rattling noise and fell silent. Rose backed away looking horrified, then grabbed a glass of whiskey from the bar with trembling fingers and downed it in one gulp.

"Well, Pox, seems like working for you can be hazardous to a man's health," Nate said with a smirk, then took another bite of stew.

"What's that supposed to mean?" the rustler growled.

"Nothing, except Sloan wound up dead a few weeks ago and now Moses. I also see Randy's got a bloody neckerchief wrapped around his arm. You're a dangerous man to work for." Nate toasted him with a spoonful of stew before popping it into his mouth. "You had yourself another run-in with Denning, didn't you?"

"Yeah, and I'm gonna kill that son-of-a-bitch next time I see him. I'll kill that bitch he's working for and her entire family, too."

"Nope," Nate said over another bite, "I'll tell you what's going to happen. You're going to get several more men killed, if there's still anyone stupid enough to work for you…then you'll get yourself killed."

"He's right, Pox," Earl said angrily. "I told you to leave that widow's cattle alone. You got exactly what you deserved."

"Well, now," Pox came to the bar next to Nate and leaned close to his face. He smelled of a nauseating combination of stale sweat, tobacco and whiskey. "You claim to know this Phillip Denning, and I hear he came here looking to kill you. Why don't you just ride out there and kill him yourself and save us all a little trouble; that is, unless you're not as good as you say you are?"

"First of all," Nate paused to pour himself a drink, "I never said how good I was. You just assumed I thought that because I refused to join your little band of thieves. To answer your question, I will meet Denning. But I'll do it on my own terms, and not to rid you of having to deal with him. In fact," he paused to down his whiskey, "I just might postpone my meeting with him until after he's killed you." Nate pointed his finger. "I'm like Earl, in that I hate a highbinder who's low enough to steal from a widow."

"Agh, I'll go out there and kill 'em myself, the whole lot of 'em. Then we'll see how tough your friend Denning is." Pox pounded the bar with his fist and gave Nate a taunting glare. "Come on, Randy, let's go where our company is appreciated." He started toward the door but stopped when the boy refused to move. He was still staring at the dead man on the floor.

"Randy! He's dead and there's nothing you can do for him. You coming?"

"No, Pox, I don't think I'm going to ride with you anymore. They're right. It's not good stealing from a widow, and there's no sense in getting myself killed over a few head of cattle. Besides, I ain't no killer and seeing as how you didn't even flinch killing that little girl..." he shook his head slowly, "na, you go ahead. I'll stay here and figure out something else."

"Then to hell with you! To hell with all of you," he yelled as he slammed the door.

"Well, that calls for a celebration," Nate said with a chuckle. "Set it up, Earl, a bowl of stew and a mug of beer for everyone, especially our friend Randy."

"Sure, but let's drag Moses out back. He's bleeding all over the floor." Earl reached for his mop and paused. "You say he killed a little girl? When?"

"The other night out on the trail. Pox and Moses killed a whole family just to steal what little they had. They didn't have much, and the girl was a pretty little thing, ten, maybe eleven years old. The woman had been cooking their supper when they killed them. Pox and Moses sat there and ate their food while those folks' bodies lay on the cold ground. I don't want no part of them ever again."

Pearl slid off her stool and slithered toward Randy, who had grabbed hold of Moses' arms. Nate had reached for the dead man's legs, but paused as the woman slid her arms around the boy's neck and kissed his cheek.

"Good for you. After you help Nate cart Moses out of here, we'll celebrate your freedom from Pox here in the bar. Then I'll take you to my room for our own special celebration."

She gave a throaty laugh as he blushed.

CHAPTER 35

Katherine woke late in the morning feeling almost normal. While the bout of fever and nausea had left her pale and weak, the gnawing hunger in the pit of her stomach told her she was on the mend. She pulled the curtains back and studied the sun-washed yard. Ginger was busy munching hay from the trough beside Sunrise and his mother inside the corral, while chickens pecked and scratched for bugs in the dirt between their legs. The dog that had attached itself to Phil regardless of his complaining, came out into the sunlight and stretched with a long yawn, shook itself and trotted toward the kitchen to beg a meal. The willow shading James and Abby's graves on the farther side of the barn swayed gently in the breeze. The windstorm had passed and it was going to be a beautiful day.

She allowed her attention to drift back toward the corral and her horse. The boys' horses were gone. She smiled at her own surprise, knowing their habit of storming the kitchen before sunrise and gobbling their breakfast in order to get an early start. She quickly dressed into her riding skirt and boots and made her bed hastily before heading to the kitchen.

"And where do you think you're going dressed like that, young lady?" Charlene asked sternly as she eyed Katherine from head to toe. Charlie had the sleeves of her blue house dress rolled above her elbows and was busy kneading bread dough. She had a smear of flour on the tip of her nose.

"I thought I would grab a cup of coffee and something to munch on before going for a ride. I might even be able to catch up with the boys, if I'm lucky."

"No you're not. Take off your boots and change your clothes."

"What?" Katherine said with a half-laugh.

"You're just getting over a bad case of something, and you're still pale as a ghost. So, get the idea of going horseback-riding out of your silly head."

"Charlie, might I remind you that you're not my mother. I brought you out here to run the household, not to run my life."

"That's right," she said and gave the bread dough one last punch before covering it with a towel. "The agreement was I could run the house the way I saw fit…I was going to be the boss, so I'm saying you're not going riding today."

"Charlie…" Katherine started, but the woman shook a finger at her from across the table and glared.

"I'm not arguing with you, Missy. I've spent two days mopping your vomit off the floor, changing your bed linens, and cleaning up after you. I've even washed and bathed you when you didn't make it out of bed. And I'll be hanged if I'm going to go through that again, just because you're too stubborn to listen to common sense."

Katherine raised her eyebrows and nodded thoughtfully as Charlene washed her hands in a pan of water. The woman glanced at her sideways and grinned.

"You might own this place, but I'm still older and big enough to turn you over my knee and tan your hide. I'll get you some breakfast ready while you change. How hungry are you?"

"I'm starving."

"Good. Change into something comfortable, I've got work for you inside the house."

Katherine turned toward the bedroom and glanced back over her shoulder. "You realize it's a good thing I love you, don't you?"

"I love you too. Now git!"

She changed into a peach-colored house dress with a small white flower print, and slippers. She added a white bow to her hair as an afterthought. Her stomach growled loudly as the smell of bacon and fresh coffee drifted toward the bedroom. Checking herself one last time in the mirror, Katherine skipped into the kitchen with a smile.

"Okay, Mommy, how do I look?"

Charlene laughed as she scooped two eggs onto a plate of bacon and biscuits. "You look absolutely beautiful, as usual," she said, sliding the plate toward her. "How about a glass of milk with that?"

"Fine, as long as I can have some coffee too," she said over a mouthful of egg.

Charlene poured two mugs of coffee and sat across from Katherine as she ate. They discussed their plans for the day, and what they each thought the house or ranch needed, and what they might buy on their next visit to town. Katherine had just finished her milk and was starting to sip her coffee, when the clomping of horses in the yard caught their attention. Phil's adopted dog had begun barking his greeting as Charlene looked out the window.

"Looks like Steve and Phil's back early. What in the world?"

"Why, what's wrong?" Katherine said, jumping from the table.

"Looks like Steve might've fallen off his horse."

Katherine jerked the door open and rushed outside. Phillip dismounted as Steven slid out of the saddle and turned toward his mother. He had a large black and blue welt on his right cheek with several scratches, one of which still seeped a small amount of blood.

"What in the world happened, honey? Are you okay?" Katherine asked as she inspected the wounds.

"We had a run-in with some rustlers." The boy sounded almost gleeful.

"Rustlers?" Katherine felt her blood turn cold.

"Yeah, and one of 'em took a shot at me, but hit the dead tree I was standing by. The bark flew off and caused this. It hurt at first, but not anymore."

"Oh, my Lord!" Katherine said as she folded Steve in her arms and kissed him.

"Ma," he protested and pushed her away.

"Then what happened? Was that it? Did you boys fight back or run for cover?" Charlene asked.

"No, Phil nailed the one who shot at me, and Matt winged another. They were the ones running for cover. I'm sure the one Phil shot is dead by now. He dropped his rifle and I picked it up." Steven held an almost new Winchester proudly for Charlene to inspect.

"I see it's got blood on the stock. I hope it's from the rustler."

"Well, let's get you inside and tend to your wounds." Katherine took her youngest by the arm and looked back over her shoulder. "May I see you in the office after you care for the horses, Mr. Denning?"

"Yes, ma'am. I figured you might want to talk some."

~ ~ ~

She waited to make sure Steven's wounds were only superficial before seating herself behind the massive desk. She was studying the ledger when Phillip knocked on the open door.

"Come in, Mr. Denning. I'd like to hear your version of what happened out there today."

"It's pretty much what they boy said. Matt built a small fire inside the draw where we found the cattle yesterday. He was heating the irons and making coffee when I come up on him."

"You 'came up on him?' Where were you, and why weren't all of you with the others from the Box D and Rocking J?"

"Oh, guess I forgot to tell you that part. The other ranchers figured they could make up for lost time by splitting up. Well, Matt thought we'd find more of your cows nearer the ranch and chose that wash. I'd been up top scouting around while the boys checked out the wash. The only thing is I could see the smoke from Matt's branding fire, and I guess the rustlers could too. Plus, Josh spied them trying to make off with some more of your steers. They followed him right to where everyone was. They came at us shooting, and the rest is pretty much what Steve said."

"Were they the same men we've had trouble with before?"

"Yes, ma'am, I reckon so." He nodded.

"Did you kill the one who tried to shoot my son?"

"I don't rightly know. I hit him pretty hard, so if he ain't dead, he's gonna be laid up for awhile."

"Good." She leaned back in her chair, drumming her fingers against the oak desk thoughtfully.

"Tell me, Mr. Denning, you seem to have some experience in things like this. I've had run-ins with rustlers before, and even a few Indians, but all they seemed interested in was making off with a few horses or cattle. What makes a man like this? He keeps coming back and trying to kill us."

"It could be any number of things, ma'am. A lot of men like him came back after the war to find their homes destroyed and loved ones gone. Right or wrong, the north sucked all the money out of the south. They couldn't find work, and didn't have anything but the ability to kill. They're not afraid of dying, 'cause they figured they were dead every time they went into battle. They wind up doing what they know best, and killing don't mean a thing to them."

"What would you do if you were me?"

"Well, for starters, I'd make sure all the ranchers stayed together during roundup. That'd give you more guns and those highbinders might be reluctant to cause trouble. When roundup's finished, I'd get me a posse made up with as many ranch hands as I could find and put an end to this nonsense. That's the only way to stop it, ma'am."

"Yes, I'm afraid you're right, Mr. Denning." She sat upright in her chair and studied him thoughtfully.

"They came close to killing Dusty, and almost killed my son. We still have another week of roundup. What would you suggest in the meantime?"

"You might consider letting me ride line for a few days. Kind of scout around and see if I can't stir the pot some. One man might be able to sneak up on them easier than a whole posse. It'll make you short-handed, but I might be able to get my sights on them. If I get a chance, I just might put the fear of the Lord into them."

"Okay, Mr. Denning, consider it done. Have Charlie fix you enough supplies to last several days. And if you happen to see them, make sure you send as many of them to their maker as you can without getting yourself killed."

"Yes, ma'am. I sure will." He gave her a firm nod.

CHAPTER 36

Pox Tivo sat sullenly on a rock, staring at the cattle grazing lazily below. They were his now. They might have belonged to the Rocking J or Flying K at one time, or perhaps one of the several other ranches bordering the badlands. But he had stolen them fair and square and driven them to this valley. They belonged to him. He figured he might need a hundred more before he'd have enough to build himself a large enough herd to survive the winter. The valley had plenty of grass and water, and was surrounded by high rocky walls, shielding it from the harsh wind that had devastated so many of the ranchers this last winter.

He had discovered the valley himself while running from Sheriff Crutchfield after holding up the stage outside of Denby. The sheriff acted as though the money had belonged to him personally, and hounded him all the way into the badlands. He didn't quit until Pox had woven a crooked trail across the rocky ground that a Sioux would have trouble following. That was when he discovered the valley.

He was not the first person to have visited the hidden paradise. He found a small cabin nestled back against the eastern wall, hidden from view by a cluster of cottonwoods and shielded from the wind. He also found the bleached remains of what Pox figured had been the trapper who had built the cabin, lying in the open with a Sioux arrow still poking through the ribs.

He immediately claimed the valley as his own, and that's when he devised the plan of how he'd become a rich and powerful cattleman. No one would expect someone to rustle a few head early in the season, especially after a harsh winter. The cattle would not be worth selling, and would probably not survive the trip to market. But that was when Pox decided he would strike, driving off small numbers that could be easily handled by just a few men. They would herd them into his valley to fatten for fall roundup. He also decided he would sell an even smaller amount at market, and keep the majority for breeding. Within a few years, he should have quite a herd and there would no longer be a need for rustling.

Things were going well for him too, until Denning had come along. The man had killed two of Pox's men and wounded a third. Replacing his men would not be a problem. He already had a couple in mind, but Denning had threatened to hang him, and Pox figured the man needed to be taught a lesson for causing so much trouble. He decided hanging him might be good justice. He also had a score to settle with Nate Thomas, and he would do that right after he had settled with Denning.

CHAPTER 37

Charlene had packed enough food to last a grown man a week, but Phil loved the taste of wild game and shot two cottontails late in the afternoon. When he spotted a pheasant, he killed it too. Picking a spot under a clump of cottonwoods near a creek, he made camp and spitted his dinner over a campfire. The cattle he had checked on that afternoon were doing fine, grazing and getting fat on the thick grass. He had not seen any sign of rustlers, although he had expected none. It was too soon for them to make another try after the skirmish that morning. Phil had to agree with Joshua's assessment, that the man he had shot was most certainly dead by now or dying. He had not shot to frighten or wound the man. He had fired with deadly accuracy intending to kill him. The rustler had been trying to kill Mrs. Parker's youngest son and had gotten exactly what he deserved. The part Phil had not expected was her cool assessment of the matter, and her acquiescence. He really didn't know what to expect from Mrs. Parker, but the woman was as cool under pressure as Charlie Goodnight. He'd met the rancher years ago while in Texas, and had been impressed with the man's grit. But he'd wager that Katherine Parker could hold her own with him any day of the week.

As a matter of habit, he made his bed under the trees a short distance from the fire. There was little danger of being attacked during the night, since Lucky was better than a watchdog. But he felt the small safety zone between his bedroll and a campfire gave him an advantage, since an enemy would have to search for him in the dark.

He put on a pot of coffee and turned the meat, which was now sizzling above the fire. The rabbit was almost done, and the plump pheasant gave a nice aroma. He dug inside the pack and found several biscuits wrapped in soft cotton. He wished he had some of Charlie's fresh churned butter to go with it. Lucky shuffled his hooves and whinnied slightly before Phil heard the bray of a mule.

"Yeah, I hear him. He ain't too quiet, is he?" Phil drew his pistol and laid it across his lap as he turned the meat.

"Hello in the camp," came the call. "Is it safe to come in?"

"Depends on who you are, pilgrim. If you come peaceably, sure. But if you come looking for trouble, you'll find that too."

"I'm not looking for trouble, young feller. I just smelled your rabbit and bird a ways off, and that was plenty. When I smelled your coffee, well I knew I just had to swap howdies. I ain't had no coffee in months."

"Well, come and get it. I'm not taking it to you."

"Much obliged." A grizzled old man came into the light leading a grey mule. He made conversation as he removed the mule's pack and dropped it to the ground.

"Name's Hiram Jenkins, but most folk just call me Hank. Ain't seen you around here before. You punching cattle for widow Parker over yonder? These are her cows aren't they?"

"Yeah, they belong to Mrs. Parker. You know her?"

"Not much. I've stopped by her place and seen her a time or two. I don't cotton to most folks, and stay mostly to myself. Safer that way, and I don't have to put up with a lot of nonsense. Know what I mean?"

"Yes sir, I know exactly what you mean. That's why I'm out here tonight, instead of sitting at her table. Help yourself." Phil took one of the cottontails and handed the second to Hank. "Coffee's done, and the pheasant should be by the time we pick the rabbits clean."

"Much obliged. You didn't say what your name is. Mind my asking what your handle is, son?"

"Phil, but most folks around here call me by my last name, Denning."

"Denning," Hank repeated with a nod. "Denning the lawman?"

"The same." Phillip poured himself a mug full and refilled Hank's cup. "How'd you know about me? You said you don't cotton to people much."

"Word gets around. I hear things when I take my furs into town. You ever catch the men you're looking for?"

"All but one. He's around here somewhere. You haven't seen him, have you? Big fellow with sandy-blond hair and moustache, and a fancy dresser last time I saw. His name is Nathan Thomas, but he goes by Nate."

"No, don't reckon I have seen anyone like that. I'll leave word with the widow and her boys if I do. As I said, I don't hang around white folks that much. I reckon I probably see more Injuns in a year when I go by their villages to do some swapping."

Phillip took his hunting knife and sliced a drumstick off the pheasant, passing it to Hank. They ate the bird in silence for several minutes before the trapper picked up his train of thought as if there had been no break.

"Speaking of which, I just left a small Pawnee village about four, maybe five miles west of here."

"Hum, kind of far north for Pawnee to come, isn't it?"

"Not when pickings are slim. They come into the Dakotas once in awhile. Hunters have killed off most of the buffalo, and last winter wasn't too kind to them. They'll move south once the weather starts to turn, looking for most anything they can. Don't know what them folks are gonna do once all the buffalo are gone. Starve to death, is my guess."

"Either that or change their ways. They might try farming," Phil said, slicing hunks of breast meat. "Careful, it's hot." He held a hunk on his knife tip for Hank.

"That's exactly what they used to do, back before we came along and chased them off their land. They lived mostly around Nebraska where they farmed the land and hunted buffalo. Now, they live most anywhere they can and still hunt buffalo. They're a proud people, Denning," the trapper said, shaking his head. "Huntin's all they've got left, and they're not gonna be asking for no handouts. They don't really have any land, not like white men's got. They used to figure the land belonged to everyone, that is until we started taking it away.

"Anyway, if I was looking for someone hiding up in these parts, I'd take me something they might be interested in, like a deer or elk I'd shot, and go do some swapping with them folks. An Indian will see most anyone wandering through. They might know where your man is holed up."

"Not a bad idea. I'll think on it some. There's a band of rustlers that's been botherin' Mrs. Parker and folks around here. Think they'd know where they're holed up?"

"They'd know quicker'n most. Like I said, I'd take something to swap, and talk turkey with their chief. He's a big feller called Many Coup. He don't cotton to most white folk, but he can be right pleasant once you get on his good side. They're good people to know, if you treat 'em right. I drop in on them once or twice a year and do some swapping for furs, baskets and anything I can sell. I usually meet up with them farther south, but they're hungry and looking for game."

"Huh," Phil said thoughtfully. "I'll tell Mrs. Parker. Maybe she'd like to go have a confab with the chief. Those rustlers have tried killing her and those boys a time or two. I'd like to put a stop to it before it gets out of hand. Besides, I'm heading south come autumn. It gets too damned cold here as far as I'm concerned."

"Can't say as I blame you none. I'll be wandering south myself in a couple more months. Well, I've had me a long day," Hiram said. He stretched with a yawn and scratched his unruly beard. "Thanks for sharing your vittles and fire with me. I think I'm gonna turn in and head out early." He spread his blankets near the fire and lay down with another yawn.

"That village lays four or five miles directly west of here, right on Stony Creek. They're friendly folk, but shy of strangers. I can go in there, 'cause they know me. I'd take some sort of a gift, if I was you. They're mighty hungry, so keep that in mind. Let 'em know you're friendly and visit some, before you start asking questions. Goodnight, young feller."

Hiram drifted into a peaceful sleep, wondering if he should mention the white squaw living in the village. He'd seen her on several visits, but had never gotten close or tried talking to her until today. She was a pretty little thing, and downright pleasant. He'd seen white squaws before, but what struck him about this woman, was how she was similar to what he remembered the widow Parker looking like. But his memory wasn't quite what it used to be, and it wasn't any of his concern anyway. He rolled over and began snoring.

~　　~　　~

Phil had no idea when he actually fell asleep. He woke before daylight feeling chilled. He built a fire and put on some coffee, then had a breakfast of jerky and cold biscuits ready by the time Hiram Jenkins had his mule packed. After breakfast, Phil saddled Lucky and trotted off to check on the cattle and look for rustlers. He would eventually have to return to the ranch for supplies and tell Mrs. Parker about the Indian village, but not today. He was still smoldering about a two-bit highbinder who was willing to steal a widow's cattle and take a shot at her twelve year-old son in the process. The old man's idea of visiting the Pawnee village had been a sound one. Maybe he'd pass it on to Mrs. Parker and see what she thought of the idea. He stopped under a cottonwood near the creek and rolled a cigarette. They might even be able to tell him where Nate Thomas was holed up, and he could take care of that little problem too, before heading toward Arizona. He lit the cigarette and nudged Lucky forward. The idea of visiting the Pawnee felt more appealing the more he considered it.

CHAPTER 38

Katherine fidgeted around the house, getting into Charlene's way until the maid stood with hands on her hips giving her a crooked grin.

"Well, I reckon you're well enough to go pestering the other ranchers if you want. You're worried about what's happened to Phil, aren't you?"

"Some. I'm just wondering if he's been able to locate the rustlers."

"Well, you'd best go find out."

It was now mid-afternoon, and both she and her horse were tired. She eventually found Joshua who said Phillip had ridden into their noonday camp, looking scruffy and unshaven. He had told the boys to keep a sharp eye for trouble, because he could feel it coming. All this had happened near the wash where the dead tree had fallen.

She was still feeling the effects from her bout of nausea, and wondered how long such a thing might plague a person. While she didn't feel ill physically, she tired easily, and had decided to abandon her search when she caught a faint word or two that sounded like Phillip's voice.

Trotting her horse to the crest of a small hill, she stopped to stare. The man was wading knee deep in a muddy bog at the edge of a wide creek, struggling to rescue a calf caught in the mud. He had a rope looped around the calf with the other end attached to the saddle horn. At first glance, it seemed as if Lucky was being entertained by watching his master's struggle, instead of helping rescue the poor animal.

"I said back up, you knot-head! I can't get it done by myself."

Phillip's yelling grew robust, and carried a few obscenities. Lucky just stared as the calf bawled. From her angle, Katherine caught sight of the horse's problem. A very angry mama cow was standing toward Phillip's right and shielded from his view by a clump of brush. She was watching intently and lowered her head as Phillip struggled with her crying baby. He wrapped his arms around the muddy calf and heaved as he yelled.

"Quit standing there and pull!"

The angry cow bellowed and charged. The frightened horse bolted backward, causing Phillip to fly forward. He lost his grip on the calf and landed face-first into the bog. Katherine giggled as Phillip struggled to his feet, wiping mud from his eyes. He was cursing fiercely as the calf bawled and its mother bellowed her rage. He gave no indication he had heard Katherine's giggle, so she stayed where she was and watched the show.

He staggered toward the calf as its mother lowered her head and charged. He jumped backward, landing on his back in the bog.

"Let me get my rope off, you dumb jackass, and you can have her."

He swiped at the mud on his arms before making another attempt. The cow charged again, causing him to retreat to the bog where he fell and almost sank out of sight. He was now using words unknown to Katherine, but she was certain they would never be uttered from Parson Norris' pulpit in Denby. Lucky had drug the frightened calf several feet closer to the creek bank, and the mama cow took up residence between the horse and her baby.

Katherine walked Ginger toward a gentle slope in the bank and crossed the creek near the angry cowboy.

"Would you care for some help, Mr. Denning?"

"What I'd care for is my Winchester, so I could shoot that damned cow."

"Well, I don't think that'd be a good idea. That cow happens to belong to me, and I'd rather not see her killed." She walked Ginger up the opposite bank and drove the cow back into the brush.

"There Mr. Denning, I believe that might help." She slid from the saddle and waded knee-deep into the chilly water.

"Let me give you a hand."

"Better take a look at who came back."

She turned her head toward the back as the mama cow trotted out of the brush and resumed her post. "Well, I'll be… Okay, it doesn't matter. Let's just get her baby on the bank and she'll go away."

Katherine positioned herself on the opposite side of the calf and gave Phillip a nod. He yelled at the horse and they both tried hoisting the slippery calf to safety as Lucky backed away from the creek. The cow gave a loud bellow and charged, causing the horse to jerk. Katherine fell face-first into the mud as the calf shot forward. She struggled to her feet, trying to regain her balance only to discover her boots were firmly stuck, she fell backward, sinking in the sticky goo.

"Ya! Get out of here!" Phillip yelled and hit the cow square in the face with a glob of mud. The cow darted away shaking her head before turning for another charge. By then Phillip had jerked his lasso free and dove back into the mud as the cow charged. The frightened calf darted toward its mother, ending the standoff. The mama cow bellowed loudly and they disappeared into the brush. Phillip cast a few more curses their way before turning to offer Katherine a helping hand.

"Thank you, Mr. Denning. I don't know how much help I was, but I tried." She spit a glob of mud from her mouth and retrieved her hat. "I'm afraid I've lost my right boot," she said as she tried to move.

"Here, allow me." He stuck his arm into the bog and handed her a mud-filled boot. Katherine stared at the boot a minute and burst out laughing.

"I must look a sight."

"Yes ma'am, you do. I reckon you look about as bad as I do."

Phillip's eyes and teeth stood out against the mud-plastered face. She suddenly found herself laughing so hard, she stepped backward and lost her balance. She sank chest-deep in the mud, which caused her to laugh even harder. That started Phillip to laughing and he sat in the mud opposite her. Katherine scooped a handful of mud and tossed it at him, and he returned the favor. They exchanged several globs of mud before she finally recovered from her fit of giggles.

"Oh Lord, I don't know when I've laughed so much. Thank you, Mr. Denning. I honestly enjoyed that."

"You did?"

She nodded.

"Well, I reckon I could've done without the mud, but I'll allow it was fun seeing you laugh. You ought to do it more often. You look right pretty when you do."

She stared at him. "You think so?"

"Yes ma'am, I know so. The only thing that might've made this better, was shooting that cow and seeing what Charlie could do with the carcass."

"As I said, she's a valuable asset, so that might not be a good idea. We'd better see if we can't get some of this mud off and head back to the house. We're going to be late as it is."

She turned the mud-filled boot upside-down and laughed as the contents splashed into the creek.

CHAPTER 39

The sun was beginning to set when they rode into the yard and dismounted. Charlene was standing in front of the corral gate with her hands on her hips and looking rather perturbed. She was being flanked by all four boys who, from the looks of them, were not in any better mood.

"Where in the world have you been, ma'am? We've been worried sick, thinking the rustlers might've gotten you," she said.

"That's sweet of you, but there's no reason to worry. We've been trying to rescue a stranded calf."

"Well, you shouldn't be taking off like that. Phil told the boys there's Indians camped not too far from here," she said in a loud voice.

"Indians? You didn't say anything to me about Indians."

"I'm sorry, ma'am. We were having so much fun with that calf, I simply forgot. But yes, there is a family of Pawnee camped four or five miles to the west of here."

"We haven't seen any Indians around here in years. Do you expect they will cause us any trouble?"

"No, not hardly," Phillip shook his head. "These folks aren't looking for trouble. They're a small band who's simply looking for something to eat. Buffalo hunters have killed off most of the game, and a bunch of white people ran them off their land. They're starving. I was thinking, since most Indians will see and know what's going on around them, these folks might know where the rustlers are holed up. If they do, I plan to get Sheriff Crutchfield and go take care of this little problem. That is, if it's alright with you."

"Yes, that is perfectly alright with me, Mr. Denning. I think that would be a good idea." Katherine turned toward Charlene and grinned.

"There, that's all taken care of. Is there anything else you would like to tell me?"

The housekeeper eyed her from head to foot and shook her head. "No, I guess that's about it. You two must've been having fun. Looks like you've been in a mud-fight."

Katherine broke into another fit of giggles. "Yes, that is exactly what we were doing."

Charlene returned to the kitchen shaking her head and mumbling she now had six children to take care of.

"Charlie's right, ma," Matthew said softly. "You should've let one of us know where you were going."

"Well, son, I did tell Charlie I was going to find Mr. Denning before I left the house. And seeing as I found him at the creek near the south end of the ranch, it would have been a little hard letting you know, wouldn't it? I might have sent up smoke signals, but you would have had trouble seeing them from here."

"Excuse me," Phillip said quietly. "It seems you two have things to discuss. I'll take care of the horses." He led the tired animals to the corral and began unsaddling them.

"He was here, you know," Matthew continued.

"Who was here?"

"Sheriff Crutchfield. He say's there's trouble brewing." He drew close and talked in a low, even voice. "That band of cutthroats killed and robbed an entire family out on the trail, including their little girl. There's nothing stopping them from killing you. Charlie said you were just riding out to see how things were going, and figured you should've been back hours ago. She's been half-sick worrying about you, and her eyes are all puffy and red from crying. We had fresh mounts saddled and were fixing to go look for you when you rode in. We've all been worried."

"I'm sorry. There was no need for you to worry. I'm a big girl, and can take care of myself."

"Maybe, but so was that family they killed. Please, Mother, don't ever go off by yourself like that again."

"I wasn't by myself. I was with Mr. Denning," she said as he disappeared inside the house.

Katherine stared at the door and clenched her fists as faint voices drifted from the kitchen window. She couldn't make out what they were saying, but made herself a mental note she would have a lengthy discussion with her eldest son as soon as possible. Timothy's arms suddenly slipping around her gave her a start.

"Its okay, Ma. Matt didn't mean anything. He's just upset 'cause you scared us running off like that. He'll calm down after awhile. But he was right about those rustlers. They did kill that family, and the sheriff was looking for Mr. Denning. He wants him to help track them down."

"I love you, son…all of you." She hugged him back.

Timothy released his hold and stared at his soiled hands. "I think you'd better get cleaned up. Charlie's got supper ready."

"Ma?" Steven asked as she started toward the house.

"Hmm?"

"Mr. Denning was saying he'd like me to go with him to see the Indians when we talked to him earlier. Is that okay?"

"To see the Indians? Hum, I don't know. Yes, I suppose so. Did he say why?"

"He said it might be a good idea to take a few steers as some sort of gift, like a peace offering," Timothy said with a snort. "Then Phil made some joke about taking Steve along so you couldn't have him hung for being a rustler. I don't think he really meant he wanted him to tag along."

"Did so," Steven yelled.

"Na-uh, turd-head."

"That's enough! Stop it right now! I'll swear to the Lord Almighty, I might have him take all four of you and leave the cattle. I'd have less trouble. And if Mr. Denning says he really wants Steven to go with him, yes it is okay, you may go."

"See there, stupid-head!"

"You're still a turd-head."

"Good Lord in heaven!" Katherine tossed her hands in the air. "I give up."

"Welcome home," Joshua said, draping his arm around her shoulder as he opened the door.

She hugged and kissed Charlene before offering an obligatory apology. She had expected the housekeeper to give her one of her scoldings, but she instead wiped her eyes in silence and sniffed before returning to the stove. Katherine felt crushed. She passed through the dining room on her way to bathe and change for dinner, then stopped when Phillip Denning entered the front door.

"Steven told me about the cattle."

"Ma'am?" He gave her a questioning look.

"Steven said you wanted to take some of my cattle to the Indians as an offering."

"Yes, ma'am. I just thought it might be a good gesture. The old trapper who told me about 'em, said they're near to starving."

"How many cows are we talking about?"

"I don't know, four, maybe five. Why?"

"Just curious, since it is my cattle you are thinking of giving away."

"Yes," he said with a nod. "You have every right to know, and I had planned to clear the exact number with you before I did anything. I was thinking they might have some information that might be useful, but even if they didn't, it would be a nice act of human kindness. They have women and children with them."

"Steven said you wanted him to go with you, is that correct?"

Phillip cocked his head to one side and grinned. "Yes, I reckon I did mention it. It might be a good learning experience for him. I'll take good care of him, ma'am. There's no need to worry."

"I'm sure you will. When will you be leaving?"

"The day after tomorrow, unless that's too soon."

"No, Monday will be fine, Mr. Denning." She started to leave, then turned. "And I will not have you hanged for rustling my cattle, Mr. Denning. I might throw a mud-ball at you, though."

~   ~   ~

Katherine crawled into bed sometime after eleven o'clock feeling exhausted. She had removed her soiled clothing and taken a lukewarm bath, marveling at the amber-colored water inside the tub when she had finished. She was seated at the table with the boys when Phillip entered. He had bathed and was clean-shaven with his hair slicked back, and sporting a fresh change of clothing. Not a word was mentioned about rustlers or Indians as they engaged in lighthearted conversation. Katherine recounted the story of their encounter with the angry cow and calf inside the muddy bog. Then the conversation quickly centered on Matthew's romance with Rebecca Jordan. When the meal was finished, everyone pitched in to help Charlene clean the kitchen. Steven produced a deck of cards and Charlie made a fresh pot of coffee. They crowded around the table and played Texas Hold'Em for matchsticks, until Charlene had won all the matches. Katherine's cheeks ached from laughing as she closed her eyes and drifted quickly into a peaceful sleep.

~   ~   ~

Katherine woke before sunrise feeling surprisingly rested and full of energy. She crawled out of bed, slipped into her housecoat and slippers, and lit a lamp. Pulling the curtains closed, she crossed the room to her washstand and stared into the mirror. The image looking back at her didn't match the way she felt. Her hair was a frightful sight, but at least the dark circles under her eyes left by the illness had almost disappeared. The years had left their mark with small crow's feet at the corner of her eyes and a healthy smattering of freckles across her nose and cheeks. Her once dainty hands were hard and calloused.

She dropped her housecoat and gown to the floor and continued to study her reflection in the mirror. Her once flat stomach had disappeared somewhere with five children, and while she could not be considered fat, she had certainly added pounds to her once slim physique. She used to tell herself it was *just muscle from working like a man*, but it no longer mattered. Her youthful body was gone, and Katherine Eleanor O'Hara Parker had reached middle age.

What in the world happened to you? Where did the years go? Well, one thing's for sure. You're not going to have to worry about those men knocking on your door looking for the rich, young widow any more. That woman's all grown up now.

"Why are you even thinking that way," she said to her reflection. "There is something seriously wrong with you." She had little time to entertain such foolish thoughts. She quickly dressed, filled the washbasin with water from the pitcher and scrubbed her face. She ran a brush through her hair before storming down the hall, pounding on bedroom doors.

"What's wrong, Ma?" Joshua asked, sticking his sleepy head out the door.

"Nothing's wrong. Get dressed. Today's Sunday, and we're going to church."

"Church," Steven said with a whine.

"Yes, church. We haven't been to church in quite awhile, and I've decided we need to start going."

"It's about time," Charlene said as she came into the hall tying her robe. "I'll fire up the stove and get breakfast while you corral the boys."

She peeked into Timothy's room to find him lying in bed with a pillow covering his head. "I know you heard me, so get up."

"I don't wanna go," came his muffled reply.

"I didn't give you that option," she said, jerking the pillow away and throwing the covers to the foot of the bed.

"Now get up. You boys still have to feed the animals before we leave."

She opened Matthew's door to find him dressed and whistling as he adjusted a string tie around his neck.

"I take it you're looking forward to seeing Rebecca Jordan at church?"

Matthew gave her a wide grin. "They attend every Sunday. Do you mind?"

"No, I think she's a very nice girl. How serious is this, Matthew?"

"I'm thinking of asking her to marry me."

"Oh," she said and walked to her room in a trance. She sat on the edge of the bed as the tears welled in her eyes and trickled down her cheeks.

"Hey, I didn't mean to make you cry." She looked up as Matthew entered her room. He sat on the edge of her bed and hugged her. "I thought you said you liked her."

"I do. It's hard seeing my boys grow up…that's all. I knew all four of you would someday get married and move away. I didn't think it would be this soon. Someday it'll be just me and Charlie here on this big old ranch all alone." She covered her mouth and choked back a sob.

"Well, if it makes you feel any better, Phil says I should build a cabin right here before I get married. That way, I can help run this place, and you can help raise your grandchildren. Now come on," he kissed her on the cheek, "I want to get there early enough to walk her to church."

"You discussed this with Phillip Denning before talking to me? I'm your mother."

"Yeah, but he's a guy. It's easy to talk to him, once you get to know him."

He vanished into the hall yelling for his brothers to hurry. *He discussed asking Becky Jordan to marry him before talking to me?* Katherine followed him to his room and poked her head inside.

"Matthew Henry Parker! I might be getting old, but I'm still your mother! You are supposed to discuss these things with me first. Is that understood?"

"Yes, ma'am."

"Good. Now that you're dressed, make sure your brothers are up and presentable and have their chores done while I finish dressing."

"Yes, ma'am."

"By the way." She paused as she turned away.

"Ma'am?"

"I love you."

"Yes, ma'am, and I love you too."

CHAPTER 40

The whiskey glass thrown by Rose shattered against the door with a loud bang as she released a string of curse words.

"Hey, that's enough of that! Those are hard to come by up here, and that's the third one you've broken in the past two days." Earl Tucker came from behind the bar to glare in her face. "I'm charging you two dollars for that one."

"Take it out of the pay from my next customer." She slurred her words and wobbled against the bar as she lit a cigarette.

"Na-uh, nothing doing." Earl held his palm out and wiggled his fingers. "Pay me now."

"I haven't got it on me. I'll pay you after my next customer."

"You haven't had many of them lately, Rose." Earl turned away as he cleared and wiped a table. "Maybe you should sober up some and take a bath."

"Go to hell. You haven't had anyone come in here wanting a woman. Most of them are all virgins, like Nate." She leaned across Nathan's table and breathed heavily in the man's face. He leaned away as several hard looking men laughed.

"You tell me, why doesn't Randy want to play with me? He's your friend, you ought to know."

"Geeze, Rose. I'm trying to eat my dinner. I don't know. Why don't you ask him? Go ask one of them," he motioned toward the table of laughing men, "maybe they know."

"I did ask Randy."

"Well, what'd he say?" Waco bellowed.

"All he said was he'd rather be with Pearl. Hell, she's not as pretty as me, and a whole lot older." Rose patted her tangled mass of hair and puffed angrily on the cigarette.

"She might be older, but she's got a lot less miles and trail dust, Rose," Waco said with a laugh.

"Really, well the next time you wanna sleep with a woman, go sleep with your horse."

"His horse would smell better'n you, that's for sure," one of the men said.

She screamed several obscenities and grabbed for another glass from the bar, but Earl latched onto her wrist.

"That's enough. That's exactly why no one wants you. You treat the customers like hell, you haven't been sober in a week. And he's right. You smell like a pile of horseshit."

"Aggh!" She tried clawing at his face and received a resounding slap across the cheek.

"Now, get to your room and don't come out until you're thinking straight," Earl said sternly. "I mean it, Rose. Git!"

The woman bellowed as she dashed into her room to the rear of the bar and slammed the door.

"Dirty whore," Earl mumbled as he refilled Nate's cup with coffee.

"You ain't lying on that one, Earl," Waco said. "Hell, open a window and let some fresh air in."

"She knows how to spoil a man's dinner," Nate said, pushing his plate aside. "She never was the cleanest person around, but she didn't used to be that bad. What the hell's gotten into her?"

"She's been sleeping with Pox Tivo and a couple of new guys he's teamed up with. One of 'em...what's his name…?" Earl looked upward as if the name would appear in the sky.

"It's Wah Lee, if you're thinking of the chink," Waco said, shuffling a deck of well-used cards. "He's been paying her for her services with opium. She likes the shit, and would rather smoke it than take a bath or eat." He dealt the cards with deft hands.

"Yeah, well I've about had it with her, and if she doesn't straighten up and fly right, I'm gonna toss her fat butt out of here," Earl said matter-of-factly. He paused as the sound of squeaky bedsprings came from behind Pearl's closed door.

"She's right about one thing, though. Randy spends plenty of time with Pearl. What's he see in her?"

"That's a stupid question, Earl. What's most men see in a whore?" Waco laughed loudly.

"She's clean and carries on an intelligent conversation for one thing," Nate said.

"Well, Rose has been after him since he first rode in here with Pox three months ago. Maybe she'd straighten out if Randy would bed her once in awhile."

"Would you?" Nate grinned and toasted the bartender with his coffee.

"Reckon not."

"I'm headed into Denby Wednesday morning. Want me to bring you back some more glasses for Rose to break?"

"Guess you'd better. You go in there about every week or so. You got yourself a woman you're seeing?"

"No, just expecting some mail, Earl. And when I get what I'm looking for, I'll be heading for a warmer climate," Nate said, and took a sip of coffee.

"Are you taking Randy with you? He thinks you walk on water since you talked him into quitting Pox."

"I don't know if I could pry him away from Pearl long enough to leave," he said with a snicker. "We'll see."

Nathan hadn't really intended on having any close friendships or partners while in End Of The Line, but Earl was right. Randy Houk had latched himself onto him like a shadow.

He felt sorry for the boy, and knew if he rid himself of the friendship, the boy would simply drift back to being an outlaw and eventually get himself killed. Nate had started thinking of him as an odd sort of pet.

The boy's relationship with Pearl had escalated the competition between the two women to comical proportions. Rose had somehow thought Randy belonged to her, although he seldom had talked to her, and had never crawled into her bed that Nate knew of. Pearl, on the other hand, had treated Randy as a good friend and lover. She gave the boy her services free of charge, when she wasn't occupied with another customer. She was also choosy who she accepted into her room, something Nate admired, and she never allowed Pox Tivo or any of his gang near her. Nate considered her friendship with Randy was more of a poke in Rose's eye than anything else, since the women had never gotten along.

Nathan finished his coffee and rose from the table with a yawn, stretching his lanky frame. In all, he considered Pearl Fisher to be a decent woman. Had she been dealt a different hand in life, Pearl probably would be happily married and raising a family. The only question in Nathan's mind was what to do with Randy Houk when he left. He couldn't very well take Randy and Pearl with him. He'd have to ponder the issue. Now, it was time to join Waco's card game and earn his keep.

CHAPTER 41

Phillip had the team hitched and was standing beside the buckboard by the time Katherine gave herself one last glance in the mirror. She figured she had done everything possible to make herself look presentable, and had carefully chosen a soft green dress with white lace trim around the neck, and a matching poke bonnet. She finished by placing a seldom worn pair of white lace gloves in her purse to wear once they reached the church.

"My, you look nice this morning," Charlene said as she joined her at the door.

"So do you." Katherine suspected the housekeeper only had one nice dress, which happened to be a well worn white cotton with a flour sack blue print and matching poke bonnet. She knew Charlene would never consider spending money on a store-bought dress for herself, so Katherine made a mental note to force a couple of good outfits on her during their next shopping trip.

"You ought to get that surrey out of the barn and fix it up one of these days, ma'am," Phillip said as he helped the women onto the buckboard.

"I thought about it once, but I really don't have much use for a surrey here on the ranch, Mr. Denning." Katherine slipped on her leather gloves and took the reins. "And we don't go into town very often, unless it's to buy supplies, and we need the buckboard for that."

"Mmm, you might have more use than you think right soon," he said, and motioned toward Matthew with his head. He was dressed in a black suit with a white shirt and tie. His black felt hat looked a little worse for the wear, but all in all he made a striking figure.

"Are you speaking of my son and the Jordan girl?"

"Yes, ma'am. I'm sure she knows how to ride a horse just fine, and will make a fine addition to this ranch. I reckon a lot of young brides start having babies, and it wouldn't be right to have her in the family way and riding a horse, or being uncomfortable in a wagon, would it?"

"No, it wouldn't. But that brings up another thing, Mr. Denning. Just where do you get off advising my son to get married without consulting with me first?" Katherine gave him an angry glare.

"I didn't advise him at all, ma'am. The boy came to me and asked what I'd do if I was him concerning that girl, so I told him."

"You told him you would marry Rebecca Jordan? Now, why do I find that hard to believe?" She slapped the reins and yelled, "Ya, get up there," and started the wagon rolling without waiting for a reply. It only took a minute before Phillip trotted Lucky close to the wagon and grinned at the women.

"Why does that seem hard to believe? Don't I look like a fellow who could get married?"

"Have you?" Katherine urged the team into a brisk trot and Phil kept pace.

"No. I was engaged once upon a time."

"And what happened? Why didn't you get married, Mr. Denning?" Charlene asked.

"She decided she would rather have my best friend instead of me a week before the wedding, and I didn't feel like sharing."

"You still should have consulted with me first, before advising my son."

"Maybe, but do you think I actually gave him bad directions, ma'am? There's worse things for a man to do than settling down and marrying a pretty young woman. She seems like a fine pick. He plans on them living right here and giving you and Charlie some grandsons to spoil the dickens out of. That's not so bad is it? He could become a no-account saddle-bum like me." He spurred Lucky ahead of the wagon and joined Matthew about twenty yards ahead of the team. The mongrel dog gave several barks and darted ahead, skirting the trail as it bounced through the grass and brush, disappearing completely from time to time.

"That's strange," Katherine said.

"What's strange?"

"His bringing the dog to town."

"He said he was going to start making him earn his keep, since he insists on sleeping on his bed," Charlene said.

"It doesn't sound like a bad plan to me."

"No, the dog should earn his keep, just like the horses do."

"No, I'm talking about the advice Phillip gave Matthew."

"Oh…no, actually it isn't. To tell the truth, I kind of like the idea of being a grandmother. I might even consider letting the boys have more responsibility running the ranch, while you and I spoil the babies and teach Becky how to cook and keep house."

"*You* teach her how to cook and clean house?" Charlene asked with a snort.

"Okay, I'll spoil the babies and *you* teach Rebecca. Does that sound better?"

"Some, but I still get to spoil the babies too."

"He should have talked to me first. After all, I am Matthew's mother."

"Maybe, but sometimes things just happen. Matthew asked, and Phil more than likely thought the timing was right. I think Phil's a fine addition to this ranch. I know he and Matthew had a difficulty at first, but the boys sure take to him. And he does a lot of things around here that need doing without being asked. I've never once heard him complain. I'm sure you'll discover he's done a few things you didn't know about long after he's gone. That is, unless you decide to keep him." She snickered as Katherine gave her a *go to blazes* glare.

They rode in silence several minutes before Katherine asked, "Like what?"

"What do you mean, *like what*?"

"You said I would be discovering he's done things I don't know about. What things? What could he possibly do that I wouldn't see or know about?"

"Becky Jordan for one thing," Charlene said with a grin. "Or, maybe it's the fact that you and I have a military escort into town this morning."

Katherine shifted in her seat to look at the trail behind, and spied Joshua, Timothy and Steven riding abreast military style about twenty yards behind the buckboard. All three boys had their Henry rifles drawn with the butts resting against the saddle. She turned back wide-eyed to stare ahead. She had been so engrossed with thoughts of Matthew's asking the storekeeper's daughter to marry him, she had not even noticed Matthew and Phillip were carrying their rifles the same way.

She turned toward Charlene who patted her on the leg and laughed. "Well, it looks as though Phillip Denning has had some army training, and he's passed a little of it onto the boys. Don't look so dumbfounded. Like I said, I think we'll discover something he's changed we don't know about. Most folks have their own way of doing things."

The wagon creaked and groaned the last few miles into Denby and rolled to a stop behind the livery. The church bell chimed as Katherine accepted Phillip's hand to help her out of the well-used contraption. She eyed its weathered side-boards as he helped Charlene to the ground, vowing she would either check into a nice two-seat buggy, or get her old one repaired soon. A buggy would certainly offer a softer ride for the housekeeper and her future daughter-in-law. Remembering the girl's reaction inside the doctor's office, she doubted that Rebecca Jordan would refuse Matthew's proposal of marriage. Phillip Denning was right about one thing. The girl would more than likely be pregnant within the first year or so after the wedding. Katherine Eleanor Parker realized she would simply not stand for her daughter-in-law to be in that condition and ride in the buckboard.

Katherine dusted herself off, and each woman checked the other's dress to make sure they were presentable after the ride. The boys had the team unhitched and turned into the corral by the time they had finished. Phillip ordered the dog to stay before offering his arm as they walked toward the church. She reluctantly took it and grabbed Charlene's arm with her free hand. Katherine quickly glanced over her shoulder, amazed that the dog had obeyed. She had not been able to get him to do anything since the day he had shown up at their kitchen door begging for food. She had doubted he even understood English. But there he was, sitting in the shade watching, as they made their way toward the church.

Matthew increased his stride as Rebecca Jordan appeared out of her house with her brother and parents. She sighed as the boy tipped his hat and took the girl's arm. She had carefully packaged things inside her comfortable world the past few years, and stored them away into neat little categories where they fit, making life on the *Flying K* easy to deal with. But things were changing quickly, and she suddenly felt old.

The bell stopped its bonging and the first chords of *Sweet By and By* were coughed by the wheezy organ as they entered the chapel. They sat about midway down the aisle in the left set of pews, directly behind the Jordans. Rebecca was making a pretense of sharing her hymnal with Matthew, except she seemed to be studying the boy's profile more than the page in the song book. Katherine opened her hymnal to page 169 and allowed her eyes to wander around the room, where they stopped on the pew directly across the aisle from where she was seated. There sat Silas Norton beside his father and mother. Instead of singing, the big bully was glaring toward the young couple seated in front of her, and what she saw in his eyes sent a chill coursing through her veins.

Dear Lord, please have mercy!

CHAPTER 42

Katherine would have been at a loss if someone had asked her what subject Pastor Norris had discussed that morning. Outside of *Sweet By and By*, she had trouble remembering what hymns had been sung. She did, however, know that Silas Norton had stared brazenly at Matthew and Rebecca throughout the sermon. With fear gripping her entire body, she prayed silently and more intently than she had prayed since Abby's disappearance or James' illness.

She felt ill by the time the closing prayer was said, and clutched Charlene's arm in a white-knuckled grip as they left the church. She had hardly cleared the last step when Rebecca's mother, Mary, came from behind and grasped her in a hug.

"It was so nice to see your entire family and Mr. Denning at church this morning, Katie. I do hope you will be able to join us for dinner. I have a couple of chickens…" The invitation was cut short by several shouts as Silas Norton charged toward Matthew, shoving people aside.

"I warned you, dumb-ass, to stay away from my girl!"

Matthew gave Becky a gentle push toward her father and moved quickly toward his right and away from the crowd of worshipers.

"Silas, I warned you about doing something like this," Harry yelled as he grabbed for his son's arm.

Several women screamed as the brute sent a smashing right hand that knocked his father to the ground. He then whirled and charged Matthew with what sounded to Katherine like a growl. She would have bolted after him, but Phillip grasped her in a hug and held her tightly against his body. "Believe me, you don't want to get between those two now."

She gasped as her son danced quickly to his right and hit the brute with a left hand, causing him to stagger.

The crowd made a half circle, with several men making an effort to stop the fight. Their efforts were short-lived as Silas knocked two middle-aged men senseless. Matthew gave Joshua his jacket and hat to hold and calmly circled Silas as the bully readied himself for another charge. It came with a bellow. Silas rushed forward, throwing wild punches that Matthew easily ducked under. He danced completely around and behind Silas, who looked almost bewildered as he whirled, searching for his weaker prey.

Matthew faked with a right hand, then he hit Silas with a left instead, knocking him backward. He moved quickly in, hitting him with three more jabs that brought a trickle of blood from Silas' nose.

Silas charged, throwing more wild punches, and only landing one or two that seemed to have little effect, while Matthew continued to bob and weave his way around the big man. Silas paused his swinging and received a quick left and right hand that knocked him to the ground. He staggered to his feet cursing fiercely and charged, making an effort to grab Matthew in a bear hug. Matthew danced backward and planted his boots firmly, as he landed a hard right that snapped the man's head backward. Katherine felt her stomach churn as blood gushed from Silas' broken nose. Her son was now hitting Silas at will, driving him backward. Phillip released his grip on her and grabbed Matthew as he continued the pounding.

"Whoa, son…he's had enough. Come on, it's over."

Silas sank to his knees as Sheriff Crutchfield wove his way through the crowd. He stood over Silas for a long minute before shaking his head with a snicker. "Someone mind telling me what kind of a church meeting came off this morning?"

"Well, it seems Silas Norton is under the impression that Miss Rebecca should belong to him," Reverend Norris said with a shaky voice. "He attacked Matthew because they sat together during the service. He also attacked several others when they tried to stop him, including his own father."

"That right, Harry?"

Harry Norton didn't answer out loud, but nodded his head. The weary-looking man had a swollen left cheek. Two other men had lumps and scrapes from being knocked around, and willingly shared their experiences with the lawman. The sheriff listened, then shook his head again and laughed.

"I normally would have been here this morning, but I was busy busting up a fight between the Albertson clan at the other end of town. I didn't expect anything to happen like this at a church meeting. What were you doing when this come off, Arizona?" He eyed Phillip, who had once again taken a position behind Katherine and was standing with his hands in his pockets.

"Me?" He shrugged. "I was watching just like most folks. You know me, Crutch, I was trying hard not to get involved in the ruckus."

"It was Mr. Denning who actually stopped it," Avery Jordan said.

"That right, did you stop it?"

"Mmmm…sort of, after I was sure Matt had won." He again shrugged his shoulders.

"Well, a couple of you men help me lock Silas up."

"I need to see the doctor," Silas protested and tried to jerk his arm away.

"You'll see the doctor when I say you can. Right now, you're going to jail, and I'll get Doc Krucker to look at you after he's patched up some of these men you decided to punch around, including your own father."

Silas gave Matthew a glare before allowing himself to be led away.

"I'll get you later, Parker. You keep away from Becky."

"My God, but you're a blowhard." Crutchfield gave him a shove. The sheriff glanced over his shoulder at Phillip.

"You haven't changed your mind about helping me run down Pox Tivo, have you?"

"Nope, I'm needed more here, Crutch."

"My, my, my," Mary Jordan said, clucking her tongue as the sheriff gave Silas another shove and marched him toward the jail. "I don't know what's going to happen to that boy. I hope all of you can stay for dinner. We do need to talk." She laid a hand against Katherine's arm.

"Yes, I think we'd better talk, that is if you have room for all seven. I did bring quite a crowd with me."

"Yes, we have plenty of room, and we can talk while we put the finishing touches on the meal."

"I'll give you a hand," Charlene said, slipping a hand in Mary Jordan's arm. "Katie has trouble making coffee."

"I do not!" She heard Charlene giggle as the women walked away talking. "I really don't."

"I believe you," Phillip said with a chuckle. She felt weak and took a deep breath as she watched Rebecca Jordan inspecting Matthew's bruised and scraped knuckles. The young couple was being mobbed by several excited teenagers, both boys and girls, all wanting to be near her son. He was their new hero, for at least the day.

The idea of going to the Jordan's for Sunday dinner suddenly felt nauseating to her. She would be forced to talk, and detested the idea of having to discuss her son's relationship with their daughter even more than facing the rustlers. What Katherine wanted and needed was quiet. She wanted to be alone…but quickly decided that actually wasn't really what she felt. She gave herself a quick examination as they walked slowly toward the storekeeper's house. What she really wanted more than anything was to be alone with Phillip and talk. She wanted to find out more about him. It had been a long time since she had cried, and even longer since she had had anyone to comfort her and tell her it was okay when she did. She needed to know things were going to be alright. It was one thing being boss and having people do what you ordered, but she desperately needed someone to tell her she was okay being Katie Parker. She wanted to know they liked her just the way she was, even if the person happened to be a saddle tramp like Phillip Denning. She swallowed hard as her eyes began to water. It was only a few yards from the church to the Jordan's house, but to Kate it felt like miles.

CHAPTER 43

The afternoon had been about as pleasant as one might suspect. Although Charlene and Mary Jordan had done an exceptional job frying the chicken and creating a delicious gravy to compliment the mashed potatoes, Katherine only picked at the food on her plate.

"What's the matter, honey, aren't you feeling well," Mary asked her halfway through her third piece of chicken.

"No, I'm fine," she said, shaking her head. "I guess I don't have much of an appetite. It was a little upsetting seeing my son beat on that big bully."

"He deserved it, Ma," Joshua said over a mouthful of potatoes and gravy.

"Yes, I know he did, Josh. By the way, it isn't polite to talk with your mouth full. I don't know, I guess I was afraid that Matthew might get hurt again. I also felt sorry for Harry and Mrs. Norton…having a son like that, and them having to watch him get hurt."

"Well, you have some fine boys, Mrs. Parker," Avery Jordan said. "And Matthew proved this morning he can handle himself when he needs to."

"Yes, Mr. Denning has taught him well." Katherine sent Phillip a glance across the table before studying the now cold potatoes and gravy on her plate.

"Not really. I just showed him a few things. Matt's a quick study and can take care of himself, as long as he keeps a clear head."

"Well, regardless of what happened down at the church, we're more than happy to welcome you and your son into our family." Mary Jordan patted Katherine's hand and beamed.

"Into your family? Am I missing something here, Matthew?" Katherine turned toward her son seated beside Rebecca near the end of the table. The girl fluttered her eyelids and looked down with a blush.

"Ah…yeah. I was waiting to talk to you in private when we got home. I've asked Becky's parents permission to marry their daughter, and they said yes."

She stared at her son open-mouthed for a minute.

"I knew you were going to ask for her hand. You never said you were going to ask them today. I thought you would discuss it with me first. I am your mother, after all."

"Yes, but…I thought you wanted me to marry Becky."

"I do. I love her. It's just that…"

"Then, what?"

"Nothing…" She turned her attention toward the dark-eyed girl.

"I am extremely happy you are going to marry my son. I couldn't think of anyone I'd rather have as my daughter-in-law. I do hope he will talk to you more than he does his mother. Now, if you'll please excuse me, I don't seem to have much of an appetite." Katherine laid her napkin beside her plate and walked briskly toward the front door.

"What's the matter with her?" Timothy asked.

"Mothers always cry when their sons and daughters get married," Charlene said.

"She wasn't crying," Steven said matter-of-factly.

She released her grip on the latch without opening the door and took a deep breath. Perhaps she was acting silly. Her son marrying a nice sweet girl like Rebecca Jordan was the best thing to happen in years. Matthew came and stood quietly beside his mother, before giving her a quick kiss on the cheek. Then he told her about a dance at the Grange hall next Friday, and that he wanted to take Rebecca.

"Everybody should come. I know you once told me that you used to like to dance too." The words felt like a hot knife through her heart.

"Well, son, there are a lot of things I *used to* enjoy. I really don't have time for them now. I had to raise four sons and build a cattle ranch. That's been my life, and I don't have time for much else, do I?"

"No. I didn't intend to make you angry. I just thought you might like to go."

"I'm not angry. I'm simply telling you how things are. I'm glad you and Becky love each other, and you're going to get married. I really am. I just...I'll let you know about the dance." She waved him off and opened the door.

In all the years since James' passing, not one person had asked her if she would like to attend a dance until this minute. Actually, there would be no need in her going, since Matthew was the only one of her sons that had shown any interest in learning how to dance. He would be taking Rebecca and leaving Katherine with no one to dance with.

Phillip came out onto the porch holding a pie tin filled with table scraps and asked if she would like to go for a walk. He guided her toward the edge of town and stopped at the livery where he placed the tin in front of the hungry dog. The quiet felt soothing to her.

"I'm sorry I'm such a mess," Katherine finally said. She sniffed several times while digging inside her hand bag for a handkerchief, and blew her nose. "There was simply no reason for me acting the way I did. Rebecca is a lovely young lady, and she will make Matthew a fine wife."

"Yes she will," Phillip said with a warm smile. "There's no reason for you to apologize for anything. I may not understand everything from a woman's view, but from where I stand, you've had a lot of things thrown at you that could knock a grown man for a loop. It's okay to get upset once in awhile. I'm just surprised you didn't cry. I know my sister Ruth would have. She used to cry about most things, but I've never known a stronger woman, outside of you."

"You think I'm strong?"

"Yes I do." He nodded. "I frankly don't know how you've held it inside as long as you have. You were handed a full platter all in one serving, with your husband dying and daughter disappearing. You stepped right in and took over."

"I had to. There wasn't anyone else."

He fished the makings out of his vest pocket and grinned as he began rolling a cigarette.

"Maybe, but you've run that big ol' ranch of yours better than most men could, and you've done a fine job raising those boys. You're one heck of a woman, Katie Parker. You're okay just like you are. Even if you wanted to cry…that still would be alright in my book."

"Thank you, Mr. Denning. Frankly, I needed someone to tell me that. I think you're okay too…that is for the *no-account saddle bum* you are."

CHAPTER 44

The emotional strain of the preceding day had caused Katherine to oversleep. She jumped out of bed cursing her laziness and quickly threw on her riding skirt, a white blouse and brown vest before jerking the curtains open. The sun was already casting a warm glow across the yard as chickens pecked and scratched in the dirt. She poured water into the washbasin and scrubbed the sleep from her face before vigorously running a brush through her hair. She grimaced several times as it snagged a tangle. Just payment for her laziness, she thought.

The heels of her boots clicked with precise rhythm as she marched into the kitchen and grabbed a clean mug. She blew in it once to remove any dust that might have gathered in the night, and filled it from the pot on the stove.

"Good morning, ma'am." Charlene's voice drifted from inside the pantry. "I saved you a slice of ham and biscuits in the oven. The butter's on the table. Care for some eggs?"

"No thank you, Charlie. I've got to get saddled and catch up to the boys. Did they say where they were going this morning?"

"Yes they did, and you won't need a horse and saddle to catch up with them. They're right up behind the barn working in the cemetery. You can see them for yourself," she said, pulling the curtains apart.

Katherine peered through the kitchen window to see Matthew and Joshua scraping the wrought iron fence, while Timothy and Steven followed closely behind applying fresh white paint. She could not make out clearly what Phillip was doing, as he was kneeling between the graves.

"What in the world...? What's going on?"

"It looks as though they are cleaning up the cemetery, ma'am, and I'd say it's high time, too," Charlene said. "We all should've been taking better care of James and Abby's graves. We ought to be ashamed of ourselves. Now, sit yourself down while I'll fry you a couple of eggs."

"No thank you, Charlie. The biscuits and ham are just fine."

"Are you sure? It's no trouble at all."

"I'm fine Charlie...really," she said with a smile. "Go on and do what you were doing. I can take care of myself."

She cut the ham into several hunks and placed them between the two biscuits she had sliced open, making small sandwiches. Katherine ate them as she stood quietly at the window watching the boys paint the cemetery fence. She washed her breakfast down with coffee and refilled her mug. As an afterthought, she filled an extra mug and took them both, intending to give one to Phillip. She decided to take a shortcut through the opened barn, and was nearing the rear entrance near the cemetery when Phillip's voice caused her to pause and listen.

"Well, I never knew your pa, son, but my guess is he figured he had done something he thought he could never forgive himself for. From what I understand, your sister and pa had become best friends. He taught her how to ride, punch cattle and even shoot. He might've been married to your ma, and I'm sure he loved her something terrible-like. From what I see, that wouldn't have been a hard thing for a man to do. But you're pa and Abby had become saddle-pards.

"And, my guess is, he had sent her out to do something that morning...maybe check on something for him. And that's what she was doing when that blizzard hit. Now, logically speaking, he couldn't really blame himself, cause he wasn't

God, and wasn't in charge of the weather. But down deep inside he figured it was his fault, because he was the one that had sent her to do whatever she was doing when she got caught in the blizzard. In his mind, he might as well have taken a gun and shot her in the head."

Katherine could see him through the crack between the door and rear wall as he talked. And while she had not been able to tell what he was actually doing from the kitchen window, the sight caused her lips to form a smile. Phillip Denning was busy weeding the graves, and planting fresh wild flowers. She sat the cups of coffee on a sack of feed and listened.

"There's just some things a man has trouble forgiving himself for, son. My sister, Ruth, had herself a fine boy about Matt's age. I was the sheriff of Crown Point…"

"New Mexico?" Matthew asked, cutting him off.

"Yes, Crown Point, New Mexico. Anyway, her boy Robert and me were kind of like Abby and your pa. We were best pards and hung around together. So, when I needed myself a deputy, I hired Bob, thinking it was safe. Crown Point was a nice, quiet little town, and we hadn't had any trouble in a long time. Bob wanted to be a lawman like me and I figured it would be good experience for him. He'd only been my deputy about six months when some yahoos decided to rob the bank and one of them killed Bob. I was out of town at the time on a wild goose hunt."

He paused to stare off in the distance for a silent moment.

"He would still be alive today if I hadn't of pinned that badge on him. I still see his lifeless body lying in the dirt and I can hear Ruth cry every time I close my eyes. She was covered with Bobbie's blood as she cradled and rocked him. I'll never forgive myself as long as I live. Worst of all, the man who killed him was supposed to be my friend."

He began pulling weeds with renewed vigor.

"It might be something hard for you boys to understand right now, but there's things that'll kill a man just as easily as a bullet, and they're a whole lot more painful.

They eat away at your gut and kill you slowly from inside out. I can understand your pa. I understand him real well."

"Is the robber you've been looking for the same man that killed Bobbie?" Steven asked after a minute.

"Yes, my friend Nate Thomas, and I'll find him sooner or later."

"What'll happen when you do?" Joshua asked.

"I'll kill him."

Katherine took the cups and returned the way she had come. She sat on the edge of the porch watching and thinking while she sipped her coffee. When she had finally finished, she refreshed Phillip's mug and walked briskly to the cemetery, feigning ignorance of what they were doing, and especially of the conversation she had heard.

CHAPTER 45

"So, it's all settled then. Soon you'll be an old married man," Phillip said. He scooted away from the table and grinned at Matthew as he rolled a cigarette. Katherine had only been picking at her steak and baked potato, and paused with a forkful of potato halfway to her mouth to hear what her son had to say.

"I'm only eighteen, so I'd hardly be considered an 'old married man.' That'd make me a young married man, wouldn't it?"

"Either way, you're doing things kind of backwards, aren't you?" He struck a match and lit the cigarette before toasting Matthew with his cup of coffee.

"How's that? What am I doing backwards?"

"The Bible says from the beginning of creation God made them male and female. And a man shall leave his father and mother, and cleave to his wife; then they shall become one flesh. But instead of leaving your ma, you're bringing Becky to her. That sounds kind of backwards to me."

Katherine allowed her fork to fall to the plate with a clink. "What are you suggesting, Mr. Denning? That my son should move into town when he gets married?"

"No ma'am, not at all. I'm just joshing him some. In fact, I'd say he has his head on straight and is doing the right thing. Now, if you'll excuse me, I think I'll check on that colt before calling it a night," he said and returned his chair to its proper place at the table.

"You know something about the Bible, Mr. Denning?" Charlene asked as he reached for his hat.

"Yes, ma'am…some," he said with his back toward her. He took his time adjusting the hat and buckling his gunbelt as he talked. "I've read the Bible. I used to read it every day, but sort of gave up awhile back."

"What made you stop reading it?" Katherine asked as he opened the door. He turned and gave her a crooked grin.

"I spent the greater part of the past three years looking for a man, with every intention of killing him. I don't know, but it just seems to go against all that *love your enemies* and *turn the other cheek* thing."

He cocked his head and touched the brim of his hat. "Evening, ma'am, and thanks for a nice supper, Charlie."

"You're welcome," Charlene said as he closed the door. Katherine suddenly felt chilled and rubbed both arms vigorously.

CHAPTER 46

"Well, that solves the mystery as to where some of our cattle's been going," Katherine said in a hoarse whisper. She had ridden out early that morning to make a sweep of her ranch, and hopefully find a clue that might lead them to the rustlers. It was now mid-afternoon, and they were crouched behind a thick growth of brush watching two young braves drive three steers westward toward Stony Creek.

"Yes, ma'am. Although I don't think these folks have been taking more'n a few head to feed themselves," Phillip said. "Injuns don't normally like the taste of beef. They'd rather have buffalo or a good elk stake."

"Take it easy, son," Katherine said as Steven cocked his rifle. "They don't mean us any harm."

"No, I reckon they're some of the Pawnee that old trapper told me about. He claimed they're near starving to death. He might be right. They sure took a chance by encroaching on Sioux huntin' grounds. According to that old man, their summer camp's right up there on the creek.

"You mentioned you'd like to have a talk with them, didn't you, Mr. Denning?"

"Yes, ma'am. I think it might be a good idea."

"Well," she said, shoving her rifle back into its scabbard, "I don't think we'll find a better time than now. Matthew, Josh? I want you to take Timothy and round up three more steers. We'll find out where they are headed and wait for you about where you see them now."

"Yes, ma'am." Matthew motioned for his brothers to follow.

Katherine followed the braves a quarter of a mile before seeing the smoke from the Pawnee village ascending above the trees lining Stony Creek. She caught her breath as two fierce-looking braves appeared suddenly from opposite sides of the trail. Their faces were painted, and they were mounted on ponies that were equally decorated. The men pranced their ponies in front of them, blocking the trail. Katherine urged Culpepper forward and raised her hand in an effort to show them they meant them no harm. One of the braves took a careful look into her face, then shouted something in his native language, and both darted toward the village as fast as their horses could carry them.

"Well," she said, exhaling loudly. "I wonder what that was all about. I know I'm not much to look at, but I'm hardly that repugnant."

"I reckon we'll find out soon enough. They're having themselves a confab with several others near that line of trees." Phil pointed.

"Here comes Matt," Steven said as the sound of bawling calves reached their ears. She could feel the pounding of her heart inside of her chest as several Indians charged toward them.

"We might as well take it easy and wait." She smiled as she tried to sound calm.

"Best take your ma's advice, son," Phillip said as Steven reached for his rifle. "Keep your hands in plain sight. They don't mean us no harm. Tell your brothers to hold them steers right about there."

Katherine took several deep breaths and released them slowly as the five braves encircled them. The men pranced their ponies back and forth, eyeing them carefully. One fierce-looking brave seemed particularly interested in Katherine, but not in a threatening way. She felt his stare was born out of curiosity, more than anything. They were soon joined by several other braves. The first group parted, allowing an older man in the center through. He had a collection of coup hanging from his lance that included several human scalps as well as chunks of animal fur. It didn't matter whether the scalps had belonged to white people or braves from other tribes. She knew enough to know the old man was someone who meant what he said, and would not tolerate being argued with or questioned. He was mounted on a magnificent white stallion that pranced proudly as he circled Katherine several times. He snatched the hat from her head, allowing it to hang by the drawstring.

"Mmm," he said with a nod. "You come." He turned his horse and galloped away.

"I brought cattle," she yelled, but he kept going. The fierce-looking brave gave her a firm nod.

"You come." He motioned with his head.

"I brought cattle as a gift. I know you're hungry." She shifted and pointed toward the steers. "Those are my sons, and they brought them as a gift."

"You come." He said something to the other braves as he urged her forward. The remaining braves galloped back toward the boys.

"We'd best go with them, ma'am," Phillip said as he trotted up beside her.

She glanced over her shoulder. The boys were being escorted by the braves as they drove the cattle.

"I wonder where they're taking us?" Steven asked in a soft voice.

"To their village, I suppose," Katherine said.

"I reckon that old chief might've taken a liking to your ma," Phillip said. "Maybe he wants to do some swapping with you boys. Whadda ya think your ma's worth. Ten ponies?"

She gave him a stern glare and received a wink as he laughed.

The creek flowing through the center of the village had been dammed at the upper end, creating a pond. Several naked children were busy splashing in the pond, and stopped their play as they passed. Phillip grinned as Katherine's jaw dropped when she realized two of the naked swimmers were girls, fast approaching their teens. She stopped Culpepper and shifted to watch as the boys passed the swimming hole. One particularly attractive girl gave Steven a broad smile as he passed. The shocked expression on her son's face would have been humorous under different circumstances, but the pounding inside her chest kept her from laughing.

Their escort had them dismount in front of a large teepee, where the chief began barking orders. Several women scurried about as some young boys rushed to care for the horses. The cattle were driven past and through the center of the village toward a large pasture, where several other head of her cattle were grazing among a herd of fine-looking horses.

"What's gonna happen, Ma?" Steven asked.

"I suppose we'll find out soon enough," she said as a crowd of curious women and children encircled them.

"Maybe they're gonna eat us for dinner," Timothy said with a snicker, and nudged his little brother.

"Hush, the both of you. This is no time for horsing around."

"Mama?"

Katherine turned to see a woman dressed superbly in buckskin and beads.

"Mama?" The woman rushed toward her.

Katherine caught her breath when she saw the woman's face. Then the ground suddenly opened and swallowed her.

CHAPTER 47

The inside of the teepee was dim when Katherine woke. She blinked several times before she realized she was staring into the dark eyes of the young swimmer who had smiled at Steven. The girl was holding her beautifully sculptured face only inches from her own.

"Hello," Katherine said softly. The girl caught her breath and vanished so quickly, she thought it might have been a dream.

"You're awake." The voice came from Phillip, who was seated quietly on a pallet of buffalo robes on the opposite side of the teepee.

"Yes, I'm awake. I had the strangest dream…" She stopped to take in the surroundings. "Where are the boys? And was there a girl in here? Where did she go?"

"Well," he said with a chuckle. "The boys are getting reacquainted with their sister. The girl's name is Taaka', and I reckon she went to fetch Abigail."

"Abby?" Her voice sounded high and squeaky. There were a million questions flooding her mind as the flap on the teepee flew open. The bright sunlight seemed to halo Abigail as she ran to engulf Katherine in her arms and kiss her.

"Mama, oh Mama! I thought you were dead!"

Katherine couldn't speak as she wept and kissed her daughter.

"Alright you knot-heads, back outside," Phillip ordered as he ushered the boys out.

"But she's our sister," Matthew protested.

"Yeah, and you've already had your time with her. Let your ma have a turn. He closed the flap, leaving them alone.

<u>CHAPTER 48</u>

"Mother, I would like you to meet your grandsons. This is Skiri." Abby laid her hand on the toddler. "You would say *Little Wolf*. And this is Kiwaku'." She bounced the baby in her arms. "You would call him Red Fox."

"They are beautiful!" Katherine squatted on her heels in front of Skiri. "How old are they?"

"Skiri has seen two winters, and Kiwaku' will see his first winter. He was born when the grass turned green." She said something in Pawnee and the toddler ran to give Katherine a quick hug and returned to his mother's side.

"They are darling," Katherine said with a laugh. "May I hold my grandson?"

"Yes, you may hold him all you want. I have things I have to do." She passed the baby to Katherine's arms and quickly disappeared into one of the teepees. Katherine cooed and bounced the tiny bundle, before realizing she was actually a grandmother. She jerked up as Phillip approached.

"I'm a grandmother," she said excitedly. "Can you believe it, Mr. Denning? I'm actually a grandmother."

"Yes, ma'am. He's a find looking boy; both of them are."

"You've already met them?"

"Yes, ma'am. Your son-in-law introduced me when you was having a confab with the chief. How'd that go, anyway?"

"I didn't ask about the rustlers." She shook her head and studied the baby in her arms. He had fallen asleep. "I did learn he is called Many Coup, and he was the one who found my daughter half-frozen. He took her in and she became his adopted daughter." She looked up with misty eyes and smiled.

"Did you know it is a great honor to be the chief's daughter?"

"Yes, ma'am. I reckon it must be."

"I had no idea."

The baby stirred, and she looked down.

"Ma'am?"

"Yes, Mr. Denning?"

"It's getting late, and I reckon I'd best be heading back. Charlie's gonna be worried sick, thinking something's happened to us. And someone had better take care of the stock."

"Oh, Lord. You're right. I had completely forgotten about Charlie. Why don't you take Matthew, and you'd better take Timothy and Joshua also. They will likely pull some stunt and cause an Indian uprising if we're not careful. Then load as much food and supplies as Charlie will allow, and bring them all back here in the morning."

"Including Charlene?"

"You'd hardly stop her from coming, Mr. Denning."

"I take it you're spending the night?"

"You couldn't drag me away with a team of horses, Mr. Denning."

They paused as Abby approached, leading a young girl. Katherine recognized her as the one that had been watching her inside the teepee.

"Mother, I would like to introduce you to Taaka'. I believe you have met."

"Yes, we have." Katherine gave the girl a warm smile. "I'm pleased to meet you, Taaka'. You are a lovely girl."

"You are welcome." The girl spoke haltingly, making it sound like a question. Abby said something in Pawnee that made the girl smile.

"Well, you two have more catching up to do, so I'll just grab the boys and be moseying along. Pleased to meet you, ma'am." He touched the brim of his hat and turned away.

"Mr. Denning?" Katherine called after him.

"Yes, ma'am?"

"Where is Steven? I haven't seen him for quite awhile."

"Oh, I saw him wandering toward the pasture. I reckon he's gonna look the ponies over. You know how he feels about horses, ma'am. Don't worry yourself about him."

"Thank you. I'll see you in the morning."

She handed the baby to Abby as he began to cry. "I believe my grandson needs changing. Then, perhaps you can introduce me to some of the ladies."

CHAPTER 49

Steve soon found himself being ignored and pushed aside. He didn't think he could've gotten his mother's attention with a stick of dynamite. He could understand that, and knew they had to spend time getting reacquainted. What he couldn't understand was Matthew following the women around the village as Abby proudly displayed their mother. Josh and Tim had quickly disappeared with a couple of boys, and were likely up to no good, and all Phillip seemed to want to do was to sit and roll cigarettes for the braves and talk. Most of the Indians seemed to know a little English, and tried to carry on a conversation, but they crossed their words, and he had trouble understanding what they said. What made sense was the horses.

He wandered through the herd of ponies, admiring how well kept they were, until a group of noisy boys began congregating at the far end of the pasture. They started a game of keep-away with a ball made of animal hide. The players circled the ball and walked counterclockwise, taunting each other. Several made fake attempts at grabbing the ball, that caused others to leave their spot and try to stop them. The taunting continued until one boy actually grabbed the ball and dashed quickly toward a line of cheering girls, which seemed to be the goal. He was overtaken and tackled by two boys before reaching the girls, and the ball was returned to its proper place as the game continued. It took him several minutes of watching before he realized there were two teams, and a strategy was being worked out on the field. When one boy had the ball, his teammates tried to keep the opposing players from stopping him by pushing, holding or tackling his pursuers. As he watched, a tall lanky lad snatched the ball and, proving to be much faster than anyone on the field, reached the squealing girls without being tackled. He then danced around, holding the ball high in the air, taunting the others.

Steve inched closer to the goal as the ball was returned to the starting point. One of the players spied him standing near the girls and motioned for him to join in the game. He shook his head, but the players seemed not to take no for an answer and kept urging him onto the playing field. The girls began cheering him on and one particular girl, who happened to be the one that had smiled at the pond, actually took his arm and urged him onto the playing field.

"Go," she said, pointing toward the circle of boys. She cheered and bounced up and down as he allowed her to hold his hat as he ran onto the field.

He was quickly introduced to his teammates and took his place in the circle of taunting boys. Several made attempts at the ball, and quickly retreated to the circle. Steve bucked up his courage as the circle moved to where he was opposite the goal. He could see the pretty girl now wearing his hat and clapping her hands. He bolted forward to snatch the ball, but his clumsy boots and heavy clothing caused him to move at a snail's pace. He was pounced on by several players before escaping the circle of boys, and found himself struggling for breath as all the players piled on top. They rolled off and clapped him on the back and shoulders laughing and cheering.

The ball was returned and they motioned for him to regain his place, but Steve held up a hand as he sat to remove his boots. He then stripped to the waist and ran to hand his clothing to the girl wearing his hat. Several boys grinned at him when he returned, and the tall boy, who happened to be on the opposing team, motioned toward the girls with his head.

"Taaka'? Mmm." He raised his eyebrows and nodded.

"She seems nice," Steve said and several boys laughed.

"Grey Fox," he said, tapping his chest.

"Walking Horse," another boy said. Steve nodded as each boy took their turn introducing themselves, then the circle began moving as the game resumed. Grey Fox waited until Steve was the one guarding the goal and he grabbed the ball. He was passing Steve in a flash, but instead of grabbing for the boy's arms or torso, Steve whipped a leg under the boy, tripping him. He then pounced on top and knew it was a mistake when he became sandwiched between the ball carrier and the other players. He was congratulated by each player for making such a brilliant tackle, including the lanky speedster, who seemed to regard him with respect as a cunning player.

The game continued with only two boys nearing, but none actually reaching, the goal. The play became intense as a crowd of adults gathered to watch, and the body contact was increased to teeth-jarring proportions. One of the players on his team limped off the field with an obvious knee injury that Steve hoped was not serious. The sun sank low behind the hill and each side wanted desperately to obtain one last point before the game ended.

The circle of players moved slowly as the taunting grew loud and boisterous. Steve waited for his chance and found it when one boy darted from his right and grabbed at, but missed the ball. He was shielded from Grey Fox for only a split second, and grabbed the ball at a full gallop. Grey Fox's eyes widened when he realized Steve had the ball and was right on him. Steve faked to his right, and quickly dashed left. The move gave him the advantage he needed as he darted toward the goal. Several players on the opposing team made attempts to stop him, but were quickly cut down by his teammates. He collapsed as he crossed the goal, gasping for breath. Steven quickly discovered that was another mistake as every player from both teams piled on in one last crushing dog-pile.

He was slapped on the back and praised by youngsters and adults alike. Grey Fox grabbed his wrist and gave him a firm nod of the head. He had become one of them, for at least one day. He sat on the ground to pull his boots on, as Katherine squatted on her heels by his side.

"Well, you certainly have a way with people. I was worried that your sister and I had been ignoring you. And here you became a hero by getting beat up in a ball game. You scored the winning point."

"Really? I didn't even know they were keeping score, or what it was."

The girl handed him his shirt and vest, but made no attempt to return his hat. Steve shrugged it off, considering it would be a gift of goodwill if she kept it. Besides, he reasoned, he had a newer and much better one hanging in his room. He couldn't seem to shake her, as she latched herself onto his arm and refused to leave. Although she spoke broken English, he had trouble making her understand when he needed to step behind a tree to relieve himself.

A blazing fire was built near the creek and one of the steers was brought in to roast. The animal had been quartered and skewered on sharp willow poles. The music and dancing began as drummers beat out a rhythm, accompanied by chanting and clacking sticks. Taaka' was still wearing his hat as she joined several young maidens in a dance, and gracefully wove her way around the campfire. Steve had to admit she was one of the prettiest girls he had ever met. Her slender body moved freely and her long black braids swung from side to side with the movement of her head. Her eyes sparkled like black diamonds in the firelight as she turned her perfectly sculptured face toward him and smiled.

The dancers moved toward the crowd of onlookers as the music increased its tempo, and each girl chose a male partner.

"No, I can't dance," Steve protested, as Taaka' held her hand for him to take. She gave him a pouty look and refused to leave. He was instantly urged forward by several of his teammates and found himself stomping around the fire clumsily in his boots. She moved close to caress his cheek with her palm and slithered her body lightly against his. He had never expected or experienced such contact from a girl, and it sent a strange sensation surging through him.

He sat beside his mother when the music ended and the girl sat next to him, hugging his arm.

"Looks like you've got yourself a pretty admirer," Katherine said with a chuckle.

"I guess so. I don't know what to do about it."

"I wouldn't do anything. And I mean that. Don't encourage her, but don't insult her either. Just be Steve."

He decided that was good advice and set his mind to following it. The girl waited on them, making sure they were both fed, before she helped herself to some meat and sat in a small gathering of teenage girls. She cast multiple smiles his way from the midst of the giggling girls. The meat was half raw and tasteless, but he ate it anyway. He was growing tired, and his body ached from the beating it had taken on the ball field. He was thinking of asking where they were going to sleep when Abby's husband, Kaatit, approached.

"Many Coup say you come."

"Well, guess we'd better go see what the old gentleman wants." Katherine wiped hers fingers against the hem of her riding skirt. Steven followed them to a large teepee that had been decorated with paintings depicting hunts and battles. They ducked inside to find the old chief sitting on a pallet of buffalo hides, with Abigail seated on his right side, smiling.

"Sit," he said motioning toward an empty pallet. They sat quietly, and Katherine took her time adjusting her skirt for modesty. Kaatit took a place beside Steven, causing his palms to sweat. He rubbed them against his pant legs as the chief spoke.

"We talk now."

CHAPTER 50

Many Coup made several frustrating attempts at speaking for himself, but finally allowed Abby to interpret. He spoke rapidly, without showing any outward sign of emotion.

"Many Coup says they found me the day of the ice wind. They were returning after rescuing their women and children from the Sioux. I was lying beside my pony, frozen to the ground. Everyone except Many Coup's first wife, Buffalo Woman, thought I was dead. She said there was still life in me and took me to their teepee. My skin was blue like the sky, and I became known as Tarre'uus Cka'u', the blue woman.

"Many Coup's wife took care of me, and became my mother. When I returned from the spirit world, they discovered I had great powers. Blue Dog then named me second shaman in the village, and Many Coup became my father. He gave me to become Black Crow's wife. Black Crow is second war chief in our village, and it has been a great honor."

Katherine felt a chill as she listened to her daughter, realizing the woman seated cross-legged on a pallet of buffalo skins was her daughter. Abby held her chin high and her spine ramrod straight. She spoke every word with pride, and every syllable was uttered without an ounce of emotion. Her Abigail had become Taree'uus Cka'u', the Pawnee.

"My father says he is sorry for the loss you suffered in the ice wind. He understands what it is to lose your own flesh. He had four sons, but soldiers killed them."

"Tell him I am terribly sorry," Katherine said softly.

"My father thanks you. But he also wants you to understand each loss has a gain. He lost four sons, but found a daughter. You believed you had lost your daughter, but you have shared her with others who needed her wisdom and spirit. You lost a husband, but the Great Spirit has given you another good man."

"Another good man?" Katherine cocked her head and grinned. "What good man is he speaking of?" She waited as Abby and Many Coup spoke in Pawnee.

"He speaks of Phillip Denning. Is he not your husband?"

Katherine struggled to keep from laughing, and nudged Steven as he giggled.

"No," she shook her head, "Mr. Denning is a good man who works for me, but he is not my husband. Tell him thank you, and I understand you have become an important part of their lives. Just knowing you are alive and have been taken care of is enough."

"My father thanks you. Tomorrow he will show you the place where they found me. He wants you to understand."

Katherine stepped into the cool night air and inhaled deeply. She turned as Steven joined her and started laughing.

"Hush, they can hear you inside the tent."

"It's just funny…that's all."

"What's funny?" She cocked her head.

"You and Mr. Denning. He thought you were married to Phil."

"Well, I must admit, that was rather humorous. I got the impression that your sister believed it also."

"I believed what?"

Katherine jerked around to see her daughter standing behind her.

"Oh, I didn't know you were there. Steven thought it was funny that Many Coup thought Mr. Denning and I were married. And, I said I had the feeling you might've thought the same."

"Mmm, not really married, but he is special, isn't he? It's not impossible, Mother. You said daddy's been gone for four years."

"Yes, and I've had several proposals from men I didn't care for. I'd hardly up and marry a hired hand, though. Give me some credit. As far as Mr. Denning's concerned, yes he is special. He saved our lives the day we met him. But we're hardly married."

Abby stared at her before nodding. "Okay, if you say so."

"What do you mean, if I say so?"

"It's okay. I believe you. Now, it's getting late and I have to tend my children. Taaka' will show you where you will sleep."

Katherine draped her arm around Steven's shoulders as they drifted back to the fire. They sat on the ground cross-legged and watched as a group of braves danced, jabbing at the air with their lances, depicting what Katherine decided must be a buffalo hunt or battle etched into their history. On the opposite side of the fire she could see Many Coup talking to Taaka' and pointing in their direction. The girl nodded and scampered toward them.

"Many Coup say you come," she said and reattached herself onto Steve's arm. She led them to a teepee on the far edge of the camp.

"You sleep. I build fire." She scampered away and Katherine poked her head inside. The place was pitch-black and cold.

"Might as well grab our grip and wait for her to get a fire going. We can't see a thing until she does."

Taaka' had the fire going by the time they returned with their bedrolls and was waiting dutifully outside the teepee. She held the flap open for them to enter. The tent was surprisingly roomy and the perimeter was lined with pallets of animal skins.

"You sleep." She ran to sit on a buffalo pallet and smiled.

"Yes, it looks very comfortable. Thank you," Katherine said and dropped her bedroll next to the pallet. The girl bounced up and ran to another pallet a few feet away and repeated the process for Steven.

The boy smiled and nodded. "I don't feel like going to bed right now. You go ahead, and I'll just hang around the campfire and watch the dancers."

Katherine paused in the middle of removing her boots. "Okay, but stick close to this teepee, and don't do anything stupid. I'd like to have a nice quiet visit getting re-acquainted with your sister and getting to know my grandchildren."

"I won't go anywhere. I'll be right outside the tent."

"Alright, I'm taking you at your word," she said, as Steve left the teepee. "I don't know if you can understand me, but please keep an eye on him," she said to Taaka', and the girl gave her a broad smile before exiting the teepee.

"Danged kids," she mumbled and removed her other boot. She knew she didn't have much to worry about when it came to Steven, although he did tend to be emotional and was easily led. She lay back on the soft pallet and closed her eyes.

Matthew had a temper, but he was mostly level-headed and dependable. Timothy and Joshua, on the other hand were a handful. *Merciful Lord in heaven, I wonder what Charlene must be going through without me being there.*

She closed her eyes, listening to the chanting and drumming outside the teepee. The tension of the day seemed to seep out of her body as she drifted into a deep sleep.

~   ~   ~

It was well past midnight when Steve tossed another log onto the smoldering fire and stripped to his long-johns before crawling under the buffalo robe. His thoughts still raced between seeing Abby alive and knowing his beautiful sister had become a Pawnee. It was as if he had stepped into the pages of one of the ten-cent novels Matthew had purchased at Jordan's general store.

Taaka' had drug him back into another dance around the campfire. What he had really wanted was to sit and watch, but he found the girl's presence strangely comforting. She spoke little, and seemed content to simply hold his arm in hers, leaving him to his thoughts. She led him around the fire several times after the dance, proudly displaying him like a trophy, and never leaving his side. At one point, she presented him to a rather important-looking brave with a buffalo headdress and decoration from head to foot made of beads and feathers. She simply said one word, "father," and squeezed his arm tightly.

Guessing the girl's father must be someone of great importance, and remembering his mother's warning not to offend anyone, he gripped the man's hand in a firm shake and nodded.

"Pleased to meet you, sir."

The man grunted with a nod and clasped his shoulder. Giving himself a mental pat on the back as to having somehow earned a little more respect in the village, Steve finally excused himself and headed back to the teepee. Even though he was exhausted, he lay awake thinking about Abby, and wondering what it must have felt like, having to learn a whole new way of life. It must have been scary, especially believing everyone and everything you loved had died in one afternoon. Scarier still, was being left with people you couldn't understand. He had decided his sister was a much stronger person than he could ever be, when sleep overtook him.

CHAPTER 51

Katherine stayed on Culpepper as Tarree'uus slid off her pony and stared at the spot on the bare rocky ground. Outside of the lonely beetle crawling across her path, there was no indication that anything had ever happened there in the history of the entire world. She marveled at how very Pawnee her daughter had become this morning, riding bareback and speaking mostly Pawnee. Abby glanced at her husband, then toward Many Coup before returning her gaze toward the beetle.

"This is it?"

"Yes, my daughter. That is where Low Dog first saw you. All but Buffalo Woman thought you were dead, but she sensed life still in you and wrapped you in a blanket. Your skin was the color of the spring sky, so she called you Taree'uus. Then you came back from the spirit world to be our daughter."

Abby allowed her vision to roam, surveying the horizon and surrounding area. Nothing looked as she had remembered. There was no canyon, nor streams. There weren't any cattle or house either. Perhaps the cattle all died in the ice storm that had almost claimed her, but she reasoned that some sign of the house and barn would still exist.

"Where is the place where the white family died? The ones you thought were my father and mother?"

Many Coup answered by pointing toward the south. They rode approximately a quarter of a mile through the brush to a small cabin sitting in the middle of a now over-grown yard. A large shed with a lean-to pitched dangerously to one side made her wonder what invisible force kept it from falling. The corral fence had long ago rotted and completely fallen in places.

Pain gripped Katherine's heart as she spied the bleached and scattered remains of what had once been a happy family. She dismounted and wandered slowly through the yard. She paused at what looked like a man and perhaps a boy not much over nine or ten years old. Inside the cabin she found the remains of a woman and child, causing her both grief for the horrible end of what might have been a happy family, and yet joy that her daughter had not become a permanent addition. Abigail joined her inside the cabin and choked back a sob.

"They had dreams, Mama. Just like you and daddy."

"Yes, I'm sure they did. It must have been horrible, being caught up here on the ridge, with nothing to block the wind."

Abby stepped back into the yard and once again addressed Many Coup in Pawnee. "I thank you, my Father, for bringing me here. I see why you thought these people were my white family."

"Why were you here? Where was your white family?" Kaatit asked. "We found you here. You should not have been here alone."

"I had come from the bottom of the canyon to see if cattle had strayed." Abby placed her hand against Kaatit's arm. "Come, and I will show you where my white mother lives. The place where I was born was a great valley inside a canyon. It has streams of water and grass for the horses. There is a lodge, much larger than this one, with a large barn and corral to one side. There were many cattle that roamed freely with the deer and wild game. That is where I lived until I became Blue Woman. I do not know how I came to be at the place where you found me. I could not see and lost my way when the great wind came."

"Horned Toad says there is such a place," Blue Dog said. The old medicine man trotted his pony toward the edge of the yard and pointed east. "He says it lies toward the rising sun. He and Spotted Tail were hunting and saw it. They did not enter because they saw white men with the cattle. It is a magical place with great power. It gave us Taree'uus Cka'u'."

"Hmm," Many Coup said thoughtfully. "We shall see the place that gave us Taree'uus, from the rim, but we shall not go there. It grows late and we must return to our village before the sun sets."

CHAPTER 52

The camp that had been a beehive of activity suddenly came to a standstill with the arrival of the wagon. Women and children stared as Phillip helped Charlene to the ground. Live chickens crated in the back of the buckboard clucked noisily as she tucked a wayward strand of hair beneath her poke bonnet.

"My, my." She chuckled. "You'd think they'd never seen a white woman before."

"Oh, they've seen a couple of 'em. They're just trying to figure out *who* you are, and why we brought the buckboard," Phillip said.

Katherine came from one of the teepees and rushed to squeeze Charlene in a hug that brought a grunt from her.

"Come here," she tugged on Charlene's arm, "I want you to meet someone." She drug her toward the teepee as a squaw appeared holding a baby. A toddler that seemed attached to her buckskin skirt stared at the newcomer with dark eyes.

"You remember my daughter, Abby?"

"Yes, ma'am, I certainly do." Charlene took the young woman in from her blond braids to the finely beaded moccasins. "Last time I saw you, you was a skinny little thing about so high. Now look at you. All grown up with two young-uns."

"You haven't changed a bit. Hello, Charlie." Abigail grabbed the woman in a one-armed hug and kissed her cheek.

The village seemed to erupt into frenzied activity with barking dogs and squealing children chasing each other. Women gossiped and giggled as they tended to the campfires and the midday meals they were preparing for their families. Taree'uus Cka'u' had welcomed the woman into their camp, and that was enough.

~   ~   ~

Katherine and Abby drug the housekeeper around, introducing her. She received the same greeting from Many Coup that she had gotten from Black Crow in the form of a grunt. Blue Dog had been more elaborate, and shook a rattle as he chanted a blessing on their visitor.

Matthew and Joshua stretched a large tarp from the wagon between several trees as a makeshift shelter, and that was where Charlene set up headquarters. She enlisted the help of several Pawnee children to build a fire, and began the task of helping several of the Pawnee women cook large stews for that evening's feast. One of the women invited her to share their midday meal in front of their teepee. Charlene apologized for not sitting on the ground, explaining the best she could about her hip. The woman nodded, and sent one of her sons into a neighboring teepee. He returned seconds later with a makeshift stool padded with buffalo hide.

Charlene tasted the bowl of soup, smacked her lips and nodded her approval. The woman smiled, then dished more soup into bowls and passed them to her family. Charlene yelled for Steven as he wandered past. The boy stopped and Charlene eyed the pretty girl attached to his arm.

"My, my, but ain't she pretty."

"Yes, ma'am. Did you want something?"

"Yes, go fetch me some spices from the wagon. I want a little salt, some black pepper, and some ground-up chilies."

"Yes, ma'am." He returned a minute later, and Charlene put a pinch of each into her bowl and stirred, then took another taste. She then nodded and passed the bowl to her host. The woman tasted the spicy mixture and nodded excitedly. Charlene repeated the pinches of spice for each family member, before pouring a small amount of the spices into an empty container for her host.

She spent the remainder of the afternoon baking bread in a Dutch oven. She enlisted the help of several Pawnee women, who killed and cleaned the chickens. She discovered her supply of spices was dangerously low when it came time to liven up her stew. Charlene decided sharing them earlier in the day might have been a mistake. The chickens would have to make due with a little butter and salt.

She presented the chief with a large bowl of stew, a generous portion of roasted chicken and buttered bread, then stood at attention as he sampled the fare. He took his time, thoughtfully chewing and savoring each item, before declaring his blessing.

"Well, you certainly earned his appreciation," Abby said. "He may want to make you one of his wives before long."

"I might accept, if Sheriff Crutchfield doesn't make up his mind."

"Is he still around?" Abby paused in the middle of filling a bowl for her husband.

"Around and still kicking. He's slower than wet gunpowder though, when it comes to romance. I don't know why I even care, but I do."

"I don't think any of us know *why* we care, Charlie…we just do." Abby cut and buttered a hunk of bread.

"You really love that man of yours, don't you?"

"Yes." Abby nodded thoughtfully, "I didn't at first. He frightened me. But he's a good man and yes, I believe I do love him."

~   ~   ~

Charlene slept on a pallet of buffalo skins next to Katherine, and had trouble getting to her feet the following morning. She made coffee and warmed herself next to the fire, then began the task of packing. It would be a grueling five miles back to the house with her hip giving her trouble.

"You'd best be finding a better way home, if you know what's good for you," she said as Phillip hoisted a bundle into the buckboard.

"Well, I could've found one coming, except you kept saying to hurry. Sometimes the quickest way ain't the easiest."

"You should've known what I meant, instead of taking the roughest trail in South Dakota, cowboy."

He put his hands on his hips and grinned. "Now, how in the hell is a man supposed to know what's inside a woman's head?"

"They are just supposed to know, that's all. And you'd best be listening, if you know what's good for you."

"Yes, ma'am…I'll do my best."

<u>CHAPTER 53</u>

Katherine hugged and kissed her grandsons before holding Abigail tightly. "Oh God, you don't know how much I've missed you."

"If it's anything like what I have been feeling, yes I do. I missed you and the boys something fierce. And I still miss Daddy."

Phillip cleared his throat and offered Abby his hand. "I reckon I'd best say my goodbyes now. I figure your ma's gonna take awhile."

"It was nice meeting you, Mr. Denning." She squeezed his hand. "You take good care of my family."

"I'll do my best. Oh, I have something for Little Wolf." He pulled a Saint Christopher medallion from his pocket and draped the chain around the toddler's neck. "Tell your husband it has powerful medicine."

"Yes, thank you, Mr. Denning. It is beautiful." She held the Saint Christopher thoughtfully between her fingers.

"We'll wait near the buckboard, ma'am. You just take all the time you need." Phillip touched the brim of his hat and gave Katherine a nod. She waited until he was at the buckboard before taking Abby by the shoulders.

"I want you to tell Many Coup he is welcome to move the entire village to the ranch. The large flat area lying on the opposite side of the corral is his. The men can help around the ranch and hunt the hills to their heart's delight. It will be good having you home, and I'll get a chance to spoil my grandsons."

Abby stared at her mother misty-eyed without speaking.

"What's wrong? Did I say something? What is it, baby?"

"We're leaving tomorrow, Mama. I thought I told you."

"Leaving? I heard you say something about having to move the camp because there wasn't any game, but I just thought you were looking for a different site. Now I've given you one. There isn't any reason to go anywhere."

"Mama…you don't understand."

"Understand what? What are you trying to tell me? Leaving where?"

"This isn't where we live, Mama. Our home is south of here in Nebraska. We don't live in teepees, we have a village with dome-shaped huts, covered with earth. They are quite comfortable and warm during the winter. We are on our summer hunt, and don't normally come this far north. It was a miracle you even found us at all."

"Yes, but…there's no reason to leave. Don't you understand? I'm offering a place for the entire village to live. You can live at the ranch."

"As what, Mama?" Katherine took a step backward as her daughter's manner changed. "What would you have us become? Would we be free to come and go as we pleased, or would you take care of us like the government promises to do? What are you going to do, give us our own little reservation at the Flying K?" Abby took Katherine by the arm and shook her head.

"I'm sorry, Mama. I can't ask Many Coup to do that. You don't understand what we've been through already. Please leave us with a little pride and dignity."

"When will you be back?"

"I don't know. This is Sioux territory, and we took a chance coming here at all. You are welcome to come visit us anytime you wish, but I can't promise we will ever return here again. That will be Many Coup's decision."

"I can't persuade you to change your mind? What about you and the children? Can't you stay?"

"That makes me angry that you would even ask such a thing. Would you have left daddy? Black Crow is my husband, and he is my sons' father. Look," she added as hot tears rolled down Katherine's cheeks, "you're only making this hard on both of us. You had better go, they are waiting for you. I'll tell Mr. Denning where you can find us if you want to visit sometime."

She rode the five miles to the house in silence. The green valley dotted with thousands of cattle and horses, the gurgling creek, the barn and outbuildings, nor the rambling house, none of these things seemed to matter. Not even Ginger could catch her attention, as the magnificent mare poked her head over the corral fenceand whinnied her welcome. Katherine found the solitude of her bedroom and wept bitterly.

"It isn't fair," she said through clenched teeth. "You took her from me once, then turned around and took James. Wasn't that good enough? And I don't care if you think it's sacrilege," she glared toward the ceiling, "but it isn't right. Why didn't you just kill me, instead of tearing my insides out a third time?"

CHAPTER 54

It was growing dark when Charlene rapped her knuckles lightly against Katherine's bedroom door and opened it.

"Ma,am, supper's almost ready. Oh, my word." she opened the door wide and opened the window shades. "What are you doing lying here in the dark like a mole? It's high-time you freshened yourself and spent some time with those boys."

"I don't feel like it, Charlie."

"I didn't ask if you felt like it. I know how you feel."

"No, you don't know how I feel."

Charlene lit the lamp and turned to glare at her. "How dare you say that to me," she said softly. "I know something about losing someone. I lost my little boy to the fever when he was one. I waited six years to get him, and only had him for a year. I couldn't have more babies, no matter how hard I prayed. Then I lost George, or had you forgotten about that?

"You've still got four fine boys in that other room, and you've still got Abby. She might not be living here on this ranch, but she's alive. The fact is, those boys can run this ranch a few weeks without you being here, if you'd let 'em. Come next spring, right after roundup, you and me could pack a few things and catch a stage, or maybe one of them steam engines. We could head to Nebraska to see that girl." Charlene paused at the door with her back toward Katherine.

"The fact is, the Lord's blessed you more than most folks I know, Kate. You ought to be thanking Him, instead of feeling sorry for yourself. Get out of that bed, wash your face and run a brush through that tangled mess you call hair. Supper will be ready in ten minutes."

"You do realize you're not my mother, don't you?" Katherine said through tight lips."

"Yes, if you were my daughter, I'd paddle your backside. Now get out of bed. You're not sick, and I'm not bringing supper to you." She glanced over her shoulder and gave Katherine a grin before closing the door.

~   ~   ~

Mathew talked mostly of what needed to be done around the ranch before his wedding, while Joshua and Timothy kept needling Steven about his Pawnee sweetheart.

"She's not my sweetheart," he yelled.

"Whoa, there's no need for yelling," Katherine said. "They are only teasing you. You know how they are."

"She isn't my sweetheart, Mom. I couldn't even understand most of what she was saying."

"I know she's not your sweetheart, honey. But she did seem like a nice girl, and she seemed to like you an awful lot."

"It appears to me, your brothers might be a little jealous," Phillip said as he cut his steak.

"No we're not," Joshua said with a snicker.

"Take a look at the facts. Taaka' is mighty pretty to look at, and from what Many Coup said, she's got some powerful medicine. She's third shaman in the village, right behind Abby. Folks go to her when they're ailing." He popped a hunk of steak into his mouth and talked while he chewed.

"Worse things could happen to a man than having a pretty girl hanging onto him, and waiting on him hand and foot."

~   ~   ~

Katherine took her coffee into the living room and sat in her favorite chair. Charlene had finished washing the dishes and came into the room, drying her hands on her apron, to offer more coffee. Katherine crossed her legs as she sipped the coffee, and watched the boys, who were involved in a card game with Phillip.

"Do you know anymore stories, Mr. Denning?" Katherine asked.

"I beg you pardon, ma'am?"

"I asked if you could tell us another one of your stories."

"Oh, did I ever tell you about 'ol Charlie Harte?"

"No, I don't believe you have." Katherine took another sip of coffee.

"Well, every outfit's got someone who claims to be an expert at whatever it is you're doing, and is willing to point out how they could've done it better. Charlie was ours. One day he was bragging how he was the best bronc-buster around, and there wasn't a cayuse born that he couldn't ride.

"Well, McCarty disappeared in the middle of the afternoon, claiming Tunstall needed him to run some errands. He headed into town, and returned a few hours later, leading a tinker with one of those wagons loaded down with snake-oil and trinkets. This tinker had him a pretty young daughter who could sing and dance, and of course they drew a crowd. I don't think Tunstall got an ounce of work out of us the rest of that day.

"They had 'em a pretty little mare tied to the back of that wagon that no one paid any attention to, until the tinker started taking bets there wasn't any one on that ranch that could stay on her back longer than a few seconds. Well, it didn't take long for Charlie to start bragging that he could. Of course it was all wind, 'cause he never made a move toward that cayuse, or laid down his money. That is, until the tinker's daughter forked the mare and trotted her around pretty as you please.

"Well, that done it, 'cause Charlie whipped out a silver dollar and climbed on that mare's back. He'd no more than settled in the saddle, when that hoss slipped the pack. Charlie dusted himself off, as we all hooted and hollered, and crawled on her again careful-like. At first, that hoss just stood there with one of its ears down, and that aint't a good sign.

"It wasn't but a couple of seconds before that cayuse broke in two and unloaded. She pitched Charlie clean out of the corral, and he bounced a time or two before landing right at Tunstall's boots. He told me later the only thing that gave was different parts of him when he hit the ground.

"It took him awhile to come around. Then he limped toward his own hoss and fetched his Winchester, saying he was gonna catch that mare over the eye, but Tunstall stopped him. About then, that tinker's daughter fed the mare a biscuit and forked her pretty as you please, and trotted her around the corral.

"The next morning, Charlie went out to the corral and offered this cayuse a biscuit, but the hoss just knocked his hat off. That's when McCarty told him he didn't have the right kind of biscuit.

"'That's a lady's hoss,' McCarty said. 'And being a pet, she wants those fancy little lady's biscuits. You're just making her mad offering her those sourdoughs.'

"The tinker left for Santa Fe, taking the hoss and his pretty daughter with him. McCarty told me later, the mare was part of the tinker's medicine show, and they'd trained her that way. 'Ol Charlie was madder'n a bee in a bonnet, and it took him a day or two before he'd say anything at all to the rest of us, but he quit bragging about his riding abilities."

Katherine laughed, then gave Charlene a hug and a warm kiss on the cheek before saying "goodnight." She knelt beside her bed and asked for forgiveness, and thanked God for sending Charlie her way.

CHAPTER 55

"Okay, Rose, that's it," Earl Tucker yelled as he came from behind the bar. She had just flung an entire tray of mugs and glasses against the wall, smashing every one of them, all because Pearl had once again taken Randy Houk to her room. Nathan suspected the woman did this more to irritate Rose than anything else, especially since she never charged the boy for her services.

"Go screw yourself, Earl! I keep this place open, so I can damned well do what I want." Rose staggered and grabbed onto the edge of a table for balance as she yelled. The two card players grabbed their money and moved to avoid the war.

"Used to, Rose…maybe you used to bring business in here, but not anymore. Most every man I know would rather sleep with a goat. Now get out of here and take your business elsewhere."

"Aggh!" Rose charged Earl but the wiry bartender grabbed a wrist and spun her around, twisting the arm painfully behind her back. He then grabbed a fistful of hair, jerked her head back, and marched her screaming toward the door where he gave her a shove.

"Now, stay out! I'll have Pearl toss your things out to you when she's finished with Randy."

"Aaaaah!" Rose charged the door, where she was met by one of Earl's fists, knocking her back into the street, where she lay unconscious.

"Geeze, Earl," Waco said with a snort. "What the hell'd you do to get her so riled?"

"Nothing. That's just it. I warned her if she broke one more glass she'd have to service her clients in the middle of the street…if she's got any left."

"I don't think she has," Nathan said, slowly shuffling the deck. "The only ones I've seen her with lately are Pox Tivo and his gang of idiots. I certainly wouldn't go near her."

"Hell, Nate, I've never seen you go near any woman," Waco said. "You got something against being with a woman?"

"No, Waco, I'm just a little choosy who I go to bed with," Nate said, dealing the cards. "Five Card Stud, gentlemen."

"I figure Nate's got himself a little gal in Denby," Earl said, as he swept the broken glass from the floor. "He goes in there about once a week."

"That right, Nate? You got yourself something going in town?" Waco asked over the top of his cards.

"Could be Waco, or it might be something else. Place your bets."

He'd taken up gambling once again, more to pass the time than anything else. But he had also discovered he was a pretty fair player when sober, and had cut a deal with Earl to keep his glass filled from a special bottle filled with cold tea so he could match the others drink for drink and stay sober. Waco and his partners were only hack players, and Nate kept them coming back to his table by allowing them to win approximately thirty to forty percent of the time.

Pox Tivo burst through the door yelling. He was followed by the Chinaman and a giant of a black man called Tuck.

"What the hell's Rose doing out in the street? What happened to her, Earl?"

"She tried busting up the place again, so I threw her out. That's what happened," Earl yelled back.

"You hit her?" Pox laid his hand against the butt of the gun in his holster, and froze as the bartender calmly pulled his shotgun from under the counter and pointed it at him.

"Yes, I hit her. She tried to scratch my face so I hit her and tossed her into the street. Anymore questions Pox?"

The half-witted rustler glanced around the room in search of some support, but found none. He snarled as Nate laid his forty-five on the table before tossing five dollars into the pot.

"What's that for, Nate? You taking Earl's side in this?"

"Pox," Nathan said with a sigh, "your brain cavity wouldn't make a drinkin' cup for a canary bird. Yeah, I'm taking Earl's side. I probably won't have to use it, since Earl's ten-gauge will clear a pretty big path. Now, it only has two shells, and there's three of you, so I thought I'd clean up the leftovers, if there are any."

"Huh," the rustler said indignantly, "I guess we'd better go where our company's wanted."

"Where might that be…hell?" Waco said with a snort.

Pox turned toward the door and paused as Earl yelled.

"Take Rose with you. I don't want to see her back here again. Got that?"

"I'll just do that. I like her better than anyone here."

"Geeze," Waco said with a laugh after the man had left. "Someone open a window. He smells like something dead."

"And to think that's what Rose has been sleeping with? No wonder she lost all her customers," Earl said, propping open the window with a stick.

"Well, she'll probably die right along with the rest of them soon enough," Nate said tossing his cards in. "I fold gentlemen. Three kings are the winner." He pushed the pot toward Carl. The big man grinned as he drew his winnings toward himself.

"What makes you say that?" Earl asked.

"That they'll be dead?"

The barkeep nodded.

"She'll smoke herself to death with whatever the Chinaman's giving her. She's half dead now. And Pox'll get himself and the other two killed pestering that widow Denning's working for."

"Think so?"

"I know so. It's just a matter of time. Same game, gentlemen," he said dealing the cards.

CHAPTER 56

Katherine woke the following morning much later than she had planned and quickly dressed into her tan riding outfit before rushing into the kitchen. She paused in the doorway as Charlene flipped two eggs in the frying pan.

"Morning, ma'am," Charlene said with a smile and set a cup of coffee on the table. "Sit yourself down. I'll have your breakfast ready in a minute." The table was piled with dirty dishes and bread crumbs. Charlene slid a plate of bacon, eggs and fried potatoes in front of her.

"I'm sorry about the mess. The boys just finished and rushed out the door a minute before you walked in. I'll have it cleaned up in a jiffy."

"Don't worry about it, Charlie. Grab yourself a mug of coffee and sit down. I want to talk to you."

"Oh? About what?"

"Nothing special," Katherine said, buttering a biscuit. "We never really sit and talk. We always have things to do, and I thought we should visit once in awhile. We live under the same roof."

"Okay." Charlene sat and stared at her over the steaming coffee mug. "How are you feeling this morning?"

"Much better. Thank you for swatting my backside last night. I guess I was acting childish."

"No you weren't, not at all. It's a hard thing not having your children around, especially when you're seeing them for the first time in years. I thought you handled yourself better than most women would have.”

Katherine stabbed a hunk of egg and stared at Charlene before plopping it into her mouth. “If that’s true, why did you force me out of my room last night?”

“Because those boys needed to know things were okay…that you weren’t going to fall apart on them. They were sitting in here all gloomy, and didn’t cheer up until you came out to join them. You’re all they’ve got Kate. This ranch isn’t the same without you knocking around.”

“Now, if that’s true, they’ll be in a heck of a fix when I get old and die, won’t they?” She grinned at Charlene and sipped her coffee.

“Most men are in a fix when their women aren’t there. We’re what holds things together. You and me are alike in that respect, Kate. We don’t change. We’re like rocks those boys can tie onto when things get rough.”

“Huh, I never thought of it that way, but maybe you’re right. Speaking of which, did either of them say where they were heading this morning?”

“Phil said something about the upper end of the creek. That’s all I know. By the way,” she added as Katherine scooted away from the table. “We’re just about out of everything. Someone’s going to have to make a run into Denby right soon, or you’ll be eating dirt.”

“Make a list and we’ll go tomorrow or the next day. I promise. Besides, it will be up to us to help Mary Jordan plan Matt and Becky’s wedding. You know those men will never do it.”

She left the house knowing another trip to town would make her oldest son very happy. She urged Ginger into a lope and crossed the canyon in a matter of minutes. According to her husband’s watch it was approximately seven-thirty when she rode out of the yard. It was much later than she had wanted to leave, but still early enough to get a full day’s work in. She made herself a mental note to make sure the watch was properly wound and time set according to the grandfather clock inside Jordan’s store when they were in Denby. That way Charlene could set every clock in the house accordingly, and maybe she'd quit complaining. The only times that really mattered on the ranch were sunrise and sunset. They were always correct.

She slowed the horse as she neared the waterfall cascading down the rocky canyon wall, but there was no sign of Phillip or her boys. Shading her eyes against the morning sun, she spied a lone rider moving slowly upward and out of view where the trail crested the canyon.

Katherine turned Ginger and climbed the trail up the side of the canyon. She crested the hill, but the rider had vanished. She sat quietly for a minute, looking and listening for any indication as to where he might have gone. Hearing and seeing nothing, she spurred the horse back into the lope, figuring the mare could catch whoever it was before they had gone far. She was nearing the fork in the road the rustlers had taken when she heard a quick buzz and the sickening sound of a bullet striking flesh. It was immediately followed by the roar of a rifle as her horse collapsed under her. Katherine found herself being propelled through the air and everything went blank as she crashed into the hard-pack ground.

CHAPTER 57

Katherine tried shaking the cobwebs from her head, but the loud ringing in her ears continued as a bullet bounced off the road with a whine, inches from where she was lying. She rolled on her left side to see her horse down several feet away, in the throes of a struggle between death and life. She scrambled on her hands and knees back toward Ginger as another bullet bit into the road dangerously close to her fingers. Another shot buzzed close to her head as she reached safety behind the dead horse. She made a quick reach for the Henry, and dove back as a bullet almost took fingers.

Another bullet slammed into the horse as she reached over its body and pulled the rifle from its sheath. Katherine leaned back against the horse and injected a shell into the chamber, then gave the gun a quick once-over. She could see the shooter kneeling on a small rise to the north of where she was pinned. She rolled and pulled the trigger, then cursed as the bullet kicked up grass and dust several feet to the right. She had never missed this badly, even while learning to shoot. She quickly checked the sights on the rifle and found them to be out of alignment. Another bullet slammed into the horse directly behind her head, forcing her to duck lower.

Katherine tried adjusting the sights as a bullet passed overhead to kick up dirt a few feet beyond where she lay.

She finally gave up aligning the sights, as it would be impossible without the proper equipment and a set of targets to sight them on, and she had neither. What she did have was someone trying to kill her. She rolled and snapped another shot by sighting down the barrel. She must have gotten close, as the big man dove to lie flat on the ground. He was a large man with red hair and looked vaguely familiar. Katherine tried to remember where she'd seen him before, as she sighted down the barrel at the spot where the man was lying.

The big fellow rose slightly in an effort to fire another shot and Katherine pulled the trigger. The bullet fell just short of the mark, kicking dirt and grass into the man's face. He jump to his feet cursing and retreated in a full run down the back of the hill. Katherine tried leaping to her feet to run after him, but fell against Ginger as Phillip and her boys crested the canyon at a full gallop. Matthew and Steven raced to where she was lying as Phillip led Joshua and Timothy in a charge toward the fleeing gunman.

Matthew leaped from his horse to grab her by the arms. "You okay, ma?"

"Yes, I'm fine…I think."

"You don't look okay," Steven said as he poured water from his canteen on his bandana and washed the blood and dirt from her face. "You got buggered up some."

"Did you see who it was?" Matthew asked.

"Yes, yes I did. I didn't believe it at first, but I'm almost positive it was Silas Norton."

They jerked around as several gunshots rang out. A few seconds later Phillip and her boys appeared and trotted their horses toward them.

"Did you get 'em?" Steven asked excitedly.

"Naw, they got away," Joshua said.

"Phil shot the hat off one," Timothy said with a laugh.

"It could've just blew off in the wind," Phillip said as he knelt beside Katherine.

"You said they. How many were there?" Katherine asked as Phillip studied her face closely.

"Four," Phillip mumbled.

"Ma says the one doing the shooting looked like Silas," Matthew said.

"It was. I got a good look at him. He's taken up rustling. At least that's who he rode off with." He gently forced one of Katherine's eyes open wider and stared at her pupil. "You hit the road pretty hard, didn't you?"

"I think my eyeballs are still in their sockets, Mr. Denning. Do you really think it is necessary for you to stare at them this closely?"

"Yes I do. I've always thought you have pretty eyes."

"Really?" She pushed him away and sat upright.

"Sure, but I was actually checking to see if you have a concussion."

"Well, what's you diagnosis, Doctor? Am I going to live?"

"I reckon you still have a few brains left," Phillip said, "but you're going to be sore for awhile. We'd better take it easy getting you home." He stood and offered her a hand.

"I'm fine, Mr. Denning." She ignored the hand and jumped to her feet, only to fall backward and sit on her dead horse.

"No you're not." He turned to Steven. "You'd better double up with me and let your ma ride your horse."

Katherine took a slow look around her before realizing the animal she was sitting on belonged to her.

"Oh my God, Ginger! They killed Ginger!" She tried to stand but staggered and fell to her knees beside the dead animal. They allowed her a few minutes to grieve before helping her to her feet.

"We'd best be going, ma," Matthew said. "Those rustlers might still be out there. They could come back and finish what they started."

They helped her onto the brown gelding Steven had been riding, and Steven climbed on Lucky behind Phillip.

"My saddle. What about my saddle?"

"We'll come back and fetch it and take care of Ginger for you," Matthew said. "Right now, we need to get you home."

"Josh, you and Tim had best ride close to your ma," Phillip said. "She's still kind of wobbly from getting bonked on the noggin. You'd best fetch your ma's Henry," he added as Steven started to mount Lucky. "No need leaving it for the rustlers to kill us with."

CHAPTER 58

"Ya! Get away from there," Phillip yelled as he fired his pistol in the air. The sky was instantly filled with a cloud of vultures that had been helping themselves to Ginger's cold carcass.

"Christ Almighty!" Matthew leaned in the wagon seat and rid himself of the ham and fried potatoes he had finished a half an hour earlier.

"That's why I only wanted coffee. Makes things a little easier to handle," Phillip said, dismounting. He took a rope and looped it around the horse's neck.

"Unhitch the team and bring 'em over here, Matt."

"Why, what are we gonna do?"

"We're dragging your ma's horse off into that wash over yonder, and cover her with rocks." Phillip took a second rope and tied it to Ginger's rear legs.

Matthew led the team into position, then paused to stare at the mutilated carcass.

"What about the saddle? Ma's gonna want to keep that."

"Yeah, we'd better take it back with us. But we're gonna have to remember to stop at the creek and give it a good scrubbing," Phillip said as he tied the ropes to the harnesses. "It's covered with blood. I don't know how we're gonna explain the teeth marks. Looks like some other critters were here before the buzzards run 'em off. Of course, we could just bury it and say the rustlers came back and took it."

"Boy, that'd sure make ma mad. She paid a lot of money to have this rig made." Matthew unhooked the cinch and gave the saddle a tug.

"I reckon so, but there's just some things that womenfolk don't need to know…that is if you really care for them. And that goes for that pretty young thing you're fixing to marry."

"Becky? I don't have any secrets from Becky," Matthew said as he tossed the blood-covered saddle into the wagon.

"Didn't say you did, and you shouldn't. Okay," he said as Matthew started the team forward, "right over there to that low spot." He pointed. "Stop them about here while I get the shovels." He grabbed two spades from the buckboard, handing one to Matthew, and started to dig.

"How deep are we going? Ginger's a mighty big horse."

"Deep enough to get a few inches of dirt on top, then we'll pile some rocks on her, to keep the critters from digging her up again."

"What kind of secrets should I keep from her?"

Phillip paused his digging, as Matthew tossed several shovels of dirt aside. "You speaking of Becky, or your ma?"

"Both…but mainly Becky."

"Well, sir," Phillip said as he resumed his digging, "not much on both counts. Just mainly things you think will really hurt them. Take the hurt and pain life dishes out for yourself…as much as you can stand. There's some things they are going to have to know, like when your sister came up missing, and your pa died. Or say, when Steve got barked by that rustler. There wasn't any hiding those things. But others like her half-eaten horse and a gnawed-up saddle…it's better not to tell her about it." He paused to wipe his brow against his sleeve.

"My pa used to say God-fearing women are really princesses lent to us from heaven. And it's our job to love and protect them, just like they are a princess, because if we don't," he paused to heave another shovelful of dirt, "God's gonna ask us why we treated them badly. And that won't be so pleasant."

Matthew tossed another shovelful aside. "So, you're saying Rebecca Jordan is a princess sent by God from heaven?"

"Yes, sir, and you're her prince. Treat her like one, and you'll get along just fine. That's just about deep enough," Phillip said, inspecting the hole. "Let's get her in here and cover her up."

"What about Ma?" Matthew asked as he started the team forward. "Do you see her as a princess too?"

"Well now," Phillip said as he rolled a cigarette, "I ain't quite made up my mind about her. She's a female-critter cut from a different cloth than anyone I've ever seen before. But, yeah," he added with a nod and struck a match. "I guess she's a princess, and a mighty fine one, too. Look at all the things she's done…raising you boys by herself, and holding this ranch together. Not many women could do those things the way she has. I just don't know who's going to become her prince…or even if she wants one."

They shoveled dirt for a few minutes in silence before Matthew stopped to stare thoughtfully at Phillip.

"What about you?"

"What about me?"

"Why don't you become my mother's prince?"

Phillip burst out laughing and tossed his shovel up the bank. "That's enough dirt. The heat must be getting to you, boy. Let's get some rocks to cover the grave."

"No, I'm serious. I know she likes you."

"Huh, a lot you know. She got hotter than a burnt boot when I said she ought to stay home and let you and me bury this hoss and fetch her grip."

"Yeah," Matthew said with a strain as he heaved a large stone onto Ginger's grave. "But that doesn't mean she doesn't like you. She's always getting mad at Tim and Josh, but she still loves them. I think she likes you a lot."

"Maybe." He strained as he tossed a rock on the grave. "Listen, boy, your ma and I ain't meant for each other. We get along just fine with her being boss and me being a hired hand, and that's as far as it goes. Don't go getting ideas there might be something else, because there ain't nothing. Do I find her attractive? Certainly. She's a fine looking woman. But she doesn't have any use for an old saddle-bum like me, plus she's a headstrong woman who'd be telling me what to do. So no, she'll have to find her own prince…if she decides she wants one. Besides, I'll be moving on before the snows come.

"Now, let's get the team hitched and go put on the feedbag. Wonder if Charlie's got something hid we can munch on? I don't think I can wait for supper. My stomach is beginning to think my throat's been cut."

CHAPTER 59

Phillip was seated on the edge of the porch having an evening smoke when Matthew came to sit beside him.

"Nice night," the boy said as he began whittling on a piece of wood. The dog padded up onto the porch and lay beside Phillip.

"Yep, it certainly is."

"I'm glad you're gonna be around for my wedding."

"When's the date?"

"First weekend in August."

"Better get your cabin built to give you and your bride some privacy. A woman needs her own space." Phillip crushed the cigarette under his boot.

"Pastor Norris says he's organizing a house-raising next month. A bunch of people are coming from town, and they're supposed to finish it in one day."

"Hmm, I reckon that'll be something to see. I'd better check with Charlie and see if she wants me to butcher a beef before they all get here."

Matthew whittled in silence as Smokin' Ripplin' Rio pranced proudly inside the corral.

"Your brother did himself right proud training that colt," Phillip said.

"Yeah, he's got ma's gift, that's for sure. She was the only one of us who could handle Culpepper when she first got him." Matthew snickered and shook his head. "We used to fight to see who got to ride him once she got some of the starch worked out of him."

"Can't say as I blame you none. That stallion's a real hoss. A true cayuse. Those scars he's carrying are war maps. He probably belonged to a Comanche one time or the other. It's too bad about her losing Ginger. I was hoping your ma might breed the mare to that old cayuse. They'd sure have one hell of an offspring."

"Huh, that's exactly what she was thinking." Matthew glanced at Phillip and grinned.

"Yes sir, Silas needs hanging for killing that mare." Phillip stood and stretched with a yawn. "I reckon you'd better grow a set of eyes in the back of your head, son."

"Why's that, Mr. Denning?"

"It ain't likely Silas Norton's riding with the rustlers for the money. He's nursing a canyon-sized grudge against you, and will try bushwhacking you the first chance he gets. Most of the responsibility of keeping your folks alive is going to fall on you, especially after I'm gone. Your ma's got enough to worry about, without us adding to it. That's why I'm telling you."

Matthew tossed his piece of wood into the yard and folded the pocketknife closed as he stood. "I'd just as soon you stuck around. When are you leaving?"

"The same as always, as soon as fall roundup is finished."

"That's three or four months away," Matthew said with a nod. "Maybe you and me should take a ride and see if we can't rid ourselves of Silas Norton and the rustlers before roundup."

Phillip grinned and nodded. "I reckon. Now, I think I'll get some shuteye. Tell everyone good night for me."

CHAPTER 60

Silas Norton sat next to the fire watching the scene unfold on the opposite side of the tiny cabin. The three men were each taking their turn with Rose. There was no interest in privacy as the other two, a Chinaman named Wah Lee and a black man called Tuck, looked on. Pox finished and Wah Lee took over.

"You can have a turn when one of them two gets finished," Pox said with a snigger as he buttoned his soiled britches.

Under normal circumstances, Silas would have had nothing to do with any one of them, except they had left him with no option. He had ridden to the *Flying K* after a massive argument with his father. Harry had demanded he give up his friends, then demanded that he get a job and earn his keep. His mother had taken Silas' side, but to no avail. One thing led to another, until Silas had lost his temper and hit the old man with his fist. To his surprise, his father returned the favor. The result had been a vicious fight that had left their living room destroyed, as well as his father lying unconscious in a pool of blood.

Knowing he could never return to that house, or Denby without being arrested, Silas decided to leave the state and go south. He figured maybe even as far as Texas, but not before settling the score with Matthew Parker. He emptied his father's wallet and cashbox before riding out of town as fast as his horse could take him.

He had been on the ranch once some years ago, and remembered the road leading into and out of the valley well. He was about to descend into the canyon when he spied Mrs. Parker riding the ginger-colored horse toward him. Knowing how close-knit the Parker's were, Silas quickly rode behind a hill, grabbed his rifle and waited. He chuckled as he injected a round into the chamber. Killing her would hurt Matthew more than killing him personally.

She had just rounded the bend in the road when he pulled the trigger. The woman was catapulted into the air as her horse went down. He felt a surge of glee, knowing how she loved that animal. Silas watched as she struggled back toward the horse on her hands and knees before deciding she might make good target practice. He fired again. Killing her outright would be too quick, so his next bullet kicked up dirt next to her head. He laughed as he injected another round into the chamber. His next shot almost took the fingers off her left hand. That was when she actually made a dive behind the dying horse. His next one came close to killing her as she made a grab for her rifle.

Katherine fired from behind the horse, but her shot was so far off mark it made him laugh. Silas was drawing a bead on her when the next shot buzzed dangerously close to his ear. He quickly dropped to the ground. Her next shot kicked dust into his eyes and came close to giving him a permanent part in his hair as it ricocheted off the ground. That's when Phillip Denning and her boys came charging out of the canyon. Silas ran to his horse, cursing. He spurred the animal into a full run, and soon heard more horses behind him. Thinking it was the Parker boys, Silas beat the animal mercilessly.

The riders soon overtook him and the ugly one grabbed his reins, pulling him to a stop.

"What's your hurry, sonny? You got some sort of beef with that widow and her hired hand?"

Fear gripped his heart as he stared at the three men. They were the dirtiest and scariest men he had ever seen.

"He must have something going on. He was shooting at them," Tuck said with a snigger. He had several teeth missing in front and the remaining ones were yellow.

"Well, you just come along with us, sonny, 'cause we'd like to see them dead just as bad as you," Pox said. He then pointed to his own missing teeth and growled. "See this? That Denning fellow did this to me, and threatened to hang me. So shootin's too quick for him. I want him to die real slow, understand? I plan to hang him. You can shoot the rest if you want, I just want Denning. As I see it, you just come along with us, and we'll scratch each other's backs, so to speak."

He had soon found himself sitting inside their dirty cabin by the fire, eating canned beans and watching the disgusting scene before him.

"Okay, you can have her now."

Silas looked up into the face of Tuck.

"Go on, sonny. She won't bite," Pox said with a laugh.

Lying with the smelly woman after three other men had finished with her was not his idea of a good time. Afraid he would offend the rustlers, Silas began to disrobe as he crossed the room.

CHAPTER 61

Hiram Jenkins woke feeling weak and feverish, but attributed the feeling to his old age. He packed the mule carefully and ate a quick breakfast of elk jerky, washing it down with water. Furs and hides were becoming scarce in these parts. This would probably be his last season in South Dakota. He figured to take the meager wages of his labor to Denby and head west. He had heard a rumor that the game was still plentiful in the Rockies and figured that was where he should be. On a good day when he was feeling strong, it would take him most of the day to reach Denby from where he was. He figured age was beginning to catch up with him, and Hiram did not like the feeling.

He paused while making sure the pack was tied down securely, wondering exactly how old he was. Things like time and age had never meant much to him. When you were living in the wilderness, seasons passed and years came and went, but everything stayed the same. He did not even know what year his mother had given him birth.

He traveled slowly, resting frequently and hoping the feeling would pass. It was midday with the sun directly overhead when he neared Many Coup's village. Having already traded with the Pawnee earlier, he had planned to bypass their village and head directly to Denby, but he was feeling weaker and turned toward the small cluster of teepees. A hot meal and a good night's sleep might be just the thing he needed. The Pawnee were eager to see him as always, and welcomed him with open arms.

Upon hearing his old friend was not feeling well Blue Dog brought herbs mixed in warm water for him to drink, and shook his rattle while chanting magic over Hiram. He thanked Blue Dog and promised he felt better already. Instead, Hiram found himself rushing to a clump of bushes an hour before sunset to relieve himself. His stool was nothing but brown water and his fever was growing worse. He sat on a log, trying to regain control of his mind. He vaguely remembered refilling his canteen a day earlier from a stagnant pool and thinking the water tasted funny. Drinking stagnant water was something he never did, but he had run out of water and it had been a particularly warm day.

He slowly made his way back to the village and accepted a bowl of stew from one of the ladies. He sat on a pallet of buffalo robes inside Blue Dog's teepee and spooned a few sips of broth into his mouth. Blue Dog mixed more herbs and said more chants but nothing seemed to help. Many Coup came to visit, as well as Black Crow, and they passed around the pipe as they made small talk. Hiram was growing continually weaker and the fever was worse. The last cogent thought passing through Hiram's fever-ridden brain was the one word that he had been refusing to acknowledge throughout the day, *cholera*. He had known Many Coup and Blue Dog quite a few years, and considered them his close friends. Hiram might have thought it funny, if it wasn't so tragically ironic. He had done his best to protect his red brothers from the evils of the white man, and unwittingly had been the one to bring the deadly disease into their camp. He prayed God would forgive him as the delirium overtook him.

CHAPTER 62

Taree'uus woke early to the sound of wailing. She quickly slipped into her buckskin dress before nudging Kaatit awake. Normally, her husband's movement would have been what woke her. She found it odd that on this particular morning, when the mourner's wail sounded in the camp, that Black Crow should be the one needing to be awakened.

"What's wrong?" He wiped a hand across his face and leaned on one elbow before falling back to the buffalo robe.

"Listen," she said. "Something is wrong. I must go."

Tarree'uus left Black Crow still lying in bed and followed the wailing toward Blue Dog's teepee. A small cluster of mourners were gathered. She took Taaka' by the arm and pulled her aside.

"What is wrong? Why is everyone singing the mourner's song?"

"It is the old trapper. He has brought an evil spirit of sickness among us. He died during the night and now the evil spirit has possessed my father and mother."

Tarree'uus pulled the flap of the teepee open and entered. The stench of dysentery and vomit was almost overpowering. Hiram Jenkins' cold corpse still lay on the buffalo robe where he had died. Blue Dog and his wife were lying next to each other shivering. She lay a hand against the old man's brow to find him burning with fever.

"Dear God help us." The prayer escaping her lips was an honest one. Abigail had seen this sickness once before when she was twelve years old. A neighbor living in a small house at the edge of the badlands had come begging for help. Her husband had returned from a hunting trip burning up with fever. Abigail had watched as her mother and father attended to the ailing man and remembered them calling the sickness cholera. They were not able to save the man, but had kept his wife and her children from catching the sickness. She prayed again that God would help her remember what measures her parents had taken.

She exited the teepee to find that nearly everyone in the village had gathered, and they all had their expectant faces glued toward her. Blue Dog, their powerful medicine man, had been stricken with an evil spirit of sickness, and she was next in line. She had shown great powers of healing in the past and now they were looking to her for answers.

"Grey Fox," she called toward a tall lanky youth standing at the edge of the crowd. "Do you know the way to the valley where I was born…where my white mother now lives?"

The boy nodded.

"Good. Take Walking Horse and go. Tell my white mother of the sickness. Tell her it is important that she comes immediately. She has powerful medicine and can help. Hurry now."

She waited until the boys had ridden out of the village before re-entering the teepee. Her first order of business was to dispose of Hiram Jenkins' body. She had several men carry him a distance from the camp and cover him with stones. She then told them to do a ceremonial bathing in the swift-running creek. Next, she ordered the buffalo robe which Hiram had been using as a bed to be burnt, as it had contacted the evil spirit. Blue Dog and his wife both died around midday, and she repeated the orders as Taaka' wailed the traditional mourner's prayer. They were supposed to be moving the camp this morning and going home. This wasn't supposed to happen.

It wasn't until mid-afternoon that someone brought her word that her own husband, Black Crow, and several others, including Many Coup, had been stricken with the same evil spirit. The cholera had taken root in the small tight-knit village where everyone was considered family and often shared food and clothing. Abigail worked and prayed like she had never done before. It had been eight long years since her parents had helped the neighbor. She racked her tired brain trying to remember every detail about their treatment of the disease. Taree'uus knelt beside her husband and bathed his fevered brow with cool water, praying, and desperately needing her mother.

CHAPTER 63

Silas Norton leaned against the rotting cottonwood log and laughed hysterically. He paused and stared at the figures across the campfire and laughed some more. From where he sat, it looked as though Wah Lee and Tuck were sitting in the middle of the fire drinking from the same bottle. Tuck took a long pull from the bottle then passed it on to Wah Lee and laughed.

"Hell, the son-of-a-bitch is crazy as a loony bird," Tuck said, wiping his lips against his shirtsleeve.

"Can't handle the Chinaman's magic seeds, that's for sure," Pox said with a snort.

"Yeah, that's what it is…magic," Silas said, waving his hand in the sky. "I see elves dancing in the fire. Big elves, a black one and a yellow one." He tilted his head back and roared with laughter.

"What the hell's he talking about?" Tuck asked with a growl.

"He thinks we are inside the fire," Wah Lee said, passing the bottle to Pox.

"Well, I just might open his head for him, and let the pixies out," Tuck growled.

"Hell, let him be. That pipe's making him see things," Pox said, then paused to take a long swallow from the bottle. He gasped and passed the bottle back. "Besides, we might need him as a distraction when we visit the widow. When we're finished with her and her friend Denning, you can do whatever you want with him."

Silas heard the words but they didn't register or cause him concern. He had taken his first drag from Wah Lee's opium pipe a week earlier, merely out of curiosity to see what the big deal was. The rush to his head, along with the feeling of floating in air, had caused him to desire even more. The joy of smoking the pipe had become a ritual with him to pass the boredom of sitting around the rundown cabin with his new-found friends. The stolen cattle more or less took care of themselves in the small canyon, which left them with nothing to do. He missed the busy life and friends he had in Denby. The boredom had been driving Silas crazy, until he tried Wah Lee's pipe.

The feeling caused by the opium had grown stronger with each experience, and tonight was even better. He was a little boy and the world was made out of candy. It all belonged to him. He was floating high over the meager campfire in front of the cabin, looking down and seeing his own body leaned against the log, laughing. The scene was so hysterical, it caused him to laugh even harder.

"Come on, let me share." Rose scooted close and took the pipe stem from his hand to draw deeply. "Ah, yeah," she sighed and leaned her matted head against Silas' shoulder. Silas looked at her, and she was suddenly beautiful. The whole world was beautiful, and there was music floating inside his head. He had no idea where it had come from. He just knew it was beautiful.

"I wanna dance." He jumped to his feet and grabbed Rose by the arm. "Come on, dance with me Rose."

"Dance? There isn't any music to dance with." Rose said with a whine that Silas normally found irritating but tonight, even it sounded beautiful.

"Sure there's music," he said, looking skyward and spinning in a circle. "Can't you hear it? There's music all around us. You can hear it, can't you Pox?"

"Sure, there's plenty of music," the rustler said with a laugh. "Go ahead and dance with him, Rose."

"Yeah, now I can hear it." Rose staggered forward and gripped Silas by the arms, breathing heavily in his face. "Let's dance."

The two staggered in a crazy dance, laughing and pawing at each other as the three rustlers cheered and urged them on. Silas felt powerful and happy. He was the best dancer of the lot, and was holding the most beautiful woman in the world in his arms. She must love him, because her hands were roaming all over his body, making him feel even more powerful and happy.

"Take your clothes off and let's dance naked under the stars," Rose said, as she unbuttoned her dress and kicked it aside. In a matter of seconds, the two were staggering in the same crazy dance stark naked, as they fondled each other. Silas didn't feel the chill of the night air as he danced, and didn't mind the laughter and cheers coming from the opposite side of the fire. He finally gave into Rose's urging and laid on the ground as the whore had her way with him. She was beautiful. The world was beautiful, and Silas was happy.

CHAPTER 64

Charlene was slicing onions, carrots and potatoes in preparation for chicken soup when she heard the pounding of unshod hooves. She glanced toward the window in time to see two young Indians dismount and dash onto the porch. One of them banged on the front door with his fist.

"What in the world…?" Charlene laid the butcher knife aside and opened the kitchen door. The boys rushed forward speaking rapidly in Pawnee.

"Whoa, hold on there," she said raising her palms. "Slow down. Now you," she pointed toward Grey Fox, "I know you know a little English. Tell me what's wrong."

"Taree'uus send for mother. Bad sickness. Come quick."

"Katherine is with Phillip and the boys in the winter canyon. You'll have to go fetch her." She pointed toward the trail leading to the canyon. "I'll pack some things while you go. Wait…," she said as they started to leave. "What kind of a sickness is it? How do the sick people feel?"

The conversation between the boys was rapid and animated, with Walking Horse mimicking someone in the throes of heaving his dinner.

"Old man called Hiram brings evil sickness when he comes. His skin is like the fire and his…his stomach…" Grey Fox finally gave up trying to find the correct word himself and mimicked Walking Horse's portrayal.

"I got that. What else. Are their bowels loose?"

The boy blinked several times and stared at her.

"Does he use the bathroom a lot, and is it runny…like water?"

Both boys nodded.

"Go get Katherine and Phillip. This is a bad sickness and we must go."

Charlene didn't know for sure what might be ailing the people, but she had been around Indians enough to know it didn't take much to devastate a small village. A simple cold could cause havoc. What the boys were describing sounding like influenza, or maybe worse. Charlene had seen an influenza outbreak wipe out nearly half the population in a Sioux village when George was alive. One of the officers at the fort had called the outbreak ghastly, and she reckoned it was as good a description as any.

The boys leaped on their ponies and raced out of the yard. Charlene grabbed her shopping basket and began stuffing it with anything she thought might be helpful. She was just finishing the task when the entire family including Phillip rode into the yard looking dusty and tired. Katherine almost ran into the kitchen and stopped to stare at the heavily-laden basket on the table.

"I stuffed about everything I thought we might need, ma'am. It sounds like influenza, or maybe worse. I'm fixing to fill the other basket with food, if you don't mind. I figure you and the women at the village will be so busy with the sick, they might need a cook."

"You're an angel, Charlie. I don't know what I'd do without you."

"I don't know either, but we'd better rustle. It won't take long until those boys are the only survivors of that village."

~   ~   ~

Phillip and the boys had fresh mounts saddled and a team hitched to the wagon by the time she had finished packing. They helped load the wagon with food, medicine and blankets. Katherine sent Steven and Joshua to fetch Doctor Krucker. Katherine felt a twinge of guilt as they pulled out of the yard. She had been hoping and praying to see her daughter again, but had never dreamed it might be caused by something like this.

She prayed for God's mercy as the buckboard groaned and rocked over the rough ground, pitching the women from side to side. Grey Fox and Walking Horse soon grew impatient with the wagon and disappeared over a rise, not to be seen again until late in the afternoon when they finally pulled into the village.

Katherine sat next to Charlene staring at the scene. Women, young and old alike, were wailing the mourner's cry as bodies were being carried from teepees to the cemetery. The bodies were hoisted upward and placed on elevated beds toward the heavens. The stench of death was everywhere.

"Oh my God, Charlie, it's worse than anything I've seen or imagined," Katherine said, grabbing her wrist. The maid grew teary-eyed and nodded. "Come on, we'd better lend a hand."

Taaka' appeared from no where and grabbed Katherine by the hand. She led her toward a decorated teepee as Charlene barked orders to the boys. She entered the tent to find Abby kneeling beside her husband. She was mopping his brow with cool water and talking softly as the boys played quietly on a buffalo robe on the opposite side of the teepee. She knelt beside her daughter and slipped an arm around her.

"How is he?"

"Dying. He knows he's dying, Mama. That old man brought cholera into our village. We are a close people and share many things. Many Coup and Black Crow smoked the peace pipe with him last night. So did Blue Dog. I know he was our friend and didn't mean to, but Hiram killed us. Nearly everyone in the village has cholera, Mama. I've tried...but I can't stop it."

She sobbed and Katherine hugged her tightly and kissed her cheek.

"It looks like you've done a fine job, Abby. Now, I'll sit with your husband for awhile. You take my grandsons and see what Charlene has for them to eat."

"Charlie's here?" Abby asked in surprise.

"Certainly. The whole family is, including Phillip. We wouldn't leave you alone. I sent Steven and Joshua to fetch Doctor Krucker. He should be here soon. Now, run along while I visit my son-in-law."

~   ~   ~

They divided the village into sections, moving those who did not yet have symptoms into one area, with those who only had symptoms but not yet ill into another, and isolating the violently ill. Many Coup and Abigail's husband were both placed in the latter group.

Doctor Krucker arrived an hour before sunset and set to work immediately. Matthew and Joshua stretched a large tarp from the wagon between several trees as a makeshift shelter, and that was where Charlene set up headquarters. She enlisted the help of several Pawnee children and began the task of cooking several large stews.

With the arrival of Doctor Krucker, Taaka' had a chance to sit and rest. That was when exhaustion and the impact of losing both parents hit her. Steven held her in his arms while she cried and prayed, wishing her mother and father well in the next life. It did not matter that she had only seen thirteen winters. Blue Dog had been her father and taught her many things. That put her second next to Taree'uus as shaman in the village. The people would now look to her for spiritual advice and healing.

<h1 style="text-align:center">CHAPTER 65</h1>

Phillip sat beside Many Coup's pallet and rolled a cigarette. The old man's fever-ravaged body would soon give up and quit breathing. From the short time he had known the war chief, he admired the hell out of him. He had an inner strength and character Phillip had found lacking in most men, white or red. The chief was now awake and almost completely lucid. Phillip licked the paper and propped the cigarette between Many Coup's lips.

"You are good man, Denning," he said as Phillip struck a match and held it to the cigarette.

"There's some that would argue with you about that, Chief. I know I'd have to grow some to reach your stature."

He held the cigarette as Many Coup coughed, then returned it to his lips.

"I have fought many battles, Denning, and won them all. This is one battle I cannot win."

"Maybe, but I'd venture to say you'll win."

"No, I am dying, my friend. I have seen the other side and I will soon join my grandfather. I cannot win this time."

"But you already have. You led your people well. Look at your daughter and your grandsons. They are fine people and they carry a lot of you inside. They will remember you and act accordingly. I don't have anyone to remember me. So, I'd say you won."

"You must take a woman, Denning. A man should be remembered for what he is." He coughed and it took him a minute to catch his breath.

"We both were good warriors, Denning. It would have been good to ride into battle with you."

"It would have been better than riding against you. I wouldn't have wanted to be in that fix. I think I might've lost that one."

"It would have been a good fight, my friend." He coughed again and lay quiet several minutes. Phillip tossed the cigarette away and was about to leave when the old man gripped his hand.

"My daughter, Tarree'uus. I must say goodbye."

"Is it time to cross over, Many Coup?"

"It is time."

CHAPTER 66

Doctor's Log: 28 July, 1893
Attending Physician: Benjamin A. Krucker
Pawnee Village, approximately five miles northwest of Flying K Ranch, Denby South Dakota. Case: Severe cholera outbreak.

I was informed of the outbreak approximately 11:45 a.m. on the 28th of July by Steven Parker inside my office. I immediately cleared my calendar of all appointments, and having loaded all available medical supplies I deemed necessary into the buggy, my wife and I followed young Steven to the village, arriving approximately mid-afternoon.

We found that one Abigail Susana Parker, wife of Pawnee War Chief Black Crow, had already taken steps to isolate the disease. She was being assisted by her mother, Katherine Eleanor Parker, Katherine's sons, Matthew Henry Parker, Joshua Laurence Parker and Timothy Eugene Parker. They were also being assisted by Katherine's housekeeper, Charlene Georgina Thompson and ranch hand Phillip Anthony Denning. The young Pawnee girl called Taaka', daughter of the Pawnee medicine man, Blue Dog, and Steven Michael Parker also assisted as much as we would allow.

The outbreak is suspected of being introduced by one Hiram Jenkins, a trapper by trade. Mr. Jenkins died sometime during the previous night and was buried. Medicine man Blue Dog and his wife passed mid-morning and were buried according to traditional Pawnee custom. Leading war chief, Many Coup, passed approximately eight o'clock on the *evening of the 28th. Second war chief, Black Crow, and husband of Abigail Susana Parker, passed approximately ten-twenty-nine, the evening of the 28th. Those who were not ill mourned their passing greatly, and I have no doubt these men will be remembered for several generations, perhaps even longer. Their leadership among their people will certainly be deemed a success by the survivors.*

The effects of the disease began dissipating by noon of the third day, but the devastation it caused will forever be etched in our minds. In all, out of a village of thirty-five Pawnee, counting women and children, only eight survivors remain, including Abigail Susana, her children, and the Pawnee girl known as Taaka'. I have not listed all the dead at this point, but will log their names after Abigail and Taaka' have finished their period of mourning, and are able to assist me in the task. Katherine Parker wept bitterly when the plague was ceased. So did we all.

Benjamin A. Krucker, M.D.

CHAPTER 67

At the urging of her mother, Abigail finally relented and moved the survivors to the ranch. Doctor Krucker came just short of demanding that all teepees, buffalo robes and any items that could possibly be burnt be put to the torch in order to halt any future outbreak of the disease.

"I simply cannot destroy every sentiment or memory of their past, Doctor Krucker. These people have been through enough as it is," Abby said.

He finally allowed them to keep the items that could be boiled in water, and several of the smaller teepees, with the promise they would be scrubbed with soap and hot water once they reached the ranch.

Katherine's heart ached for her daughter like she had never known. There had been little time for either Abby or Taaka' to mourn their losses. The few remaining members of the village had immediately begun looking to them for guidance, and they had proven themselves equal to the task. Her own experience told her that both girls would soon feel the crushing weight of pain once everyone had settled into some sort of routine at the ranch. It had taken several days for the loss of James to fully hit Katherine. The emptiness grew to unbearable proportions in the middle of the night, especially in the middle of the winter when the canyon winds blew against her bedroom window. Watching the two young women organize and lead the small band toward the ranch, Katherine decided the most she could do was pray for them and make herself available when that time came.

~   ~   ~

Rebecca's parents and Doctor Krucker insisted they postpone Matthew and Rebecca's wedding until late August, in order to give Abigail and the Pawnee children a chance to adjust to their losses. Katherine wasted no time in getting the young Pawnee men acclimated to ranch life and refused to allow a small barrier such as language to stand in his way. She used Taaka' and Abby as interpreters, which Charlene thought was a good thing, for it allowed little time for brooding. Charlene agreed to watch Abby's boys, but the energetic youngsters proved to be too much for her to handle and still meet the demands of cooking and cleaning for the increased family. Abby, Taaka and Katherine decided to split their time watching the children in order to give the woman a reprieve.

The sleeping arrangements were handled by the use of the teepees. Katherine however, quickly deemed them impractical, especially considering the past winter. She sent Matthew and Joshua into town to hire several carpenters to construct a large addition onto the main house, over Abigail's protest.

"Mother, you have no idea how strong or warm a teepee can be. They can withstand a gale-force wind if they are constructed right."

"I don't care. I am not allowing my daughter and grandsons, or those precious children out there, to sleep in tents in the middle of the winter, especially while I am sleeping in a warm bed. Besides, I'm your mother, so don't argue with me."

CHAPTER 68

A week after Abigail had moved to the ranch, Katherine looked out her kitchen window to see her daughter kneeling inside the cemetery. She placed her freshly poured mug of coffee on the table and made her way toward the kneeling figure. She paused at the opened gate to listen. The words pouring from her daughter were Pawnee, mingled with an occasional sob. Katherine moved silently to kneel beside her daughter.

"What happened, Mama?"

"Your father seemed to pine away and quit living. We looked for you from sunup to sundown seven days a week for more than a month. We even had the help of dozens of people from town. You were simply gone. If we had had just a clue…a body….anything, it might have been different. We found your horse, but not you. There was nothing." She looked at her daughter through watery eyes. "Your father couldn't stand not knowing."

She sniffed.

"I overheard Mr. Denning telling your brothers he suspects your father had sent you out that morning and blamed himself for what happened. Maybe that's true. I don't know. I only know he was dead long before he quit breathing. He didn't seem to care about me or your brothers or the ranch…. I almost hated him for a long time."

She sniffed again and smiled.

"I'm over that now. I miss him, and feel sorry."

She sat quietly listening to Abby cry, and finally asked, "What happened, honey? Tell me about it."

"Daddy had asked me to check the east range for strays. He was worried we might have missed some. The storm hit all at once, and I was caught in it. I was so cold, Mama. I couldn't see and it was hard to breathe. I kept trying to find my way home. I was riding Sally, my little grey mare. She was a good horse, but even she didn't know where we were. She finally just stopped and toppled over. I tried to get her up, but couldn't. She just laid there, Mama. It was so cold. I finally snuggled up beside her, praying for someone to find me, and wishing the cold would stop."

She sniffed and Katherine gave her a handkerchief.

"I woke up with strange faces staring at me. They were speaking a language I couldn't understand. I knew they were Indians and I was scared. I tried to scream, but I couldn't make a sound. I was scared, Mama." She grabbed Katherine's arm and squeezed it tightly. "I was only a little girl!"

"Anyway, when I finally got where I could talk, I couldn't understand them, and I couldn't make them understand me either. All I wanted to do was cry. Many Coup's first wife, Buffalo Woman, used to beat me, trying to get me to stop…but I couldn't. Finally, Many Coup made her stop. He was a kind man, and spent hours trying to teach me, and learn English. He finally made me understand they found me frozen. He said they had also found my family all dead. I was the only one who lived. I finally understood that must be true, because no one had come for me. I was alone, except for these Indians."

She heaved a great sigh. "I woke the next morning, knowing you and Daddy must be dead, and were never going to come. And if I was going to survive, I had to become Pawnee. I learned to speak and think Pawnee. I learned to cook and became Many Coup's daughter. I called him father, and he treated me well. One day the men were on a hunt and one of the boys had gotten bit by a spider. I remembered how you use to pack a poultice of baking soda on insect bites to draw the poison out, so I made one out of clay and dry herbs and packed the bite. I also prayed real hard to Jesus. When the men returned the women told Taaka's father that I had made medicine and chanted magic over the boy. He removed the poultice to discover the swelling was gone, and the boy was fine. Blue Dog declared I had returned from the spirit world with great magic, and I became second shaman in the village.

"Many Coup gave me to be Black Crow's wife, which was a great honor." She stopped to stare at her mother.

"You have no idea what it was like, Mama." I was only fourteen when I became his wife. I was a little girl and was frightened to death of him. I was Pawnee though, and I had to become his wife. He was good to me, and only beat me twice. I learned to be a good wife and keep him happy. He loved me, Mama, and I learned to love him. I wish Daddy could have known him."

"I am so sorry, Baby." Katherine folded Abby in her arms and cried until she could find no more tears. They wiped their eyes and blew their noses, using the same handkerchief and laughed at their predicament. They started toward the house arm in arm but stopped when they realized Phillip Denning had been standing quietly by the cemetery gate.

"Mr. Denning," Katherine said. "How long have you been standing there?"

"Long enough."

"Oh, please excuse us," she said, and started to leave.

"Aren't you forgetting something, ma'am?"

"What would that be, Mr. Denning?"

"What would you like me and the boys to do with Abigail's marker? Since she's standing right beside you, there isn't much sense in keeping it here. Besides, it's not everyone who gets to remove their daughter's headstone. It's sort of like witnessing a resurrection, isn't it, ma'am?"

"Yes, I suppose it is, Mr. Denning. I'll let Abigail make that decision, and I'm sure she'll let you know."

CHAPTER 69

The Denby Grange Hall was a large building with a wooden floor and a raised platform at one end to accommodate speakers or, as on occasions like this, local musicians. The hall had been built for the farmers and cattlemen to conduct their business, but had gradually been pushed into service as a community center. She had no idea how many tons of wheat, maze and soybeans had been sold inside the building. Katherine herself had made quite a bit of money buying and selling cattle and horses not too far from where she was presently seated. She had also heard several speeches given by red-faced politicians hoping to be elected, and a few traveling evangelists out to snatch souls from the fires of hell, but tonight was no such night. Tonight, a makeshift orchestra consisting of three violins, two guitars, a slightly out of tune upright piano and a bass-player had taken center stage.

Katherine heaved a sigh and allowed her eyes to survey the room as the musicians pounded out a lively version of *Skip To My Lou*. Taaka' had caused a minor stir when she entered the hall dressed in one of Abby's white gowns. She fearfully clung to Steven's arm amid stares and whispers, and she refused to ease her grip as he got two glasses of punch. He had finally gotten her to relax by dragging her onto the dance floor and skipping around the room to the beat of the music. Katherine grinned politely and nodded her greetings toward the townspeople, realizing that the girl would have to deal with the whispers and disdainful looks for the rest of her life.

Katherine took a sip of punch and craned her neck, trying to get a better view of one particular couple. It was difficult to get a view of the entire floor from where she was seated beside Charlene. She relaxed when her efforts were rewarded, as Matthew spun across the dance floor holding Rebecca Jordan in his arms. The girl looked radiant in her white dress and black slippers. Her long chestnut hair had been pulled back and held in place with a black satin ribbon to compliment the slippers. Katherine sighed again as they passed near her.

Charlene leaned close to her ear in order to be heard over the piano, and asked loudly, "They make a handsome couple, don't they?"

"Yes, they certainly do," she said, raising her voice.

"Matt dances pretty well. Where'd he learn?"

"I taught him."

"Well now," Charlene said, shifting to study her face, "I learn something new about you every day. I just found out that Katherine Eleanor Parker isn't just cattle and business. She knows how to dance."

"I did have a life before coming to South Dakota, Charlie," Katherine said with a snort. "I wasn't born old, with a litter of rowdy boys and a ranch to take care of."

"You're far from being old, Katie," Charlene said with a laugh. "Try living inside my body for awhile."

The music stopped and the dancers drifted to different parts of the building to await the next tune. Matthew and Rebecca took chairs next to Katherine and the girl sat fanning herself, trying to catch her breath. Katherine studied her profile a minute before patting the girl's arm.

"You dance very well...both of you. And you look lovely, as usual."

"Thank you, Mrs. Parker. So do you."

The music started and Matthew jumped to his feet to offer Rebecca his hand.

"No, let me catch my breath. Why don't you ask your mother to dance?"

"Wanna take a spin, Ma?"

"Well now," she said with a crooked grin as she handed her glass of punch to Rebecca, "I would love to dance with my son." She brushed a few wrinkles out of her skirt and took Matthew's hand. They were about to step onto the dance floor when Phillip Denning approached.

"Huh, I was about to ask you to dance, but I see this handsome lad beat me to it." He eyed Matthew from head to foot and grinned. "The boy cleans up pretty good when he dudes up, don't you think, Miss Rebecca? He ought to put on the good hoof more often."

"Do you dance, Mr. Denning?" Katherine asked as Rebecca giggled.

"Some." He slipped past her and took Charlene's hand. "I'll show you if this handsome woman will accompany me onto the floor."

"I certainly will, if you don't mind my bum leg." Charlene jumped to her feet and followed him onto the floor. Katherine watched her housekeeper and hired hand until she was pulled onto the dance floor herself.

"What's the matter, Ma? You don't mind if Mr. Denning dances with Charlie, do you?" Matthew asked.

"No, I was just surprised to learn he dances. I guess he must have had another life too."

"What?" Matthew scrunched his face as he swung his mother to the right in rhythm to *High, Betty Martin* as the fiddles screeched. She moved easily across the floor as the caller called the dance moves.

> *Ducks in the river, goin' to the ford,*
> *Coffee in a little rag, sugar in a gourd.*
>
> *Swing 'em once an' let 'em go,*
> *All hands left an' do-ce-do.*

"Nothing, just something Charlie and I were talking about," she said as they moved closer.

She could only catch glimpses of Phillip and Charlene as the couples passed on the floor. There was little doubt the housekeeper was having the time of her life. It was evident that the man was a charmer as well as a good dancer. The music ended and they made their way back toward their seats. It was plain that Rebecca was feeling rested, as she immediately slipped her arm through one of Matthew's and hugged it tightly.

"Now, may I?"

Katherine glanced up at Phillip's voice to see he was offering her his hand.

"Yes, Mr. Denning. I believe you may." She took his hand as the band began play *Paper of Pins*. He held hers lightly and placed his right hand against her waist, using just enough pressure to help guide her across the floor.

First couple to the right,
Cage the bird, three hands 'round,
Birdie hop out an' crane hop in,
Three hands 'round an' go it again.

She was amazed at how easily the man moved to the rhythm of the music. He seemed to glide, rather than shuffle, and she suddenly found herself lost inside the melody and the gentle touch of his hands. The music ended all too soon for her, and Phillip escorted her back to her chair.

"Thank you, Mr. Denning. You are a wonderful dancer."

"So are you, ma'am," he said with a warm smile. "Hope we can do it again sometime."

"I'd love to…" She let her voice trail off as he took Rebecca Jordan by the hand.

"But first, I'm gonna steal Matt's gal for a few minutes." He pulled the giggling girl to the dance floor as the band began playing *Go Tell Aunt Rhody*.

"Well, looks as though he's making the rounds tonight," Charlene said with a chuckle.

"Yes, indeed he is," Katherine agreed. She watched as he swung Rebecca easily through the lively steps and across the crowded floor.

"Well there's my gal," Sheriff Crutchfield said, slipping through the crowd and offering his hand to Charlene. "I thought maybe a couple of old folks could teach these young-uns' a thing or two about dancing. Care to take a spin with me?"

"It's about time, Bill Crutchfield. I thought you'd forgotten all about me," she said, taking his hand with a big grin.

"Not hardly. You wouldn't let me if I tried." He laughed and danced her onto the floor.

Katherine suddenly found herself being dragged onto the floor by a dusty-looking cowboy she had never met, and although the man tried desperately, he couldn't dance a lick. She found it an effort to keep from having her feet trampled beneath his well-worn boots. That seemed to set the pace for the rest of the evening, as she found herself being pulled onto the floor by different men, most of whom Katherine suspected learned how to dance either inside a saloon, or not at all. She began to think the evening couldn't get any worse, when a drunken cowboy stepped fully on her right foot, causing her to cry out in pain.

"Gosh, I'm sorry, lady. Where're ya going?" he asked loudly as she limped toward the nearest door. "Ma'am?" he said reaching for her arm, but Katherine brushed the hand away.

"It's okay. Just…leave me alone for a minute.

The door opened onto a rear patio where cattlemen and farmers normally drank and smoked while they discussed informally what was taking place inside the building. She leaned against the railing and gulped the cool night air into her lungs, trying to will the pain in her crushed toes to go away.

"Are you okay?" She jerked around to see Phillip hovering over her.

"Actually no, I'm not. I think every toe in my right foot just got broken."

"Yeah, I saw. Sit on the bench and let me have a look."

"I beg your pardon?" she said haughtily.

"I would like to see how bad your toes are," he said, forcing her down onto the bench. He knelt in front of her to unbutton and remove her slipper, then stopped as several people crowded close for a better look.

"Would you mind?" Phillip barked loudly.

"We was just wondering…" one young cowboy with a giggling girl hanging on his sleeve began, but Phillip waved him away.

"Go wonder somewhere else and give the lady some privacy!"

"What's he doing?" some one asked as they crowded back inside.

"Don't know," came the reply. "My guess is he's proposing."

"Sorry," he said to Katherine with a chuckle. "People are curious critters."

"Why, may I ask, do you wish to see my foot?"

"Because, if the skin is broken, you could be bleeding inside your shoe."

"I'm sorry, I didn't think of that." She grimaced and gave a short cry as the shoe came off.

"I'm sorry, I know it hurts." He held her foot in his hand to examine the damage. "Well, there's no bleeding. Let me see you wiggle your toes." He gave a short nod as she obeyed.

He stared at the white stocking covering her foot and gave a crooked grin.

"Ah, perhaps you'd better remove the stocking yourself."

"I certainly will not!"

"Well, my eyesight isn't good enough to see your foot with it on, so you'll have to, that is unless you'd like me to take it off." He hiked the hem of her skirt just slightly, and she caught her breath.

"Mr. Denning, I'll do it myself! You'll have to close your eyes or turn away."

"Okay, how's this?" he asked, staring toward the sky. "Sure a pretty moon tonight. Did you happen to notice?"

"No I didn't. You may look at my toes now."

"Yes, ma'am." He cradled her foot in his hands and examined it closely.

"Well, doctor, what's the verdict?"

"I don't think he actually broke your toes, but you've got a nasty bruise and it'll be sore for a few days."

"It's your fault. You realize that, don't you?"

Phillip gazed at her as he massaged her foot. "I don't quite follow you. How is it my fault that Nevada stomped your foot?"

"Was that the boy's name?"

"Yes, ma'am."

"If you had not wandered off dancing with every woman in the building, I would have been dancing with you and would not have gotten trampled by that herd of men inside," she said matter-of-factly.

"Well, I suppose that might have a little truth in it. I remember my pa saying I should ask every woman to dance at least once, because some of them never get asked, and they can't be having a good time. Besides, think of all the men you made happy tonight, by allowing them to dance with the prettiest woman in the building."

"Now, that has to be the biggest line of hogwash I've ever heard, Mr. Denning."

"What, my dancing with women who never get asked, or you dancing with every man in Denby?"

"No, Mr. Denning. About me being the prettiest woman in the building," she said with a short laugh.

He stopped massaging her foot and gazed at the starlit sky as she worked the stocking back over her bruised foot.

"Well, ask yourself this. Why was it that every man in the building was fighting to get you onto the floor?"

"They didn't at first. I sat beside Charlie for quite awhile until you and Matthew asked me to dance."

"That's because they didn't think you would dance with them. There's a rumor going around that you don't particularly like men. Some are saying you even tried to shoot a man simply because he proposed to you."

"Ah, that's not true!" she said indignantly.

"You didn't try to shoot anyone?"

"No…well, I did threaten a couple of men with Charlie's shotgun, but they deserved it." She clenched her teeth and glared as he laughed.

"They were uncouth and vulgar men who actually deserved to be shot for the things they said to me."

"I have no doubt that is true, and I would probably have whupped 'em if I'd been around at the time. But, Miss Kate," he said taking a seat beside her, "they were afraid you didn't want to dance with them, and that's why no one asked. But once they saw me dance with you, I would've had to shoot a couple of them to get another chance with you. That's why I didn't ask you again."

"Really? And did you want to dance with me again, Mr. Denning?"

"Certainly, but seeing that foot, I don't guess you'll be dancing for a few days."

He put the slipper back on and stood to offer his hand with a warm smile.

"Come on, let's go join the others before Charlene thinks I've kidnapped you."

~   ~   ~

Katherine wrung the washcloth semi-dry and bathed her face and neck, savoring its coolness. She dipped it again into the porcelain washbasin, then ran it across her breasts and under her arms, and repeated the process several times, bathing her tired body as best she could before slipping into her nightgown. The noisy alarm clock on the nightstand said it was fifteen minutes past midnight when she stretched her tired body in the bed and pulled the blanket up to her waist.

There was no crack in the hotel ceiling for her to study, so Katherine remained awake until the early hours of the morning, replaying her dance with Phillip over and over again in her mind. She could feel his hand against her waist as he guided her across the floor and his gentle fingers as he massaged her feet. What seemed to matter most was that he had said she was the prettiest woman in the room. She knew it was vain, and it mattered little to her whether or not he actually believed she was that pretty. Phillip Denning had said it, and that's what seemed to matter at the moment. She suddenly found herself wanting to return to his arms and allow him to guide her across the dance floor once again. There was another dance scheduled at the Grange Hall next month. Perhaps she could persuade him to attend that one also. If he did, she would certainly handle herself differently. If what he said about his father and the cowboys who danced with her was true, there would be a lot of lonely people inside the room that evening, for she planned to monopolize Phillip Denning's time from the beginning tune to the last.

CHAPTER 70

Pox Tivo sat on his horse shielded from view by a thin growth of cottonwood trees, and watched as the stage crept into view. He had picked the perfect spot. The driver always slowed the mules to a walk while rounding the hairpin curve in order to cross the creek directly in front of where Pox was sitting. One Wells Fargo driver carrying a full strongbox, and knowing the spot was a favorite spot for bandits, decided not to slow for the turn and overturned the coach. There happened to be no bandits on that particular day, and several passengers were hurt, including the guard, whose shotgun discharged during the accident and killed him. Since then, orders had been given for the drivers to slow to a walk, regardless of the amount inside the cashbox.

"Okay, get ready," Pox said, as he pulled and cocked his rifle. "I'll get the guard and you can have the driver."

He took careful aim through a small clearing between several branches, and squeezed the trigger. The guard lurched in the seat and slumped as the shotgun clattered to the hard-packed road. The driver yelled and slapped the reins in an effort to flee. A bullet from Tuck's rifle sent him pitching completely off the coach to land in a pile of dried tumbleweeds. The mules labored under the heavy load as they rounded the curve, where Wah Lee and Silas Norton appeared from the thick growth lining the creek and grabbed the lead animals, bringing the coach to a halt.

One of the passengers leaned through a window to point a pistol at Wah Lee, but another shot from Pox's rifle killed him before he could pull the trigger. Tuck jerked the door open and grabbed a young pregnant woman, pulling her to the ground. She screamed and he gave her a hard slap across the mouth.

"Shut your mouth, bitch!"

"Alright, the rest of you," Pox yelled, "outside...now!" He climbed off his horse and waited as a gray-headed woman and a petite teenage girl with a full head of chestnut hair climbed out of the coach. They were followed by a middle-aged man with blood splattered across his cheek and jacket.

"Line up against the stage," Pox said as he pointed with the rifle. "You too, ma'am," he added with a glance toward the pregnant woman.

"You heard the man, get over there," Tuck yelled. When she continued to sit on the ground crying, he grabbed her by the arm and flung her against the stage.

"Okay, now that's better," Pox said with a toothless grin. He paused as Silas tossed the dead guard to the ground and heaved the strongbox down with a loud grunt.

"Sounds heavy, don't it?" he asked the passengers with a chuckle. "Now Tuck is going to check you for guns and valuables while I open the box. I would advise you to give him anything you have when he asks for it, because he gets kinda mean when people don't do as he says. Ain't that right, missy?" he asked the pregnant woman with a chuckle.

The middle-aged woman gave a short scream as Pox blew the lock off the strongbox, then leaned heavily against the coach as Tuck jerked her handbag away and dumped its contents on the ground. The glass mirror inside her compact crunched under his heavy foot as he jerked the small handbag from the teenage girl. He then belted the man in the stomach when he protested having to hand his billfold over. Tuck took the billfold and pocket watch, then cleaned out his pockets.

"Oooeee! We hit the jackpot. Look at this, Tuck," Silas yelled as he allowed several gold coins to dribble through his fingers.

"Yes sir, we'll be living good tonight," Pox said. He tossed a stack of legal papers and bank notes aside and closed the lid on the strongbox. You boys un-hitch one of the mules and tie the box on so we can get out of here."

"What are we going to do about them, Pox? They know what we look like," Tuck said with a growl.

"Well now you're right, Tuck. They do know what we look like, don't they? Now, that's never bothered me too much, but I get your point. Especially the pregnant one. We just can't leave a pregnant woman stranded out here in this heat, can we? What do you suppose we can do about her?"

"Huh, that's simple enough," Tuck said and plunged a hunting knife into the woman's stomach. The teenager screamed as the woman crumbled to the ground with a groan.

"Well now, that wasn't exactly what I had in mind, but it does solve the problem, don't it?" Pox snorted and chuckled. "Hey Wah Lee, you get the old woman. What do you want to do with her?"

The Chinaman paused tying the strongbox to the mule to glance at the woman, before drawing his pistol and shooting her. He then returned to securing the strongbox to the mule.

"You have to excuse Wah Lee. He doesn't talk much, but he gets the job done. Now, what about you?" Pox caressed the teenager's cheek with his grimy fingers. "What do you suppose we could do with you? You're closer to her age, Silas. What do you think?"

"Take her with us. Then there'll be two women."

"Yeah," Pox laughed loudly, "I thought that's what you'd say. You go with us," he said and flung the girl toward Silas.

He stared at the man who was just now regaining his breath. "That leaves only you." Pox swung the rifle around and pulled the trigger.

CHAPTER 71

"What is she doing?" Katherine asked, as Taaka' perched herself in the center of the children. They were seated in a circle on the living room floor.

"She's getting ready to tell a story. This is something I normally do, but I've asked her to be the storyteller tonight," Abby said.

Katherine listened intently, as the young girl began in her native tongue, using voice inflection and hand motion to capture the children's attention.

"She's telling of the Woman Who Became a Horse," Abby said, and began to interpret.

"There was a village, and the men decided to go on the warpath. Their journey took them several days toward the south. They came to a thickly wooded country, where they found wild horses, and among them was a spotted pony.

"One man caught the spotted pony and took care of it. He took it home, and instructed his wife to look after it, as if it were their chief. She obeyed her husband, and grew to like the horse very much. She took it where there was good grass. In the winter she cut young cottonwood shoots for it to eat, so that the horse was always fat. On cold, stormy nights, she would cover the horse with a blanket and stuff dry grass under the blanket, so the horse never got cold. The horse was always fine and sleek.

"One summer evening she went to where she had tied the horse, and she met a handsome-looking man, who had on a buffalo robe with a spotted horse pictured on it. He smelled fine, like the sweet grass and wilderness.

"She followed him until they came to where her husband had caught the horse, and the man said, 'You went with me. I am the horse you've been caring for.'

"She was glad, for she liked the horse. For several years they were together, and the woman gave birth to a spotted pony. When the pony was born, the woman discovered she had grown a tail like that of a horse. She also had long hair on her body. When the colt sucked, the woman stood like a horse.

"For several years they roamed where the sweet grass grew, and had more ponies that were all spotted. At home the man mourned for his lost wife. He could not understand why she would leave.

"The people went on a hunt to the same country many years afterward, and discovered these spotted ponies. They did not care to capture them, for among them was a strange looking animal. As they hunted and watched the horses for several days, they finally decided to catch them. The ponies were fast and hard to catch, but they finally caught them, all except for the woman, because she could run faster than them all. When they had finally caught her children, she gave in and was caught.

"People said, 'This is the woman who was lost.'

"And some said, 'No, it is not.'

"Her husband was sent for, and he recognized her immediately. He took his bow and arrows out and shot her dead, for he hated seeing his wife with the horse's tail. The other spotted ponies were kept, and as they increased, their offspring were also spotted. So the people had many spotted ponies."

Taaka' finished the tale with a fine flourish that received the nodded approval of Abigail and cheers from children. Abby turned toward Katherine with a grin and mischievous twinkle in her blue eyes.

"And that, Mother, is why we Pawnee have so many spotted ponies."

CHAPTER 72

Seventeen-year-old Geraldine Mc Kenney had listened to the Chinese laborers on her father's railroad crew speak of the existence of a seventh hell, but never knew what they had meant until she met the bandits who held up the stagecoach. She believed things couldn't get worse, when the ugly pock-scarred man had given her to the smelly young man named Silas and killed her father with his rifle. She had been terribly wrong. Her terror escalated the moment they reached the filthy cabin littered with empty liquor bottles and cans. A horrible looking woman with matted hair was sitting on the dirt floor and leaning against a crude log bench when they arrived. She took a drink from the bottle in her hand and staggered to her feet to glare at Geraldine.

"What the hell's she doing here, Pox? You went and found yourself another woman, did you? After all I've done for you, to hell with you! To hell with you all!" She ranted with slurred words and threw the almost empty bottle at the leader, who laughed as the projectile missed badly.

"Aw, shut the hell up, Rose. It was Silas that decided to bring her along. I'd just as soon have left her for the buzzards like we did the others. Besides, you can have her when we're done. Maybe you can make a good whore out of her, and we'll open our own stable."

"Really? And where in the hell you gonna get the money to do that?"

"We've got the money," Silas said, dropping the heavy cashbox on the ground. "And, we've got two girls…you and the new one. Maybe you can give her a few pointers."

"Maybe I can at that," the woman said, and grabbed the front of Geraldine's dress and gave it a jerk. Geraldine found herself on the ground as Rose ripped and tore at her clothing. The men laughed as she screamed and begged for help. Finally, her anger overcame her fear as the shock of losing her father wore down, and she fought back. The struggle only lasted a few seconds, before Geraldine realized she could easily overcome the crazy woman. She kicked Rose off, pounced on her, and hailed on her with her fists. Rose screamed and clawed at her with dirty fingernails, but Geraldine hardly felt the scratches as she pounded the dirty face time and time again. She was suddenly grabbed and pinned to the ground by Silas, who held her wrists in a steel-like grip. Rose wiped the blood from her nose against her soiled arm with several curses, then finished tearing at her clothes. Geraldine soon found herself stripped of all clothing, and what followed was unimaginable.

~   ~   ~

Geraldine woke in the smoky dawn with every inch of her bruised and battered body aching. She had been abused multiple times by the four men and the woman, who took pleasure in what she called special instructions. She was forced to endure and participate in things that had never crossed her mind, and was sure they had been invented only to torment her. She raised her head from the filthy pallet she was lying on, to find she had been tied to a spike driven into the log siding. She tugged at the knotted rope with her teeth, wishing her captors had killed her when they finished their torments. She uttered a whimper as a bug crawled across her bare leg, and bit her tongue as Silas stirred at the sound.

She was cold…very cold. One thin blanket had been tossed over her, barely covering her nude body. She prayed for the warm sunlight, then quickly changed and asked for death as the pock-faced man rolled over with a snort and smacked his lips. Rose crawled from beneath her blankets and staggered to the door. Geraldine could hear the woman as she relieved herself in front of the cabin. She came back inside and made sure to pass in front of her on her way back to her own blankets, taking time to kick at Geraldine with her dirty toes as she passed. Gerry had never known what it felt like to really hate anyone in her short life. Her mother and father had made sure she had no need to. She decided what she felt at that moment must be what it was like to genuinely hate. She promised her father she would not despair, and would hold out hope for her own rescue. Then, if at all possible, she would kill them all, especially the woman.

CHAPTER 73

Katherine rose early and had made coffee before Charlene shuffled into the kitchen.

"Morning, ma'am. Did you sleep well?"

"Yes, Charlie…yes I did sleep well. How about yourself?" She smiled and poured two mugs of coffee.

"Thank you, ma'am." Charlene accepted one of the mugs and took a sip. "Yes, I was pretty tired last night, and passed out the minute my head hit the pillow. They paused as Taaka' drifted silently into the room. The girl hardly made a sound when she moved about the house, and Katherine found herself jumping at the girl's presence from time to time.

"Good morning, Taaka'," Katherine said as the girl pulled several plates and coffee mugs from the cupboard.

"Good morning, Mother," she said hesitantly, carefully pronouncing each word. "How today are you?"

Katherine glanced at Charlene, who chuckled warmly.

"I did not say words correctly?"

"No, Taaka', you said them perfectly." Katherine held the girl by the shoulders and smiled. "We just thought it was cute the way you called me mother." She kissed her on the forehead.

"When I am Steven's woman, I am your daughter. That is Pawnee custom."

"Well, that's something new," Katherine said. She cast a glance toward Charlene who raised both eyebrows and cocked her head and grinned. "That is our custom also, but it isn't our custom to allow our children to get married so young. What makes you think you and Steven will get married?"

"I have chosen him."

Katherine glanced toward Charlene again. The woman smiled and toasted her with her cup. "Sorry, ma'am, this one is on you."

"Does my son know this?"

"No." Taaka' shook her head.

"Oh," Katherine said quietly. "When you see Abby, tell her I would like to speak to her."

The girl stared at her blankly.

"Taree'uus," Charlene said. "Tell Taree'uus that her mother wishes to talk to her."

Taaka' smiled and flew silently through the door, then disappeared inside the barn.

"Well, you were a big help," Katherine said.

"I told you that this was your problem. Steve's your son, not mine. What are you going to tell Abby, ma'am?"

"Hell if I know. Excuse the language, but I really don't have a clue. I knew Steve and Taaka' liked each other, but I thought they were only friends. I had no idea she felt that way about him. They're only children. What would you do?"

~   ~   ~

"She's a princess, mama," Abigail said over the brim of her coffee mug. Katherine had summoned her into the kitchen and immediately ran Charlene and Taaka' out of the house. "She's nobility and her mother and father are dead. She can make that choice if she chooses."

"Yes, I guess she can, but they are too young to be thinking that way. Take a look at them."

"I have, mother. Is it because she's young, or that she's Pawnee?"

"That was uncalled for!" Katherine glared at her daughter across the table.

"I am just asking. You never told me how you feel about me being Black Crow's wife and having Pawnee grandchildren. How do you feel?"

"I felt shocked, to be honest with you. It took a little getting over. But I will be eternally grateful for Many Coup saving your life, and I couldn't love my grandsons any more if they were white. All I am saying is Steven and Taaka' are too young to be thinking about such things."

"I agree," Abigail said with a nod.

"What?"

"I said I agree. She won't be old enough for marriage for at least three years. Then Steven will have to prove he is worthy of her. I have taken Taaka' as my daughter, and I will make that decision for her."

"Oh," Katherine said, and took a sip of coffee. "Then why did she say she wanted to marry Steve?"

"She's a little girl, mama. He's been nice to her, and was there when her parents died. Look," she added with a snicker, "didn't you ever see a boy and wish you could marry him when you were her age? I certainly did."

Abby grinned at her as she sipped her coffee.

CHAPTER 74

Nathan Thomas sat at his favorite table inside The Snake Den, drinking coffee and playing a friendly game of five card draw with Randy Houk and Pearl Fisher as he explained his plans for leaving South Dakota.

"Well hell, Nate, that sounds good to me," Randy said eagerly. "I'd just as soon go with you as stay here."

"What would you do when you got there, boy?" Nathan glanced at him as he expertly shuffled the deck. He dealt the cards as a round of raucous laughter broke out at the table next to the window, where Waco was busy dealing Black Jack to Texas Bob, Mexico and Willie Jack. No one knew the men's real names, and Nathan wondered why he had chosen to use his own while on the run. Waco had claimed the table near the window as his own, as Nathan had claimed the one where he was seated, for much the same reasons. Nathan chose to have his back toward a blank wall where he could keep an eye on the door, while the window allowed Waco a clear view of the narrow street.

"Well, I hear folks are still finding a lot of gold in California. I figure I could just go stake my own claim on some creek and get what I want when I need it."

Nathan glanced at Pearl, who grinned. "Well, let me tell you something about California, son. I've got a sister who's lived there for years. She says there never was that much gold in the first place, and what's there is hard to get. Nearly every claim worth having has been already taken by big mining companies. You might be able to find a little by scratching around in the dirt by some creek, but not enough to make a living. The people who make it there all have jobs doing something. So, let me ask you once more," he paused to look at his own hand, "what are you going to do once you get there?"

"I don't know. I just figure I'll look around and find something. Maybe the town you're going to needs a deputy. I can shoot."

"Yeah, guess you can at that. Dealer takes two." He tossed the discards to the middle and waited for the others to study their hands. "It takes a little more than shooting to make a lawman. What else can you do? How about reading? I've never seen you read anything. Can you read and do your sums?" He dealt three new cards to Pearl as she discarded three.

"Yeah, some. I never finished school, but I can read and add and subtract, as long as they're easy." Randy discarded four and Pearl moaned with a snicker. Randy looked up from the single card in his hand.

"Why, what's wrong?"

"Four cards? Jesus, Randy, I'm not a gambler, but I can read cards better than you can, and I can't even see your hand. You threw away a pretty good hand." She grabbed the cards and flipped them over to reveal a duce, three, four and five of Clubs, causing Nathan to laugh.

"Christ almighty, Randy, you threw away the makings of a small straight? You couldn't make it gambling, that's for sure." He laughed as he dealt the boy four cards.

"What he needs is me taking care of him," Pearl said with a snort. "Maybe I ought to go with you and look after this egghead."

"Sure, Pearl, the more the merrier. Think California needs another whore? What do you plan on doing once you get there? Three Aces," Nathan said, spreading his hand on the table.

"That beats my two pair," Pearl said, tossing her cards to the table. "No, I don't plan on whoring any more than I have to. I was a school teacher once upon a time. I've been thinking about going back into teaching, but I need someplace fresh where nobody knows me, in order to start over." She turned to glare at Randy who was still studying the cards in his hand.

"Lord Almighty, either play that hand or give it to me."

"Don't rush me, I'm thinking."

"Thinking about what? Nate's got three aces and I folded. Either you can beat three aces or you can't. It's as simple as that." She snatched the cards from his hand and fanned them on the table to reveal four Jacks, then banged her head on the table several times. "Shit, shit, shit! I need a drink."

Nathan laughed as the woman rushed to the bar and poured herself a drink. She took her time sipping from the glass and glaring at them.

"Hell, Pearl, maybe he does need you to take care of him. Think you're up to the challenge?"

"You dealt him those cards on purpose just to get my goat, didn't you? You bastard."

"You'll never know," Nate said as he scooped the cards into a pile.

"Now, you're not calling Nate a cheat, are you, Pearl?" Willie Jack asked, with a short chuckle.

"No, everyone knows there ain't no cheats here at End Of The Line," Texas Bob said, as Waco rose from his chair to get a better view of the street.

"Aw hell, Pox Tivo's headed this way. Better open the windows to air the place out, Earl."

"You're kidding," Earl said. He automatically checked the shotgun for loads and leaned it within easy reach of his vantage point behind the bar.

"Na, he's not joking, and he's got the whole gang with him, including Rose," Waco said.

"Geeze, someone get a bar of lye soap," Mexico said with a hoarse laugh. "Rose wasn't nothing to look at when she was here, but she really looks like dog shit now." Willie Jack jumped from his chair to peer over Mexico's shoulder and laugh.

"Na, no dog would crap something that ugly. Say who's the new girl with them? She don't look half bad."

"No, but someone's beat the hell out of her," Waco said, and checked the loads in his Peacemaker. "I hope you don't mind me killing that son-of-a-bitch, Earl, if he's done what I think."

"Just do it outside. I don't want lead flying around in here."

Earl reached for the shotgun and laid it on the counter as Pox entered. He stood in the middle of the room and surveyed the occupants as the rest of his gang sauntered inside. Nathan felt his stomach turn as the sour smell of whiskey and body odor filled the room. Pearl gagged and covered her nose and mouth as she carried her drink back to the table where she sat next to Randy. She took another sip of her whiskey and turned to glare at her former stablemate.

"My gawd Rose, go take a bath…all of you."

Rose answered by giving Pearl an obscene gesture.

"That's real intelligent Rose. How long did it take you to learn how to do it?" Waco said with a snort. "But for the record, Pearl's right. You do need a good scrubbing." He laughed as Rose gave him the finger.

"What do you want, Pox?" Earl said.

"What do I want? Now, that's no way to treat one of your best customers, Earl. We came here to have a drink and talk over old times, ain't that right boys?"

"Okay," Earl said, filling several glasses. "Have your drink and get out of here. There ain't no old times for you, and especially Rose. I told you both I never wanted to see her around here again."

Nathan removed the leather thong on the shoulder holster of his Smith and Wesson and eyed the young girl wrapped in a dirty blanket as he shuffled the cards. From the bruises on her arms and face and the glassy look in her eyes, it wasn't hard to imagine what had taken place. Pox downed the glass of whiskey and slammed it against the bar.

"Think I'll have myself another."

"Not without paying. Show me the money," Earl said with a glare.

"We've got plenty of money. Pay for the drinks Tuck," Pox said in a loud voice. The black man tossed the heavy saddlebags on the bar and removed several gold coins.

"There, now pour the drinks."

"Where are you from, girl?" Nathan asked as the frightened girl moved closer to their table.

"Na-uh," Pox said as he grabbed her by the wrist and flung her against the bar. "You don't get none of this without paying for it. She's mine."

"Please mister…help me!"

Nathan flew across the room and clubbed Pox to the floor with his .38 before he realized he had even left the chair. Silas Norton grabbed for the girl but froze as Nathan jammed the gun against his forehead and cocked the hammer. The room was instantly filled with the sound of scraping chairs and cocking weapons as Waco and his companions drew their guns and pointed them toward the rustler gang. Nathan glanced around to find Randy Houk also had his gun drawn and was covering a moaning Pox Tivo, as the man held a hand to his bleeding head.

"Go on, pull on that shooter and see what happens," Waco said as Wah Lee's hand drifted toward the pistol tucked in his belt.

"Don't be a fool, Lee," Tuck said in a shaky voice. "They's got enough firepower to kill Grant's army."

"I warned you about trouble inside my place. Now help your boss to his feet and git!" Earl Tucker leveled his shotgun across the counter and cocked both hammers.

"Better listen to him boy," Nathan said, and nudged the gun harder against Silas' head. "The girl stays," he added as Silas gave the frightened girl's arm a tug. "Clean the hunk of garbage off the floor and git, before I lose my patience and decide to open your head."

"Pox ain't gonna like having to leave her," Rose barked. "He's gonna be real mad."

"Like I give a hot damn what Pox Tivo likes. He can come back anytime he wants, and I'll be glad to send him to hell."

They kept their guns drawn until Wah Lee and Tuck had drug Pox from the bar and helped him onto his horse. Pox mumbled something to Silas and the boy returned to the bar, but paused at the door as Nathan again jammed the Smith and Wesson in his face.

"Pox says he wants our money."

"It isn't their money," the girl yelled. "They robbed the Denby stage and killed everyone out of pure meanness, including my father. Then drug me off to…to…" She covered her mouth and burst into tears.

"You sonofabitch!" Nathan pulled the trigger and the bullet ripped a chunk of Silas' right ear off. "I ought to kill you!"

Silas screamed in pain and ran for his horse as his partners spurred their mounts into a full gallop. He reached the horse as Nathan fire again, hitting him in the left leg. Silas grabbed hold of the saddle horn with a cry of pain and clawed his way up on the animal's back. He beat the horse mercilessly as he galloped out of town. Nathan took careful aim and fired what would have been a killing shot if the girl had not flung herself against him. Nate's eyes darted between the girl and Pearl Fisher several times as she clutched him with both arms and wept uncontrollably. They finally landed on the saloon girl, who cocked her head to one side and grinned.

"Seems like you've found yourself a girlfriend, whether you wanted one or not."

~   ~   ~

"I should have killed the bastard when I had the chance, instead of shooting his ear and leg," Nate said, sipping his coffee.

"Hell, we should've done lots of things, Nate," Waco said with a chuckle. "If we'd had any brains, we would've killed the whole gang."

"Na," Mexico said shaking his head. "Then we would've had to bury their sorry asses, and I ain't touched nothing that smelly in my life."

"I was downwind from you the other day when you took a crap. That's pretty smelly," Texas Bob said.

"What I crap out my ass still ain't that dirty."

"Well, if you want to see justice, take these saddlebags and that girl to Denby and tell Bill Crutchfield what came down here today," Earl Tucker said. "The fact that they robbed the stage and killed all those people, and what they did to that girl, will cause them to go after those bastards and hang them."

"Since when did you get so righteous, Earl?" Waco asked. "And who said anything about turning over all that money? The way I see it, it belongs to us now."

"Not unless you want the whole town of Denby up here," Nathan said. "I know Crutchfield, and Earl's right. He won't let this thing rest. Neither will Denning. He's been chasing me now for three years, because I held up a bank in New Mexico. He sort of takes things personally." He looked up from his coffee and grinned, but turned his attention toward Pearl as she came from her room.

"How is she?" Earl asked.

"Sleeping. I saw that she had a hot bath and found something for her to wear. She fell asleep in my bed. Guess I won't be working this afternoon," she added with a grin.

"Hell, you could use Rose's old bed," Texas Bob said, pouring a drink.

"I wouldn't lie on that mattress for that whole bag of money," Pearl barked. "That thing needs to be burnt. So," she looked at Nathan and grinned, "what are you gonna do with her? She seems to belong to you now."

"Take her and the money to town, like Earl suggested. I don't think Crutchfield or Wells Fargo would mind too much if Earl counted out some sort of reward to split amongst ourselves for recovering their stolen money. Do you Earl?"

"No, not at all," the bartender said and dumped the contents on one of the tables.

"Say Earl, how come you got so angry when you seen that girl all beat up and all?" Mexico asked as they divided the money.

"I had me a daughter once, just about her age." He turned to stare at Pearl's door for a minute. "Some bastard raped and killed her. We never caught the sonofabitch either. I want to personally see Crutchfield hang Pox Tivo, even if I have to get arrested and spend the rest of my life in prison.

CHAPTER 75

Phillip woke early to the sound of the metal washbasin hitting the wall, then clanking several times as it skipped across the hard-packed ground. An open shutter on the barn banged mercilessly in rhythm to the gusting wind. He lay still for a few seconds listening to nature's symphony as the conductor brought the entire orchestra into play. A high-pitched whistle appeared as air gushed between a gap in the boards in the tack house siding. The dog whined at the foot of the bed and stared at Phillip with sad brown eyes.

"Yeah, I know and I feel the same way. Come on up here," he said patting the bed. The dog happily obeyed and snuggled beside him with his head against Phillip's chest.

"Ain't gonna be any fun working outside in this, is it boy? I guess I should've thought up some sort of name for you, but saddle bums like us don't really need proper names, do we? Guess I'll have to take you back to New Mexico with me when I leave, won't I? I've been seriously thinking about paying Ruth and her family a visit before heading on to Arizona. I think you and me both would like a little warmer climate.

"Say," he said propping himself on his elbows, "does that mean we're getting old? How old are you anyway? I never asked." He got a tail wag out of the mutt.

"Yeah, I guess it was a stupid question, wasn't it?

He rolled out of bed and donned his hat before slipping into his britches and boots. He took his time buttoning a red flannel shirt and vest, then strapped on his gunbelt. He stared at the dog, who seemed to read his mind and gave a whimper as he scrooched lower in the blankets.

"Na-uh, you don't get to stay inside by yourself. I've already stepped in one of your messes, and it ain't happening again. You're dressed, so come on."

He repeated the command three times, then finally scooped the animal in his arms and scooted him out the door. A strong gust flung his hat across the room, and the dog rushed back inside and dove under the bed as Phillip found his hat. He uttered several curses at the dog's refusal to come out from under the bed and pointed a finger at the dark snout.

"I'm warning you. If I have to clean one pile off this floor, or smell you're pee when I come back, I'm shooting you and giving your carcass to Taaka', and she'll make doggie stew out of you. Got that?"

He held his hat down tight as he opened the door and dashed across the yard toward the kitchen. Charlene and the Pawnee children were seated at the table with Katherine and her family, eating breakfast.

"Well, there he is. I thought you might've decided to stay in bed this morning," Charlene said.

"I've been trying to get that dog out from under my bed. He refuses to go outside, and I can't say as I blame him. But I'd rather see him having to put up with a little wind than me having to clean a mess when I get back this evening." He grabbed the steaming mug Taaka' offered. "Thank you." He took a sip and savored the flavor as he found a seat at the end of the table.

"Taaka' honey, go see if you can get Phillip's dog outside and latch his door," Abigail asked with a smile. The girl grabbed a piece of bacon from the platter and dashed out the door.

"Your table's starting to shrink a might, ma'am. You might consider serving meals in shifts, or build a chow hall," Phillip said as Charlene cracked two eggs into the frying pan.

"We were discussing that very fact when you came in," Katherine said over the rim of her cup. "Abby was suggesting she should eat with these precious children after her brothers and I have eaten our meals. I think it is important for families to eat together. What do you think is proper, Mr. Denning?"

"Well, it appears that question is loaded with buckshot, and I'm going to ruffle someone's feathers no matter what I say. But I'd have to agree with you, ma'am. And I'd be willing to eat my meals on the front porch or in the tack house before splitting you folks up."

"Thank you." She grinned and gave Abby a firm nod. "There it's settled, and I'm not going to hear another word out of you on the subject."

"Alright, mother. But you had better get a bigger table. Matthew will be getting married in a few weeks."

"Well, I do hope to be eating a few meals inside my own house with my wife alone," Matthew said with a smirk.

"I'm sure you will," Katherine said as the door flew open and Taaka' bounded inside. The girl sat down and began nibbling at her breakfast without a word.

"Well, could you get him outside, or do I have to shoot him?" Phillip asked, after watching her eat for a minute.

"All done." She smiled sweetly.

"Huh, guess that dog ain't so dumb after all." Phillip took a bite of bacon and crunched it in his mouth.

"And why do you say that, Mr. Denning?" Katherine asked.

"Most men would follow a woman who looks like Taaka', especially if she was offering him some good grub." He took another bite and grinned.

CHAPTER 76

Rose woke in the middle of the night shivering. The howling wind sent dry leaves scattering across the yard and against the cabin. The chinks between the logs had long been overdue for repair, and allowed the wind to seep inside with an eerie howl. Every inch ached as she wrapped the dirty blanket around her trembling body. Had she not been in the pains of opium withdrawal, she would have discovered the wind was somewhat warmer than usual for that time of year. It had been two days since the Chinaman had let her smoke his pipe, as he was getting low on his supply, and needed to buy more. But that took money, and they had fled The Snake Den leaving the money behind. Rose felt terrible.

What was even worse was the way Silas Norton had carried on most of the evening, moaning like a little baby because of his wounds. Normally, when Rose had smoked the pipe and was feeling good, she found the big man handsome and a good lover. But this night, with every fiber of her body crying out for the magic smoke, she hated the sight of him and hated listening to him whine. Sure a hunk of his ear was gone, and he had a hole in his leg. But there was no need to cry and carry on the way he had. The Chinaman had finally gotten him calmed down by giving him a pinch of the ashes from his pipe mixed in some water. Whatever it did, Silas not only calmed down, but looked more like his old self, even joking about his missing ear.

Rose fumbled with an empty whiskey bottle and drained the last few drops before tossing it aside. What little there was did no good, and she felt like she was going to die. Her stomach was on fire and she tossed the blanket aside and bent over, sweating. Another chill quickly followed the sweat, causing her to scramble for the blanket. That was when she saw the pipe, sitting on the ground next to the cold fireplace where Wah Lee had left it.

Rose grabbed a cup and filled it half full with water from the canteen, then carefully removed the lid from the pipe. Just a pinch, if she remembered right. She stirred the dark concoction with her finger and took a swig. It tasted horrible and made her gag, but in a matter of seconds, the fire inside her stomach went out. She took another sip and the aching in her arms and legs ceased. Rose drained the cup and discovered she felt good…more like her old self, happy and cheerful. She had to fight off an urge to burst out singing.

She stared at the pipe and suddenly felt cheated that Wah Lee had not told her about the magic ashes. She vaguely remembered seeing him dump the cold ashes into a small tin and place it in his saddlebags, but had never given it much thought. She stared at the pipe a minute or two longer before removing the lid and dumping the contents into her scarf. She would hide the ashes inside her handbag and keep them for emergencies like this one.

She was busy stuffing the scarf inside the bag when she paused. If she felt this good after one little pinch, what would two pinches make her feel like? She grabbed the cup and added more water and untied the scarf. Just one pinch? Hell, why not two…or maybe three?

She lost count of how many she added, or how big the pinches were. Then she downed the cup and suddenly found herself flying. She was completely out of her body, floating near the ceiling and looking down on the cabin. She could see Pox and Tuck fast asleep on the opposite side from where she had been sleeping. Wah Lee was lying near Silas who really looked like hell with the bloody bandage wrapped around his head to cover his missing ear. She wanted to laugh, and so she did. She laughed hysterically, and continued laughing as she floated away and through the ceiling.

It was Tuck who discovered her stiff body the next morning. Wah Lee only offered a shrug and emptied the ashes that were inside her purse into his tin. Pox and Tuck tossed her body into a wash and covered it with some brush. The wind blew the brush away the moment the men returned to their cabin.

CHAPTER 77

Katherine kept herself busy indoors, writing letters and doing paperwork, as the wind howled outdoors. She had just finished balancing the figures in her ledger and reached for her coffee mug to discover it was empty. She found Taaka' washing pots and pans as she entered the kitchen.

"Is there any coffee left?"

The girl smiled as she poured her a cup, and returned to the hot soapy dishpan. The coffee was stale and bitter. Katherine set the mug on the table after only a few sips and studied the girl. Last night she had been able to satisfy the girl's fears about her father's soul wandering the spirit land alone by reminding her how many people actually knew Blue Dog.

"My father will have died with no one to remember," she had said in tears.

"That's not true, Taaka' honey. A lot of people will remember your father. I will always remember him. So will Steven and his brothers. So will Charlene and Mr. Denning. There's also Taree'uus and her sons. A lot of people will remember your father. But most of all, you will remember, and be able to tell your children about him and his wisdom. They will remember their grandfather by your words."

The girl had thrown her arms around her waist and clung to her for what seemed an eternity. Watching her this morning, it was easy to understand how her son might have been attracted to Taaka'. Her unbraided hair hung like black silk down her back and glistened with each movement of her body. The sleeves of Abby's old house dress that she wore were pushed above her elbows, revealing slender copper-colored arms. Her bare feet moved noiselessly across the floor as she dried and stacked the plates in the cupboard. Steven had never shown any interest in girls that she had been aware of, and claimed he and Taaka' were simply friends. But Katherine suspected his feelings toward her might be more that he was willing to admit. The girl was simply gorgeous.

"Do you know where Mr. Denning and the boys are working?"

"Yes, Mother," she said with a nod.

Katherine waited as the girl scrubbed a bread pan, and finally asked, "Where are they?"

Taaka' glanced at her and scampered to the kitchen window to point. "There."

"The barn?"

She nodded and returned to her dishes. Katherine watched her work awhile longer then decided to satisfy her own curiosity. She grabbed her hat and snugged the drawstring before opening the door and making a dash toward the barn.

She shut the barn door and waited for her eyes to adjust to the dim light. The boys had shuttered the windows against the wind and a lantern in one of the stalls at the far end of the building cast an eerie glow. Katherine could hear voices as she started toward the light. Steven poked his head out of the stall and disappeared back inside.

"Its Ma," she heard him say. She paused in front of the stall to stare. They had removed the wheels from her old surrey, and had it perched on crates. The vehicle had been scrubbed and cleaned from top to bottom. The black lacquer glistened in the dim light. Matthew was busy applying a healthy dose of grease to the axles, while Steven and Timothy were using saddle soap on the leather seats.

Abigail poked her head over the top of the surrey and grinned. She was standing on a stepladder, polishing the leather with a rag. "Hi. I thought you were busy with the books."

"I finished with them." She took her time circling the surrey, making sure to stay a safe distance from the greased axles. The vehicle had not looked this clean and shiny since the day James pulled it into the stall five years earlier.

"My, I must say you certainly have the old contraption looking nice. Do you think it will actually hold together, Mr. Denning?"

"There wasn't anything wrong with it, ma'am. The wheels were a little dry, so Matt and Josh have them soaking in the horse trough out back. We might have to take them into the blacksmith in Denby to have the rims tightened, but other than that, they're in pretty good shape. Some critter's been gnawing on one of the rear straps, but we'll soon have that fixed." He adjusted a piece of leather on a board which was sitting on sawhorses. "Hold it tight," he said to Walking Horse as he sliced the leather with his knife.

"Do you think it will be ready before Matthew's wedding?"

Phillip paused his cutting to look at each boy. "What do you boys think? Think the new bride and groom can use it?"

"We'll have it back together in a couple of hours, Ma," Matthew said, "as soon as the wheels have finished soaking."

"Oh, then perhaps you and I can take it for a trial run, Mr. Denning. As soon as you say it's ready."

She returned to the house grinning. The expression on Phillip's face when she asked for the ride had been priceless. She spent the rest of the afternoon reading *David Copperfield*.

CHAPTER 78

"Are you ready, ma'am?" Katherine looked up to see Phillip standing by her chair. He had bathed and was clean-shaven, and wore a fresh change of clothes. They had eaten supper almost an hour earlier. The entire family, including the boys, had pitched in and helped clean the kitchen, and were now gathered in the living room in a lively conversation. Katherine herself had gotten engrossed in her book.

"Am I ready for what, Mr. Denning?"

"Your test ride in the surrey, ma'am."

"Oh." She marked her place and closed the book. "Do you think it's ready?"

"Yes, ma'am, I have a pair of horses hitched, and took it for a short spin. It seems to be fit as a fiddle. The wind has quit blowing, so now would be a perfect time."

"Okay, Mr. Denning, let me get my shawl."

She hurriedly grabbed her gloves and shawl, and as an afterthought, tied a white poke bonnet on her head. She was adjusting her gloves when she entered the living room and stopped. Her entire family, including Charlene, Abby and the Pawnee children', had formed two lines on either side of the door. They were standing at attention, and waiting for her to walk down the isle. Matthew proudly opened the door for her and simply said, "Mother."

"Have a nice evening, ma'am," Charlene said as she passed. Katherine stopped in the doorway to glare at them.

"I know you had something to do with this, Charlie, you and Abby. None of my boys would have thought of it by themselves. I'll get you for this. I promise."

"I have no idea what you're talking about, ma'am," Charlene said as Matthew closed the door. She could hear them laughing as she made her way toward the surrey.

"What's going on in there? Are they giving you a hard time about something?" Phillip asked as he helped her into the rig.

"Yes, and don't pretend you knew nothing about it, Mr. Denning."

"Okay, but actually, I didn't." He climbed in beside her and took the reins, giving them a gentle shake. "What were they doing?" he asked as the surrey started forward.

"To put it bluntly, they are acting as if you are a suitor, who came to court me. I'll swear a person can't even take a simple buggy ride, without them making something out of it."

"Ah-huh, that *is* funny," he said and urged the horses into a trot. "Nice night, isn't it?"

"Yes, it is. We have a full moon."

They rode in silence as he took the fork to the right and across the valley toward the road to Denby. He slowed as he crossed the main creek and urged the team back into a trot. A small herd of cattle parted as if by magic as they neared, and the surrey climbed higher. The night air had a slight nip to it, and Katherine pulled her shawl tighter.

"Why is it funny, Mr. Denning?"

"Why is what funny, ma'am?"

"The thought of you being my suitor?"

"Oh, that," he said, and took his time turning the surrey around on a wide flat area halfway up the canyon wall.

"Would you take a look at that," he said, stopping the rig and locking the brake. "You sure have one pretty ranch, Mrs. Parker."

The moon cast a soft glow, turning the several streams and ponds into silver ribbons that crisscrossed and dotted the valley floor. Cattle and horses moved like silent shadows, as a wolf howled it's mating call in the distance, and received an answer seconds later. Katherine could see the yellow glow of lamplight shining through the ranch house windows in the distance, giving her a happy welcome. It had been a long time since she felt that welcoming call and her heart suddenly felt full.

"Yes sir, it sure is pretty," Phillip repeated. "About as close to heaven as I'll ever see."

"I doubt that, Mr. Denning. By the way, you never answered my question."

"What question was that, ma'am?"

"Why the thought of you being my suitor was humorous."

"Oh, that question." He chuckled and rubbed his chin. "I just never figured you wanted a suitor, and even if you did, you sure wouldn't have me as one."

"Oh, so you think I didn't need any knight in shining armor to come rescue me, is that it?"

"No, ma'am. I never figured you needed rescuing." He shook the reins and started the surrey back toward the valley.

"And why is that, Mr. Denning?"

"I think you can do most anything you set your mind to. You were pretty successful before I showed up on your doorstep begging for a handout like that old mongrel dog of yours. I kind of figured I was the one needing rescuing, not the other way around."

"Yes, you were pretty shabby looking at that," she said with a laugh. "And what about the rustlers? Didn't I need to be rescued from them?"

"Maybe, but you didn't know they were stealing your cattle the day I rode in, until I told you. If I hadn't told you about them, you would have lost some cattle, but you still would have gotten along."

"Yes," she said with a nod. "That all might be true Mr. Denning, and thank you for saying I didn't need to be rescued. I believe you are the only person to actually say that. I want you to know that you have done an awful lot for me and my family. I might not have seen my daughter again, if not for you. And you certainly have been more of a father to my sons than James ever was. He loved them, and every one of us loved him terribly. The last year, though, before he died was simply miserable. I hate to say this, and I hope you don't think me horrible for admitting it, but I was actually relieved when James passed away.

"Then you showed up looking like something the cat dragged in, asking for a job. I had no idea you felt part of your job was to teach my sons what it's like to be a proper man. I shall be eternally grateful for you doing that, Mr. Denning."

"You're welcome, ma'am, but let's don't forget Taaka'. That girl's got her brand set on your youngest boy. You might have gotten a little more you bargained for."

"That's right!" Katherine laughed. "Lord have mercy. I was watching her do dishes this morning and thinking the same thing. I just wonder if Steven's feelings toward her are more than he's letting on."

"They are." He pulled the surrey to a halt in front of the ranch house and set the brake.

"What are you saying, Mr. Denning? Is it something I need to worry about?"

"No, the boy's too scared to do anything about it. I'd keep an eye on them. They're still young and easy to keep corralled. You're gonna have your hands full a couple more years down the road, though, and might consider letting them get married then. You've got Abby and Charlie to help out, but yeah, the boy's pretty smitten with her."

He climbed out of the surrey and offered his hand.

"I hope you enjoyed the ride, ma'am."

"Thank you, Mr. Denning." She took his hand as she stepped down. "I do believe this has been one of the most pleasant evenings I've had in a long time…only second to seeing Abby. I'm sorry it has come to an end."

"Thank you, ma'am. It's been a pleasure to me also."

He touched the brim of his hat and began unhitching the team as she disappeared inside.

CHAPTER 79

"I reckon you must be popular with the folks in Denby," Phillip said as the procession of wagons loaded with building supplies and people pulled into the yard. They were here to build the honeymoon cabin. Women and children piled out of one special rig with baskets of fried chicken, biscuits and jars of gravy. Avery Jordan unloaded a fifty pound burlap sack of potatoes.

"I've made some friends since moving here, but they're also pretty fond of the Jordans," Katherine said. She turned as Charlene came from the house, shouting and directing the ladies toward the kitchen where she kept everything. Charlie was particular about her kitchen and the way she kept the house, and this house-raising party was going to be tough on her.

"Better get the boys and split some more firewood," she said.

"Yes ma'am. We're gonna need lots before this day is through." Phillip finished his coffee in one gulp and set the mug on the railing. Then he walked briskly toward Steven. The boy was watching the proceedings from the corral with an open mouth. Katherine started to return the empty mugs to the kitchen for Charlene to wash, then decided to give them a quick rinse at the pump instead. Her friend was going to have enough to do without her adding to it, and the kitchen was too crowded to squeeze inside.

A large Swede named Lars Jorgensen was the ramrod for the project, and barked orders as Katherine helped unload the wagons. She was soon handed a carpenter's belt and hammer by one of the men, and found herself on her hands and knees nailing wood flooring as the cedar logs were laid on foundation stones and attached into place with long bolts. The big man knew exactly what he was doing and how he wanted it done. Katherine marveled that she could not remember seeing him look at a single plan as the construction proceeded. They had the entire floor constructed and several exterior walls framed by the time the noon dinner bell rang.

Katherine sat across the table from Matthew, who was almost giddy. The wedding was only three weeks away and the boy could not seem to contain himself. She had taken the hammer away from him earlier in the day, after Matthew had hit his fingers several times.

"Here, hold on, son. You're going be a cripple before the wedding. You won't be able to slip the ring on Becky's finger. Go help them haul lumber." He made several trips carrying boards before informing her that Charlene was out of firewood, and he was going to help Steven split more.

"No you're not. You've already busted your fingers with a hammer. I'm not letting you anywhere near an ax. I'm not rushing you to Dr. Krucker's after you've whacked your leg off. You keep hauling. I'll help Steve."

The framing was complete by mid-afternoon. Katherine and several women and young people were put to the task of nailing siding as the men worked on the roofing. The cabin would be small with only two actual rooms, but could be easily expanded as the need arose. The living quarters would consist of one bedroom and a large living room with a potbellied stove for heating and cooking. Phillip climbed down the ladder and stacked several bundles of shingles on his left shoulder, then paused as Katherine nailed a piece of siding into place.

"Looks like you've done that sort of thing before, ma'am," he said as she flushed the nail with four whacks.

"Yes, Mr. Denning, I've driven a few nails in my time," she said with a smile, and reached for another board. "I stood beside James and helped build every building on this ranch. We did hire some help from town, but James and I did most of it ourselves. How about you? You look familiar with a claw hammer and saw."

"Yes, ma'am." He gave her a grin. "Most anyone who's worked on a ranch knows something about sawing and whacking boards for fencing and what not. My pa knew how to build things and taught me some. You folks did a fine job building this place. It's got a good lay, and it's downright beautiful. I don't know if I've told you that."

"No, you haven't, Mr. Denning. Thank you. This cabin will be a fine addition to the ranch."

"Yes it will." He gazed at the ranch house and outlying buildings for a moment and heaved a huge sigh.

> "Work, build and worry
> Act insane to give it birth
> Deliver a building
> Who remembers the man when
> He is dead, who drove the pegs?"

"What's that, Mr. Denning?" Katherine held her hammer poised to drive another nail.

"Oh, just a little poem I learned from John Tunstall. I complimented him on how beautiful his ranch was one day and he quoted me that proverb. He said it was a loose translation of an ancient Japanese saying. I asked him what it meant, and he told me to go find out."

"And what did you decide?" she asked and drove her nail flush with three whacks.

"I don't rightly know if he'd agree, but I think it means we don't actually matter. What matters is what we leave behind…the little good we do to help others while we're here. So we shouldn't worry too much what folks think about us right now."

"Amen, brother," Reverend Norris said as he climbed the ladder with a bundle of shingles.

"Reckon I'd better quit talking and get busy," Phillip said with a grin.

He followed the minister up to the roof to nail shingles. Katherine stared thoughtfully at the empty ladder before cocking her head to one side.

"Huh." She finished nailing the board and reached for another piece of siding. *A lawman, a killer, cowboy, carpenter, and now a philosopher. What else am I going to discover about you, Mr. Denning?*

CHAPTER 80

"How long do you think it will take him to come down?"

Katherine jumped at the sound of his voice, sloshing coffee over the brim of her mug. She had been standing on the porch in the cool evening breeze and watching Matthew clean the newly-built honeymoon cabin, when Phillip had slipped up behind her. The townspeople had constructed the cabin in a single day, and the last wagon had no more than pulled out of the yard, when the boy began sweeping and dusting. He had only nibbled at his supper and continued the tidying up by lamplight.

"My guess is somewhere around one or two o'clock in the morning. It might last into tomorrow. I reckon we won't get any work out of him tomorrow either way."

"Yeah, you're probably right. I never thought much about it before. I guess it must be just as exciting for men to get married as it is for women."

Phillip moved up beside her and brushed against her arm as he watched her son at his frenzied work. "Of course, I wouldn't know," he said with a chuckle. "I've never been married, but I've seen some of my saddle partners get hitched, and they were like your boy. They weren't any good a week before the wedding, or a month afterward. Marriage did something to their heads."

"Ah," she said with a slow nod, "you're saying women make men crazy. Is that it, Mr. Denning?"

"Yes, ma'am," he said with a grin.

"And I suppose you have developed some sort of remedy to stop that from happening to you."

"Yes, ma'am, I certainly have."

"And may I ask what that remedy is? I may want to impart it to Joshua and Timothy before the craziness strikes them."

"Well, I'm afraid you wouldn't like the cure anymore than the cause," he said with a chuckle and took a sip of coffee.

"Perhaps. Why don't you tell me anyway?" She stared into his face with soft blue eyes, but her tender expression fled with Phillip's answer.

"It's simple. I climb on my horse and leave before the craziness gets me." He tossed the remains inside his mug into the yard and grinned.

"Well, reckon I'll be doing the work of two men tomorrow, so I'd better be calling it a night. Goodnight, ma'am."

"Good night, Mr. Denning." Katherine stood on the porch long after Phillip had left, watching her son attack the cabin with frenzied passion.

You're wrong about one thing, Mr. Denning. You don't need to mount a horse to get away from the craziness we women create. You know how to do it very well while one is standing right beside you.

CHAPTER 81

Geraldine McKenney tugged at the top of the dress and stared at her image in the mirror. The first twelve hours tucked in Pearl Fisher's bed inside the tiny room in the rear of The Snake Den had been spent in a fitful sleep. She woke with every laugh or tinkle of glass coming from the bar. Even the sound of a deck of cards being shuffled made her jerk. Once she thought she had heard a gunshot and jerked upright, until someone was scolded for slamming the door. Then, when complete exhaustion had taken over, she spent the following twelve hours in a dreamless sleep. It was now one o'clock in the afternoon and she was feeling starved. Having refused anything offered by Pox Tivo and his companions, it had been three days since she had eaten a bite.

"Tugging on that thing isn't going to make the cloth grow, honey," Pearl said from where she sat on the bed watching. "I'm sorry, but that's the most modest dress I have. The men who come around here don't like seeing females in any kind of clothes."

Geraldine turned with a start.

"Oh, don't worry, nothing like that's going to happen to you. They will treat you with more respect than they gave their own mothers. Everyone in the bar was ready to kill Pox and his entire gang when they found out about you. Nate would have certainly killed Silas if you hadn't grabbed hold of him the way you did."

"What's going to happen to me?"

"Well, I'd say that's up to you," Pearl said. "Here, let me help you." She tucked a lace scarf into the neckline of the dress and pinned it into place.

"Well now, what do you think? Is that modest enough for you?"

"Yes, it's very pretty. Thank you."

"You're welcome." Pearl backed off to admire her work. "You're a little taller than me, so the hem rides up a little more than it should. It's supposed to cover most of your calves, but it's showing quite a bit of leg. Oh well, it's the best I can do until we get to town and get you a new outfit. Besides, you've got pretty legs. Come on, let's get you fed before you blow away."

She ushered Geraldine through the door and toward Nate's favorite table. The young girl paused in the middle of the room as every man inside The Snake Den rose to their feet. She cleared her throat twice before speaking.

"Thank you, gentlemen…thank you for your kindness. I will never forget it."

"You're quite welcome, young lady," Earl said as Nate held a chair for her to be seated at his table. "Now let's get you fed. I've got a nice pot of elk stew. Randy Houk shot the critter early this morning before daylight, so it's nice and fresh," Earl said as he scooped a bowlful of the steaming concoction. "It's got onions, potatoes, and about everything I could get my hands on that was worth eating."

He set the bowl in front of her with a large spoon and a cloth napkin. "I also made a pan of cornbread. Would you like to try some of that, too?"

"Yes, I would. It smells delicious. Thank you, Mr. Tucker."

"You're quite welcome, young lady." He rushed to the bar, scooped a hunk of bread onto a plate and brought it to the table along with a large glass of milk.

"That's fresh out of the cow this morning. I milked her myself."

"Thank you…that's very kind of you. And the stew is delicious."

They allowed her to eat in silence for a few minutes while Waco and Texas Bob resumed their game of five card stud. It was Geraldine herself who broke the silence.

"What's going to happen to me now?"

"We're going to take you to Denby as soon as you feel up to it," Pearl said with a warm smile. "I thought I told you inside the room."

"Well, yes you said something about getting new clothes in town but… Can you go to Denby? Isn't this some sort of outlaw place?"

"Yeah, I reckon we've all been called that by some," Waco said with a laugh.

"Hell, you've been called a lot worser than that, Waco," Texas Bob said.

"Won't they arrest you if you go to Denby?" Geraldine glanced around the room.

"Not Nate," Waco said with a glance toward their table as he dealt the cards. "He's got some sort of thing going with the sheriff. My guess is he knows something about the lawman that he doesn't want to get out. Ain't that right, Nate?"

"Maybe. I knew Bill Crutchfield back in New Mexico along with a few others. The fact is, we've all got a little something in our pasts, Waco. I borrowed some money from a bank without asking permission, and Crutch knows all about it. I know a few things about him that I haven't spilled the beans about, and probably won't. I'll see the young lady gets to Denby and is able to tell her story. Then, I reckon I'm heading toward California."

"California? Going gold-hunting, are you? Well that's about the riskiest business I've heard about," Earl said.

"No, I'm not hunting gold, Earl," Nathan said with a chuckle. "I'm going to be a lawman exactly like Bill Crutchfield."

"Geeze," Willie Jack said with a laugh. "Just what we need, another crooked sheriff. I always knew lawmen were no good. They get a star pinned on their vests, but they're all just like us."

"Na," Waco said as he tossed a couple of chips into the pile. "They're smarter and do their stealing legal-like. I knew a fellow awhile back down in Texas who got himself elected sheriff of a nice little town. They had a couple of saloons and whorehouses, along with every other kind of business a town might need. He kept the peace alright, just so long as he got a ten percent cut from everyone in town. That is, until one man who owned a little restaurant decided he didn't want to pay and his place burnt to the ground.

"Now you take fellows like you and me. We're just as crooked, only we're not as smart as that lawman. We steal things right out in the open and get sent to prison or hanged for our trouble. Nate's the smart one. He'll be able to walk down the street, tip his hat to women, eat at the parson's table. Hell, he might even get married and have a passel of kids. You'll become a respectable member of the community. Won't you, Nate?"

"Maybe I'll become exactly what you say, Waco. Or, maybe I'll get shot in the back just like the last two sheriffs in that town. That's why they're willing to hire me. No one wants the job." He grinned and toasted them with his cup of coffee.

"Well, if you're leaving for California when you get her to Denby, guess I'd better start packing," Pearl said.

"Packing? Where are you going?" Earl asked.

"To California with Nate and Randy."

"I didn't know I asked you to come," Nathan said with a chuckle.

She leaned across the table and gave him a toothy-grin. "You didn't, but that isn't going to stop me from going."

"Do you have money for train fare? I've got just enough for mine and Randy's tickets."

"I've got money, Nate. I've been saving like mad to get to someplace besides End Of The Line."

"Well, what about me?" Earl came from behind the bar to confront her. "I lost Rose and now you? I need a girl, Pearl. Who's gonna work here?"

"My hell, Earl, you can always find another whore. This might be my best chance at another life."

She turned to give Geraldine McKenney a soft smile.

"Don't pay any attention to him, honey. We'll see you safely to Denby, and the sheriff will contact your family."

"That might be hard to do," Geraldine said laying her spoon aside. Her voice quivered as she spoke. "My mother died when I was born, and my father was all I had. Now he's dead. I've got one aunt somewhere in San Francisco, but I never got along with her and haven't heard from her in years." She gave Pearl a weak smile and almost whispered, "I honestly don't know what I'm going to do."

CHAPTER 82

It was in the middle of the afternoon when Katherine went to the kitchen for a cup of coffee and found Charlene and Abigail staring out the window. The aroma of ham and baked bread caused her mouth to water and she wondered how long before the meal was done. She opened the oven door for a peek before pouring the coffee. She turned to find the women still staring out the window as the sound of chopping wood drifted through the opened window.

"What are you two up to?" she asked, and crossed the room slowly so as to not spill her coffee.

"We're sinning," Abigail said.

"You're what?"

"Take a look and tell me if you're not tempted to lust," Charlene said as she pulled the curtain back a little farther. Phillip had removed his shirt and the warm afternoon sun caused the muscles in his arms and back to glisten as he swung the heavy maul. Matthew and Joshua were cutting a log into fireplace-sized hunks with a bucksaw while Steven and Taaka' hauled the split hunks of wood in a wheelbarrow and stacked them beneath the lean-to next to the tack house.

"Isn't that the prettiest thing you ever saw?" Charlene asked as Katherine took a peek.

"Why Charlene Thompson, you ought to be ashamed of yourself," Katherine said, turning away.

"Oh, come on, mother," Abby said. "We might be widows, but we aren't dead. Neither are you, for that matter.

And you can't lie and say you don't find that appealing, 'cause I've seen you sneaking a peek at him every now and then when he isn't looking."

"I do no such a thing," Katherine snapped in reply, and felt a flush run through her cheeks.

"Now you're really sinning, 'cause you just told a whopper," Charlene said. "Besides, I really don't see the harm in it myself. Now admit it…you'd like to take another look right now, if we weren't around, wouldn't you?"

"No…well maybe, but no," she said shaking her head.

"Well which is it? Either you've still got some blood flowing in your veins, or you're ready to join folks in the cemetery. I wouldn't mind seeing a little more of him, myself." Charlene grinned as she turned back to the window.

"Charlene!" Katherine said with a giggle, and sat down at the table. "How long have you felt like this?"

"Oh, quite often to be honest," she said, pulling the bread from the oven. "I'm gonna have to tell him to quit cutting wood while I'm baking. I almost burnt this loaf. I'm not going to do anything about it, if that's what you're worried about. But then," she cocked her head to one side thoughtfully, "if he started it…"

"Charlene…oh my word," Katherine said, covering her mouth and laughing.

"Let's be honest, Ma. Didn't you find that the least bit appealing…exciting…just a teeny bit?" Abby asked, sitting across from her.

"Well yes, to be honest. I have found Mr. Denning quite attractive at times, and his company has been pleasant. I haven't really sat down and entertained the idea of having another man in my life, other than what he is…a hired hand."

"And may I ask why?" Charlene asked as she refilled her coffee mug. "You're still young and pretty. It would be easy for you to find a good husband, if you wanted. Don't you get lonely some nights?"

"Yes, to tell the truth I get lonely. As far as that goes, what about Abby? She's younger and prettier. Are you thinking about getting remarried?"

"Quit changing the subject. My husband died a month ago, and I hardly think it would be proper for me to be looking at other men. And it will be much harder for me if I decide to get remarried, because I have two Pawnee children to think of." Abby shrugged and stared into her coffee.

"Yes, and they are darling. I wouldn't trade them for all the cattle in South Dakota." Katherine reached across the table and held her daughter's hand. "The right man will come along some day. To answer your question, yes I like Mr. Denning fine. I'm just not looking for a husband. This ranch keeps me busy enough as it is, and I don't have time to think about things like that."

CHAPTER 83

It took a week and a half of hard labor, from sunup to sundown, but Katherine finally had her road. While it was little more than a narrow pathway, it descended gradually from the brim of the canyon to the mouth of the cave. She had insisted that it should be wide enough for a person to safely walk during the icy winter without danger of falling, and that no one would be allowed on the trail without hobnailed boots once the weather turned cold.

"Well, that leaves us out," Abby said happily.

"And why's that?"

"We Pawnee wear moccasins." She kicked one foot waist-high and grinned. "You and the boys will have to do that chore."

~   ~   ~

After seeing what a painstakingly slow job it was for the boys to cut hay by hand, Katherine decided to visit Clayton Jones at the Rocking J. He had purchased a mule-drawn mowing machine several years ago, and she figured to either borrow or rent the machine if it was not in use. Clayton stared at her in silence for what seemed an eternity before speaking.

"No, I can't let you rent it from me, or borrow it for that matter. I'll let you buy it, though, mules and all," the old man said matter-of-factly.

"But why, Mr. Jones? Don't you plan on using it anymore?"

"No, I don't. I've had it, Katie. I've had it with the whole mess. Between the past two winters and the rustlers taking what little I had left…I'm busted. They even came near killing Dusty Moore. You remember that, don't you?"

"Yes, I remember, Mr. Jones. I thought Dusty had fully recovered. Why should that make you give up your ranch?"

"Dusty quit me along with everyone else, and I can't say as I blame him. I don't have any cowboys, and I don't have the money to pay them if I did. To top it off, I don't have any cattle. I don't have anything. Sarah and I are packing up and going south. We're too old to start over, but I've got a brother in Texas who's been doing pretty well and he says we can stay at his ranch and work for him."

"Well," Katherine said, "I really don't know when I've been more insulted."

"Insulted?" Sarah said with a laugh. "Why's that, my dear?"

"Both of you were there for me when Abby vanished and James died. Now, don't deny it," she added quickly as Sarah started to speak. "I don't know how many times the both of you let me cry on your shoulders. And you came to stay at my house for days on end, Sarah. You cooked and cleaned and took care of Steven while I was out taking care of the ranch. And you, Clay, taught me more about ranching than anyone, including my husband. You were there to advise and answer a million questions. You even loaned me a few hands when I needed extra help, and wouldn't let me pay their wages. Now, that I'm well capable, and you're the ones needing an extra hand, you insult me by not letting me repay a little of the kindness you showed me."

"Well, we didn't mean for you to take it that way, Kate," Clayton said.

"How else could I take it, Clay? I'll buy the danged mower, if that's what you want. And I'll buy any cattle you've got left. But I'll chase you down and shoot you in the foot if you try leaving before I've had a chance to work a few things out."

"What do you plan to do, my dear?" Sarah asked.

"I don't quite now yet. Give me a few days…you can wait that long." She started to leave, then stopped to point a finger in Clayton's face.

"And you'd better damned well stay put until I get back. I'm serious, Clay."

"Yes, I know you are, Kate," he said with a laugh.

CHAPTER 84

She spent the next two days visiting the neighboring ranches and soliciting pledges from each rancher to pitch in and help their neighbor through this difficulty. Some were willing to pay overdue bills, while most pledged to give breeding cattle to rebuild Clayton's herd. Donovan himself had not only pledged cattle, but offered to pay three months salary for two hands to help the old man finish the season. She returned to the Claytons on the third day with Bill Donovan.

"Na, I agree with Katie. You've been a good friend and neighbor to us all, and willing to offer a helping hand when we needed it. Now, you're planning to leave in your time of need without saying a word? What you're doing is a sinful thing, Clayton Jones, and an insult to us all. And I'm ashamed to be calling you my friend." Bill Donovan shook his head slowly and stared at the floor. Katherine glanced toward Sarah and knew the woman was struggling to keep from laughing.

"I've got these pledges from all our neighbors." Katherine passed a piece of paper with the signatures and pledges to Clayton. "Now, we're all willing to step in and offer a hand. All we need from you is a promise not to quit, and give us a chance."

"I...I don't know what to say." Clayton shook his head as he read the paper. He passed it to Sarah with a trembling hand.

"Yes would be the right thing to say," Donovan said as he pulled a flask from his coat pocket. "Now, why don't you get four glasses, Sarah darling, and let's seal this with a nip of good Irish whiskey."

343

CHAPTER 85

The machine was proving to be one of Katherine's best investments and the boys were only spending a fraction of the time cutting hay as they had by hand. She had insisted on having the bank appraise the mowing machine. She paid half the appraised value and drew an agreement where she would be a joint owner with Clayton of the equipment and mules. According to the agreement, she could buy the second half if Clayton chose to quit ranching. Katherine also had a first right of refusal on the Rocking J property if he did decide to quit.

"You don't leave anything out, do you?" Clayton eyed her over the top of the contract.

"I've learned that it pays to make sure you've covered every possibility, Mr. Jones. Now, what do you say? Are we partners?"

"I reckon I don't have much choice. You'd probably hunt me down and shoot my foot off if I tried quitting now." He signed the paper and passed it back to her.

"Is there anything else?"

"Yes." She nodded.

"Let's have it."

"If you really want to quit raising cattle, you could raise hay. I'd give you full ownership of the mower, and even help buy a second, if you decide you need one. You've got plenty of flat land…a lot more than I have, and I'm sure every ranch around here would buy all the winter feed you could raise. You wouldn't have to put up with rustlers.

"Think about it," she added with a grin as she pulled her gloves on.

~   ~   ~

The wagon made regular trips throughout the day, dumping the straw over the side of the cliff. Although stacking the bundles of hay was much easier work than breaking a new horse, Katherine had failed to consider the barrage of bundles coming from above, as the boys pitched them from the bed of the wagon. She had several bundles nearly hit her on the head during the first day of stacking. While they did no real physical damage, the girls teased her about making her head a target. She returned to the house that evening caked with dust and sweat, and straw-filled hair. She was sitting on the porch next to Abby, Taaka' and Charlene, sipping a glass of lemonade, when Phillip approached. He stood a few feet away and grinned, but the grin quickly turned into laughter.

"I know, I know. I must look like a scarecrow. I'm really beautiful, aren't I?"

"Well, actually…if you must know," he said, pulling several stems of hay from her hair, "I was thinking of how perfect you are." He gave the women another grin and went into the house.

They sat in silence for a long minute before Charlene spoke.

"I'll marry him if you don't."

"You might have to fight me first," Abby said and took another sip of lemonade.

CHAPTER 86

Katherine finally relented when Charlene took her by the hand and showed her the empty pantry.

"You know I only like going to town once…maybe twice a month, Charlie."

"Yes, but we've got a much larger family now. And you promised your son you would talk to Rebecca's parents about the wedding. Those children are getting married in two weeks. We've postponed their wedding twice now, and we can't do it again. It wouldn't be right."

"Oh, alright. Get a list together and we'll go," Katherine said. She started for the door and stopped to glare at her friend.

"You'd better figure out something, because I'm not making that trip every week."

"You could have those men who are fixing to build the addition onto this house add a second pantry. But that'd mean we'd need a second wagon to haul the extra supplies. Or better yet," she poked her head out the door and yelled as Katherine left, "you could go to church every Sunday, and make Avery open his store just for us. Matt's marrying his daughter, you know. "Have Avery deliver your order right to the house. He'll be family soon," she yelled louder.

In the end, Katherine felt it was up to Charlene to get whatever she and Abby thought they needed.

~   ~   ~

They were inside Avery Jordan's store filling their list, while Katherine eyed a bolt of blue cloth. It might make a nice dress for the wedding. She unwound several inches for a better look, when several riders passed the front of the store. Phillip was studying a Winchester, which he laid on the counter with a loud clunk and rushed toward the window for a better look. He immediately checked the chamber in his pistol as he headed toward the door.

"What's wrong, Mr. Denning?" she called, but drew no reaction from him. She hurried to the door to see him walking briskly toward the riders, who were now dismounting in front of the sheriff's office. Katherine shielded her eyes against the sun in time to see two men and two women enter the office, while Phillip increased his pace.

"Oh no," she said, and took out after him.

"What's wrong with Mr. Denning, Ma?" Steven asked as he joined her side.

"I don't know, but we had better go stop him before something bad happens." She tried weaving her way through the bodies on the crowded sidewalk. Finally, she chose to run down the middle of the street instead. She reached the sheriff's office as Phillip entered and grabbed hold of the doorpost to steady herself and catch her breath.

"Well, hello Arizona," Sheriff Crutchfield was saying. "Pull up a seat. You might find this interesting."

"No need for that. I think you know what I'm after. Are you going to arrest Nate, or are you going to leave it up to me?" Phillip allowed his hand to rest against the butt of his pistol. The younger of the two women released a strange cry as the other pulled her toward the safety of the wall.

"You touch that gun and I'll have to kill you Phil," the sheriff said, as he leveled his own pistol across the desk. "Is that what you want?"

Phillip allowed his eyes to drift from Nathan Thomas to the pistol in the sheriff's hand and back again.

"I didn't think so," Crutchfield said with a sigh of relief. "Now, sit down and listen."

"Howdy, Arizona," Nathan said with a toothy grin, as Phillip sat in an empty chair. "It's good to see you don't hold grudges."

"Don't you go prodding him, Nate, or I will toss your carcass into a cell and let him cart you back to New Mexico." He glanced up at Katherine and smiled.

"Come in, Mrs. Parker. You'll be interested in what's going on, and you might as well know what your cowhand's got himself tangled in."

Katherine carefully seated herself on a bench along one wall in the tiny office. The two women squeezed in next to her. They both looked like saloon girls, and smelled of cheap perfume. The clunking and scraping of boots caused everyone to turn toward the door as Katherine's boys, minus Matthew, crowded inside for a look. Sheriff Crutchfield gave the boys a pleasant grin.

"Well now, since you boys are interested in helping, I'm going to put you to work. Tim, run next door and grab Judge Walker," he paused to check his pocket watch, "he's probably eating his dinner at the café about now. He likes to keep things punctual, as you know. Anyway, tell him I need him here immediately. I've got us a first-hand witness to the stage holdup, and I need several warrants for arrest.

"And you," he pointed to Joshua, "run over to Ben Krucker's and tell him to clear his waiting room and whatever he's got scheduled, unless it's some dire emergency. I'm going to need his evaluation on what they did to this young lady. I'll send her over to him as soon as she gives her story to the judge. Go on," he added, when Joshua stood staring.

"Where's Matthew," Katherine asked Steven as Joshua ran to carry out the sheriff's orders.

"With Becky Jordan. Where'd you think?"

Judge Herbert Walker rushed into the room. He was still wearing the soup-stained cloth napkin tucked into his collar. "Is what this boy said true?"

Sheriff Crutchfield nodded.

"Well, now that's what I call God's intervention. Maybe, with this young lady's help, we'll be able to put a stop to all this killing."

Phillip offered his chair and the heavyset man plopped into it with a breathless "thanks," then began rummaging inside a carpetbag for a tablet and something to write with. He abandoned the search and accepted the pen and bottle of ink offered by Sheriff Crutchfield.

"Now, what do we have here?" he said, glancing around the room.

"Let Doc Krucker inside and close the door," Sheriff Crutchfield said, as the gray-headed man knocked softly on the door. "Then you and your brothers had better leave yourselves."

"Aw man," Timothy whined.

"I'm sure your Ma will fill you in soon enough. I need you to stand outside and don't let anyone come in. Especially him," he said walking toward the door and pointing toward a man worming his way through the crowd. It was Earnest Enfield, the publisher of the local newspaper.

"Hey, Sheriff, what's going on in there?" The publisher yelled, as the doctor squeezed into the tiny room. Crutchfield poked his head through the door to address the gathering crowd outside his office.

"Y'all will know right soon...I promise. Run along now."

"At least let me in, Sheriff. The citizens need to know what's going on here," Earnest Enfield said with an air of importance.

"You'll know right along with the rest when I make my statement. We believe we have an eye witness to the stage holdup the other day, but we're not sure of anything until we gather all the facts." He closed and locked the door.

Part of the crowd ran to grab guns and horses should the sheriff call for a posse. A few others sauntered away grumbling.

"He isn't going to like being left out of the room, Bill," Judge Walker said.

"That's what he gets for telling all those lies about me during the last election. Now, let me tell you what you've got here, Judge." Crutchfield sat down and pointed toward Geraldine McKenney, "This gal is an eye witness to the holdup. Now maybe you'd better pass those writing implements to Kate and listen real close, 'cause you're going to need to hear this. You too Doc, 'cause I want you to take Miss Mc Kenney to your office and give her the once over real good. She was a passenger on that stage, and the bandits held her captive for a couple of days before Nate and his friends rescued her."

Phillip glanced toward Nathan Thomas in disbelief.

"It also seems from what little I was able to gather from her, before Phil came busting in here and raising all sorts of hell, that Silas Norton was part of that gang. So, we can add murder charges to the list of things he's wanted for."

"Oh," Katherine said covering her mouth with her fingers. "His poor parents…"

"Poor mother is more like it," Crutchfield said with a glare. "You probably haven't heard this yet, but he beat the hell out of his father and stole his parents' money before leaving. He beat the old man so badly, he died. We buried him yesterday."

"Oh, my God…I…I'm so sorry."

"You can add attempted murder to the list," Phillip said sullenly. "He tried bushwhacking Mrs. Parker and shot her horse out from under her."

"He didn't kill Ginger, did he?"

Katherine nodded as she wrote the date and time at the top of the page.

Crutchfield uttered several obscenities as he wiped a hand across his face. "Okay," he said studying Katherine closely. "Think you're up to being the Judge's scribe, Mrs. Parker?"

"I'll do my best."

"Good enough." He turned his attention toward the young girl seated beside Katherine. "Tell us your story, and take as much time as you need. Start out by giving us your name, age, who your father and mother are, and where you live."

"My name is Geraldine Susanna McKenney," she said softly. "I turned seventeen on the nineteenth of January. My mother died during my birth, and my father never remarried. He was murdered by a man called Pox during the stage robbery."

The girl spoke in a low monotone as if she were in a trance. Katherine took notes quickly, but had to stop her several times in order to blot her own eyes and blow her nose. When Geraldine McKenney had finally finished telling of her ordeal, Katherine signed the paper and passed it to the judge.

"Now, when do we go get these murdering sons-of-bitches?" she asked matter-of-factly. Everyone jerked their heads to stare at her as Pearl burst out laughing.

"Amen, sister." The saloon girl said as she lit a small cigarillo.

"We? You're sure as hell not going," Crutchfield said.

"I'd like to know how you're going to stop me? They've been stealing my cattle and they've tried killing me and my boys twice. Now, they've done this to this nice young lady? I'm fed up with their nonsense, Bill, and there's absolutely no way you're going to stop me. I'll go by myself if I have to."

The sheriff looked toward Phillip for some help, but the cowboy only shrugged.

"Better let her go, Crutch. The lady always says what she means. Besides, she can probably outshoot most men, and she's got the ranchers organized. She can get you an honest-to-God posse with men that can shoot.

"Alright, Kate, you're in. But I'm still in charge, and you'll do like I say. Got that?"

She nodded.

"Good. Now, can you can see why I told you to leave off trying to finish your war with Nate?" Crutchfield asked Phillip. "We got ourselves bigger fish to fry, and I want both of you to help me fry them."

"Na, you've got plenty of folks out there that can ride and shoot. I'm heading to California," Nathan said.

"Maybe I can get a posse together, but I need someone who's been down this road before and knows what they're up against. If I have to go after Pox Tivo and the Norton boy with some of those folks gathered in the street, I'll only get them killed. I rode through Lincoln County with you boys, and know what you're capable of. I'd like you two riding with me when I go, if you're willing."

"As much as I hate to admit it, Mr. Crutchfield is right," Katherine said sullenly. We've dealt with Pox Tivo a couple of times, and he's pure meanness. And I'm sorry I stopped Mr. Denning from hanging the man. I thought we could turn him over to Sheriff Crutchfield, except he escaped. I can't help feeling what happened to Miss McKenney is partly my fault."

"She's telling the truth, Nate. I was with Pox that day, and I thought for sure he was gonna hang me," Randy said with a nervous laugh.

"I would have," Phil said as he rolled a cigarette.

"We can't go around blaming ourselves for something that a snake like Tivo will do, Kate. What we can do, is make things right by huntin' him down and making sure he's dead. What do you say, Nate, are you going to help us out?" Crutchfield asked.

The gambler glanced toward Pearl.

"Go help him take care of Pox, Nate. I'll take Geraldine shopping and get us some decent clothes and a hotel room. Two women shopping…what can go wrong? Besides, we'll all sleep better, even in California, knowing Pox Tivo is barking in hell."

CHAPTER 87

The two women left the doctor's office and cut a beeline toward the bank, where Geraldine withdrew a sizable amount of money from her father's account. They then walked arm-in-arm into Jordan's Mercantile and began to raid the racks of clothing.

"Oh no you don't. You put that away." Pearl Fisher looked up from the roll of bills in her hand to see Geraldine glaring at her.

"That would be nice, but I don't think this man is going to let me walk out of his store carrying these dresses without paying for them."

"No, but I asked you to go shopping with me, and I am not going to allow you to pay the bill."

Avery Jordan let his gaze bounce between the two women as they glared at each other, then cleared his throat. "Excuse me, Ladies, but I have another customer waiting. Let me know what you decide."

"There's no need in our waiting, Mr. Jordan," Geraldine said and slid Pearl's package containing several changes of unmentionables next to hers then grabbed the dresses. "I am going to pay for these."

"Gerri, I am quite capable of..." Pearl started but the young woman cut her off by clamping onto Avery's wrist as he reached for the money in Pearl's hand.

"I said I was going to pay, Mr. Jordan. Believe me, neither of you want to argue with me."

"No, ma'am. I'm not one to argue with either of you," he said, raising both hands with a laugh.

"Good," Geraldine said, digging into her handbag. "Just give me a total for everything, and toss in the green hat Mrs. Fisher was eying."

"Gerri, that thing is overpriced," Pearl hissed in a low tone.

"Not if it makes you look good…which it does. It also complements the green dress you're getting."

"May I ask why you are doing this? I'm supposed to be the one taking care of you. Not the other way around," Pearl said as Geraldine paid their bill.

"Because, I want to. Besides, you were the one who took me in and helped me after my experience with those men. Now," she said with a grin, "this is just the first step. We've still got more shopping to do." She took Pearl by the arm and guided her toward the door.

"Excuse me, ladies?" Avery said as they walked away.

"Yes?" Geraldine said.

"What should I do with your packages?"

"Send them to the hotel."

"Yes, ma'am," Avery said as they vanished through the door. He had never been asked to do such a thing, and stared at the packages until his wife came and removed them.

~   ~   ~

"Is this what you're looking for?" The clerk inside the hardware store placed a small Smith and Wesson .31 caliber revolver with a holster on the counter. The holster had two small straps instead of a belt. "It has a short barrel and is designed to attach to your leg. A lot of women in the larger cities are using them."

"Exactly," Geraldine said with a nod. "I'll take two of them, one for me and one for my friend. I'd also like a dagger, if you have one."

"Yes, I think I can accommodate you," he said and crossed the room to a glass-covered display."

"My, but you're going heavily armed, aren't you?" Pearl said with a laugh. "What makes you think I need, or even want a gun?"

"My father was an excellent shot and taught me how to shoot, although he seldom carried a gun. He believed you would never have to use one if you did not carry one. He had his revolver stored inside the luggage on top of the coach the day our stagecoach was held up. In fact, there was only one person inside the stage that had a gun. Perhaps things might have turned out different if we had all been armed." She looked up with watery eyes. "I swore to Almighty God, I'd rather die than go through another experience like that one."

The clerk returned with a shiny dagger and laid it on the counter.

"Will this do? It comes with a boot sheath, or some women prefer to strap it to their leg. Careful, it's razor-sharp," he added as Geraldine picked up the knife.

"Yes, it will do nicely. Thank you."

"Forget the leg holster for my gun," Pearl said as she examined one of the revolvers. "I'll just carry it inside my handbag. Do you have bullets and a place we can practice?"

"Yes, ma'am," he said rushing toward a locked cabinet. "I have plenty of ammunition and a small shooting range out back. Give me a few minutes to lock the door, and I'll give you personal instructions. We'll have you both shooting like a professionals in no time at all."

CHAPTER 88

The first week of August came with humidity, and heat that ranged well into the nineties. Katherine swiped the sweat from her eyes against her sleeve as she scooted on her stomach to peer over the rock ledge. A sizeable herd of cattle were grazing freely on a thick blanket of grass in the fertile bottom of the small canyon. "Well, I guess we know where your cattle went, Clay." The old cattleman eased up beside her and uttered a curse under his breath. Randy Houk had led them to the canyon Pox was using as a hideout. The size of the herd there held them in amazement.

"I'd say he's got some of yours there also. Sure is a pretty place. Maybe we can use it as a summer pasture after we give this Tivo feller a good send-off."

Bill Donovan crept up beside them and instantly turned the air thick with loud curses.

"Quiet down, Bill," Sheriff Crutchfield ordered. "You want to warn them we're here?"

"I'm sorry, my friend, but do you see? The man's a bloody thief!"

"I'd say," Phillip said with a snort. "That's what rustlers usually are."

"Well, let's go pay him a visit," Crutchfield said, and began barking orders to the thirty ranchers and cowboys that had gathered in an effort to put an end to the rustling. When he was satisfied they were ready, he gave the signal to move in.

"Kate, you stay close to Arizona. I don't want any woman killed on my watch."

"I suppose seeing one of these men killed would be somehow better?" She levered a shell into the chamber of the Henry and eased the hammer down before injecting a round into the magazine.

"Just do it," he ordered and slid over the ledge.

"Okay, let's go," she said and bounced down the steep slope from bush to bush, and rock to rock, pausing only seconds to make sure they had not been seen. Katherine had celebrated her forty-first birthday the previous night with a cake Charlene had baked. She received a braided necklace made from strands of Taaka' and Abby's hair, which they had decorated with beads taken from the girls' dresses. She paused in the stifling heat behind a clump of brush and tucked the necklace safely inside her blouse. She glanced back to make sure Phillip was close at hand. The man had given her a blue silk scarf, which he said matched her eyes. She shook her head as she bounded further down the hill. Why would he give her such a personal gift?

They reached the floor of the canyon and paused behind a clump of brush. She could see Matthew and Steven beside Clayton and Dusty Moore to her right. Joshua and Timothy were somewhere with Jerry McCoy and Lucas Martin of the Circle M. Sheriff Crutchfield was approaching the cabin from the rear and slipping through a grove of cottonwoods.

"Look," she said, pointing her rifle toward a window. It was hidden from the sheriff's view by a clump of brush. She heard Phil catch his breath as she darted across an open area and dove behind a leaky water trough.

"You do that again, and I'll turn you over my knee and paddle your backside," Phillip said as he slid in beside her.

"That might be a difficult thing to do, Mr. Denning. But you followed."

"I'm trying to keep you safe."

They jerked their guns over the trough as Crutchfield kicked the door off its rotting hinges. Bill Donovan led a charge across the open area followed by ten cowhands. Several men entered the cabin and came out shaking their heads.

"It's empty. They're gone," Sheriff Crutchfield yelled. Katherine and Phillip eased the hammers back down on their rifles and approached the cabin as men suddenly appeared from everywhere.

"Well, I reckon we get our cattle back," Lucas Martin said.

"I reckon. Why don't you and Clay organize a roundup and cattle drive while I have me a talk with Kate?" Crutchfield's stern glare brought a grin to Katherine's lips.

"What in the hell did you think by running across the open like that? Arizona? I thought I told you to take care of this woman!"

"How am I supposed to do that, Crutch? The woman's my boss, and has her own ideas about such things."

"I was getting into position to cover the front door and that side window. That's what I was thinking."

"You ever do something like that again, and I…I'll…"

"Mr. Denning has already threatened to spank me." She cocked her head to one side and grinned.

The sheriff glared at her before turning away. "Damned woman!"

CHAPTER 89

Pox Tivo wiped the sweat from his eyes with a grimy hand and cursed. The men below in his beloved canyon were rounding up the cattle. "They're a bunch of damned thieves," he mumbled. He had driven the cattle into the valley personally, and fattened them on his grass, and now they were taking them.

"What are we going to do about it, Pox?" Silas asked.

"Do? Are you crazy, boy," Tuck said with a snort. "We ain't gonna do nothing."

"Tuck's right," Pox said as he scrambled away from the rim of the canyon. He seated himself in the shade of a small willow and pulled the cork from a fresh bottle. He took a swallow and passed it to Lee.

"They must have twenty or twenty-five men down there. There's only four of us. What do you think we *can* do?"

"I count thirty, including the woman," Tuck said.

"Woman? What woman?" Pox sat up straight.

"Same woman that's got that gunman working for her."

"I'll be damned and go to hell! I didn't see her down there. How'd I miss that?"

"Does she have those boys of hers with her?" Silas asked as he scrambled toward the canyon rim. The dirty bandage on his leg was still oozing blood.

"I reckon. Hell, I don't know boy. Take a look yourself." Tuck went to fetch the bottle and took a long swallow.

"They are. I think that's Matt riding the paint. Son-of-a-bitch!" Silas limped to his horse and pulled the Winchester from the scabbard.

"Now, what do you think you're gonna do, you fool? You gonna take on that whole posse down there by yourself?" Tuck laughed loudly.

"No, I'm just gonna kill that oldest boy of hers."

"No you're not," Pox said sullenly. "Put that thing away."

"But…"

"But nothing. I said put it away. You're gonna do exactly what I say." Pox waited until Silas had the gun back in the scabbard.

"Sit down and listen." He took another swig and passed the bottle to Silas.

"They might've stolen our cattle, but it's gonna take them another day or two to round them up and organize a drive. And it don't look like that sheriff's in any hurry to get back either. He's probably hoping we're stupid enough to come riding in while they're camped out there. So, we'll do the next best thing. He's stealing our cattle, so we'll just show up at the bank in Denby and steal their money."

CHAPTER 90

Katherine tied Culpepper to a scrub willow near a pool and pulled the Henry from the scabbard. She ran to a clump of rocks protruding from a small rise and injected a round into the chamber, then waited. Sheriff Crutchfield had pitched a royal fit when he had arrived in Denby and discovered the Tivo gang had robbed the bank while they were away. It was a wonder that they hadn't killed anyone in the process. He had immediately gathered a second posse, much larger that the original one, consisting of townspeople and ranchers alike, and had begun scouring the country side. While the group she was riding with had not discovered Pox and his gang, they had run across another band of rustlers, stealing Box D cattle.

She could see Dusty and Curly crouched behind a clump of bushes to her right. Phillip had Steven and Timothy with him somewhere to her left. Sheriff Crutchfield had several men with him, including Matthew and Joshua, opposite from where she was hiding. She readied herself as the sheriff's loud voice carried on the breeze.

"Okay boys, drop the burning iron and put your hands in the air!"

The air was instantly filled with gunfire and the smell of burnt gunpowder. She could hear several horses coming toward her as the men tried to make their getaway. Dusty and Curly rose from their positions and opened fire, but quickly ducked as the rustlers shot back. One man fell from his horse as Phillip's Winchester barked. They were right on her as

Katherine fired from a kneeling position. One of the men pitched backward as the bullet slammed into his chest. The second man fired a pistol but missed badly. He was past her now, and Katherine levered another round and squeezed the trigger. The man slumped and fell from the saddle.

"Good shootin', ma'am," Dusty said as he and Curly ran toward her.

"I heard him take a shot," Curly said. "He didn't wing you, did he?"

"No, I'm fine." She tightened her grip on the rifle as her hands began to shake and took a deep breath. She could see two men lying on the ground farther up the draw near the campfire.

"I hope that isn't any of our men."

"Nope, you can quit worrying," Phillip said as he and Joshua appeared at her side.

"Hey, this one's still alive," Steven yelled. He was standing over the second man she had shot. Katherine heaved a sigh of relief as she approached. He was bleeding from a gaping wound high in his left shoulder.

"Oh God, that hurts," he whimpered.

"Hell yes, it does." Dusty laughed. "That's what .44's are supposed to do. I ought to know. It took me a month to get over one some damned rustler put in my back."

"What are you going to do with me?"

"It's up to this man," Katherine said as Sheriff Crutchfield joined them.

"Hang the son-of-a-buck," Bill Donovan said.

"No, that'll be up to the judge to decide. He'll go back to Denby and stand trial."

"You've changed from the Lincoln County days," Phillip grumbled.

"Yeah, Arizona, I guess I did. When you pin on a badge it does make a difference. You ought to know that as well as anyone."

She could hear Donovan's loud voice as she walked slowly to her horse and shoved the Henry back into the scabbard.

"I hear you're getting married this Friday. Is that right, my boy?"

"Yes sir."

"Well, that calls for a nip of good Irish whiskey."

Katherine watched as Matthew took a swallow and grimaced.

"It reminds me of my courting days in Ireland. There's a tunnel near Killarney they call 'The Kissing Tunnel.' Legend says if you kiss your sweetheart inside the tunnel, you'll be in love forever. But me cousin Sean says he doesn't believe a word of it. 'You don't believe it?' says I.

"'No,' says he. I kissed Mary O'Leary in that tunnel and she married my friend, Albert.'"

The men laughed and passed the flask as Katherine took her canteen and sat on a rock. She pulled the cork, swished a mouthful of water and spit. It didn't help as the bad taste in her mouth remained. She took a swallow and shoved the cork back into the spout, then leaned forward and hung her head between her knees.

"Are you okay, Ma?" Timothy's voice sounded distant.

"Let her be, son," Phillip said softly. "Killing a man isn't an easy thing to live with."

No it isn't, Mr. Denning. Katherine heaved a deep sigh as she raised her head. She had killed two Sioux and wounded a third in a raging gun battle when they tried to steal her horses. She had also severely wounded a rustler who wanted to make a fight of it. This somehow seemed different to her.

She returned the canteen to the horse and began tending to the wounded man. Bill would take him back to stand trial and they would find him guilty and hang him. He didn't look any older than Matthew.

CHAPTER 91

Thursday arrived with Katherine feeling as blue as the dress she had decided to wear. She rented several rooms at the hotel in preparation for the wedding the following afternoon. Then she busied herself helping Mary Jordan as she scurried around smiling. She thanked everyone who offered their congratulations and hid her real feelings. She kept thinking Abby should have been there. Her daughter had refused to come. She said it might be a little too much for her to show up after five years, especially with two Pawnee children. Everyone agreed, and as much as Katherine hated to admit it, Abby was right. Her presence would indeed cause a stir.

But she was about to give her oldest son to another woman, and Abigail should have been there to see her brother get married. Nothing seemed to be turning out the way it should.

Late Thursday afternoon found her seated next to Charlene in the small corner café. There was a steaming coffee cup painted in the window. She had only been picking sat the slab of beef smothered in gravy, while Charlene, on the other hand, seemed to be enjoying her meal. Katherine wondered how the woman found so much energy to chew.

"I'm sorry to ask, but the place seems to be packed. May we join you?"

Katherine looked up into the face of Geraldine McKenney. She was standing next to Pearl Fisher, but they looked different. Both women were finely dressed and looked very much like proper ladies. She would not have recognized either one had she passed them on the street. It was Geraldine's soft voice which carried a slight rasp that had caught her attention.

"Certainly, please do," Charlene said quickly. "You'll have to excuse my friend here. Her baby's getting married tomorrow, and she's lower than a lizard's belly." She waited until the women were seated then added, "Might as well eat her dinner. I don't think she's going to."

"I'm sorry," Katherine said with a slight grin. "I didn't recognize you…either of you. You both look so…"

"Like honest women?" Pearl smiled as she folded a napkin in her lap.

"I didn't mean it as an offence. It's just that…"

"I know what you meant, and believe me, none is taken." Pearl reached across the table and gave Katherine's wrist a small pat. "In fact, I take it as a compliment. You are looking at the new Pearl Fisher, school teacher. At least that's what I will be doing when I reach California. I have no idea what Miss McKenney plans on doing. I don't think she has decided yet."

"Get a job working for the railroad my father helped build," she said with a shrug. "Actually, he owned quite a bit of stock in the company and willed it all to me. I could live quite comfortably if I chose. I've always worked by his side, and I don't think I can simply sit around doing nothing. I need to be busy."

"Well, I do wish you both good luck, and I will be praying for you," Katherine said with a smile. She had meant it as a way to end the conversation and slip back into her cocoon, but Charlene kept the conversation lively, so Katherine finally relented and joined in. By the time they had finished, she discovered she had actually eaten most of her tasteless dinner.

~   ~   ~

The wedding went as planned and Katherine thought it couldn't have been any better. Rebecca Jordan was stunning in her simple white gown, and Matthew was her tall handsome prince. At the end of the ceremony, when Pastor Norris pronounced them man and wife, Taaka' slipped out of the pew and made her way to the bride and groom. She placed Rebecca's right hand into Matthew's, and wrapped a buckskin ribbon that had been decorated with beads and drawings around their hands. She then chanted something in her native language and sat back down next to Katherine.

The reception was held outdoors, and Katherine was busy chatting with the guests when she discovered that Taaka' was missing. She was starting to panic when she heard Steven issue a low moan. She asked what was wrong and he pointed toward two women at the edge of the crowd. Martha O'Dell and Shirley Hall, the town's biggest busybodies, had Taaka' pinned between them and Pastor Norris, and were giving the minister a piece of their minds. The girl had the look of a frightened deer.

"Well ladies," Reverend Norris was saying as she approached, "I actually found it touching. I had heard of the custom, but had never seen it. As I understand, the strap wrapped around the hands and wrist is a symbol of the couple being bound together for life. I fear the day may come when we forget that. I may include something similar in my future ceremonies. Oh, hello Katherine. We were just discussing the ribbon this young lady used at the end of the wedding."

"Yes, I gathered that." Katherine slipped an arm around Taaka's shoulders and pulled her close.

"We don't mean to offend you, Kate, but..." Shirley started.

"Sure you do."

"I beg your pardon?"

"I said, certainly you mean to offend me and my family. If you didn't, you wouldn't be attacking Pastor Norris and this child. I'm a big girl though, and I can take it, so go ahead."

"Why, I never..." Shirley said with a flare.

"Well I certainly don't mind saying what needs to be said," Martha O'Dell said. "You should consider the whole wedding tainted. May I add, you should have taught this savage better before bringing her, or better yet, not brought her at all. Furthermore, I certainly hope you don't adopt a pagan symbol into your marriage ceremonies, Pastor. Taaka' (or whatever her name is) had no business saying a pagan prayer inside a Christian church. And if Katherine Parker is going to allow her to live under her roof, she had better keep an eye on her sons, especially her youngest. I've seen the way he looks at her, and he's quite taken with the little savage."

"Taaka'," Shirley said with a snigger. "What kind of a name is that? It sounds like a cat trying to cough up a hairball."

"It means Swan," Katherine said, and took a small bite of wedding cake. A crowd had now gathered, surrounding them.

"I'm sorry, what did you say?" Shirley asked.

"I said the English translation for Taaka' would be Swan, or Little Swan. And what you witnessed inside the church was simply her way of giving Rebecca and Mathew her blessing. Her father happened to be Asakis. His English name would be Blue Dog, and he was the leading medicine man in their village. The fact that her father and mother both passed away a few weeks ago has been weighing heavily on her. Coming to the wedding today was a real sacrifice. And just so you'll know a little more about her, the war chief, Many Coup was her uncle. You've heard of him, haven't you?"

"Well, that might be, but she's still a savage pagan, and you ought to he teaching her some Christian values, especially if you're going to bring her to church with you."

"Why Martha O'Dell," Katherine said with a laugh, "what better place to learn about Jesus than inside this church? Besides, Taaka' is learning about God and Jesus at home. We have a habit of reading several chapters out of the Bible and praying every evening. Taaka' always insists on being one of the readers. She is a highly intelligent girl, who is eager to learn. I'm very proud to know her." She smiled and kissed Taaka' on the top of her head.

"But, of course I might be a little prejudiced. As you probably know, our Abigail disappeared during the Children's Blizzard, and we never found her." She gave a little shrug. "We thought she had died somewhere, and even held a funeral and put a grave marker for her next to James'. As it turns out, Taaka's family found Abby and saved her life." A murmur rolled through the crowd as Katherine continued.

"They found an entire family who had frozen to death not too far from where they had discovered Abigail. They naturally thought the family was hers, and took her in to live with them. She stayed with them for the next five years, believing we were dead.

"I know it might be hard for you to understand, but Abigail is alive. She's home right now. In the five years she lived with Taaka's family, she taught them about Jesus, and how to speak English. Abby got married and has two wonderful little boys. Her husband was Taaka's cousin. It's not the marriage or family I would have pictured for my daughter, but it was hers, and she was treated well. Most importantly, she was happy, that is until an outbreak of cholera took her husband. It was the same outbreak that took Taaka's parents. There were only eight survivors, and I've invited every one of them to live at my ranch. And I will be forever thankful they saved my daughter's life."

Katherine handed the cake plate to Steven and held Takka's cheeks between her palms and smiled.

"I love this child as my own. And if she should choose to marry one of my sons, I will be proud to call her my daughter."

She found herself meaning every word as she stared into the girl's dark eyes.

CHAPTER 92

Abigail was busy collecting eggs when Walking Horse rushed to her side.

"Four men watch us from the hill." He pointed toward the southwest.

Abby shielded her eyes and looked without seeing anything, but knew better than to question the boy's word or judgment.

"Do you know who they are, or what they want?"

"No, but they mean harm. They watch like hunters and have guns. They are there a long time now. If they wanted peace, they would have come already."

"I'm afraid you're right, Walking Horse. Go find the others and meet me behind the barn. It is best if they don't find us when they come. We will wait for my mother and brothers. They will know what to do. I will get my children and meet you. And oh," she said as an afterthought, "bring the rifles. We may need them."

CHAPTER 93

"They're gone and the place is empty. I checked every room," Tuck said with a grin. "We can empty the whole damned ranch, horses and everything, and be gone before they return."

"Yeah, we could do that," Pox said thoughtfully, "but that ain't what I've got in mind."

"What then?" Tuck asked with an exaggerated shrug.

They had come to the Flying K main house and headquarters to more or less spy it out. The small band of rustlers had been dodging the posse for a week now, and today was the first day they hadn't see them. In fact, they hadn't seen a soul outside of a couple of Indian children crossing the yard, and it had been awhile since seeing them. That was bothering Pox. They had waited most of the day, watching and hoping to see Denning and the woman. It was time to pay them both back for causing him so much trouble, except they were not to be found.

"Where in the hell are they? Where's Denning and the widow and where's them Injuns we seen earlier?" Pox asked no one in particular.

"I don't know, but they ain't there for sure. None of 'em. I checked every room."

"You already said that, Tuck. What I want to know is where they are right now. There should be someone. The cook or one of them kids of hers…anyone at the ranch. People just don't leave their place alone, especially when they have animals to take care of."

"They're at a wedding," Silas said sullenly.

"Weddin'?" Pox turned toward the ragged-looking man who was leaning against a rock and reading the newspaper Tuck had brought back from the empty house. Silas looked like hell, with a bloody patch over his missing ear and a bloodstained pant-leg. They had done their best at doctoring him, but he kept reopening the wounds. Now, Wah Lee suspected they were infected. He had told Pox that Silas would soon die if he did not get proper treatment. The part about him dying didn't bother Pox too much, because he figured everyone was going to die sooner or later. What concerned him was that the infection had grown worse and caused them to slow down and alter their plans once or twice. If it got any worse, he would end Silas' misery himself.

"How do you know they're at a weddin'?" he asked.

"Because it's right here in the paper." He held the paper high and punched it with his fist. "That son of a bitch oldest boy of hers stole away my girl, and they're getting married today. That new house belongs to them," he said pointing. "They'll probably be back some time late this afternoon."

"Well now," Pox said with a smile, "that answers a lot of things. I guess you're good for something after all. You say he stole your girl?"

"Yeah, he stole my girl. What of it? I'll kill the son of a bitch first chance I get."

"Well, how'd you like that chance this afternoon?" Pox had suddenly become animated and pranced around grinning.

"I can't. My leg hurts too damned bad," Silas said with a grimace.

"Hell, don't let that stop you, boy. Wah Lee will give you some of his magic liquor and that'll fix you right up. Won't you Wah?" He gave the Chinaman a wink and he immediately began digging into his saddlebags for the tin of ashes.

"Now, here's what we're gonna do," Pox continued as Wah Lee mixed his potion. "We're going down there and hide our horses inside the barn out of sight. Then we'll just help ourselves to whatever's inside the house and wait for them."

"We're gonna kill 'em all, ain't we? Women and kids?" Tuck asked. "Look what happened the last time we decided to let someone live and took her along. We got ourselves into a passel of trouble."

"You can kill every damned one of them yourself, Tuck. All except for Denning. I want to kill him personally. Shootin's too quick and easy for that son-of-a-bitch. I wanna hang him. Yes sir," he said with a laugh, "when they get home, we'll give them a wedding present they'll never forget."

CHAPTER 94

"There was really no need for you and Mr. Thomas to ride all the way out to our ranch, Mr. Crutchfield," Katherine said. It was growing late and the sun cast shadows across the valley as it crept lower in the sky. She had planned to have a quiet evening at home. Katherine soon realized, though, that was not going to happen. Not only had the sheriff volunteered to accompany the small group of celebrants on their journey home for extra protection, but Pearl Fisher and Geraldine Mc Kenney had also come. The women had mentioned casually that they wanted to see the ranch, so Joshua had invited them. While her son was openly smitten by Geraldine, Katherine suspected the young lady was only being polite. Whether it was out of genuine curiosity or mere politeness, the women were seated behind her in the back of the surrey, chattering happily. The presence of Nathan Thomas and the women also meant that Randy Houk had tagged along. Katherine heaved a deep sigh as the vehicle rocked and bumped over the rough roadway.

Sheriff Crutchfield had reminded her repeatedly that they still had not caught Pox Tivo, and since the man had made several attempts on her life, he felt that extra caution was necessary.

"I don't mind your company, but I know how to take care of myself. Besides, Mr. Denning and my boys have been doing a pretty good job of protecting us."

"Yes, ma'am, I reckon they have," Sheriff Crutchfield said as he trotted his horse close to her surrey. She had rented a new shiny buggy for Matthew and his bride to make the journey in, and the couple was approximately twenty yards ahead of her surrey. Phillip, Steven and Taaka' were riding guard between the two horse-drawn vehicles. The sheriff had been following the women, with Joshua and Timothy following the sheriff. Phillip and Nathan Thomas seemed to be all over the place, riding ahead and to the sides of the small caravan. All of the horsemen were armed with rifles. Katherine glanced at her own saddle-gun propped against the seat next to Charlene's shotgun. Only a fool would attack such a heavily armed group of travelers.

"I reckon Arizona's been a big help in more ways than one," Crutchfield said. "I know he's a pretty danged good cowhand, or at least used to be. Too bad you can't talk him into staying on."

"He insists that our winters in South Dakota are too harsh for him," Katherine said as she shook the reins.

"Well, I can't argue about that, especially last winter. I thought I was near to turning into a block of ice myself a time or two. I don't know what kept folks like you from losing everything."

"Well, it might've been a little easier on you if you had yourself a nice woman to keep your bed warm at night, Bill," Charlene said with a grin.

Katherine shot Charlene an angry glare as Pearl Fisher cackled behind her. "I'm sorry about her, Mr. Crutchfield. She seems to lack tact."

"Oh, no need to apologize, ma'am." The sheriff chuckled. "What she's saying does make some sense. You take that young couple up there for instance," he gestured toward the buggy, "they'll snuggle up this coming winter and keep each other warm. They'll be able to talk and cuddle, share a cup of hot coffee or tea…might even share a book of poetry or sing to each other. Folks like us, on the other hand, will jump into a cold bed and shiver until the covers warm up. Unless you're like ol' Phil up there. He's got that mangy mutt tagging along beside him. He told me that hound's been sleeping on his bed at night. That might be okay for some, but I'd rather have a nice-smelling woman instead of scratching fleas all night long."

Katherine laughed and swiped at a dust particle in the corner of her eye.

"I didn't know you were such a romantic, Sheriff, especially when it came to poetry. Do you really enjoy a good poem?"

"Certainly, and I've got a couple of books of poems I've just about worn out," he said haughtily.

"What I want to know is, where have you been hiding yourself, and why didn't I know about this sooner," Charlene said. "I like coffee, tea and poems myself. I can also whip you up a breakfast that'll knock your socks off."

"Charlene…I…what's got into you?" Katherine said as the lawman roared with laughter.

"I'll tell you what, ma'am," he said to Charlene, "after we catch Tivo, I'm coming around and collect on one of your breakfasts. Now, if you ladies will excuse me, I think it might be good if Phil and I take a quick ride around the ranch and make sure things are safe." He touched the brim of his hat and spurred his horse into a gallop.

Katherine watched as the lawman motioned toward Phillip, Nate and Randy. The four men rode away at a fast gallop, with the dog chasing after them. The men had not returned by the time they were approaching the main yard. The place looked deserted. She wondered where Abby and the children were. She grinned and shook the reins as the rented buggy increased its pace. Matthew must be in a hurry to show his excited bride how he had decorated their first house. Katherine slapped the reins. She wanted to witness the look on Rebecca's face when the bride saw the lace curtains she and Charlene had made for the living room. She knew Becky would be surprised.

CHAPTER 95

Matthew drew the buggy to a halt in the middle of the yard and stared at the main house as Steven and Taaka' trotted their ponies past and dismounted near the corral.

"Is something wrong, honey?" He felt Rebecca's fingers tighten against his wrist.

"I'm not sure. Wait here." He pulled her fingers loose and reached for the rifle tucked behind the seat. The front door to the house was standing open, and the fact that Abby and her children were not there to greet them gave him an uneasy feeling. He injected a shell into the chamber as his mother pulled the surrey to a stop next to the buggy.

"Matthew?" Katherine called. He frowned and motioned for her to stay put as she started to climb down.

"Matthew, what's wrong?" she called again.

"Just wait," he ordered and continued toward the house. Becky poked her pretty head out of the buggy to watch her husband. Nothing like this had ever happened in Denby and it frightened her. He had almost reached the porch when the door to the honeymoon cabin swung open and someone fired a gun. The bullet slammed into him, spinning him around and to the ground. He blinked hard as the air erupted with gunfire and screams from the women. Becky leaped from the buggy as the frightened horse bolted, and ran toward him. She fell at his side with a cry, clutching at his coat in an effort to see how badly he had been injured. She whimpered and dropped across his body as a large black man whacked her across the head with his rifle and grabbed her by the arm.

Matthew clawed at his own rifle lying a few feet away, only to have it kicked away. He grabbed for Rebecca as the big man pulled her away. Something suddenly flashed across the sky and hit the man with a loud clank. He let go of Rebecca and the rifle as he toppled like a tree a few feet from where Matthew was pinned beneath Becky's body. Matthew could feel his life draining out as his blood began to puddle beneath him.

"Oh God, help us," he cried as things began to turn black. This was supposed to be the happiest day of his life, not the end.

CHAPTER 96

Pox Tivo uttered a string of curses at the sound of the first gunshot. This was not what he had planned, nor what he wanted. Phillip Denning was not with them, and he had no idea what Pearl Fisher and Geraldine McKenny were doing here. He didn't care much about Pearl or the McKenny girl, their presence was simply a curiosity to him. But Denning's absence meant he was still out there lurking somewhere, and the gunfire would act as a warning to him. Pearl's presence also meant Nate Thomas and the Houk boy would be close at hand.

"That stupid bastard's messed everything up," Tuck growled, as two of the widow's sons continued a barrage of rifle-fire, backing neatly toward the tack house like well-trained soldiers. The fact that most of the women seemed to be well-armed and capable of putting up a fight was an added problem they had not counted on. He had allowed the opium-intoxicated Silas to stay inside the honeymoon cabin, thinking it would get him out of their hair, but he never thought the idiot would start the ball rolling without receiving the signal Pox was going to give personally.

"Maybe, and maybe I should've let him rot away out there with Rose, but I kind of figured on using him as a diversion. What we need is a slight change in plans," Pox said as he peered through the opened door. The pretty girl seated inside the buggy sprinted across the yard to fall across the wounded boy lying near the house.

"Grab her, Tuck. We'll use her as a bargaining chip."

The gunfire up to this point had been coming from, and directed toward, the new cabin sitting a few yards east of the main house. An Indian girl darted across the yard, when a bullet from Silas' gun knocked her off her feet. Tuck poked his head through the door for a quick look and slipped into the open. He gave Rebecca a quick rap on the noggin with the barrel of his Winchester rifle and she slumped across the limp boy with a whimper. He grabbed her wrist and glanced up quickly as something darted from behind the corner of the house. His entire head seemed to explode as the metal spade caught him flush in the face. He pitched backward and lay on the ground, vaguely aware of the battle raging around him.

CHAPTER 97

Steven's horse bolted for parts unknown at the sound of the first gunshot, carrying his rifle with him. He made a vain effort to give chase, but abandoned the effort when he rounded the corner of the main house and saw his horse leap the fence and race away. He grabbed the only weapon he could latch onto, which happened to be a blunt-nosed spade leaning against the wood siding. He raced back and around the opposite corner of the building to see Taaka', who had been putting her pony inside the corral when the shooting started. Steven watched as she dashed across the yard toward his mother and Charlene. Silas Norton staggered into the yard from Matthew's honeymoon cabin firing his pistol. He roared with laughter as one of his bullets caused Taaka's head to snap backward, knocking the girl off her feet.

"No!" Steven screamed and charged into the open. He swung the spade blindly as a huge black man loomed in front of him. The blow knocked the man to the ground and he continued his charge across the yard. He swung again as Silas turned toward him. The spade clanged against Silas' head, and flattened him also. Steven raised the awkward weapon and drove it downward several more times, the last of which almost severed Silas' head. He flung the spade at the black man who was now struggling to his feet. The blood-stained blade hit him in the back, causing him to drop to his knees with a howl.

Steven grabbed Taaka' by the arms and dragged her toward safety behind the tack house, where Joshua and Timothy had set up a line of defense. A continuous barrage of gunfire was now coming from the house as well as from his brothers and the women. The black man had miraculously worked his way to the porch without getting shot and was attempting to get inside. The bloodstain on his back grew larger as he crawled on all fours. Steven was cradling Taaka's head in his lap trying to will her back to life, when Sheriff Crutchfield and Nathan Thomas charged their horses into the yard. Tuck pulled a pistol and made an effort to shoot, but Sheriff Crutchfield's first shot hit him in the side, taking him down. Then Randy Houk fell from his horse as a shot from the house slammed into his chest.

"Aw, hell!" Nathan yelled as the men leaped from their horses and ran toward the tack house amid a hail of gunfire. Another bullet hit Sheriff Crutchfield and he fell near Steven.

CHAPTER 98

Joshua and Timothy had both returned fire the instant the first shot had been fired. Their action had been directed toward Matthew's honeymoon cabin, and they were not aware that Pox Tivo and the others were inside the main house. Joshua leaped from his horse grabbing the reins from his mother's hand. He crouched near the surrey, trying desperately to hold the frightened team in check. Timothy continued firing as he ushered Pearl and Geraldine to safety behind the tack house. His mother grabbed the Henry from the surrey and fired twice before leaving the buggy. Likewise, Charlene unloaded both barrels of the shotgun and retreated amid a string of oaths. She reloaded and fired again before dashing to safety.

Joshua dropped the reins and ran behind the watering trough as the team bolted out of the yard, taking the surrey with it. He crouched near his mother and reloaded his rifle. Her face was streaked with tears as she injected another round into the Henry and fired. He glanced up as Pearl Fisher calmly aimed and fired a small .31 caliber pistol toward the cabin.

"That won't do much good at this distance," Timothy said as he fired his rifle.

"You don't mind me using it, do you?" she asked with a grin and pulled the trigger.

Joshua cursed and ordered everyone to hold their fire as Taaka' suddenly appeared from the corral and darted toward them. Silas Norton staggered from inside the new cabin and shot her. Steven's yell and charge into the yard caught everyone by surprise. Joshua had not even seen the giant standing near Matthew until Steven hit him with the spade. The man was so large, he didn't believe the shovel would have much of an effect, but he fell as if he'd been shot. He watched for a split second as his little brother attacked Silas. Timothy's gunfire, mingled with the boom of Charlene's shotgun, turned his attention back to the house where Pox Tivo and the Chinaman had made an attempt to exit. They were driven back inside by the hail of bullets as Steven drug Taaka' to safety.

His mother passed the rifle to Geraldine Mc Kenney and knelt beside Taaka'.

"You know how to use that thing?" Joshua asked as the girl cocked the rifle.

"I'm a native born Texan, Mr. Parker. I could ride and shoot while you were sucking your thumb." She aimed, fired, and injected another shell without the gun leaving her shoulder, then fired again.

Joshua glanced toward his mother as she tore a chunk of her petticoat loose and held it against Taaka's head. "She's still alive and I think she will be okay, honey. Keep this pressed tightly to stop the bleeding."

Sheriff Crutchfield charged his horse into the yard on the heels of Nathan Thomas. The men fired their guns and young Houk was knocked to the ground by a bullet the instant he rode into the yard. Crutchfield and Nathan dismounted and fired as they retreated toward the women. The sheriff collapsed with a cry of pain as he passed Joshua's point behind the watering trough.

"How bad are you hit, Crutch?" Nathan asked as he ran to help the fallen lawman.

"Just my leg. Dammit, I hate getting shot."

"We all do, Crutch," Nathan said with a snort and returned fire. "Especially Houk."

"How bad is he?" Pearl yelled over the gunfire.

"He's dead, that's how bad he is," Nathan hollered back.

"Here, let me take care of him, Mr. Thomas," Charlene said, and shoved the shotgun at Nathan. "You go ahead and kill those bastards for me."

"Yes, ma'am."

"Pox?" Sheriff Crutchfield yelled as Charlene cut at the seam of his left pant-leg with a knife. "Pox Tivo?"

"Yeah, that's me, Sheriff. Whadda ya want?" The voice came from inside the house.

"Toss out your guns and come out with your hands up. I'll see to it you'll get a fair trial."

The laughter sounded hysterical and ended with a cough.

"Hell, you must think I'm an idiot, or you're even more stupid than I thought. There ain't no way I'm gonna give up without a fight. The first thing you'll do is hang me."

"No, I'll see to it you get a fair shake. Besides, you're out-gunned, and there's no way you can make it out of that house without getting yourself killed. Better toss out your guns and come out with your hands raised. It's your only chance."

"No, you've got that wrong, Sheriff. That girl and boy lying on the ground are still alive, and I've got a clear shot from where I'm sitting. I'll plug 'em both if you don't toss down your guns…all of you, and come into the open with *your* hands raised."

"The son of a bitch will do it anyway. I know him," Pearl said.

"Matt's already dead, Ma," Timothy said.

"No he isn't!" Katherine yelled. "Don't say things like that."

Nathan tucked his pistol into his belt behind his back and turned to grin at Sheriff Crutchfield.

"Loan me your pistol for awhile, Crutch?"

"Sure, something wrong with yours?"

"No, it works just fine. But I can't shoot it if I toss it like he wants, now can I?"

"Okay, Pox, I'm coming out," Nathan yelled and held Sheriff Crutchfield's gun high. "See? I'm tossing my iron out."

He gave the sheriff's pistol a toss. "It's me you really want anyway, isn't it?"

"You've got that right, Nate. I want you and Denning both. Where is he?"

"Hell, I don't know. He rode off toward the creek earlier. I figured he'd be here by now."

"Well, he'd best get here. Now I want to see the other guns. Come on now. I mean it. I'll bore this happy couple if I don't see them all, including the shotgun."

"Do as he says," Nathan said.

"He'll kill us all if we toss out our guns," Pearl protested.

"He'll kill the boy and girl if we don't."

They jumped as Pox fired, kicking up dirt dangerously close to Rebecca's head.

"That was just to prove I'm not lying. I can get 'em both real easy from where I'm sitting. So, what's it gonna be? The guns or the boy and girl?"

CHAPTER 99

Phillip spurred Lucky into a full run at the sound of gunfire, but pulled him to a halt as he crested the small rise near the cemetery. He was in time to see Randy Houk get shot from his horse and Crutchfield fall. He tied Lucky to the willow and grabbed the Winchester. Crouching low, he ran toward the rear door of the barn, and opened it gingerly. He caught his breath as the barrel of a gun was jammed into his ribs.

"Uh," Walking Horse said with a nod of approval, and motioned for him to follow as he ran to the other end of the barn. Abby and Grey Fox were standing beside a partially opened window, both armed with rifles. Phillip eased up beside them and peered over Abby's shoulder. He cursed under his breath as Katherine tossed her rifle into the yard and walked boldly toward Matthew and Rebecca lying in the yard.

~   ~   ~

"Well, that certainly makes it easier," Pox said with a laugh. He watched as she knelt beside her son and began unbuttoning his jacket. "What the hell do you think you're doing?"

"I'm going to see about my son."

"No you're not." He burst into the open and jerked her to her feet by the hair. The action brought a cry of pain from her lips as he jammed a pistol against her head.

"Let me tell you what you're gonna do. You're gonna stand there until I say different. And if those others don't toss out their guns, and if Denning doesn't show himself, I'm gonna splatter your brains all over this yard. Got that?" he yelled loudly. "I wanna see the guns right now!"

"Okay Pox, take it easy," Nathan said. "They'll toss them out. You'd better do as he says," he added over his shoulder.

One by one they tossed the remaining guns into the yard. Joshua relinquished his Henry next to last and cringed as Geraldine tossed hers into the yard. He grinned as the girl quickly stepped back behind the building and pulled a small handgun from one of her boots. She held it tightly against the folds of her skirt as she stepped forward. Joshua followed suit by slipping the hunting knife from his boot and stepped forward, satisfied they were not going down without a fight.

"Where's that youngest boy of hers?" Pox yelled.

"He's back there tending to Taaka', the Indian girl Silas shot. She's hurt pretty bad," Charlene said.

"Get him out here. I wanna see him and no tricks, understand? 'Cause if any of you try anything…and I don't care what it is or who starts it, this woman's dead. Got it?"

"Yeah, I got it. What about the girl? She's hurt pretty bad," Charlene said as Nathan moved slowly into the yard and away from the others.

"Hell, she's just an Injun, let her die. And you stay put, Nate. I don't want you trying to wander off somewhere."

"Steve? Better do as he says," Charlene said and motioned for him to join them.

He waited until Steve had joined Charlene's side, then gave Katherine's hair another tug and yelled loudly.

"Denning? I know you're out there. Better show yourself right now, or I'm gonna blow this woman's head off. You hear me, Denning? You know I mean it!"

CHAPTER 100

"Dammit!" Phillip said in a hoarse whisper. "I can shoot him from here, but he's got that gun cocked. It might go off and kill your ma anyway." He pulled away from the window and stared at the straw inside the stall for a few seconds.

"Okay, here's what we're gonna do. I don't plan on getting myself killed, so listen close. I'm going out there, and he's going to shoot me first, because I'm armed and I threatened to hang him once. Be ready. The second he pulls that gun away from your ma's head, shoot him." He waited for a nod from Abby and turned toward Walking Horse.

"You and Grey Fox climb up to the loft and take the other two. The minute Taree'uus pulls the trigger, you boys open up." The boys nodded and scampered up the ladder.

"Okay, let's do it." He squeezed Abby's shoulder and opened the door.

CHAPTER 101

"Denning!" Pox yelled. "I'm not gonna wait no longer! Either you show yourself or I'm killing every one of them!"

"Calm down, Pox," Phillip said as he walked into the open. "I've been here all the time."

"Well now, you ain't the yellow coward I was figuring you for." Pox jerked Katherine around, using her as a shield and pointed his pistol toward Phillip. The action blocked Abby's aim, so she darted across the barn toward a different window.

"I was hoping to hang you, but you'll be dead just the same." Pox raised the gun, and screamed as the dog shot across the yard and leaped over Katherine's shoulder. The pistol in Pox's hand discharged as the man fell to the ground, desperately trying to fend off the dog as it ripped at his flesh.

Phillip dropped his rifle as he felt the sting of the bullet burn across his left shoulder. Grey Fox and Walking Horse opened fire and the porch seemed to explode as splinters of wood and glass flew into the air. Phillip drew his pistol and shot Tuck in the chest as he tried to escape. Katherine scooped Matthew's rifle from the ground as the dog retreated to take a stand between her and the rustler, growling. Pox grabbed for his pistol as he struggled to his feet and Katherine pulled the trigger, shooting him twice before he fell. Nathan emptied his revolver into Wah Lee as he tried to retreat back inside the house. It stopped as quickly as it had started, and they stood transfixed in silence.

Geraldine rushed forward and stood over Pox Tivo. Phillip was certain Katherine had killed the man, but Geraldine fired her last bullet into the rustler's head, then dropped the revolver as she burst into sobs, rubbing her palms against her skirt.

"It's okay," Nate said, holding her tightly. "It's all over now. Go ahead and cry."

Sheriff Crutchfield leaned heavily against Charlene as she helped him to the porch. Abigail and the Pawnee children rushed to Katherine's side.

"You liked to scared the hell out of me, ma'am," Phillip said as he knelt beside Katherine. "The way you came strutting out here…he might've killed you."

"Yes, Mr. Denning. I realized that. But I had to see about my son." She finished unbuttoning Matthew jacket and shirt. She looked up at him and swiped at the tears in her eyes with the palms of her hands. "We did what we had to do. Now, I need someone to ride into town as fast as they can and bring Doctor Krucker. Matthew and Taaka', as well as Sheriff Crutchfield, are badly hurt. How bad are you hurt, Mr. Denning?"

"It's just a scratch and it can wait."

"I'll go, Ma," Joshua said, and rushed to find his horse.

"Take Culpepper," she yelled. "He's the riding-est horse we've got."

"You be a good boy and sit here," Charlene said as she helped the lawman onto the bench. She promptly followed Katherine's example by tearing her petticoat into shreds and handed one piece to the sheriff.

"Keep that pressed down tight until I've had me a look at this boy. I think he's hurt a might more than you."

"I think you're right. I'll just wait while you ladies do your thing." He snapped his head upward as Nathan raised his voice.

"Na-uh, Arizona, I'll just keep that for awhile." He pointed his gun toward Phillip and grabbed the pistol Phillip was attempting to reload. "It's not that I've got a bone to pick with you, understand. It's just that you've been chasing me for three years, and now that Pox has cashed in his chips, you just might decide to finish with me." He tucked Phillip's gun inside his own belt. "I'll give it to Crutch before I leave. You can get it from him."

"Keep it as long as you want," Phillip said with a shrug and turned to watch as Walking Horse and Grey Fox dragged Pox off the porch and into the yard next to Silas.

"Huh?"

"I said keep it, if you want. I could've shot you anytime the past couple of weeks while we were playing posse. I could also grab one of these guns lying here on the ground and continue our war. That is, if I wanted to, but I ain't got the heart for it anymore. The killing's got to stop sometime, Nate. And there's been way too much as it is."

"Amen," Sheriff Crutchfield said.

"Someone get this boy into the kitchen and lay him on the table," Charlene said. "And help Steve with Taaka'," she pointed toward the tack house, "I think she's awake now. That poor girl's gonna have one hell of a headache. Abby, can you give me a hand honey? You know something about fixing wounds."

Timothy offered to help Steve with Taaka', but his younger brother refused, and carried the girl in his arms into the house by himself. Timothy shrugged and stood between Phillip and Nathan as Charlene barked orders and the women rushed to and fro to make sure they were carried out. Phillip laid a hand against his shoulder and grinned.

"It's best to stay clear of women when they get like this son. We'd only be in their way."

CHAPTER 102

Charlene came from the house carrying two large mugs of steaming coffee and perched herself on the wooden bench next to Sheriff Crutchfield. She passed one of the mugs to him and they sat silently sipping their coffee, watching the sun turn the eastern sky pink as it began to peek over the rim of the canyon.

Doctor Krucker and his wife had rushed to the ranch as soon as Joshua had brought word, working well past midnight removing bullets and stitching wounds. The tired couple was now sleeping in Katherine's bed, while Katherine slept next to Taaka' in Charlene's bed. The living room sofa had been taken by Geraldine McKenney, and the remaining guests were scattered everywhere, including the floor in front of the fireplace. Matthew and Rebecca were spending their first night alone in their own house. This was one night Charlene was certain the young couple would never forget.

The doctor had pronounced his approval of the women's emergency care prior to his arrival, as they had more than likely saved Matthew's life. The boy had lost a large amount of blood. Fortunately, the wound high in his left shoulder had not broken any bones or severed any major arteries. He would, however, require extensive care and rest for awhile. Rebecca had a lump on her head that would be sore for a few days, but would be fine. Taaka' had a mild concussion and received several stitches at her hairline. The young Pawnee boys joked that they were caused by a white man's sloppy attempt at trying to scalp an Indian. Sheriff Crutchfield's wound was not life-threatening, although it was painful. He, like Charlene, had not slept. He had limped around trying to help, but finally decided to get out of the way and retreated to the bench on the porch where they were now seated. The tired housekeeper had made sure of everyone's comfort before brewing the fresh coffee they were drinking. The sun inched its way higher, bringing with it the promise of a good day.

"Here, try some of this," Charlene said, pulling a flask from her apron pocket.

"Lord Almighty. You're an angel, Charlie. You were reading my mind."

She poured a generous amount into each mug and they continued their silent meditation.

"I got kicked out of my own kitchen," she said after a few sips.

"Really? By who?"

"Phil and Nate. They said I looked tired. Can you imagine that?" She chuckled. "They said they would cook everyone a cowboy breakfast like they did while working for John Tunstall."

"Lord have mercy," Crutchfield said with a laugh. "That'll finish everyone off for sure. I ate one of their campfire dinners. Nate always burnt the biscuits and Phil couldn't even make a decent cup of coffee."

"That's right. I remember you saying something about working for Tunstall with those two," she said as she poured another shot from the flask into their mugs.

"Yes, ma'am. I cowboyed most of my life. It was the Lincoln County war that caused me to change, but I miss it. I guess once you're a cowboy, you'll always be one." He inhaled deeply and sighed. "I miss this. The open skies and open range. I even miss the smelly cows."

"Why don't you quit and go back to wearing spurs? You could stay right here. Mrs. Parker will be needing a good hand, especially with Matthew laid up and Phil still claiming he's leaving before the snow falls." She paused to sip the coffee and turned away. "Lord knows I could use the company. I miss having someone my own age to talk to."

"You're a mighty handsome woman, Charlie. I've never figured why you didn't get remarried after your husband died."

She turned to give the sheriff a long glare before speaking.

"Bill Crutchfield, you are one miserable old fart! You know that? Here I look like something the cat drug in, with my hair a mess and Matthew's blood all over my apron, and you say that to me? Especially after the times I prettied myself up and tried to get your attention when we were in town? I ought to shoot you in the other leg."

He laughed and squeezed her hand. They sat in silence a few minutes more, watching as Walking Horse and Grey Fox pitched hay into the corral and pumped water into the trough.

"You really did that?" he asked.

"Did what?"

"Tried to get my attention?"

"You know, you are about as dumb as Phil's dog. Yes, I tried getting your attention." She laughed and uncorked the flask. "Here, might as well finish it off." She emptied it into their mugs.

"If Nate wants to be a lawman, why don't you pin that star on him and come work for us?"

"I just might do that. He'd be a shoe-in after this Pox Tivo thing. Besides, I'm tired of getting shot. This is the third time you know. Someday one of them's gonna get lucky and finish me off."

Charlene jumped up at the sound of a loud clank followed by some curses coming from the kitchen, but Crutchfield grabbed her arm.

"Let 'em have at it, Charlie. Come on, sit and keep me company."

She forced herself to sit silently sipping her coffee as she listened to the men's voices inside her kitchen.

"Did she really kill her husband?" she asked after a few sips.

"Who, Pearl?"

She nodded.

"That's what they claim."

"Why didn't you arrest her?"

"She didn't kill him in Denby. Oh, I could've locked her up and shipped her off to Sioux Falls, but Judge Henry said he figured that gambler she was married to deserved killing. What I heard was, he'd get drunk and lose his money at cards, then come home and take it out on Pearl. Two of their neighbors claimed he was beating the hell out of her the night she did for him. I don't think any jury would have convicted her, if she hadn't run off."

"Maybe she should go back and make things right."

"Maybe."

They grew quiet and listened as Katherine scolded the men for making so much noise. He again gripped her hand as she tried to go to the rescue, and didn't let go when she relaxed.

"What about you Charlie? What's in your future? You gonna stay here the rest of your life?"

"It's a good place to be, Crutch. Maybe you should try it."

"Maybe, except I don't wanna be sleeping in the tack house with a dog like Phil. Think I could find a comfortable bed with someone to keep me warm?"

She glared at him a long time before grinning. "I really ought to shoot you, you old coot." She held up her left hand and pointed at the ring finger.

"Put something on that finger, and we'll see."

CHAPTER 103

September arrived bringing with it strong winds mingled with rain. Katherine had stopped the work on the addition until repairs to the front of the main house and the honeymoon cabin were made. Now that the weather had turned, the construction had all but ceased. She was near certain the Pawnee children would be spending the winter in her living room.

Matthew was growing stronger and sat on the porch of his cabin teasing his brothers and the young Pawnees about having to work in the miserable conditions. His teasing always turned to restlessness bordering on depression once they had ridden out of the yard. Only Rebecca's presence seemed to cheer him, and his sour mood would return once she left his sight. Nothing Katherine or Abigail tried seemed to help. Finally, during the second week into fall roundup, Rebecca lost all patience and exploded into a rage.

"You won't listen to Doctor Krucker, or your mother or your sister…you won't even listen to me and I'm your wife! All you care about is making everyone miserable. You're a spoiled brat, Matthew Parker! You want to make yourself sick and die? Go ahead," she threw his jacket in his face, "saddle your horse and go rope cattle with your brothers! But don't expect me to baby you when you catch pneumonia."

Katherine and Phillip agreed that Matthew's work should be somewhat restricted. The simple fact that the boy believed he was contributing improved his spirits considerably.

His being out from underfoot around the house improved Rebecca's spirits also. Charlene laughingly remarked that the young couple was fast discovering what married life was like.

They found the Pawnees eager to work and learn about the ranch, but the language problem between them proved to be a stumbling block. On the third day of the roundup, Katherine motioned Phillip toward the campfire and handed him a steaming cup of coffee.

"Raising your voice and shouting won't turn your English into Pawnee, you know that, don't you?"

"How's that, ma'am?"

She took a sip and stared at him over the rim of the cup. "I said, yelling won't make those boys understand what you're saying, no matter how loud you raise your voice. It will only make them frightened of you. Abigail and Taaka' are both capable hands, and they both speak Pawnee better than either of us. Why don't you just tell one of them what you want our Indian drovers to do and forget about it?" She climbed back on her horse with a grin and rode away, leaving him to wonder why he hadn't thought of it first.

~   ~   ~

Sheriff Crutchfield paid a visit and brought news of Pearl Fisher's court appearance in Sioux Falls. He said Geraldine McKenney had dipped into the sizable bank account her father had left to purchase a new wardrobe for Pearl, and to obtain the services of her father's personal attorney. Pearl Fisher walked into the courtroom looking like the perfect lady. It was also apparent she had been well-coached by the attorney, as she presented herself well. By the time the silver-tongued solicitor had finished presenting her defense, he believed Pearl could have run for mayor of Sioux Falls and won easily. She also received four proposals of marriage by members of the jury following her dismissal, and accepted one from an elderly widower who was rumored to have a sizable bank account. He also said that Geraldine McKenney had not gone to San Francisco. She was still in Denby, near Nathan

Thomas. He figured whatever Nathan decided to do would be fine with her.

~   ~   ~

A small tornado skirted the rim of the canyon the second week of the roundup, forcing them to take refuge inside the cave. The twister continued on its way, causing no damage to the houses or barns. It did, however, make the rest of the day miserable by dropping a large amount of hail and rain. The following days proved almost as bad, with a constant drizzle and gusting winds that whipped the rain into their faces. While it had not yet officially turned fall, the wind had a bite that promised autumn was coming and bringing with it another cold winter to follow.

It was the middle of the third week when Katherine sat on a damp log sipping coffee from a tin cup. Abby and Taaka' were busy pushing the last of the cattle into the winter range, while Phillip and the boys applied the branding irons. The smell of burnt hair and hide, and the barking of Phillip's dog mingled with the bawling of cattle, had once again become music to her. She knew she loved this place and would never leave it. Her sons would bury her next to James under the willow behind the barn. Her family was healthy and happy, they had plenty of hay for the harsh winter, and Abby was back. God had indeed been good to her.

Abigail dismounted and gave orders to one of the young Pawnees, then poured herself a cup of coffee and sat next to her mother on the log. She sighed as she warmed her fingers against the tin cup.

"It's getting colder," she said after a long minute.

"Yes it is," Katherine said. "You and your Indian friends will have to move into the main house if they don't finish your addition in time. Do you think it's big enough?"

"Mother," she said with a snigger, "you could sleep a regiment of soldiers in that thing. I told you it didn't have to be that large, and we do have the teepees for that matter. My only worry is having enough firewood to heat the place when they finish it."

They sat silently watching the branding for a few minutes. Phillip yelled at the dog as it darted after a wayward calf and chased it back toward those awaiting their turn with the hot iron.

"He's trained that dog well, hasn't he?" Abby asked.

"Yes, he has. I didn't think he would, from the way he complained when it first attached itself to him."

"So, are you just going to let him go?"

Katherine stared at her daughter a minute before asking, "Let who go? The dog?"

"No silly. You know who I mean. Mr. Denning. He's leaving, you do know that don't you? We'll be finished today, or tomorrow at the latest. The boys can finish anything we might have missed. I heard him telling Steven about it, and I think he's leaving tomorrow morning."

"I'm afraid I don't know what you're talking about. He hasn't said anything to me about leaving."

Her daughter smiled sweetly and stared into the cup.

"I learned quite a few things living with the Pawnee. They are a simple people who have learned to accept life as it is. They don't have much, so they don't complicate things. They've also learned to be honest with themselves. You and Mr. Denning are not being honest with yourselves. I've watched you both. You are different when you're together. He's a good man and he's been good for you."

Katherine stared at the man branding cattle. She must have known he would leave. He had told her many times, but it had not dawned on her the day would actually come when he really would go. He had become such a part of her life that she had taken it for granted he would always be there for her to argue and laugh with. Her eyes began to water, and she blinked as Abigail yelled something to one of the boys in Pawnee. Abby sighed as the boy stared at her. She passed the coffee cup to her mother and stood as if to leave.

"Here, you finish this. I've got to show him what I meant. Think about what I said, Mama. He will leave in the morning and it will be too late. You can't tell him how you feel if he isn't here."

CHAPTER 104

Katherine walked briskly to the campfire and gave Abby's now lukewarm cup of coffee to Taaka', who was attempting to clean a cup that had been dropped in the mud. She smiled and Katherine kissed her on top of the head and turned toward Phillip as he grabbed the branding iron from the fire.

"Let the boys finish that, Mr. Denning, and come with me. I'd like to show you something."

"Yes, ma'am. I've been wanting to talk to you." He passed the iron to Joshua and followed her to the horses.

They rode in silence back to the house, where Katherine dismounted next to the freshly painted fence surrounding the tiny cemetery. Phillip stood beside her and held the reins to both horses in his gloved hand as she talked.

"I don't know how much you know about us, Mr. Denning, or what happened. When Abby came up missing during the blizzard, we searched for weeks, literally a whole month…perhaps even more, but couldn't find her. She was simply gone," Katherine shrugged. "It was devastating for all of us, most especially for James." She turned to stare into his eyes.

"I heard you that day talking to Matthew and the boys as you painted the fence. I don't know how you knew it, but what you said was exactly what happened. James had sent her out that morning, and he never stopped blaming himself."

"Just a lucky guess," Phillip said with a grin. "I've usually got a hunch about people, and…"

"No, don't say anymore. Please, I need to say this."

"Okay, I'll listen."

She took a deep breath and continued.

"James was a good man, but weak in some ways. He simply gave up living and became a ghost of what he had been. He said he could still hear Abby's voice." She shrugged. "Perhaps he did. Anyway, someone had to be strong. We had four boys depending on us, so everything fell to me and I took over. We watched as James pined away. I dug his grave myself when he died. Let's go inside out of the rain. I still have a few things to say."

Phillip turned the horses inside the corral where they could get under the lean-to and out of the rain. He scraped and stomped the mud from his boots before opening the kitchen door. She was engaged in a hurried conversation with Charlene, but the women drew silent the instant he entered the room. The housekeeper gave him a warm smile and left. Katherine poured Phillip a cup of coffee and asked him to sit. She stared out the kitchen window for a minute and heaved a sigh.

"As you can probably tell, autumn is on its way," she finally said with a small chuckle. "I can always tell by the angle of the sunlight shining through the laced curtains."

"Ma'am, I need to..."

"Please, Mr. Denning. I've something to say and it is going to be difficult at the least." She pulled the curtains aside and stood facing the window with her back toward him.

"I don't know if you knew it, but we were having a time of it when you rode in here looking like a scarecrow. Oh, I had plenty of money in the bank from the good years. On the other hand, I knew we were losing cattle, and the winter had hit us all extremely hard. There is no reason for it, but I had begun feeling like a prisoner, stuck on this ranch. I didn't really know what to do, and simply did not have the heart to fight anymore." She shrugged her shoulders. "I guess I was becoming like James." She turned to face him and leaned against the wall with her arms folded across her chest.

"In short, Mr. Denning, you're arrival helped us a lot. I know I haven't been the easiest person to get along with, and I drive you crazy at times. I've probably caused you more trouble than the rustlers in my own way, but I do appreciate everything you've done for us…all of us. You gave us back our lives. You even gave us Abby, and I don't know what we would have done without you, or how I could ever repay you."

She took a deep breath and heaved a long sigh.

"Abigail says she overheard you telling Steven you're leaving in the morning. Is that true?"

"Yes, ma'am. That's what I need to discuss with you."

"Before you do, please let me finish."

He nodded and she started, but covered her mouth and stared at the floor a minute before speaking.

"Last winter was especially difficult for me. Not just the cold…the snow and wind. I have never felt so alone. Even with my sons and Charlene here, I couldn't shake the feeling. Lying in my bed and listening to the canyon wind whip the snow against my window, there were times I honestly wished I could die. Then you arrived, and I had someone to argue against and laugh with. You changed things, Mr. Denning. You changed my life."

She again covered her lips with a trembling hand and stared at the floor.

"What I'm about to ask you, Mr. Denning, will sound as bold as the wind. I don't want you to leave. I want you to stay, but not as my hired hand, or for my children or anything else. I want you to stay for me. I know I'm not much of a catch. I'm bossy and opinionated, and probably not someone you would choose to spend your life with. But I want you to hold me and protect me from the wind when it blows snow against my window. I want you there to talk to on cold winter nights. I want you to be my special friend. You were right, Mr. Denning, I don't need to be rescued from anything, but I do need to feel appreciated for who and what I am.

"Then," she shrugged her shoulders, "if there's no love there when spring comes, I guess there won't be anything left to say. You'll be free to go."

She caught her breath and turned away as he stared at her for what seemed an eternity. She heard his chair scrape against the floor and was positive he was leaving when his hands against her shoulders made her jump. He was smiling when she looked up.

"You had better understand one thing, Katie girl. I've loved you from the first time I laid eyes on you, and I've never stopped. I didn't feel free to tell you, because I came here to kill a man, and that's not much to offer a woman. I was the one needing to be rescued, not you. If I ride away tomorrow, it will be the most difficult thing I've ever had to do. But, if I spend the winter as your special friend like you said, it will most certainly be as your husband, and I will not be leaving when spring comes. So, you had better be certain of what you are asking."

The sound that escaped her lips was something between a giggle and a sob. She took her time composing herself, then wrapped her arms around his neck and grinned.

"And that, Mr. Denning, is exactly what I was hoping you would say. You may kiss me now."

End

About The Author

MAJOR MITCHELL is the author of six novels and two children's books. He lives with his wife, Judy, in Northern California. A member of The Western Writers of America and a frequent guest speaker at historical meetings and schools on the West Coast, he has also written several songs, and takes the stage on rare occasions as a singer.

More about the author, his books and photo gallery may be found at www.majormitchell.net.

Correspondence should be addressed to:
Shalako Press
P.O. Box 371
Oakdale, CA 95361-0371